THE STONE OF SHADOWS

R. A. FINLEY

ISBN: 0-9893157-0-3
ISBN-13: 978-0-9893157-0-8
eBook ISBN: 978-0-9893157-5-3
Library of Congress: TXu001876993

Published by Hickory Tree Publishing

Book Design by R. A. Finley
Cover Design & Artwork by R. A. Finley

10   9   8   7   6   5   4   3

Third Hickory Tree Publishing Edition

To my parents, who once sent me on a grand adventure with the understanding that it would end up in a book.

THE STONE
OF
SHADOWS

The shell must break before the bird can fly.

Alfred Tennyson

CHAPTER 1

Perched atop the ferry terminal, Cormac ruffled his feathers against the wind's knifing chill. The sky above the small harbor town was already thick with gray, the sun only a vague memory behind the storm blowing in from the North Sea. Dusk was hard on its heels, soon to mark the end of another wasted day.

Bobbing in almost overwhelming frustration, he let loose a series of squawks. The sharp winds would shred the sounds before they could cross the street, never mind pass through the old glass of the hotel's dining room window, so he didn't worry they might alert the woman seated on the other side. Not that it would matter if they did. She was far from stupid. She had to assume he was close.

Alert to her every move, her every expression, he watched her lift her spoon to take a slow, untroubled sip of chowder. Exactly as she'd been doing for the past forty minutes.

He squawked again.

Why so long? He had first assumed she was taunting him, flaunting her inaccessibility by seating herself where he could not help but see her. But even if he allowed for how this much-aged Leticia tended to linger over her food, this was ridiculous.

He figured she was waiting for someone—considering what was at stake, perhaps several someones. Yet, so far, no one had joined her and she had showed only a passing interest in anything beyond her food and what appeared to be a local guidebook. The other diners—the few he could see, at any rate—might as well not exist to her. The pedestrians, the cars in the street—none of them received more than a casual glance. Cormac, a lone raven on a rooftop, did not rate even that much.

Which didn't mean anything, of course. She wouldn't give away the game by showing a particular interest. Leticia McDaniel was an experienced player. She knew the stakes, knew Cormac had no choice here but to win.

He watched her take yet another mincing spoonful of soup, then dab absently at her mouth with her napkin. He could feel his frustration working its way to anger, threatening his control over his altered form. The emotions of a man (or near enough to one) did not fit easily into the body of a bird. He flapped his wings to expel some of the inner tension. Too many hours spent watching, waiting. He didn't look forward to dealing with whomever Leticia might have called for help, but at least it'd be something. He'd had enough of her tricks, of lost opportunities and wrong turns. Enough of being left behind.

Wind gusted sharply and he crouched low, dug his talons into the grooves of the roof tiles. Hard to believe this had all begun but a few weeks ago.

His house had felt particularly empty that evening, the reality of his life too present to be ignored, so he had walked the not inconsiderable distance to the village. He had taken his time about it, admiring the rural landscape beneath the setting sun, relishing the feel of the land he had chosen for himself—and that Idris grudgingly allowed him to inhabit. The woodlands of oak and ash, the rain-swollen brooks, the soft breeze that rustled the drying grasses beside the road and carried the rich scent of peat smoke.

The Oak and Thistle's mullioned windows had glowed in welcome, and as he'd approached the red-painted door, he'd stepped aside to allow several people, laughing as they wrestled for a lighter, to stumble out. With them came the din of lively conversation and someone's earnest but questionable attempts on a fiddle.

He remembered taking hold of the door only to remain standing, momentarily caught on the threshold between the solitude from which he had come and the potential of the evening ahead: a few drinks, some good-natured arguments with the gents over some sport or another, a little flirtation with the ladies. For a few hours, at least, he had expected to forget himself. But no sooner had he stepped into the bright, crowded warmth than the summons had come and he was back to being Idris Cathmor's errand boy.

No choice, no say whatsoever over the course of his life.

He supposed Leticia didn't consider that she had a choice here, either. It was a shame she was involved—and not just because she had proven herself to be tough competition over the years. No, it was a shame because he had *enjoyed* that competition up to now. Enjoyed her whimsical, often playful nature and the challenges it presented. But there was nothing enjoyable about this. She was running him ragged, forcing him into near constant use of disguise-craft, frequent spellwork, and shifts to raven-form with little chance to replenish the energies each depleted. He had reached exhaustion days ago—which was more than a little humiliating, considering Leticia was full human and eighty if she were a day. She ought to be the one exhausted, the one terrified of failure. Yet there she sat, for all appearances content, confident in her victory.

With good reason, he had to admit. The wards she'd erected around the hotel were some of the best he had seen. To get through them, he would need a lot of supplies and a lot of time. The latter was out of the question, and as soon as he left to collect the former, she'd leave. He couldn't risk letting her out of his sight. Not as long as she had the relic.

Several blasts of an air horn sounded in the distance as a North Isles ferry approached the harbor. Storm-wrought swells had the large ship bobbing like a child's toy on the channel's dark, foaming water. He watched for a moment, studied the curtain of rain that tracked the ferry's path. Figured he had about a half hour before he would need to seek shelter or resign himself to a good soaking.

Was Leticia waiting for the ship? Its being twenty minutes behind schedule might explain why she had lingered so long at the window.

She couldn't expect to sail on it tonight; this was its last run until morning. She *could* be waiting for someone on board, he supposed. Chances of that were slim, given that the ferry was coming in from the outer islands—but, then, "slim chance" was Leticia's weapon of choice, and one she wielded with enviable ease.

The ferry pulled alongside the pier with a belch of diesel exhaust, the opening note of an industrial symphony that was hell on the heightened senses of Cormac's raven form. Clanking metal, grinding gears, the squelch of the pier's rubber guards against the ship's steel side. The acrid stench of a laboring engine. A surprising, worrisome boom—the lowering of the drawbridge for the vehicles on board, their motors already running, emitting their own noxious clouds.

People, their voices adding to the tumult, emerged from the shelter of waterfront shops, parked cars, and the terminal itself.

Cormac blinked stinging eyes and, fighting sensory overload, contemplated the growing crowd below. Add to that the number of passengers amassed at the ship's rail and the sum total could equal disaster. Too late, he returned his attention to where it should have remained: Leticia at her table by the window...only she wasn't at her table.

She wasn't anywhere he could see.

Dread settled like gravel in his stomach. With so many people as cover, Leticia could slip away in one of the waiting cabs or, worse, hand the relic over to someone with Cormac none the wiser. He'd have no trail to follow at all then. *Slim chance, indeed.* He scanned the area near the hotel, just across from the pier's exit. Was she still inside, hiding, waiting? Or had she already made her move, already blended in with one of the groups milling about the entrance to the hotel's pub?

A worker's shout heralded the securing of the gangway and the potential for disaster doubled, trebled, as the exodus began.

Damn her—and damn him for not anticipating this.

At the pier's terminus, people scattered like billiard balls in a well-executed break. Some veered toward the parking lot while others rushed to jump into the vehicles currently fighting for space with those leaving the ferry. By far the largest number, a mix of passengers and the pedestrians who had come to meet them, cut through the congested traffic in the street to walk into the town proper. Even with the visual acuity of a raven, it was impossible to track every person, every movement. He was fighting something like panic when a flash of familiar colors drew his eye.

Leticia's scarf.

Maybe. It was gone before Cormac could be sure, swallowed in the stream of people going up Bridge Street. He took flight. Thankfully, it was easy to locate the jewel-toned swirls in the midst of so many drab grays and browns. It was almost as if the locals hoped to blend in with the stones of their buildings. Leticia, with such garishly dyed cashmere fluttering about her neck, couldn't have blended *less*.

He contemplated that as he circled to keep her in sight. Didn't she want to lose him? Not exactly a reassuring thought, if so. Had she gotten rid of the relic already—given it to someone in the crowd? Hidden it somewhere for one of her Brigantium cronies to pick up? Had she become merely a decoy? Cormac felt his heart stutter, choking on a flood of adrenaline until he noted the way she clutched her timeworn satchel to her side. An unusual gesture for her, and a revealing one. His heart settled into a more assured rhythm.

This would end here.

He flew to a solitary tree at the end of the long block, well ahead of Leticia's part of the crowd. Mostly sheltered from the wind by the buildings, the gnarled branches currently hosted a conspiracy of ravens and made it the perfect place to hide.

Or not, as it turned out. Cormac's landing set off a chorus of harsh protests from several territorial juveniles. Then, before he could do something about that, one of the elders noticed Cormac's eyes—a mix of vibrant blues, atypical to say the least—and set about making a spectacle in which the rest enthusiastically joined. They clucked and cawed and hopped, jouncing branches and raining dried leaves onto the sidewalk below. People looked up—some intrigued enough to stop. The flow of traffic slowed, drawing even more attention Cormac's way.

He screeched, his fury palpable enough to scatter the flock. In a confusion of flapping wings and scolding chatter, they regrouped, then flew high overhead, west toward the Peedie Sea.

A bell jangled somewhere to his right, and he looked over in time to see Leticia enter a narrow stone building at the start of the block. The post office. Its door closed sharply behind her.

Cormac flew to the building's sole window—a high thing, less than a foot wide, set next to the door. The ledge was too narrow but he gave it a shot anyway, beating his wings while his feet scrabbled on the crumbling masonry. Leticia's back was to him, blocking his view of whatever was transpiring between her and the clerk...until she took something from the counter and, turning slightly, tucked it into her satchel. A booklet of stamps, it looked like, and what was probably a receipt.

Stamps? This outing couldn't be so innocuous as that. Why wait all day to run an errand—and time it with the arrival of the last ferry? While carrying around the relic, no less. Before he could theorize, she turned away from the counter and began walking back toward the door.

He flew up to the roof, out of sight, to wait. She, more than any of her Society, knew of his knack for taking raven form. She had to have noticed the ruckus in the tree.

Most shops had or were nearly shut, their proprietors busy turning out lights and pulling down metal security gates. The last of the ferry passengers, with nothing to interest them, were moving quickly through the area.

The bell announced Leticia's exit.

Cormac peered cautiously over the rain gutter, watched her wave to the clerk as the door closed. Instead of moving away as expected, she paused, still facing the building, to adjust her scarf. Cormac held himself motionless, hardly daring to breathe, but she didn't so much as glance up. Apparently satisfied, she turned away and continued up the street. Whatever her plans, they were taking her towards St. Magnus, not back to her hotel.

With a few pedestrians still near enough to cause trouble, Cormac forced himself to hold back, to observe. Did she plan to return the relic to its hiding place? Add her own wards to the considerable craft that already protected the building? Until help from her Brigantium arrived, it would be the wisest thing for her to do. He couldn't let her.

When she turned into the alleyway behind the cathedral's walled grounds, he pursued. Trees had been planted along the interior side of the high wall, their bare, twisted branches overhanging the entire path. He landed on one, timed it so Leticia was directly below. She, with her gaze once more intent on the cobblestones, did not appear to notice.

This was it. Complete isolation, distracted prey.

With his heart pounding triple time, he initiated the shift and dropped. Illusion vanished, replaced by truth. Behind Leticia, his own booted feet hit the pavers. At the sound, she startled and began to turn. He didn't want that. Didn't want to see what loss looked like in her eyes.

"Don't, love," he said, surprising himself, and then planted both hands against her back and shoved. She stumbled into the wall opposite, her cry of shock morphing into one of pain. Belatedly, his hands registered the feel of her. The thin, light bones.

He had forgotten for a moment that her appearance was no illusion. That she was no longer the woman he had met all those years ago. Leticia McDaniel had grown old.

As she crumpled, her knees buckling, fingers scrabbling on the rough, vine-covered bricks, Cormac wrenched the satchel from her arm—pulling her entirely off balance—and ran. Above the hard pounding of his steps, he heard the slap of her hands on the pavement, her soft moan. He kept running. Regret served no purpose. He would not look back.

Nearing the alley's exit, he reached into his coat pocket for the chip of stone taken earlier from the Bishop's Palace, and he triggered the spell to send himself there, several circuitous blocks distant. Far enough to prevent Leticia from reaching him in time—even if she were able.

He arrived at the ruin in the span of a blink and, disoriented, let his head drop forward and his eyes close. He used his Sight to make sure he was alone. Tourists would have been asked to leave hours ago, but a guard or caretaker could still be about. Worse, there could be someone else like him—someone up to no good. But his search turned up no other presence. He allowed himself to relax slightly, to turn his concentration toward breathing slow and deep while his body adjusted to its new surroundings.

Icy wind, the crest of the storm, swept into the roofless Great Hall to cut through his clothes as if they were nothing. His muscles constricted, forcing a painful shiver. He opened his eyes. The dizziness had passed. The world remained steady. Jagged-topped stone walls beneath a pale sky.

Feeling exposed to more than just the elements, he crossed to the tower. He was almost certain there was no danger imminent, but when he went through the satchel, he might disturb or inadvertently destroy whatever magic was masking the relic's power. Should someone—Leticia or an unknown—sense it and come calling, Cormac wanted to be somewhere more defensible.

Gravel crunched beneath his feet as he walked and various aches asserted themselves. He hadn't done his body any favors today. His ability to take raven form was a natural talent, one of the odd gifts from his mother's side. But as with all magic, it wasn't without cost. The trick was in balancing such costs with the potential gains.

He adjusted his hold on the worn leather satchel. What was inside more than made up for the past weeks. Would Leticia forgive him if she knew his reasons? He hoped so. Theirs had always been a friendly rivalry.

Friendly, as in...friends? His foot caught on an exposed piece of the original slate floor.

Nonsense. To think he and some upstart, impetuous slip of a girl—no, an old woman now. He didn't bother finishing the thought. It didn't matter.

He jogged up a set of modern steps leading to the tower's entrance. What was past was past. Over. No good ever came from looking back. He ducked under the lintel of the open doorway and turned left into the windowless dark of the base of the tower stairs. The enclosed air of the winding passage was thick with the prickly scent of cold, wet stone. He began to climb, sweat beading on his skin despite the chill.

What did he know of friendship, anyway.

By the time he reached a tiny alcove, his lungs and muscles burned—one more sign he'd been pushing himself beyond his limits. After he handed over the relic, though, he would be able to get all the rest he wanted and then some. He would be free to go anywhere. Do anything. A dangerous, tantalizing warmth began to build in his chest, and he could have kicked himself for indulging in such hopeful thinking.

Hope, for all of its pleasures, was a weapon. One which could cut deeper than any other, especially when wielded by such a master as Idris Cathmor. Everything depended on the man upholding his part of the bargain, and nothing in their mutual history gave any assurance that he would. Quite the contrary, really. But it wasn't as if Cormac could've refused.

At a small alcove, he took a moment to catch his breath. Autumnal twilight shone through a tiny window, blearily illuminating the remnants of a bird's nest scattered upon the ledge. He set Leticia's satchel down on them. Here was secure enough—although, admittedly, an unwillingness to face another climb factored heavily in that estimation.

As did impatience. With an unsteady hand, he unlatched the satchel's single clasp and reached inside.

He pulled out an odd collection: the guidebook he had seen through the hotel window; a packet of tissue; several eyeglass cases; a toffee-covered biscuit, fuzzed with lint and half-wrapped in a paper napkin. The detritus of an active, chaotic life, he thought, a smile tugging at his reluctant lips. Folded pamphlets for sightseeing tours. The folded receipt from the post office and the packet of stamps. Smooth pebbles he had watched Leticia collect days earlier on Papa Stronsay while the wind had whipped strands of silver hair out from under the scarf tied about her head.

Though she had bent down to investigate whatever objects happened to catch her eye, she'd moved with the caution of asking too much of old bones.

He had noticed it then. He'd known it in the alley. Yet he

had shoved her without concern.

There was nothing for it now—and indeed it was ridiculous that his thoughts had gone there again. Time was wasting, the Oak and Thistle awaited, and...and he wasn't finding anything remotely like a relic. His fingers combed through the remaining jumble with increasing agitation. This was not right. His heart beat a tattoo of anxious denial. The relic had to be here.

It had to be. He overturned the bag, dumped everything. Coins rained, some bouncing out the window, others pinging their way down the stone stairs. Papers fluttered, settled in the shadows at his feet. He shook the bag. Nothing. His breath catching, he thrust his hand inside, felt only cloth lining and grit. Biscuit crumbs. Sand from Papa Stronsay.

Nothing more.

Cormac's head spun, the world going ass over teakettle as reality's cold wave thrust him towards a bleak, rocky shore. His fingers shook as he unfolded the paper from the post office.

She had played him for a fool, after all.

● ○ ●

Lettie still couldn't believe she had pulled it off. But she had. Tricked Cormac right and proper and given herself the time she needed to get away.

Her hands clutched the steering wheel too tightly, the pain in her bones reminding her why she had essentially retired to Oregon and set up shop years ago. She was far too old for this kind of thing. The tires hit another chuckhole, jounced her back in the seat.

She quickly leaned forward again, her chest nearly against the wheel, her eyes straining as she tried to peer beyond the uselessly short beams of the headlights. So far, she had caught no sign of the tiny harbor where a fishing boat and its well-compensated captain waited. But it couldn't be too far.

The island wasn't that big.

Softly, she directed a curse at the cheap rental car, although in fairness, she knew where the blame more properly rested: her own aging vision and the careless absence of her distance glasses. Cormac had those now. He had *all* her glasses. When she had tucked necessities into her traveling bag earlier, she'd neglected to include them.

What else might she have neglected?

That troubling thought was shoved in with the many others she had locked away for later consideration. Thoughts which, if allowed to run around now, might lead to second-guesses and panic—two luxuries she couldn't afford just yet.

Her worried sigh was cut off by the hard bounce of another hole in the asphalt. She squinted as the whole car began to vibrate and steering became even more of a wrestling match. Not asphalt anymore. Hard-packed dirt and stone.

If the consequences of failure were not so dire, Lettie might have thought this a grand adventure. Alone in a bucking, speeding car she could barely handle on a narrow, pitted track; racing against things she barely understood yet sought to control; leaving behind the closest friends and allies she had ever known. Thrilling, really. If only it all weren't so close to falling apart.

The car splashed through a flooded dip in the road. Muddy water coated the windshield. She could barely see at all now, and the odd, illuminated symbols on the controls failed to suggest to her how she might engage the wipers. Something else she had failed to do in her haste—to properly acquaint herself with the car.

Another wave of fear threatened to swamp her. Had desperation caused her to do a terrible thing?

"Oh, Thia," she murmured. "I *am* sorry, dear."

Should everything go as planned, however, there would be no need to be sorry. Everything would be resolved before her grandniece could be pulled into the mire. Or so Lettie hoped. Timing was everything, and time was moving altogether too quickly these days.

Evil was at work. An insidious evil that had slipped past all the Brigantium's defenses to take root deep within. Yet Lettie had no proof. She didn't even know exactly what form it took, or who might be behind it.

She was keeping secrets from her compatriots—her *friends*—because of a few groundless suspicions. It was terrifying.

It was treason.

But had there been another way? Things had happened so quickly, had she not given this enough thought?

Her mind preoccupied, she took a curve too fast. The wheel shuddered in her grip as the car went wide, its right side tires tracing the edge of the rough track. When it straightened—and the car seemed content to stay on it—Lettie blew out a relieved breath, said a prayer of thanks.

And shrieked.

She was about to hit a man.

Her foot stomped on the brake, mashed the pedal to the floor as she wrenched the wheel to the right. The car shimmied, resisting, only to careen off the road and down a grassy slope. The front dropped abruptly into a ditch and the car slammed to an immediate, shocking stop. The seat belt locked, holding Lettie fast as her breath whooshed out and her head whipped forward and back, then forward again. Her teeth clunked together, the hollow sound reverberating through her skull.

It took her a moment or two to pull herself together, to process what had happened and that she was no longer in motion. She bent forward to rest her head on hands that continued to grip the wheel.

She hurt. Everywhere. Like the dickens.

The sputtering motor died, and with the ensuing silence

came a horrific clarity of thought. The man in the road. She knew him.

She should have run him down.

Her slowing heartbeat sped again. Surely the postal form and its false trail should have kept Cormac occupied longer than this. And how had he tracked her so quickly, in any case?

Sitting up, she forced her wildly trembling fingers to turn the key in the ignition. He would be furious. Her skills were nothing to his. Her only hope was to evade. She turned the key again.

Clicking. Grinding and clicking. No matter how hard she cranked the key, no matter how hard she willed it, the motor would not catch. Instead, the lights went out. Next, the key jammed, refused to budge. Superior magic at work.

"*Brigid*, help me," she prayed, and scanned the vast field before her. With her blurred vision, she could just make out a cluster of lights on the distant shoreline—the harbor at Tingwall, she realized. Her intended destination. Perhaps she could run.

"Silly old fool," she whispered. She couldn't outrun a normal man. She certainly would not outrun Cormac. Why couldn't her deception have lasted just a little longer?

There was nothing for it now. Taking a pained breath, she prepared to leave the car's illusion of shelter. Her muscles locked as something deep within screamed in protest.

She told it to hush.

Shoving open the door, she eased her legs out over the threshold, felt a sharp twinge in her back when she turned to look up the hillside. The car hadn't traveled all that far, she was surprised to see. That was the way of frightening events; things became distorted. What had seemed a great distance was only the matter of a dozen or so yards.

Cormac stood watching from the edge of the road. Even without her glasses, she could see every detail of his face, from the harsh set of his jaw to the triumphant gleam in his dark, cruel gaze. What magic was he employing that enabled her to see so clearly? Such a spell could have saved her a fortune in lenses over the years. If she wasn't so afraid of his present anger, she'd have asked him. They had long been opponents, but never truly enemies—not until this terrible business.

And, until tonight, they'd met only once before. He looked the same. Starkly handsome with a lean, athletic body. The sharp planes and angles of his face accented deep set, piercing eyes and an elegant, bitter mouth. His hair was styled differently—short and tousled, in keeping with current fashion. It must have cost him a fortune in some trendy salon.

Something tickled the back of her mind, caused her to look more closely at his face. Not exactly the same, she realized. His eyes were wrong. Though moonlight robbed her vision of color, she could tell that the irises were too dark—brown, most likely, when they should have been a striking mixture of blue. As unforgettable as the North Sea in a storm and just as moody. Why, of all his features, would he change only them?

And how had he done it? According to the information on file, eye color was the one aspect of his appearance he *couldn't* alter. It was a fixed part of his nature.

Lettie nearly groaned at her idiocy. Colored contacts were a dime a dozen these days. "*Enough,*" she told herself, and braced her hands on the door. "No more procrastinating."

She began to stand. Her feet sank into the ditch's foul mud but she managed to keep her balance as she stepped away from the car and raised her head to meet Cormac's stare once more. A slow smile spread across his face. Cocky bastard, she thought. Anger flared and her mouth opened of its own accord, ready to tell him where he could stick that over-confidence.

From behind, an arm wrapped around Lettie's chest to pin her arms to her ribs. Crushing force pulled her off balance. She couldn't kick at her attacker, couldn't even stand. Clawing at the woman's arm, she tried to twist free. Her feet slipped, slid in the mud. Something popped in her chest and she couldn't breathe.

She had been stabbed. The pain of it exploded through her, made her head swim.

Her pendant, Lettie thought desperately, refusing to believe even as the evidence mounted. Her pendant should have prevented this—should have at least warned of the woman's approach, not to mention the strike of her blade. It should be acting now in defense.

"Not...possible," she rasped, struggling to breathe. She was going to be sick, even as blood filled her lungs.

The hilt of the knife pressed harder against Lettie's back. She couldn't turn her head, couldn't see anything of Cormac's partner. Lettie had assumed he was working alone. He *always* worked alone.

How she longed to say something to wipe that smirk off his face. But she hadn't enough breath to speak. And what *could* she say without giving anything away? She had lost, yes...but he hadn't won, even if he thought he had. Her laugh was more of a spasm, but her murderer translated it well enough.

"Something amuses you?" The woman's taunting voice, although whisper soft, rang a bell.

Understanding dawned, sharp and cold.

Lettie went numb from it. The implications were too terrible, the situation far worse than she had dared imagine.

"Not the eyes," she said, the words nothing but strangled sounds as blood bubbled in her throat. She coughed, tried to pull in a breath. "The rest of it. Not the eyes." Blood surged into her mouth, trickled down her chin. She would have wept had it not been too late.

Oh, Thia. Forgive me.

The arm pulled away and Lettie's body dropped, sliding off the knife to land facedown in the stagnant muck.

CHAPTER 2

The packing tape was gone. Just...gone. Thia McDaniel rooted through the desktop clutter in bewilderment. This was crazy. She had just set the roll down a few seconds ago. She picked up a folder stuffed with invoices, found two pairs of scissors and a half-eaten candy bar. No tape. She stared at the chocolate a moment, seeing it as another indication of a life fallen inexplicably out of order. Her normal self would never leave milk chocolate with nut-truffle crème lying around.

Nor would her normal self tolerate a workspace this messy, she thought as she slapped the folder down on a stack of catalogs—one of several stacks the office had acquired since her great-aunt had left on a buying trip.

Thia missed normal. And her great-aunt, she admitted—and then acknowledged the incongruity with a wry smile. As one of the world's foremost eccentrics, when Leticia McDaniel walked into a room, "normal" went out the window.

That she and Thia had gotten along so well, not only working but also living in close quarters, had been both a surprise and relief. To Thia, anyway. Lettie hadn't seemed anything but delighted from the moment her grandniece had arrived, as if she had expected them—veritable strangers aside from a few childhood visits and phone calls—to have nothing short of a grand time.

"Ms. McDaniel?" Stefanie's tentative voice came through the door.

Thia bit back a groan. Nothing made her feel older than her thirty-two years than the unfailing formality of her great-aunt's clerks. "Come in," she called and, as Stefanie entered, gave one last try: "Please, as I've said before, call me Th—"

"Ms. McDaniel," the girl wailed, ignoring her in the rush up to the desk. "People are still going through the decks. Look. Look at all this." She held out several packs of Tarot cards and a large wad of cellophane.

Lettie had hired Thia to set up and run Eclectica's website and online sales system, but in her absence, Thia had become more and more acquainted with aspects of the "brick and mortar" store itself. This was one of the more peculiar. And, unfortunately, it came up a lot.

She indicated a relatively clutter-free spot on the desk. "Go ahead and put them here. I'll add them to the list."

Stefanie set the opened cartons down with the cellophane on top. Immediately, the wrinkled plastic began to shift and expand with soft, foreboding crinkles.

"I guess the sample book isn't working, huh?"

"No," Thia said. "Maybe the stock should be kept in one of the—"

"Ms. McDaniel, um, since it's not too busy right now, I was thinking it would be a good time to, you know, um... smudge." Stefanie's eyes were alight with fanaticism. Or addiction. To sage smoke? Was it possible?

"I think we're still good from yesterday," Thia said carefully. "But if you need something to do, Abby mentioned a lot of pocket stones have found their way into the polished stone display."

"Pocket stones," Stefanie repeated with a frown. "Those are the ones with words put into them?"

"Engraved. Yes." For reasons that remained a mystery, the simple things were one of the website's best-sellers.

"You're sure you don't want me to smudge?"

Thia hadn't felt so sure of anything in days. She shook her head, called up a phrase she'd heard Lettie use. "Energies are good right now." Whatever that meant.

"Oh. Okay, Ms. McDaniel. I'll do the stones thing, then." Shoulders slumped in disappointment, Stefanie made her way out of the room.

"Thank you." Thia kept a straight face until the door clicked shut. It wasn't nice to find amusement in another's misery, but there it was.

Her grin faded when she caught sight of the ruined Tarot cards. She would have to count to be sure, but she figured there were now more packs in Lettie's office than out in the store.

She stuffed the cellophane into the trash and then made a quick list of the particular sets. Dragon Tarot. Renaissance. Fairy Oracle. Two Ryder Waite decks. Oh, come on—two? Thanks to movies and TV, even *she* knew what those cards looked like.

She dropped the lot into the drawer to join the rest awaiting pickup by Mrs. Sharpe's art students for use in their end-of-term collages.

Maybe they could take some of the catalogs too, if Lettie wouldn't mind. Thinking to ask her later, Thia pulled a new roll of tape from the supply drawer and returned to prepping the day's shipment.

An esoteric tradition of the Tarot was costing the store real money. Thia wasn't sure she'd make the same decision Lettie had. Sure, if it were true that previously handled cards could be dangerous to their new owner, then of course customer safety came first. But it seemed nothing more than superstition.

Thia tore off a strip of tape, laid it over the mailing label on a box destined for Maryland. Inside were a whimsical ceramic toad and a wand made by a local artist, if she remembered correctly. Amazing to think she was in a small Oregon town and doing business with—she read the label— Megan Wilcox, someone who had likely never set foot inside the store itself. Although, true enough, the Shakespeare Festival attracted global visitors. The University did pretty well with that too. Thia made a mental note to add a "how did you find us" question to the website. Maybe all these online orders *were* from people who had visited.

Tallying the boxes—seventeen, many of them packed with multiple items—she did a final check to make sure they were securely sealed, the labels protected, and then she worked to form a stack she might conceivably carry the three blocks to the post office.

When she got back, she would talk with Abby about moving whatever Tarot decks remained out for sale into one of the locked cases...assuming room could be made. Not in one of the herb cabinets, obviously, since those were currently over-stocked in anticipation of a pre-Samhain rush. Maybe they could find a place for the decks at the counter, leave the sample book as it was.

Her mind on the various problems associated with that, she shrugged into her jacket, took up the tower of boxes, and crept out of the office. The store was bustling with midday shoppers. Narrow pathways, overflowing displays—this could prove to be the day's biggest challenge. Thia shuffled along, alert for any sign of impending doom. She should make two trips, she knew that. Unfortunately, she also had a preference for making one difficult journey instead of repeating several easy ones.

Anyway, this would be fine. If she craned her head just so and looked out of the corner of her right eye, she could see enough of the ground ahead to avoid obstacles as long as she took really small steps. Which she was. Inching her way around the stairs, she plastered a humble expression on her face and apologized to the many people she heard move out of her way. "Excuse me. Sorry. Thank you. Excuse me. Sorry. Thank you."

"Of course, dear," came a soft, accented voice.

Lettie?

Thia stopped, shocked speechless, and maneuvered her way around to face her great-aunt.

No one was there.

"Isn't this lovely?"

The same voice, more distant and to the left. Thia turned, saw an elderly woman holding up a gilded Celtic cross. The man to whom she was speaking, her husband probably, nodded appreciatively. Thia had never seen either of them before. She let out a pent-up breath and resumed her shuffling walk.

She had been so sure it was Lettie. Why? The slight British accent combined with the voice's obvious age? Lettie wasn't due back for weeks.

Thia moved past the main counter where, from the sound of things, a new roll of receipt paper was being loaded into the cash register. The plastic lid closed with more force than necessary—and that told her immediately who was trying to perform what for anyone else was a simple task. Somehow, for Abby, it never turned out that way.

"I'm going to take my lunch after I get done with this," Thia told her, although she figured any fool could tell she was off on her routine trip to the post office—and Abby, Eclectica's manager, was no fool. She was also, despite a couple of early disagreements over the online sales process, someone Thia had come to consider a friend.

"Sure thing," Abby acknowledged, and then swore as the clattering of the register stopped short. Paper jam. "I did not say you could bend, you stupid piece of—"

"Watch your 'negative energy,'" Thia warned lightly, thinking of Stefanie. "Don't give her an excuse."

"Oh, hell—I mean, heck. I thought she was still on break." Something (Abby's hand, from the sound of it) slammed onto the register hard enough to ring the cash drawer's bell.

Thia winced. "You want me to give that a try?"

"No, no." Paper tore. "I'm going to get this. I really am." More tearing. "Even if it takes"—*click*—"all"—*bang*—"day."

"Okay. If you're sure." Her smile safe behind the cardboard barricade, Thia continued on her way.

When she got to what she estimated was a few steps shy of the door, it opened to admit a chill breeze. She stopped. Eclectica didn't have automatic doors and no one had passed her on their way out—therefore someone was coming in. She eased herself to the side of the aisle to make room to go by.

No one did.

Puzzled, she looked down. Just as she located two beaded slippers at the threshold, an unmistakable, patchouli-based fragrance crept around the boxes.

"Hello, Madame Demetka," she said.

"Thia, *darlingk!*" The accent was unidentifiable. Perhaps something Eastern European. Perhaps not. "You carry very much for one, yes?"

"Maybe a little." Thia shifted carefully and, peering around the boxes, brought the town's most popular spiritual medium into view.

Wild, burgundy hair swirled around an upper-middle-aged face caked with foundation and painted with bold strokes of color. Dark, almost ebony eyes glinted beneath lashes so coated with mascara as to be nearly united—one giant lash per lid.

"Are you reading today?" Thia asked, sidling past and out the door. "I didn't think you were scheduled until—"

"Oh, but *miri kushti,* you are not leaving now, yes? I have come most urgently to speak with you."

Strong fingers latched onto Thia's wrist, initiating a brief, ill-fated dance. With her reflexive backward step, the box mountain began to sway and Madame Demetka, instead of letting go, tightened her grip and pulled.

The topmost boxes flew outward while the middle tier slid. Dropped. Larger, heavier boxes landed with a solid thump on the cement while smaller ones bounced, scattering. In a matter of seconds, Thia held only one box—the former base of her careful assemblage—while the rest rocked to a stop at her feet.

●　○　●

Pall Mall, London

Eight in number, they sat motionless at the round table, their attention rapt on a trio of fat white candles. There was no other illumination, no sound but the sharp hiss of flames consuming dry wicks, their reflections dancing on the highly polished dark of the wood.

"We humbly seek to know of Leticia Phyllida McDaniel," Beatrice said at last, her voice solemn and, to Quentin's ears, unwelcome. One more reminder of a night he often thought he would do anything to forget. Her voice had gone out into the dark for that ritual, too. Right before all hell had broken loose.

He took a slow breath, concentrated on the task at hand. Emotions, especially the volatile kind, had no place here.

The beeswax melted slowly at first and then more quickly, running down the outsides of the candles to mar the table's surface. Knowledge always came with a price. Sometimes small, as in the finish of a table. Sometimes not. And all too often, in Quentin's experience, unexpected.

The three flames began to twist, snapping and spiraling frantically as they rose and fell in the still air.

"What of Leticia?" Beatrice asked again.

The flames immediately ceased their dance. Breaths caught.

Clasped hands tightened, including those gripping Quentin's own, their fingers crushing the fine leather of his gloves. He gritted his teeth, worked to tamp down his resentment. By rights, he should no longer give a damn what happened to the Society; yet here he was, concerned.

Someone cried out as, in a crackling rush, the flames elongated. Growing strong and bright, they reached an impossible height above the small wicks. Golden light filled the room, illuminated tense faces beneath woolen cowls. Quentin had time to note that Beatrice's mouth gaped, an unusual sight on a woman known for self-control, before the flames winked out.

Not one flame, but all three.

Several voices exclaimed in the sudden dark, and then fell silent as the divination's message sank in. Confirmation that Quentin's vision had not been of a potential future but of a particular past. One event, unchangeable and now undeniable: Leticia McDaniel was dead.

Murdered.

Quentin pulled his hands free, the first to break the circle. He heard the rest follow suit.

"Lights!" barked Arthur, retaking control.

With the snap of fingers, the chamber was bathed in opulent light, the crystals of its chandelier painting rainbow-edged shapes onto dark wood and robes of silver-shot white. Thin tendrils of smoke drifted up from the candles' dead wicks.

Hoods were pulled back, and Quentin wondered if his expression showed any less shock than could be read on the others' faces. To imagine a Brigantium without Leticia was difficult enough, but to imagine that she would be murdered? Even having experienced flashes of it in his vision, it was hard to accept this pronouncement as fact.

He looked to Arthur, sitting motionless with bowed head. The older man was either paying his respects to their fallen associate or gathering his thoughts (or both), but because of the table's mirror-like surface, he appeared to be frowning at himself.

Quentin drummed his fingers, the action winning a glare from Beatrice. It lacked its usual force, however, diluted as it was by tears.

With her ice-blue eyes deeply shadowed despite the skillful application of make-up, she looked tired. Old. She seemed not to care that her hood had frizzed her iron-gray hair, tugged it loose from the confines of her habitually and intricately woven plaits.

Feeling a tingle of...something, Quentin stilled his hand, shifted his gaze to the woman staring at him from her seat to Arthur's left. Cassandra Swinton. If he was not mistaken, her brown eyes were bright with a very particular kind of interest. He acknowledged it with a slight nod. Her full lips quirked, not unattractively, before she broke contact, turning to listen to something her brother murmured to Eben, Head Archivist and their mentor.

"Don't even think it," came Beatrice's harsh whisper.

Turning to her, Quentin lifted a brow in inquiry. Damian, unlucky enough to be seated between them, made a point of staring straight ahead.

"You know very well what I mean." Beatrice's eyes narrowed. "Just...don't. She's more than a pretty face."

"Very much more, indeed," he quipped. It was almost knee-jerk with her, his argumentativeness. "I'll be sure to keep that in mind."

She made a quiet sound of exasperation, but wisely let the subject drop.

Quentin looked at his hands, resting easily on the table when he felt inclined to throttle someone. The rumors were true; the Swinton twins were being groomed for positions of high rank—perhaps even directorship should Arthur get around to taking his due retirement. Not so long ago, that had been *him*, Quentin thought with surprising jealousy. Some dreams, it seemed, were harder to kill than the rest.

At the snap of opening locks, he looked up to see Arthur remove a stack of papers from an attaché case. Once those had been arranged to satisfaction on the table, Arthur cleared his throat and, in a formal, dispassionate voice, began.

"When Lettie last reported, she claimed to be on her way to Edinburgh to visit one of her dealers about some documents and"—he checked his notes—"maps. Through a search of her home, we have since learned that she believed she was on the trail of an item connected to the Cailleach. A relic."

Damian raised a hand. "Of her followers or—"

"Of the goddess herself."

And wasn't *that* a particularly nasty bit of news.

Quentin gauged the others' reactions. Grim faces all, but most exhibited no surprise. So it would seem that everyone but Damian and himself had known already. He couldn't quite decide about the woman seated to his immediate right. Leslie was clearly distraught, yes, but had been since the beginning. Devoted to the cataloging and painting of pillywiggins, she was not the sort who belonged in tonight's events.

So why had she been included? Were they that desperate for powerful mediums? (The fact that the guileless woman *was* one proved life's ironic bent.) Or was there another reason for this odd assembly? The Brigantium had an entire Bureau of Divination, after all. And yet not a single member of it was present tonight.

"What *I* do not understand is what Leticia was doing with matters of the Cailleach in the first place," Eben said, clearly working himself up to a high level of outrage. "Why was I not made aware of her acquisition plans? As head of Archives, I should be notified of any such—"

Beatrice cut him off with a weary gesture. "I'm sure she

meant no slight to your position, Eben. Leticia has always been impetuous." She shot Arthur a look. "And as one of our oldest living members, she was often given certain liberties when it came to travel and procurements."

"Not that we did not try to rein her in," Arthur said. "And we most certainly did not know she was involving herself in matters of the Cailleach. Project Monitoring believed she was on a routine buying excursion for her little shop in the States, coupled with a bit of continued research into localized Celtic deities. They gave her the usual budget for the latter and classified it as historical and of minimal import. We were as taken aback as you, Eben, to discover that her official reports were less than forthcoming."

Quentin did his best to hide his astonishment. What sort of game had the old bird been running? The sort that had gotten her killed, obviously. But why? He'd known her all his life—first as a guest in his mother's home and then through the Society itself. She had been a frequent lecturer in his classes and, even after her semi-retirement, an ubiquitous presence in libraries and archives throughout London.

She had devoted her life to the Brigantium. And, after his vision, Quentin had thought she had lost her life to it as well. But if she had gone out on her own, that might account for the first message the flames had presented. When they had all gone out, they had affirmed Quentin's vision of her death. The spiraling that had preceded that, however, signified false friends.

"So it was intentional," Eben declared. "Leticia McDaniel was using the system to her own advantage. Do we know to what end? Was she working for someone else?"

"Brigantia's spear, Eben," Beatrice snapped in a rare show of temper. "This is Leticia we're talking about. *Leticia.* One of our finest."

Spots of red mottled Eben's cheeks. "If she were that, she would have followed the rules. The monitoring system was established for good reason. To prevent confusion, improve efficiency and oversight, and cut down on danger to those in the field. She knew that well enough, and yet it appears she went against it—indeed, used it so no one knew what she was really doing. With something as important as a relic of the Cailleach at stake! And look what she got for it. *Killed* by a—"

Leslie's sob startled them all—Eben to the point of silence. When she buried her face in a delicate, lace-edged kerchief, Quentin felt temper rather than pity. It was about time the woman got her head out of the flowers and took a look at the rest of their world.

"I have spoken with our people in Edinburgh," Arthur said, apparently setting aside Eben's aspersions of treason as easily as he did the top page of his notes. He pushed up his glasses, consulted the second page. "They verified that she did indeed stay there, but she left over a week ago. I've got calls in to our other safe houses but so far no one else mentions having seen her." He fixed Quentin with a look. "Are you certain you can't pick up on the location?"

"Night. Clouds filling the sky. Grassy hills, perhaps. A few lights in the distance." He shrugged. "Smell of the ocean. Cold." Inside and out.

Leslie made another noise. How ironic that the woman who communed with flower fairies should be such a watering pot. His loud sigh earned him another one of Beatrice's looks.

"You believe, Quentin, that you saw Cormac? At the...at the moment of death?"

"It was a highly broken sequence," he told Arthur, a repeat of what he had said to Beatrice earlier. "Incomplete pictures, most often blurred. No sounds. Few sensations." For which he was grateful, even if they might have provided additional clues. He cleared his throat. "But, yes. At the moment of death, she was looking at Cormac. His image came through clearly."

Almost too clearly, but Quentin saw no point in mentioning

that yet. If at all.

Arthur removed a photograph from one of his files, slid it across the table. "You saw him?"

Quentin pulled it closer with the tip of a gloved finger. It was a bit grainy and out of focus—obviously taken in a hurry. A young man, slight of frame and perhaps average of height, had been captured mid-stride, looking directly at the camera.

"Yes." He pushed the image away.

"Everyone should have a look," Arthur advised, and Damian took up the photograph. "This is the only image on record. Taken nearly fifty years ago. Is it still accurate?"

Quentin nodded. "The hair is a little different. And I can't speak for the color, obviously. Otherwise, he looks the same."

"B-but surely," Leslie sputtered. "It's been fifty years. Surely he—"

"He's half-*Sidhe*, dear," Beatrice explained, her singularly patronizing tone setting Quentin's teeth on edge. "It would seem he ages as they do."

Leslie's eyes were wide. "How different from the pillyw—"

"Yes," Arthur broke in. "Naturally, of utmost concern, is his connection to Idris Cathmor."

Leslie showed no reaction whatsoever, the evil of the man apparently never having reached her magical garden. Lucky her.

As Cormac's photograph continued its slow circuit, Arthur handed a folio to Damian. "I'd like you to go to Edinburgh. See if you can't pick up Leticia's trail and get more details on those documents. It does appear that she didn't want us to be aware of what she was doing. Until we know what that was, we won't know what befell her. Or why." The last was directed pointedly at Eben.

Damian, his expression unreadable, inclined his head and tucked the papers into the sleeve of his robe. He was one of the country's greatest sorcerers, but no one would think it to look at him. With his white flowing beard and hair, he was something straight out of a children's tale. Especially when he wore his cloak of blue velvet embroidered with gold stars and crescent moons. Which he frequently did. Quentin had yet to decide if it was a quirk of fashion or brilliant subterfuge.

"We all saw the spiraling of the flames." Arthur gestured toward the candles. "If Leticia was targeted, or if it had to do with what she sought, or our Society in general, we need to know. And we need to know what *she* knew. What she was attempting, what her motives were, and what went wrong. We need to know what we're up against." He paused to cast a meaningful look around the table. "If it could happen to her, it could happen to any one of us."

Leslie moaned and, with her arms wrapped protectively about her chest, began to rock while Damian—likely headed into immediate danger—merely looked thoughtful. "What of the documents Lettie was after?" he asked, smoothing a hand down his beard. "Did she describe them at all?"

"More to the point," Eben said, "did she describe the relic? Did she *find* it?"

"No, to the first. To the second, we do not know," Arthur replied, uncharacteristically sharp. "If she did, we can only hope she put it someplace safe and that we can find it before anyone else. As for the documents, we know only that they were new to the market, pulled out of an estate undergoing renovation, and that at least two maps were involved. One of those may or may not have involved a cathedral. Somewhere." He said the word like a curse and glared at Eben. "Keep going through her effects. Look for anything that could shed light on this. Put people on her family if you have to, as well as the people at her damned shop. She may have mentioned something to them."

"Or been working with them outright," Eben put in. "We need to send people there, Arthur."

"Yes, of course." He directed a look at Beatrice.

"I'll make the arrangements," she said.

Unless the Brigantium wanted to risk an incident of untold proportions, they could not operate within another country without first performing an intricate, bureaucratic dance.

Arthur closed his notes. "In the morning, I will be sending out an official notice of Leticia's passing and advise caution. Security here and at the safe houses has already been alerted. We will put Diviners on it, but they will need guidance." He frowned at Quentin. "The more specifics you can get them, the better."

There would be no getting around it. Quentin nodded and then, "Are we certain Idris is behind this?"

"We've got Cormac. That's certain enough."

Again, Quentin was tempted to voice his concerns about that part of his vision. But, as he well knew, stress—traumatic death in particular—could bring on such extreme clarity as he had perceived.

"What of her family?" Leslie asked, apropos of nothing. For a moment, Quentin thought she was suggesting they were involved in the killing. Others must have thought that, too, given the stunned silence which followed.

Looking bewildered, she clarified, "They should be told of her passing."

Arthur shook his head. "The regulations are clear," he said. "There can be no exceptions."

"Could we contact them anonymously? It isn't right, leaving them to find out on their own."

"No, my dear," Damian broke in before Arthur or Beatrice could respond. "Even if it were not against the rules, in the case of a suspicious death—especially one without a body—it would only bring trouble. If her family were to contact local authorities and demand justice, perhaps speak to the press...." He let his voice trail off and then, gently, "You see why we cannot risk it?"

"Our protocols are in place for good reason." Arthur, having removed his glasses, took a moment to adjust the bend of an earpiece. "Her family will learn of her passing in their own way."

"When she doesn't answer letters, or call on the phone?" Leslie's eyes were wide. "It's too cruel. Surely we—"

"It is how it must be," Beatrice said over Quentin's groan of exasperation. His hip was reminding him—strongly—how long he had been seated. "Leticia understood that her family was not to know of her life with us. To make contact would not only break our trust but hers as well."

Arthur replaced his glasses. "Take extreme care, everyone. Keep several people informed as to where you will be at all times and try not to go out alone. Reinforce any protections on your homes and anything you might carry. We have been taken by surprise in this. That must not happen again." He returned the papers to his case, engaged the locks.

Quentin reached for his walking stick.

"I will be planning Leticia's memorial service," Beatrice told the room at large. "Something to honor her spirit. If anyone has any suggestions, please email them to me. Thank you."

Ignoring Leslie, sobbing anew, Quentin pushed himself to his feet and made his way out of the room.

● ○ ●

Cumbria, Northern England
There wasn't time for this, Cormac thought bitterly. If Idris expected to get the relic before Samhain—only three bloody days away—then he needed to leave Cormac alone to deal with what had become a complete cock-up. Instead, there it was, the undeniable prickling as the old man requested his presence.

Request. Such a polite term with its implication of choice. A surge of anger caused the stippled glass in Cormac's hand to shatter, dousing him with vintage Armagnac. Flames hissed,

feeding on the precious drops, as a dissonant rain of glass fragments fell upon the hearth. What should have been savored,
gone in an instant. He hurled the broken stem into the fire,
watched it strike a brick of peat and then roll to an anticli-
mactic stop against the grate. Hot anger drained, leaving cold
fear in its wake.

Cormac inspected his hand for damage; finding none, he
looked to his coat. Bits of glass and drops of brandy glistened
on the black velvet. That would never do. He vanished them
all with a tiny pull of power and a flick of his wrist. Only then
did he accept the summons.

The transition occurred almost instantly. He opened his
eyes to inky, absolute blackness. Still, he knew exactly where
he had materialized. The stale, icy air reeked of dank stone
and age old fear. The silence held a particular weight, oppres-
sive and familiar; sound did not travel well through miles of
winding passageways carved deep into the belly of a mountain. Cross Fell, it was called now. The older name was more
apt.

Fiend's Fell.

"Home again, home again, jiggity-jig."

At his muted voice, bespelled crystals flickered to life and
showed he had been right: the summons had set him outside
the Sorcerer's chamber. As usual—and despite the urgency—
he would be forced to wait. More proof of his subservience
or some such rot.

His breath misted in the chill while he glared up at the two
statues that bracketed the chamber doors. Matching granite
representations of the man himself, obnoxiously oversized.
Each outstretched hand held a glowing orb: The powerful
Sorcerer offering illumination to the lowly. So very preten-
tious, really—and threatening, too, if one interpreted the orb
to symbolize *bælcraft*. Energy collected and shaped into a form
which could then be "thrown" with degrees of accuracy and
strength that depended upon one's skill and strength. Magic,

weaponized.

Cormac adjusted his cuffs. Use of his Sight would get him a rough tally of the mountain stronghold's current inhabitants, but it would also land him in even more trouble if detected. Given his luck lately, it would be.

All he'd wanted was one night at home. One damned night so he could replenish his energy and consider how to keep his errors with Leticia from becoming catastrophic. Instead, he'd had less than an hour, only enough time to eat his Sainsbury's ready meal and pour himself the brandy.

His jaw clenched. That had been a favorite glass, the last of a set from 1763. Irreplaceable.

Metal clanked inside the chamber as the lock disengaged. Cormac drew himself up, head held high, and clasped his hands behind his back. As the doors eased open, wood sliding across stone, a wave of power-fueled rage struck him with the force of a speeding lorry. He staggered across the threshold— not at all the entrance he'd wanted to make—only to be hit again.

So much power. Wave after wave, flowing from and returning to a single source at the other end of the room.

As suddenly as it had begun, the assault ended. The energy currents continued to swirl through the vast, nearly empty chamber, but they no longer targeted Cormac. He strove to regain his composure along with his previous pose: shoulders back, hands clasped, expression neutral. The look of a calm, confident man.

Pretense, every bit of it.

He began the long walk to the dais, his boot heels clicking the deliberate, easy rhythm of his stride. The wall-mounted orbs gave off only a faint, wavering light. Hardly enough to see by. Idris preferred it that way, sadist that he was. A blow unseen, unanticipated, carried more force.

At the base, Cormac halted, kept his gaze respectfully low

while unease skittered down his spine. His mouth was dry to the point that he had to swallow before speaking. "*Athair.*"

The reply came in the form of increased anger, accompanied by a contempt that far exceeded the usual. It was easy enough to translate: Somehow Idris had learned of the events in Scotland.

Per routine, Cormac knelt and dropped chin to chest. The act grated—always had—but while subservience might not be in his nature, self-preservation was.

The lights flickered, brightened a bit.

His cue.

He rose and mounted the eight steps to the summit. Dread made his body heavy, his movements stiff, as he closed the short distance to the foot of the bed. It was a monstrous thing, the bed. Fit for a medieval king—literally. If memory served, it had been taken from Caernarfon Castle in payment for one favor or another. It had held up well, considering.

The same could not be said of the man occupying it.

With long, thinning white hair and nearly transparent skin that alternately wrinkled and stretched over sharp, forbidding features, Idris looked like death. The spells and rituals which had long preserved his life could no longer do more than the bare minimum to preserve his body.

"*Athair,*" Cormac said again, and watched Idris's eyes open. The man's expression, as usual, was neutral. Blank. Only the eyes held any emotion.

Unsurprisingly, that emotion was disgust.

«*You lost it.*»

The words, spoken silently, cut through Cormac's mind like a blade. He took a slow breath through the pain. "There has been a temporary setback, yes."

«*Insolence.*»

A vicious slap of power snapped his head back. The world spun. Settled. He swallowed again. "The parcel she handed over to the post office in Kirkwall was a decoy. Nothing but tissue inside."

A good bit of time had been wasted discovering that. Not only had the break-in taken longer than expected, thanks to some protective spells of the local variety, but Cormac had had to deal with the ones Leticia had placed on the package itself—along with what seemed like at least a half roll of tape.

"I believe she also posted the real thing," he continued, "but through another means, earlier. Morning, probably."

«*To where?*»

"The decoy parcel was addressed to her London house," he said carefully.

Not carefully enough.

«*You do not know.*»

Cords of rage shot from Idris's motionless hands to wrap around Cormac's chest and squeeze. He couldn't breathe.

"Worthless," Idris said aloud. The word echoed, bouncing from wall to wall as the room itself began to tremble. "Tell me why I should let you live."

Cormac hadn't the breath to respond. Blood trickled from his nose as the room grew even darker. Or maybe it only seemed to. He was near to passing out.

He had been a fool, thinking he had any chance against his father.

«*Culén.*»

Abruptly, the cords vanished.

Knees buckling, Cormac grabbed hold of a bedpost, sucked in a much-needed breath. Full consciousness returned on a rush; he came to understand his lingering unsteadiness was not his own but due to the room's continued, temper-driven trembling.

"The McDaniel woman is missing," he managed to rasp a moment later. Perspiration slicked his skin. He forced himself to straighten. "There is no trace of her rental car and I can't sense her beyond an isolated point on a road. Violence has been done there."

«*She is dead.*»

"So it would seem." As if he couldn't care less, he pulled a handkerchief from his sleeve, proceeded to dab at the blood on his face. "I intend to leave for London again tonight. I've found some new things to try against the protection wards around her home." He tucked away the soiled cloth.

«*And if you fail?*»

"Her absence should be noted soon if not already. Leticia McDaniel was one of their best. They'll panic. Mistakes will be made." And Cormac would be ready.

«*Fools.*» The orbs nearest the bed began to brighten, rattling in their holders. «*Samhain nears. You will finish this.*»

"Of course, *Athair.*" Or die trying.

He would be dead, anyway, if he failed.

Triggering the transportation spell, he bowed deeply—and was knocked off the dais by an unexpected lash of power. He landed hard on the floor below.

In the stunned moment before the pain registered, Cormac returned home. The cold marble of his father's chamber was suddenly the Persian carpet of his own, while the old man's laughter rang in his ears.

CHAPTER 3

Thia stared, dumbfounded, at the boxes now scattered on the sidewalk. Madame Demetka made a sound of dismay and flew into action, clapping her heavily ringed hands at a growing crowd of pedestrians.

"Everyone, everyone," she cried, gesturing wildly, her kaftan sleeves flapping like the wings of an angry swan. "The boxes! Please now to get the boxes!"

"No, it's okay," Thia protested as people, some looking quite dazed, moved to retrieve the fallen shipment. No one paid her any attention. "Please, don't trouble yourselves. I can—"

"That one! That one!" Pointing here, whirling to point there, Madame Demetka wove through the crowd like a tempest of silk and velvet. "No, not yet—you in the sport hat, take that one! Yes, yes, yes. No, the other!"

Thia murmured quiet thanks as the mountain was rebuilt in her arms.

When all was done, Madame Demetka bellowed, "Many, many thanks! Many blessings!" to the hastily departing crowd and then, for Thia, lowered her voice...slightly. "My sorrow is great. *Miri mora,* please, you must tell me nothing has broke."

She seemed so distraught, Thia would have said everything

was fine even if it were not. But, considering she had packed everything to withstand use in a football game, she said with confidence, "It's all fine. Thank you." She moved to go. "I'll see you when I get back, okay?"

"No, no, sweeting—I must talk with you now." Madame Demetka reached out a restraining hand, only to pull it back with an understanding nod at Thia's flinch, and instead took a step closer to say in an amazingly loud whisper, "My guides tell me there will be trouble for you. Trouble this day. Very clearly this comes through."

Thia smiled. "Trouble, like dropping boxes?"

"You joke, but they do not. Not this time. Oh, *maw!*" Her hands fluttered in irritation. "They will not tell me more. Not here, they say. I will ask for more details, and meantime, you will be careful. Promise this."

"Of course," Thia agreed easily, figuring that after so many years in Los Angeles, she was always careful. Well, careful enough. Granite Springs was a safe town. Quite odd at times but safe.

Madame Demetka leaned in even closer, her face only inches away. *Too* close. The scent of patchouli was dizzying, while the woman's features distorted so that all Thia could see were big, dark eyes. Bottomless pools. She had heard that description before but never fully understood until now. Thia needed to step back, to create some space, but couldn't seem to move. She felt really strange. A bit nauseous. Light-headed. Was she about to faint? Please, no. She'd drop the boxes again.

Madame Demetka blinked, and Thia felt herself snap out of...whatever she had snapped into. Although she did still feel a little weird. Shaken. "Did something—"

"Wait one moment." Raising her hands, Madame Demetka tilted her face toward the sky and closed her eyes. A sudden wind blew through the liquid amber trees that lined the sidewalk. Red and orange leaves trembled noisily overhead, some blowing loose, and Thia ducked her face against the boxes.

Several leaves slapped against her head on their way by.

"Answer they do not," Madame Demetka said as the wind died down.

Thia lifted her head. "Your guides?"

Madame Demetka nodded gravely. "We will both think on this, you and I, until they do."

"Sure, of course." Thia had no idea what the woman was talking about. She turned to go. "See you later."

"You will be careful," Madame Demetka called after her. "Trouble comes this day. Trouble in shadow and storm. No lie, this. Be wary! Be wary of the bird!"

What in the world? Frowning, Thia turned back, but Madame Demetka was already darting up the street in the opposite direction, fabric snapping around her like colorful flames. No wonder her readings were in such demand. She had a true gift for the theatric.

But, really, what was that about? Thia didn't know whether to be amused or concerned. She supposed she could sort it out later—after Madame Demetka had consulted her "guides" or whatever it was she really did. According to the invoices in Lettie's office, her legal name was Sally Wilson, so there was no telling where the line between truth and fiction lay.

Three blocks later, after shoving and bobbling past the post office's tight-hinged exterior doors, Thia was still pondering that—and what to make of that whole episode. None of it made any sense. She pushed through the service area's equally tight-hinged doors to go straight for the unattended counter. She managed to get the whole tower of boxes onto it without incident. Things were looking up.

"Hey, Dave," she called as the postmaster stepped out of the back office, a bundle of envelopes in hand.

"Thia." His heavy, white beard split in a grin, and he gave a nod to the boxes. "Web business doing good, huh?"

"It is, thanks," she replied, matching his grin with her own.

There was something infectious about his good humor. "And thanks for that advice on the delivery options. We've already seen a pick up in sales."

"Glad to help—even if it makes my job harder," he joked, the merry twinkle in his eyes giving no doubt as to why he was said to be a shoo-in for the role of Santa in the town's Holiday Parade.

She watched as he typed on his computer. "How was your vacation?"

"Cold," he answered with a chuckle. "We were in the north of Finland for most of it. Peg has family there. Now"—he reached for the topmost box—"what have we here?"

Packages were weighed; routine security questions, asked and answered; stamps, printed and affixed. An efficient ten minutes later, Dave handed over a pile of tracking slips and transferred the boxes to a waiting pushcart.

"See you tomorrow," Thia told him and, stuffing the slips into her pocket, turned to go.

He stopped her with a wave. "Not so fast—I got something for you. Came in this morning. I'll just be a sec." He took the cart with him when he went, disappearing into the silent back of the building.

Thia tried to think what the "something" could be or why it wouldn't have gone to Eclectica along with the rest of the midmorning delivery. To make life easier, she and Lettie had all mail directed there, personal and otherwise.

Trouble comes this day.

"Here you go," Dave said, returning. He held a small, square box wrapped in brown paper and coated with enough tape so as to be entirely waterproof. Thia didn't need to see the British stamps and words "Royal Mail," to identify the sender. Only one person had a more paranoid hand with tape than she did.

"Funny she sent it here, isn't it?" Dave passed Thia the box and then, saying something about seeing her tomorrow, went back to his office.

"Thanks, again." She looked at the box in her hands. Heavier than she'd expected for something so small. She gave it a little shake by her ear. Nothing rattled. She frowned. There, under several layers of glossy tape, was the curious direction, "hold for pickup," written in Lettie's elegant hand.

It was a silly thing to wonder about, especially when Thia could simply ask her about it later.

On the way back to Eclectica, she turned her imagination toward a more intriguing subject—namely, what might be *in* the box. She didn't doubt it was a gift of some sort; Lettie typically gave her some sort of trinket from her buying trips. Which was odd really, considering the rest of the family got things like socks and...well, socks.

It must really be something if Lettie didn't want to wait to deliver it in person. Thia ran a finger along the thickly taped surface, looking for any potential way in while she waited for traffic to clear at the crossing. But without something sharp, there was no way.

She waved her thanks to a stopped car as she jogged across the street.

After a quick trip to her London house in early summer, Lettie had given Thia a small collection of Roman coins and glass beads. Fairly common, she'd said they were, and not fine enough to be of interest to historians, but Thia thought them fascinating.

She pulled open Eclectica's door to find the sales floor overrun with exuberant teenagers. A school group—possibly two, given the numbers. At this time of year, the Shakespeare Festival attracted at least eight groups a week. Abby, barely visible beyond the cluster at the main counter, spotted Thia and made a dramatic pantomime of relief. The noise level was incredible, with the super-energized students picking up and exclaiming over anything and everything while carrying on conversations regardless of distance. Thia stashed Lettie's box beneath the counter, shut off the store music that couldn't be heard anyway, and found herself volunteering to retrieve a porcelain dragon's original packaging from the stock room.

Forty unchaperoned teens with time to kill.

Trouble, indeed.

● ○ ●

Near Russell Square, London

Seated on a bench in the neighborhood's central garden, Cormac touched the screen of his phone, maintaining the pretense of texting while he kept an eye on Leticia's town-house across the way. Men and women, their white jackets emblazoned with the logo of an interior design firm, had been streaming in and out all day, taking packing crates and storage boxes to the lorry parked at the curb. A bit of renovation, they'd cheerfully informed inquisitive neighbors. Some work scheduled while the owner was away. Yes, it should look quite grand when it was done.

It was a clever ruse, and an elaborate one, but it didn't fool Cormac. No one outside the Brigantium could pass through Leticia's protection wards unharmed without first destroying them; and as his Sight revealed, the air around the townhouse continued to shimmer with her distinctive magic, its semi-transparent colors in constant motion like a dreamy, deadly soap bubble.

When Cormac had arrived that morning, bleary from the turbulent British Midlands flight out of Manchester, he had expected to find Leticia's house deserted and to spend the better part of the day getting through security measures both magical and practical. Instead, he'd been forced into the role of frustrated observer yet again.

Concerns amassed in his mind like clouds gathering before a storm. The Brigantium he knew was not capable of such speed, such efficiency as this—and they sure as *ifrinn* didn't possess such numbers.

In its early days, the Society of Brigantium had been little more than a London-based aggravation. Mired in institutional traditions and academic musings, most of its people had proven no more bothersome to him than meandering cattle: a temporary obstruction requiring little effort to remove. A small push, a distraction, and they'd wandered out of his way.

That would not be the case today, he thought darkly, his fingers in constant, random motion on his phone. Though it was nearly ten o'clock at night, there were still a few people in the private neighborhood park—some on mobile phones, like him; others out for a smoke with the dog. Any one of them could be Brigantium. He couldn't risk putting anything past them now.

When had they changed?

Sometime after the Great War, presumably. He hadn't had many dealings with them since then. Aside from Leticia, of course. She had always been, or so he'd thought, the exception which proved the rule. A singular bright spot, a lively and unpredictable adventurer among bumbling academics.

The Brigantium had been a dull, slow-moving bureaucracy more inclined to study than to practice. Prone to inaction, not action.

The smoothly orchestrated activities here suggested quite the opposite.

He had dealt with them only on an individual basis for so long, he had lost track of the whole. Here, as with Idris, more attention should have been paid. Much more.

So many people, working tirelessly, for all of their youth and uniformity looking like members of a battalion. Their movements were focused and precise, with none of the little wanderings, the breaks, one might expect from a casual workforce. No chats by the van. No personal phone calls. No trips to grab a snack or a warm drink. Just in and out. In and out.

Cormac shifted uncomfortably on the bench. As traditional London shops had sold out to make way for chain stores; as building facades had been torn down to be replaced by giant panes of glass and illuminated lettering; so too, it seemed, had the Brigantium changed. Become sleeker. More efficient.

More threatening.

It had taken hours for a weak spot in their security to reveal itself—or, rather, *her*self. Just when Cormac neared his wits' end, a harried looking girl had emerged from Leticia's house, consulted a scrap of paper, and then shown an advantageous lack of concern for her surroundings as she had trotted down the street.

He'd been quick to pursue, confident that with his slicked-back hair, colored contact lenses, and quintessentially boring suit he looked both distinctly unlike himself and not liable to arouse concern. Three blocks later, the girl had gone into one of those commercial sandwich shops that had popped up everywhere, seemingly overnight, back in the 90's.

Franchise buyouts, the toadstools of the commercial world.

He had kept his distance in the shop, pretended to read the ingredients on a bag of crisps while the girl collected items as directed by her scrap of paper. Gathering dinner for the troops, he figured—the implication being that they planned to work into the night. No one bothered to feed people who would soon be at home.

When he'd seen her having a bit of trouble at the beverage case, Cormac had made his move. With a smile forced all the way to his eyes, he'd stepped up and gallantly freed the jammed bottle of Orangina. From then it had been a simple matter to silently recite the charm's trigger word and transfer a small amount of energy to the glass before he set it in her basket.

If the girl had felt his use of magic, she'd given no indication during her effusive thanks. She had blushed a bit, which Cormac supposed he should have found flattering, but under the circumstances hadn't felt anything at all. He'd bid her a polite good evening and returned to the garden to wait.

And there she was, finally, hurrying back with two over-stuffed plastic sacks in each hand. In one of them, unless she'd become wise to the trick, was the Orangina bottle and his key into the house.

With some trepidation, he watched her move through the propped-open iron gate—and when she paused at the top of Leticia's front steps, he worried outright. But she was only adjusting her grip. That sorted, she entered the house and Cormac felt the sharp prick of the charm breaking through. The tiny hole it created in the wards began healing almost immediately, so that by the time the girl moved out of sight, it was as if it had never been.

Should the protection wards be under careful monitoring, even that tiny breach would be detected. Indeed, if the neighborhood as a whole was under surveillance, the smallest use of magic might set of alarm—hence Cormac's solely practical disguise. Clothing and lenses instead of a glamour.

Yet as seconds passed, the workers kept to their routine, carrying items out of the house like ants looting a picnic.

While Cormac put away his mobile, he took a chance and preternaturally reached out to the charm lodged in the glass, felt the energy of it travel farther into the house. Still no noticeable change outside. Workers came out with boxes, went back in without. The door remained open.

He expanded his awareness and, using the glass as a focus, reached out to its immediate surroundings. Soon he could feel the people moving around the bottle: getting close to it; quickly falling away. Coming to fetch food and drink; leaving to return to work.

Time was limited. Once the Orangina was consumed, the bottle was liable to be put out in the recycle bin. Outside the wards, it would be no use to him. He expanded his Sight to its fullest and rapidly searched the house's multiple stories. Of the many isolated spots, few seemed viable. This method of scanning a destination point was imprecise at best, much like looking through thick fog at night. One wrong transit and Cormac might find himself bisected by, crushed between, or impaled upon any number of household items or architectural features. Since he'd rather avoid that, he had to choose a large, open area—a room as opposed to a crawl space or closet—and hope he could find cover before someone happened by.

Uttering the spell's trigger, he sent himself flowing through the glass to what he very much hoped to be a deserted attic.

● ○ ●

Granite Springs, Oregon

Thia scraped a scissor blade along a strip of metallic ribbon and, after it sprang into a mound of tight curls, handed the gift box it adorned to Stefanie for stickering and then hurriedly grabbed another. Wrap ribbon, snip ribbon, curl ribbon, hand to Stefanie. Wrap ribbon, snip ribbon…Thia had no idea how long she'd been at it but by the looks of things, she would be at it for a good while longer. That didn't bode well for Mrs. Blumquist's matinée seat—or those of the increasingly impatient customers waiting behind her. The Shakespeare Festival had a strict policy on late seating (namely, there wasn't any).

Madame Demetka hadn't been kidding about trouble. Along with the school tour, a group from the Crystal Hills Retreat and Wellness Center, and an unusually large number of locals looking to prepare for Halloween parties and Samhain celebrations, Natalie Blumquist—binge shopper extraordinaire—had arrived for what Abby had described as an annual spree.

"Are you certain you wouldn't like to pick these up after the show?" Abby asked for the third, maybe fourth time.

Mrs. Blumquist gave a blithe wave of her hand. "I'm sure it's fine. I need to know what goes where." Her manicure matched the color of her beehive updo: lavender. Somehow, the older woman managed to carry the hairstyle off. Thia bit

back a smile. She imagined the people who would find themselves seated behind her at the plays would like to carry it off
as well—to somewhere far, far away.

"We're labeling them, Mrs. Blumquist." She tapped scissor
points on a slip of paper tacked to the bottom of the latest
box. "Easily removed when needed."

Mrs. Blumquist's brows lifted. "That's all well and good, I'm
sure. But I still need to know what everything is. The labels
could fall off."

"Of course." Thia's smile felt brittle. Before she could
resume curling ribbon, someone near the back of the line
cleared his throat.

A man in an argyle sweater held up an inexpensive garden
statue. "My wife just wants this one frog," he said. "She'll kill
me if I miss our show."

"I only have postcards," a bespectacled woman chimed in.
"The sign said I could get five for a dollar. So I picked out
five—and have a dollar right here. There's no sales tax, right?
And I don't need a receipt. Can't I just go?" She stacked four
quarters on the counter while the man behind her waggled a
tiny pewter figure. "I promised my daughter this fairy thing,"
he said. "She's waiting out there with her mother. We'll all be
late."

Panic began to spread through the entire line.

Thia glanced at Abby, who was diligently peeling off price
tags and entering the amounts in the register. The number of
items left to ring up was dwindling, but not quickly enough.
The grandfather clock across the aisle showed fifteen minutes
to curtain, and the theater was a two sizable blocks away.

"Lynette?" Thia turned to the young clerk currently packaging already-tallied items. "Would you take everyone up to
the café and use the register there? Just make sure you keep
track of the total." It would make for an accounting hassle
at the end of the day, but it was better than ruining so many

peoples' afternoons.

"Sure thing." The clerk hurried out from behind the counter and gestured toward the stairs. "If you'll please follow me, we'll get you on your way."

With audible relief, the line reformed itself behind her.

"Just one frog," the man could be heard to say as he climbed. "Just one little frog."

Thia resumed her manic curling. The scissor blade flashed. Ribbon streamed through her fingers. Next to her, Stefanie tore into a new roll of stickers.

"It all comes to twelve hundred thirty-nine dollars, sixty-three cents, please, Mrs. Blumquist," Abby announced above the register's rapid printing. Stefanie grabbed the last item, swathed it in tissue, and stuffed it in a box. Thia wrapped ribbon around it, racing for the finish.

Mrs. Blumquist tapped a lavender nail on the counter. "I do wish you hadn't sold all those darling papier maché gnomes."

"There's always next year," Thia said cheerfully, and snipped the last length of ribbon.

"Yes, yes, that's true." Smiling the smile of a fanatic, Mrs. Blumquist signed the charge slip. "Next year."

Four sturdy bags were crammed full to bursting and then handed to their new owner. "Oh my," Mrs. Blumquist said, chuckling. "This is quite a haul, isn't it?"

"Would you like some help with them?" Abby asked, already holding open the door.

"Oh, no, dear," the other woman said, trotting toward her. "I'm sure I'll be fine."

"Thank you so much, Mrs. Blumquist." Thia waved, scissors still in hand.

"Until next year!" Bags bouncing at her sides, she left the store.

"Enjoy the play," Abby called after her, and then let the door shut with a jingle of bells. She staggered over to the replica of a medieval throne and threw herself down onto it with a low moan. As her eyes closed, her head tipped back. Curls of dark hair stuck out from several clips to give her an unusually frazzled look.

Natalie Blumquist had come and gone. Thia felt like it might take her a whole year to recover.

Oh, but what about—"Did everyone get out?" She raced for the stairs.

"Let it go. Let it go," Abby pleaded. "It's two fifteen. Time for our break."

"Time for our *lunch,*" Thia corrected from the base of the stairs. She looked up at the second floor but it was impossible to see the register area. She couldn't hear anything, either, but took that as a good sign.

"Lunch?" Abby groaned. "More like breakfast for me."

Back at the counter, Thia bent to retrieve Abby's purse. "I don't know how you can get through half the day on just a latte and a muffin."

She had forgotten about the package from Lettie, but there it was, waiting—no, *begging*—to be opened. Her fingers itched with compulsive need, worse than any kid's on Christmas.

"What's the matter?" Abby headed over.

Thia didn't know how to answer. She had picked up the box and her pulse was pounding, her chest constricted with an anxiety that had no place at all in this situation. Lettie had sent her a gift, for crying out loud. A simple, most likely wonderful gift. Abby—all-too-observant Abby—was looking at her like she thought Thia had gone off the deep end.

Maybe she had. "I—I just realized maybe no one has had lunch yet," she lied. "Do you know? Has anyone had—"

"What's that?"

Thia followed her friend's gaze to—right, obviously—the box in her hand. "Something from Lettie." She shrugged, not wanting to make a big deal of it. Because it *wasn't* a big deal.

It really wasn't. "What should we do about lunches? If no one has had any, I could stay."

"Nonsense." Abby took up her purse, slung it over her shoulder. "Management always goes first. Don't be such a damn martyr."

"I heard that!"

At Stefanie's voice, Abby's mouth snapped shut, most likely on another curse. Already, tendrils of sage smoke were wafting toward them...with Stefanie, her fingers tight on a lit smudge stick, close behind. "I thought this would be good after all that stress, Ms. McDaniel," she said, happily zeroing in on the counter.

Thia hurried out from behind it. "Do you know if anyone took lunch?"

"Yeah. I mean, I'm pretty sure everybody did." Stefanie blanketed the cash register in smoke. "We took turns grabbing stuff from the café."

"See, Thia?" Abby said hoarsely, blinking watery eyes. Her hand waved frantically in front of her face. "We can go. Let's go."

Thia's fingers tightened on the box, almost as if they had a will of their own. "Sure," she said, but her anxiety symptoms had only grown worse. She had to open the box. Not out of interest but out of *need*. What the hell was wrong with her? "I just, um, have to take care of something. If you want to go ahead, I can meet you. Wherever you want."

Abby's brow went up. "Mediterranean Rose?"

"That'd be great." She began walking to the office. "I'll see you there."

Abby accompanied her. "I'll wait for you. Not patiently, but I'll wait. You can show me what's in the box that's got you so weirded out, and then we'll go." She turned, heading left. "I'll be in the gnomes until you're ready."

Nothing much got past Abby, as Thia was coming to know.

It made her fantastic at her job but, at other times, perhaps a bit too perceptive.

Once inside the office, Thia went at the box with a cutter. Several deep slices had the paper peeling away from what was a cardboard shell crafted out of a shoebox lid and another astonishing amount of tape. There was a note folded and stuck to the top. Its instruction—"Read First"—had been embellished with several exclamation points and underlines.

"Okay, Lettie." Thia smiled as she detached the paper and prepared to read the usual ramblings about weather and innocuous retail activities—things like scouring a local artisan's market or finding a new jewelry supplier.

She couldn't have been more wrong.

Hello, Dearest. I hope this missive finds you well. It had been my intention to go with you to retrieve this parcel from the Postmaster and thus reclaim both it and the responsibility it brings. If you are reading these words without me, it signifies a great calamity has occurred, and I am so very, very sorry. Everything falls to you now.

There are those who would do anything to possess what I hereby place in your care. They must not get it. At all costs, Thia, my dear. At all costs. Legend calls it the Stone of Shadows, though its true name has been lost to time. It is a relic of the Cailleach and holds much of her power. Outside of a ritual, that power cannot escape——nor can it be detected if wrapped, as I have done, in specially charmed cloth. Tell no one what you have. Tell no one I have contacted you.

There is so no time now to explain. I am still hopeful that I can reach you and must hurriedly away, as the saying goes. Take all precautions with your safety.

All my love,

Lettie

P.S. If you are not wearing the pendant I gave you years ago, please do so. It can offer some measure of protection.

Thia's hands shook, rattling the letter as she went over it a second and then third time. What was Lettie talking about?

A relic of great power. A calamity. Precautions. Charmed cloths and protective pendants.

Had Lettie lost her mind?

Thia's fingers went to the silver charm she habitually wore around her neck. The metal, although it lay directly on her skin, was cool to the touch.

She had been twelve when Lettie had given it to her. There had been no mention *then* of magical powers. Thia hadn't even considered it a charm; but, okay, since its subject was the gorgon of Greek myth, that probably meant it was supposed to be one. But that was *superstition,* like carrying a rabbit's foot for luck. It might make someone who believed in such things feel better, but it didn't actually do anything. Did it?

No. Thia had taken to wearing it simply because it had been a gift from Lettie, whom she had near to idolized at that time in her youth. And so Thia had put on the medallion, with its garish depiction of a woman's face with fangs and oversized eyes, and had imagined she could be just like her great-aunt. Free-spirited. Adventurous. She continued to wear it now out of habit. Nothing more.

She was used to its weight, its presence, and missed it when it wasn't there, that's all.

She let go of the necklace, set down the letter in order to pick up the box. Whatever was in there was not what Lettie claimed. It couldn't be. Thia sliced through the thick tape and cardboard with increasingly unsteady motions. Lettie always seemed so on top of things...but she was in her early eighties. Even a brilliant mind could fall prey to senility.

Heart in her throat, Thia reached into crumpled wads of tissue and pulled out something hard and small and wrapped in white silk. She removed the cloth, sending a scrap of paper fluttering to the counter, and found herself holding a rock.

A nice rock, to be sure—some sort of grayish brown crystal, carved into a sphere and polished to a glassy smoothness—but a rock nevertheless. There were several quite like it in a display case near the register. They were popular with the New Age crowd, said to bring clarity to dreams, attract love, stimulate creativity, and the like, depending on the type of stone.

Oh, Lettie. With tears pricking her eyes, she brushed a finger across the sphere's glossy, dark surface.

Something like static electricity shot through her, holding her in place for a bleak, terrifying moment while the world seemed to fall away...only to slam back in place.

Hard.

She blinked, dizzied, her arms tingling as a strange warmth moved up them, soft and seductive. Unable to resist, she lifted the Stone to the light.

No longer dull and opaque, the crystal glowed the color of well-steeped tea. Strange shapes, like captive shadows, swirled as she rotated it between her fingers and thumb. It called to her, somehow. A thing of mysterious beauty, whispering of potential. She was tempted. So tempted. It was hers, whatever it was. *That* she knew without question.

It thrilled. And it frightened beyond words.

Hastily, Thia re-wrapped it in the cloth. The odd sensations faded, leaving her shaken and somehow...empty.

"So, what is it?"

At Abby's voice, Thia nearly jumped out of her skin.

She whirled to find Abby holding open the door, her brows drawn in what Thia took to be understandable impatience.

"I'm so sorry," Thia said. Her voice was rough. She cleared her throat. "I completely lost track of time." Surreptitiously, she tucked the cloth-wrapped crystal into her pocket. "I've got to make one quick phone call, and then I can—"

"Not so fast." Abby pointed to the packing scraps and stepped into the room. The door closed behind her. "We had a deal."

Thia cringed. Lettie's note might be full of crazy...but what if it *wasn't?* After what had just happened, Thia didn't know what to think.

"It's just a travel souvenir." Unable to maintain eye contact, she busied herself by scooping up the mess of paper and cardboard.

"Really."

"Yep. Just a...paperweight." Thia shrugged and shoved the debris into a drawer. The note followed.

"A paperweight."

She shut the drawer. "Uh-huh."

Rapid knocking cut through the uncomfortable silence.

"Hold on." Abby gave her a side-eye that said this was not over, and moved to answer.

A worried-looking Lynette stood outside the door. "There's someone asking to buy the last of the wormwood. He isn't on the list, though, and doesn't want to wait for the approval process."

Abby sighed. "Okay. I've got this," she told Thia. "You make that phone call. And then we go to lunch. By three." She tapped on her watch for emphasis and followed Lynette out.

"Thank you," Thia called out as the door clicked shut. Her great-aunt had potentially lost her mind—and Thia might have lost hers as well, to consider for even a moment that such nonsense might not be nonsense. And now she had lied.

Trouble comes this day.

"Ah, hell."

CHAPTER 4

Cormac pulled open the drapes to admit the amber light of the streetlamps outside. This room was no better than the others he'd explored. Shelves laid bare; drawers pulled from chests to sit empty, one atop the other; books in haphazard stacks; paintings propped against naked walls; rugs rolled up; cushions carelessly overturned on sofas and chairs. A grievous overreaction to a missing persons case—or even a death.

Again, he felt a niggling unease, a suggestion he wasn't seeing the whole picture. Leticia had always been an upstanding, if unusual, member of the Brigantium. This comprehensive and rather desperate search...it was as if her own people held her under suspicion.

Of what, though, he could not fathom.

He wandered over to the desk, not that he expected to find anything. But he needed something to do while the search-and-seizure crew finished its work below.

A stack of photographs, frames dismantled and set nearby, came as a pleasant surprise. He began to leaf through them, and came to understand why they'd been left behind. They were personal, mostly snapshots of Leticia in various locales, sometimes with people, more often posing solo. He found himself flipping through them more quickly, seeing Leticia at different ages, different aspects. Same exuberant smile, though. The same as on that long ago day when sheer luck on her part—and curiosity on his—had put them face to face in Lancashire. Here, tonight, in the skeletal remains of her home, the memory became like a living thing, at once powerful and achingly fragile.

Full of energy, she had come striding down the coal-stained streets as if all the world was a fresh, unspoiled adventure. He had spotted her in plenty of time and identified her as a Novitiate—easy enough to do when one knew the signs. And it would have been easy enough, too, for him to have avoided detection. But he had been intrigued, he remembered now, as a melancholy smile tugged at his mouth. She had seemed so vibrant, not at all the sort to shackle herself to the stodgy bunch of bookworms and curators that was the Brigantium. So, on a whim, Cormac had stepped out, undisguised, from his hiding place between two boarded up buildings.

Her reaction had been deliciously surprising.

She had walked right up, her bright, blue gaze meeting his without a hint of alarm although she had to know who—and what—he was. And then, before he could decide what to do with her, she'd smiled and thrust out her hand.

"Forgive me for introducing myself," she'd said, her voice had been as clear and guileless as the rest of her. Her accent had been distinctly American that day. She would lose it over the course of the decades to come. "I'm Leticia McDaniel."

And then she had grinned, reminiscent of a child presented with an unexpected treat; he had found it impossible not to smile in return. Certain all his shields were in place, he had clasped her hand lightly and made a simple bow. "Cormac," he'd said, and promptly returned his hand to his side.

"Yes. I know," she'd replied with a little laugh. And then she had surprised him again, this time with a graceful curtsy. "It is an honor. Truly."

He recalled now that he'd nearly said the same. Thankfully,

he had stopped his tongue before it had done anything so foolish. Instead, because it amused him and he couldn't see the harm, he had shifted into his raven form, taking to the air right before her eyes. Her cry of delight had stayed with him long after he'd flown into the countryside. Long after Leticia would have discovered he had beaten her to the illuminated manuscript she had been sent to retrieve. Her laughter and his triumph. He hadn't been sure which had pleased him more.

Still wasn't, although that didn't warrant much thought.

Their chance meeting had seemed of little import at the time; in the scheme of things it had been akin to the handshake before a chess match—one whose games had been played over decades and, more often than not, at a substantial distance. Since Lancashire, they had not met face to face. Not until, of course, four days ago. He felt a pang of something best not considered and set down the photos.

Several phones rang in tandem, one on the desk and, more faintly, others on the lower floors. Cormac set his hand on the receiver, ready, while hearing to people scramble throughout the house, their excited voices asking what to do. From the sound of it, they were gathering in the front entryway where the tinny sound of a recorded greeting played. No digital messaging service for Leticia, apparently. Her voice went on, uninterrupted long after the footsteps quieted, and Cormac entertained himself by imagining the Brigantium's people staring anxiously at a technologically ancient machine. Maybe even one with a cassette tape—something so outdated and uncommon that the youngest might think it magical. A beep sounded. When Cormac heard the caller begin to speak, he picked up. The machine downstairs, already engaged, would continue to record and broadcast for all those close enough to hear.

"It's me, Thia," the woman said, and Cormac's interest was pricked. Her voice was tight. Nervous. And somehow—the register, perhaps, or the accent—reminiscent of young Leticia.

"I had some...questions," the woman said, clearly rattled. "I don't understand what you...what it is I should do. About the—about things."

Beyond her verbal struggle, her distress was palpable, like a cold mist settling on his skin. She was hiding something, that much was obvious, and all of his instincts were screaming. Despite the risk of alerting the people below, he reached out with his senses—something that had been much easier to do before the age of fiber optics and computers, when phone lines had provided an actual, physical bridge.

In the span of a heartbeat, a surprising speed of connection, he got a fuzzy, muted sense of her. Alone in a small, cramped space. Surrounded by...*magic.* So much of it. Different types, different strengths. Objects, he realized, making up a much larger area around her. People moved among them, separated from her but close. Music played softly in the background, accompanied by the sharp rat-a-tat of...a printer? No. A cash register.

A store.

Phone cradled on his shoulder, he spread out the photos, searched for the one he'd seen with—

There. A young woman, tall and slim with untamed, russet hair, grinned up at him in a way very like the Leticia he'd met in Lancashire—so like, Cormac had mistaken them on his first look-through. Behind her was a store window filled with exactly the sort of things he sensed. The name "Eclectica" was neatly painted on the glass. *Leticia's* store. Cormac turned the image over. Blank. She had revealed her first name— Thia—but Thia what? She was clearly related to Leticia, but how closely? How involved in this might she be?

It was all Cormac could do to refrain from speaking, from doing more than his tentative sensory exploration. The need to make contact built, threatening to overcome reason. He forced himself to pull back entirely.

There was a drawn-out silence, one so weighted that he

grew concerned. Was she sensitive, aware of the connection made and then roughly broken? Could she use the Sight?

"Please be all right," the woman begged, her voice suddenly hushed and raw with emotion. Cormac felt the sting of something which, if he hadn't known better, he might've mistaken for a conscience. Leticia, as he knew and Thia clearly did not, was as far from all right as one could get.

He could tell her she was wasting her time and energy on worrying. He could save her the pain of that—but, no, that would give greater pain. The Brigantium could tell her as easily as he. More, really, since they were in the house legally. He'd make himself a target with the first syllable he uttered.

He was being ridiculous at any rate. What did he care about her, whether she knew or—

"I love you," she said, soft in his ear.

He jerked, shocked. The phone dropped from his shoulder. He bobbled the catch, shoved it awkwardly onto its cradle, ending the call. Only when it was too late did he curse himself for a fool.

Those words had not been meant for him.

In the quiet, Cormac took a slow, steadying breath. Thia's face in the photo seemed to stare up at him from the desk. A narrow oval with delicate features. On the pretty side, but not inherently beautiful. It was her expression which gave *that* impression. Hazel eyes, bright and inviting. A Cupid's-bow mouth curved into a familiar grin. Leticia's grin. Yet Leticia had never gotten to him like that. Never left him feeling so unsteady.

He smothered a derisive laugh. She hadn't even known he'd been on the line.

Or had she? Had she been playing some sort of game, trying to...to what?

Footsteps sounded downstairs—people spreading out to investigate the noise on the line, if not that of the receiver hitting the cradle. He needed to leave. Immediately.

He had ruined his chance to explore the rest of the house tonight, but thanks to the charmed glass ball he'd stashed in the attic, he could return whenever he wished. After he dealt with the woman.

The woman who said not enough and far too much.

The Brigantium might already know her identity, might be able to trace her location through phone records. He needed to get to her first.

Thia.

Wood creaked at the end of the hall. Photo tucked in his jacket pocket, Cormac sent himself from the house.

● ○ ●

Granite Springs, Oregon

Thia blinked, stared at the phone in her hand as if it held the answer to what had just happened. Beneath skin gone strangely hot, her pulse raced.

If someone had been on the line—and who would it have been if not Lettie—then he or she would have spoken.

No one had been listening; no one had hung up on her. When her message had gone on for too long, the machine had cut off, that's all. She sat back in the chair, took a deep breath.

And just because Lettie didn't answer, there was no reason to jump to conclusions. Lettie was fine. She was out, that's all.

Thia checked the time, did a quick calculation. It would be after midnight in London, but she had no idea what sort of hours her great-aunt kept there. Lettie could be out with friends—or on the road, visiting local markets. Despite what the note said, there was nothing to worry about.

She managed to believe that for all of six rings, after which it became clear Lettie wasn't going to pick up a call to her cell phone, either.

● ○ ●

Bloomsbury, London

Seated in a crowded Starbucks with his gargantuan cup of tea balanced on the chair's upholstered arm, Cormac blinked eyes bleary from lack of sleep and tried to focus on his smartphone's miniaturized search page. With a few errors due to tiredness and haste, he typed: "Eclectica," "fine gifts," and—recalling the name of the city Leticia had set up in—"Granite Springs."

In a matter of seconds, he was offered a link to the store's website. That was new. He clicked and found himself at a simple but elegant page. It showed a more recent view of the store whose photo he had...borrowed. The exact address was given, along with driving instructions and a link to several small maps of the local area. Most of the former referenced the location of the town's Shakespeare festival.

"Another tourist trap in your honor, Will," he muttered and took a drink of bitter tea. Overpriced and inferior stuff that no amount of honey and milk could improve.

The website's administrator was identified as one Thia McDaniel. Cormac felt a moment of triumph, hid it behind his tea as he took another swig.

He went on to browse the online catalogue, not sure what to make of it. Even with Leticia at the helm, he had expected the usual sort of decorative nonsense: pretty yet powerless crystals to dangle in one's window or from a car's rear-view mirror; candles of all sizes and shapes and scents; sachets of herbs and whatnot that pretended to call forth things like winning lottery tickets and true love. He found all that and more of its ilk. He also found a surprising—and troubling—amount of the real deal.

Exactly how involved was the lovely Thia? Was she aware of every aspect of Leticia's business—in the broader sense of the word—or was she simply an employee? And even if she were "simply" the latter, the store's catalog suggested its customers held more than a passing familiarity with the magical arts. He had to figure at least some of its employees did as well. Was she one of them?

Cormac's relief at finding he was indeed on the right track faded in the midst of so many unanswerable questions. So many unknowns, with the most potentially dangerous being Thia McDaniel herself. He hadn't sensed much power during the phone call, but those who possessed the most were the best at masking it. There was no telling how formidable a foe she might be.

That was a risk he had to take, however. He clicked on the map provided and swore—softly but viciously enough to earn a wary look from the Goth-garbed youth slouched in the next armchair. Cormac had looked up Granite Springs when he'd first learned Leticia had opened up shop there. Since it was nothing to him, he'd then promptly forgotten exactly how far away it was.

Airline travel would allow him time to rest, albeit fitfully... stuck in what amounted to a aluminum can, far from the familiar energies of the earth and closer to those of the moon and sun. Surrounded by nervous people. The recirculated air. The noise. The bizarre concoctions that purported to be food or to at least be edible but were most often neither.

Cormac muttered another curse, swallowed more tea. Why could Leticia not have set her store somewhere closer—like, say, Hampstead Heath? Dammit, even New York would have been a good sight better than Oregon.

In the end, after exploring his options on a travel-booking site, he was forced to rule out airplanes altogether. With the multiple connections and layovers, it would take almost two days to get to the out-of-the-way town. He didn't have that kind of time.

His heavy sigh caught the attention of both the Goth and the purple-mouthed girl now seated on his lap, but whatever they read in his expression caused them to look quickly away. He was vaguely aware of their leaving while he opened the app for Holpnick's Charts. If there was a worse way to travel than by plane, this was it.

Leylines.

His gut turned leaden as he plotted the route. And yet, sickening as the prospect was of such a long trip, he had to admit it was amusing that modern technology was helping him do it. Technology and the obsession of one pseudo-scholar named Cyrus Pickersgill Holpnick.

Not that the poor fool had any idea what he'd really done. In a misguided attempt to prove that mysterious ship and airplane disappearances had been caused by portals to alien galaxies, Holpnick had managed to compile the most detailed and accurate map of global leylines—and made it accessible to everyone at first via the world wide web, and more recently through a somewhat clunky smartphone app. It was amazing, really, that he hadn't been shut down by one of the Other-worldly consortia that worked the lines. Then again, with so much shipping and travel business being lost to real-world methods, maybe such publicity was welcomed these days as free advertising.

It was not as if the average person could use them, in any case. Though Cormac likened the process to throwing things—namely, himself—into a rushing river, that was a vast oversimplification.

To get into a line took great, skilled effort. To leave took even more. Being swept past the intended destination was quite common, as was getting pulled into the wrong branch at major intersections. Some travelers, the ones with too much knowledge but little skill, could easily become trapped, their chances of rescue slim to none.

Cormac never used the lines much himself, and never for such a length as this, but at least it looked to be an easy route. Granite Springs was situated only a few miles from a convergence of several strong lines.

Frowning, he studied the map again. The town, given its seclusion and ease of access from a number of places on the globe, had all the makings of a major depot. Particularly if its primary industry was indeed tourism.

He sat forward. If Granite Springs *were* a depot or, worse, a smuggling hub...Ah, *ifrinn*. He should've given more credit to Leticia's choice of location. She could have made all sorts of acquaintances through her store.

People who would be willing to help her for a price.

What if she had merely been a broker for the relic? Cormac couldn't imagine she would betray the Brigantium like that, but he wasn't exactly doing well on that score. He couldn't rule anything out.

He sprang to his feet, heedless of the half-full cup on the arm of the chair. The cup which, to go by the angry shouts that followed him on his way to the exit, must have spilled.

If Leticia had sent the relic to Granite Springs—and it was becoming more and more clear to him that she had—already, any number of insurmountable things might have occurred.

Once outside, he slipped through the groups of pub-crawlers crowding the narrow street, ducked into the first deserted passageway he found, and pulled out his Ronson lighter. He needed to inform Idris of his plans. To leave the country, particularly by such means, could (and no doubt would) be interpreted as another escape attempt. It didn't matter that over a century had passed since he had tried. Since he had so much as dreamt of it.

With the blood connection, his father could summon him at any time. And, unless Cormac was within the protective charms of his home—a temporary sanctuary at best—his acceptance wasn't optional.

The only place Idris couldn't reach him was the Otherworld, but Cormac wasn't inclined to try *that* again. His first visit, and his last escape attempt. The physical scars, the result of punishment from his mother's family for daring to contact them and from Idris upon Cormac's forced return, had taken years to heal. The other scars...well, he liked to think he had become adept at ignoring those.

He was an aberration, his cousins had been all too happy to inform him when he'd begged to be allowed to stay. A thing bred for Idris and Idris alone, his part of the deal made with Cormac's mother. She got the means to pay off debts which had prevented her from joining the rest of her family in the Otherworld; Idris got the means to prolong his unnatural life. The blood of his blood that, although diluted by half, carried the power of the *Sidhe*.

The blood rituals had worked for a time...until, gradually, they hadn't. When it had become clear Idris was continuing to age and Cormac's blood on the athame no longer provided enough power, the search for new methods—new tools—had begun.

Cormac flicked the lighter, stared at the flame as he sought to open a conduit. Moments passed. Frustrating moments during which he forced himself to remain still when what he needed to do was locate the specific access point to the line running through Green Park. Roughly only four blocks away, that line would take him to a larger one, and that to a larger one, and so on until he reached the Transatlantic Line.

«*You interrupt.*»

"Your pardon, *Athair.*" Cormac rubbed his temple as Idris's annoyance took the form of a dull ache. "I wished only to advise you of a necessary journey. The old woman may have had help—a relative in the States. I go there now."

The ache dissipated, replaced by a needling intrusion as his father demanded full access. Normally this was the point when Cormac raised a token objection, giving himself a few seconds to make sure anything he didn't want to reveal was buried deep. Time was too short tonight. He let Idris in and, through the open connection, felt him sort through the day's impressions and discoveries.

The path could work both ways, if one knew what to do... and dared to risk it.

He did. Too much of this whole situation didn't make sense.

Delicately, Cormac peered through the link, into the edges of Idris's thoughts. He couldn't chance more than pinhole-sized glances, and so at first he assumed he'd encountered an old memory, one made back at the height of Idris's popularity.

The chamber, hazy with smoke. A large, central fire ringed by hooded figures. Bones, red and glistening, held out toward a steaming cauldron. Voices raised, chanting of power, *for* power, when there was already so much. Power inside the chamber. Inside the acolytes who circled the fire. Inside the two who stood like shadows in their black robes. Cormac couldn't see their faces, couldn't see—

«*None of your concern, boy. Unless you fail me.*»

Cormac startled; the lighter dropped from his hand to clatter on the cement. The flame guttered, went out.

«*Do not fail.*» The conduit snapped shut.

For what might have been a long time, he didn't move. He was too shaken, too stunned to feel fear, but it would come. Soon enough, it would come.

So much power. Fewer followers than in the past, but nevertheless an inconceivable number for the present. Moreover, Idris's memory had shown a ritual that required a high level of skill from each participant, not to mention a great deal of energy. It was well beyond anything Idris should be capable of doing without help. Without Cormac's help.

Ah. There came the fear, curling through shock's icy cold to wrap around him like an ill-fitting jacket, claustrophobic and over warm.

It didn't matter. He tried telling himself that. The ritual, the power, the followers. None of it mattered as long as he got the relic. He and Idris had a bargain, a solemn oath drawn up in the Old Ways. To be kept upon pain of death. There was no way the old man would dare break it. This would be the last thing Cormac would ever have to do for his father. The very last.

Nothing else mattered.

● ○ ●

Granite Springs, Oregon

In the end, Thia told Abby to go to lunch without her. Then she had spent the better part of the afternoon trying to locate Lettie through calls to her family. She regretted it now. No one knew anything about Lettie's recent activities—or state of mind—and Thia's nerves had only grown more frayed as she had politely endured talk of weather, vacation plans, and golf.

Everything always came around to golf.

She resisted the urge to bang her head on the desk, but couldn't hold back a groan. With rare exception, the lives of the McDaniels revolved around golf. To them, it was something akin to a religion, and they were determined to bring all strays into the fold. As if talk of thrilling tee offs and breathtaking greens could make Thia forget those three humiliating weeks as Marlindale Golf Camp's Worst Student Ever. When that final camp tournament ball had followed its comrades into the water hazard, Thia had retired her clubs and, with the hardheaded determination of eight-year-olds the world over, sworn that no one would make her take them—or any others—up again.

So far, so good.

She wished her uncle a pleasant time at Torrey Pines and then dialed the number she could no longer put off. She loved her parents, she really did, but talking to them over the phone could be...a challenge.

Her father answered after four rings and, not surprisingly,

sounded distracted. Her mother was over at the neighbors, he finally managed to communicate. That was unfortunate for Thia, since the cause of her father's distraction turned out to be a Verdict: Guilty marathon on TV.

"Hold on, honey—Dr. Steve's about to corner the mob boss in the warehouse. Ha! Fantastic tackle," he exclaimed with a chuckle. "Way to go, Steve."

Thia made an appreciative sound. Tried to, at least. It came out sounding like a cross between a sigh and a gargle.

No matter how often her dad was reminded that the people in his favorite series were not real, that on television anything was possible, that nothing would change in the never-ending stream of reruns, he watched every episode with complete emotional involvement. If he had seen it six times in the last two months, it did not matter.

"They cut to an ad for some damn thing," he said, speaking to Thia at last. "People sitting in bathtubs outside, staring at a field of poppies. Why are they doing that? Are they on drugs?"

"Sort of." There was no way she was going to get into *that* with her father. "I don't want to take up too much time, Dad. Have you heard anything from Lettie? I was hoping to ask her a few questions about something at the store, and she didn't answer when I called." By now, she had her story down pat.

"There's a time difference, you know. It's late there now."

"I called hours ago." She took a calming breath, reminded herself her father meant well. "Have you heard from her?"

"Who can even tell what this one's for?" he complained, his attention clearly back on the TV. "Where's the product name? How do they expect to sell anything without saying what it is? Scotland, I think. Futons? Tell me how that can be an ad for futons."

It took Thia a moment to pick out the pertinent phrase. "She went up to Scotland?"

That hadn't been on Lettie's original itinerary, but one sure thing about Lettie was how rarely she stuck to plan. And she often went to Scotland, Thia knew; its products were in great demand. If Lettie had gone up there, that would explain why she hadn't answered her London phone, obviously...although her cell would still work, wouldn't it? Maybe not. Thia had never been, but from what she'd seen of photos and travel shows, Scotland had a lot of rugged terrain and many isolated areas. There had to be lots of dead zones.

"Probably," her dad was saying. "Your mom called her last week or so, trying to put together our golf trip over there next spring. Might've said something about it. Good courses up there. Birthplace of the sport, you know."

Thia's eyes squeezed shut as she shook an impotent fist. Breathed. "I know, Dad. Did she say which city? Or how long she'd be?" She relaxed her hand, opened her eyes.

Too soon, as it turned out.

"Why would anyone drive a car up a mile of stairs? How is that useful? No, she didn't. Just Scotland." Her father snorted derisively. "Zero percent for the first year but what about the second? It's all in the microscopic print right there—not that there's time enough to read it. All right, there you go, Steve," he cheered, the show's music playing in the call's background once more.

Right. Thia bit back a sigh. This was all she was going to get. "Okay, Dad. Thanks—and say hi to Mom. Love you," she added, because she did.

"Will do," he said, a smile clear in his voice. "Love you too, sweets."

She hung up and, leaning back in her desk chair, slowly rotated it side to side. As her vision went soft, distant, she tried to sort out what to do next. She had so many questions, all answerable only by Lettie.

Maybe. Thia woke the sleeping computer.

CHAPTER 5

From the time he had merged onto the North Atlantic line, Cormac's foul mood had only grown worse. Speed of travel had picked up considerably, the fierce current blurring reality into a rush of swirling color and silence. The only thing he could feel was a terrible, relentless pull that threatened to rip him apart. Yet without that sole physical sensation, it would be too easy to lose all sense of self in the otherwise shapeless, fathomless place. A quick trip to insanity, and beyond. Before he could contemplate that particular horror, he noted his exit point. No way in *ifrinn* was he going to miss it.

He gathered his conscious intention and—like a car taking a motorway's offramp—veered sharply left. *Unlike* a car on a ramp, there was no slowing down, no gradual braking to a gentle stop. One moment Cormac was formless and moving; the next, he stood in a grassy field in late evening.

Sensation returned abruptly, thousands of needles pricking the underside of his skin. His muscles might as well have been treacle; he collapsed onto hands and knees. His raw lungs burned as he sucked in breath after breath of crisp mountain air. Give him an airplane any day. He was never doing this again.

His head spun viciously, and with a soft curse—all he could

muster—he lowered himself fully to the frosted ground and waited for the world to settle. Or, rather, for his body to settle in it.

He also waited to be greeted by this junction's overseer. The leylines themselves belonged to no one, but control of their access points had long been an opportunity for wealth. Tithes were charged on cargo; fees demanded of travelers. Though the individuals changed over the years, occasionally through violent conflict, there was always *someone* in charge, ready to collect.

Except here. Cormac was alone in the field. That likely held significance, but he couldn't care beyond the fact that it meant he could rest for a time in peace. He rolled onto his back, continued to let the gloriously solid, frozen earth cool his overheated body. The sun had recently set behind the mountains. While he watched, night's first stars became visible, sparkling above him in a deepening, violet sky. Winter grasses rustled in intermittent breezes.

There was power here, strength from which he could draw. Quite a lot of power, he discovered as he opened to it. A sudden idea made him smile. He had stolen many tricks from Idris over the years, used most of them with impunity. But there were some—the biggest, most intriguing ones—he had never dared for fear of being caught.

Here, with Idris half a world away, temptation whispered, *why not?* He could even try one of the old man's favorites.

Cormac got to his feet, then took a deep, steadying breath as excitement threatened to fracture his concentration.

Thoughts of failure followed close behind but were easier dealt with. The spell itself was simple, a bastardized version of a *Sidhe* spell—and, after all, what was Cormac but a bastardized version of a *Sidhe?* Besides, Idris hadn't a drop of Otherworldly blood and had done it countless times. It didn't even require all that much power, not with land such as this.

Extending his arms palm up, Cormac tilted his face skyward.

"Taim in geis. Tindscetal an gaillim."

I am the spell. Begin the storm.

As the last syllable left his mouth, a tingling began in the marrow of his bones—the spell taking hold. His face broke into a grin. He'd done it. He'd actually done it.

His laughter joined the sound of the wind rushing over the mountains.

● ○ ●

Thia typed "stone of shadows" into her laptop's web browser and got back a hodgepodge of links whose overall theme appeared to be role-playing games. Results for "cailleach" were more promising. Leaning forward, she opened one to a page on a site called Rowena's Celtic Compendium.

The term was innocuous enough, according to the first paragraph. From Gaelic and pronounced "KAHL-yuk," it meant "veiled one" and referred to an ancient Celtic goddess said to reign for part of the year—a part which began on Samhain, when she left her mountain home to walk the land. With her came cold, sharp storms, and death.

"Oh," Thia breathed. Then, after clicking a few more links to other sites, "Uh-oh."

While the Cailleach was given credit for creating lakes and mountains and protecting wild animals, much more emphasis was given to her being considered a goddess of destruction, a hag who would ride on the back of a wolf and carry a wand made of human skin.

"Terrific."

Thia knew she'd have to be crazy to consider for even a moment that her great aunt had sent something belonging to a mythical deity, but still, that was disturbing.

And the search itself, confusing and often contradictory.

The Cailleach was worshiped along with her two sisters as part of a Triple Goddess. Or not. Some argued that the three-in-one concept came with the spread of Christianity, and instead believed that the Cailleach was really an earlier, Neolithic goddess.

The Cailleach once resided in what had become Ireland's County Cork and had fifty or so foster children. Or she was of the *Corcu Duibne* peoples who lived in County Kerry. Or she was descended from the *Tuatha de Danann,* invaders of an early Ireland who had eventually moved to an underground realm associated with something called the *Sidhe.*

Thia felt the knots of tangled informational threads tighten into a headache.

This was where the internet could really mess you up, she decided, then willingly let herself drift even farther from her initial investigation in order to read more about the *Sidhe.*

Well, she'd guessed wrong on the pronunciation. Gaelic, she was learning, gave her the same trouble as did French: the letters seemed to have very little to do with the actual sounds.

"Shee," Thia murmured, trying it out on her tongue. "Shee."

Shaking off a sudden chill, she tried to make sense of various pages of solid text. The *Sidhe*—also known as *Daoine Sidhe* (no help given on that pronunciation)—were considered a super-natural race. Beyond that, there was as much disagreement as with the Cailleach. Some thought them to be gods; others, ancestors of gods in Scottish and Irish myth. Some held them to be nature spirits. Some had them as a later version of the *Tuatha de Danann,* ruling invaders of Ireland. Some called them a particular type of fairy, stunning in their beauty and fierce.

"Oh." Care was taken not to name them directly. "Oops."

Thia read on with increasing distress. She had no idea that the tiny, whimsical fairies of children's books and collectible figurines were but one part of a larger grouping—the majority of which seemed to be feared as kidnappers or, like the Cail-leach, harbingers of death. Banshees, for instance. She had heard of them before, sure. Who *hadn't* heard mention of them as hideous, shrieking things? But never had Thia seen their name spelled *bean sidhe* or heard the term "fairy folk."

No more would she wrap up a figurine intended for a child's birthday without wondering if the parents should be warned about where such things could lead.

Oh, it might start out innocently enough with cute flying things clad in flowers and leaves—but look beyond them and it was wailing madwomen, soul-taking spirits, and alluring *leanan sidhe* who (depending on the source) either doomed the humans they enamored to waste away from unrequited love or, in exchange for artistic inspiration, drained their souls to the point of death.

Not big on happy endings, these tales.

Fingers none too steady, Thia left that site, opened up a blank search page. Lettie had said people wanted the Stone. It seemed logical to assume, then, that they might revere the Cailleach, maybe even worship her in some organized fashion.

It didn't take long to see that if anyone did, they were not promoting themselves on the internet. Amidst a ton of false leads and bad links, Thia could find only three solid mentions of organized, modern-day worship.

The first sounded like harmless acts of reverence done in an isolated Scottish glen. The second had more to do with tourism and moon-gazing at some standing stones on the Isle of Lewis—Scotland, again—near a range of hills named after the Cailleach. The third was an old Dr. Who episode entitled "The Stones of Blood," which pitted the Doctor against the goddess and her Druidic followers.

Thia smiled. Lettie hadn't mentioned anything about not handing the Stone over to nonexistent science-fiction-serial characters.

And with that thought, she recognized exactly how silly she was being. Celtic faeries were one thing. Television characters come to life was quite another. Wait...no. She was confusing herself. *None* of this was real. Neither the *Sidhe* nor television programs. Good grief, was she more like her father than she'd thought? But even he didn't truly believe his programs were real. He got caught up in the stories, that's all.

Thia sighed, drummed anxious fingers on the mouse while she considered where to go next. Had the Dr. Who episode been entirely made up, or was there a reason for including druids?

Please, no, to the latter if only because it would involve more research. She could count what she knew about druids on the fingers of one hand.

They wore hooded robes and might've had something to do with Britain's standing stones. They were akin to wizards—Merlin had been a druid, hadn't he? (There she was, thinking of fictional characters again.) And they...they...Well, okay, forget hand. Unless she was incredibly generous, Thia didn't even need one finger to count what she knew about druids.

So much she didn't know—about so much. Did Lettie? What about Abby and the rest of Eclectica's employees? Did they understand the finer points of what they were offering to the general public? Or had they, too, looked at portrayals of gnomes and green-skinned witches on broomsticks and seen nothing more than harmless flights of fancy?

In reality, those were remnants of an older way of thinking. Things perhaps diluted or entirely distorted from a previous era.

At least the store took care with obvious hazards. Things like ceremonial knives and collectors swords were essentially weapons, no matter how dull some of the blades might be, and some of the herbs and potions could do harm if used incorrectly. All of those things were kept out of casual reach in locked display cabinets.

Thia's hand hovered over the mouse; her eyes stared blankly at the screen. Druids? Did she really need to look up druids?

She had a feeling it would be like opening a can of worms—a figure of speech she now understood all too well. Each new piece of information was a worm, squirming and slipping out of her grasp while more and more emerged to form a writhing mass of squishy confusion. One endless line of exploration after another, twisting together until there was no telling one from the other.

How she wished she could put the lid back on the can.

A knock on the door made her start, sending the wireless mouse to the floor. Shit. She bent down to retrieve it.

"Come in," she called—loudly, since her head was under the desk.

When she sat up, mouse and its dislodged battery in hand, Abby was taking a seat across the desk.

"Hey," Thia said, mustering a smile. She replaced the battery, shut the cover.

Abby didn't smile back. "Did you reach her?"

At first, Thia was too caught up in the tangle of what she had been reading to understand the question. When she did, she really didn't want to go into it. She set the mouse down. "Did you know most fairies are nasty, evil creatures?"

Abby's eyes narrowed at the obvious dodge, but she went along. "I told Lettie not to stock Periwinkle Glade. Anything that insipid has to be hiding some serious nasty."

"Those are flower fairies," Thia said, though she didn't disagree with Abby's reasoning. "They're fine, apparently—and supposed to be a big help in the garden. Unless they get territorial." Images from the internet swirled in her memory. "It's complicated."

"You're sure about the 'not evil' thing?"

Thia laughed. "You just don't like pewter."

"It's a metal that softens in the sun." Abby made a face. "It's inherently flawed."

"I probably shouldn't have said evil. Just dark. Disturbing.

Bringers of destruction and death. That sort of thing."

"Sounds evil enough to me." Abby leaned forward. "Which ones do the death-bringing? The ones wearing clover blossom hats and riding around on boats made of oak leaves?"

"Oh, no. How awful if that were the case. To think something so adorable was out to kill you." Thia repressed a shudder. What a horrific betrayal that would be.

"You've heard of banshees, right?" She clicked open a few web pages she had bookmarked. "Those things that scream?"

"Of course." Abby chuckled. "My grandmother was as superstitious as they come."

"Okay. Here they are." Thia turned the computer, revealing the image of wild-eyed and wild-haired women, their faces distorted with fury as they flew in dark, angry skies above an isolated cottage.

"Holy sh—shoot."

"Yep. They're considered fairies too. And these." She clicked over to a painting of the Wild Hunt, where the spirits of the restless dead chased down someone's soul on a storm-ravaged plain.

"Oh." Her face pale, Abby looked away from the screen. "What brought all this research on?"

Not wanting to see the tortured faces of the hunted—or the hunters—anymore, either, Thia closed the laptop. "You know how the internet can be. One thing leads to another, and before you know it, you're—"

"—researching death-bringing demons." Abby's violet eyes narrowed. "Right. What's really going on?"

"I can't tell you." Thia felt awful saying it, but she wouldn't lie. They had become friends, or at least were on the way to it. "I wish I could, I really do. But I can't." She held Abby's gaze, watched the woman's expression become uncharacteristically grave.

"Nothing good ever comes from secrets, Thia. Believe me."

"Sometimes we have no choice."

After a thoughtful pause, Abby nodded with something like sadness. "You'll tell me if you need help."

"I'm sure it'll turn out to be nothing," Thia said.

Unfortunately, she sounded as unconvinced as she felt.

● ○ ●

As Cormac looked down on the twinkling lights of the town tucked into dark sleeping hills, he wondered if he might be drawing unnecessary attention to himself. No one had approached him in the clearing, but that didn't mean that his presence hadn't been noted. Where there was power such as this area held, there were always those who wanted to wield it. And they might not take too kindly to a stranger, let along one who flew into town on a magic-crafted storm.

So far, though, Cormac sensed no danger, and to withdraw the storm would be tantamount to pinning a target on his back. The storm might not have been his best, most carefully considered idea, but he was damned if he was going to appear too weak to see it through.

Directing the wind, he stretched out his raven's wings and glided toward a building halfway down Main Street. Leticia's Eclectica, easily identifiable from the images on the website.

Cormac had let emotion override good sense. Not just any emotion, he was loathe to admit, but something entirely unwelcome. Something childish that he hadn't felt since... well, since childhood. More specifically, when he'd still been an awkward boy and wanted desperately to impress the pretty daughter of one of Idris's attendants.

Ridiculous. He was not a boy anymore, and though he did want to impress Thia McDaniel, it was not in the hope that she would like him. He could use his *leanan sidhe* gifts for that.

Though he would rather not. It had been a long time since he'd done anything along those lines, and he'd never enjoyed it.

Enjoyed. He let out a derisive squawk. Oh, it had felt all right in the moment. Wonderful, in fact. It was afterward he felt dirty. Sick, inside and out.

As he circled, the lights shining through Eclectica's brightly decorated windows dimmed. Moments later, the door opened and a woman stepped out, then turned around to close it and engage a series of locks. Her back was to him, her head was bent. He couldn't identify her for certain, but he suspected. No...he knew.

Thia McDaniel straightened, turning away from the store, and Cormac sent a thread of wind to catch her auburn hair, sweeping it back from her face. She glanced up, toward the clouds—toward *him* as it happened—before setting off down the street. He had glimpsed worry in her expression, observed tension in the way she carried herself. He did not sense any power whatsoever, which either meant she had none or was very skilled at concealment.

Her photograph hadn't done her justice.

He circled again, long enough to confirm her direction, and then flew to a shadowed spot between two buildings. After sensing no threats, he shifted forms and stepped out to begin making his casual way up the surprisingly busy street. Thia was a block ahead and moving quickly. From cold, most likely, rather than suspicion or alarm. She was tugging on her jacket, a thing too light to be doing much good in the unexpected weather.

His fault that, not that it bothered him.

A restaurant door to his right opened and he dodged the distracted group that spilled out. The rich aroma of fresh-baked bread and Italian spices reminded him how long it had been since he'd had a decent sit-down meal. Maybe, if he took care of things with Thia soon enough, he would dine there tonight. The large plate glass window showed a room packed with eaters, every one of them in smiling conversation, the tables before them loaded with appetizing dishes.

Ahead at the block's corner, Thia waited with several other people for the light to change. The safe thing, he knew, would be to pause and make a show of searching through his coat pockets or some such thing until she continued on her way. Instead, he stepped up behind her, close enough to touch.

Too close. An uncontrolled gust sent a lock of her hair past Cormac's face like the caress of lavender-scented silk. Need flared, a match suddenly struck. He drew in a shocked breath, his awareness narrowing to a single focus even as the crowd around him grew.

Not now, *not this one,* he argued with himself, too late. His every sense fixed upon her, warm and lithe and right there. The memory of silken hair, the slightest of possible touches, felt like a brand on his skin.

Thia shivered once, a sharp rise and fall of her shoulders, and tensed as if alerted. To him? He froze, his thoughts tumbling over themselves in confusion and recrimination.

He should have disguised himself. Cormac felt that now as keenly as a razor's edge; but since he had no idea of her skills, he'd thought even the smallest glamour would be too chancy. He should have kept his distance as well, should never have put himself in this position, trapped within a crowd. If Thia turned around, he would feign disinterest. Not easy, but do-able. But if she had been warned about him, if she knew what he looked like....

She gave herself a slight shake but didn't turn. Not in the slightest. And Cormac let out a slow exhale.

Not of relief. That's what he *should* have been feeling. But no. Much to his horror, what he felt was more akin to disap-pointment. Had he wanted her to turn?

He was afraid he had. Afraid his decision to leave off all disguise was more basic—and entirely less wise—than the reasons he had used to justify it. How long had his judgment been clouded? Since the phone call? Had he been following the wrong instincts?

Or, perhaps, the right instincts for the wrong reasons.

Next to him, a man complained about the length of the light, received a sympathetic smile and pat on the arm from the blonde draped on it.

Cormac caught another whiff of lavender as the wind continued to play with Thia's hair, taunting him with glimpses of her neck. Lithe, like the rest of her. Delicate and vulnerable. His fingers twitched, drawn. He wanted to put his mouth to her nape, to breathe her in as he worked his way to the slope of her shoulder. He wanted to—

She stepped off the curb, out of reach. Someone jostled his elbow, muttered an apology Cormac barely heard above the turmoil in his head. The light had changed and the crowd was moving on, leaving him behind.

● ○ ●

Thia crossed the street and pointedly ignored the impulse to look over her shoulder. She'd had the strangest feeling....She shook her head. It had been a long, crazy day. She was anxious and tired. Her imagination was getting the best of her, that's all.

She managed to convince herself of that all the way to the bank Lettie used for Eclectica. But at the night depository, her gaze went straight to the security mirror. No one was behind her; there was no reason at all to look back the way she had come, but she did.

A happy couple, holding hands as they hurried toward a parked car; a group of teenage girls juggling shopping bags and cell phones; a dark-haired man, the collar of his coat up to protect him from the cold wind as he moved briskly past. He didn't so much as glance her way.

Opening her purse to retrieve the pouch that held the day's earnings, she stifled a shiver. The surprise storm had brought unseasonable cold, and her lightweight jacket was *not* doing the trick.

By the time she dropped the pouch into the depository, she was officially freezing, her teeth clenched to stop their chattering. She heaved the metal drawer upward, winced at the reverberating slam.

A blast of icy wind sent yellow leaves swirling around her ankles. Thia hunched her shoulders, jammed both hands in her pockets, and set off for home. Or, rather, Lettie's home, in which she was a very comfortable guest.

Chimney smoke scented the air as residents made the best of the weather, and she promised herself she'd soon be one of them. After dinner, she'd wrap herself in a fuzzy blanket and try to relax in front of a cheerful fire. She'd put everything out of her mind until morning, when she could approach it reasonably—and, hopefully, find an email from Lettie waiting.

The back of her neck prickled. Not as sharply as while she had stood waiting for the light to change, but enough to send her pulse racing again. Yet when she darted a look behind her, she saw no reason for alarm.

Imagination, imagination, imagination.

Unfortunately, knowing she was being ridiculous was one thing. Stopping it was another.

Thia had reached the heart of what was known locally as the Railroad District. Its roots may have been industrial, but with only the occasional freight train using the tracks at present, the area had become primarily residential—and, other than that occasional train, quiet and uneventful. A dented fender on a parked car, a broken driveway light, or prank-inspired relocation of someone's recycling bucket...that was about the extent of things.

Tonight, though, the deep shadows beneath Mrs. Curdy's rosebushes seemed a haven for danger, the perfect place for trouble to lie in wait. And over in Jim Duncan's yard across the street, the lurching, hunchbacked figure on the opposite side was probably (as it had been almost every other night) none other than Jim himself, bent over to retrieve his evening paper from his rhododendrons. But, as Thia's imagination so vividly suggested, this time it might be some kind of violent lunatic.

She refused to run. That would mean she believed, and she would not—absolutely would not. Not even when the Davidsons' porch light clicked on and she uttered an embarrassing little yelp. She would not run.

She jogged.

Every order Thia gave herself to calm down only seemed to make things worse. Every scraggly branch transformed into a clutching hand. Every shifting twig held the sound of an impending attack.

By the time she entered Lettie's front garden, the world had become a mysterious, terrifying place and Thia hardly cared if the gate latched after it swung shut. She pulled out her keys on the way up the path, had the one to the house ready by the time she rushed up the porch steps, and so was able to make fast work of the front door. Inside, she not only locked the deadbolt but also set the never-before-used chain. She stood, breathing hard, shocked at how thoroughly she had frightened herself. Her heart pounded, knocking against her ribs—and for what? Nothing. Absolutely nothing.

● ○ ●

Cormac studied the small, well-maintained house and garden nestled within a white picket fence. It was all something of an American cliché: white with soft yellow trim; neat rows of shingles on a peaked roof; rosebushes along the fence line; wisteria by the porch. If not for the protection wards around the perimeter, with extra on the house itself, it would have appeared entirely innocuous. Instead, with layer after layer of expertly crafted protection shimmering in the air around it, the whole blasted thing sat there like a cruel and jagged taunt.

He could almost hear Leticia's laughter in the shifting swirls of translucent color. The wards were unmistakably her design and, damnably, even more complex than those crafted for her townhouse.

Still connected to the storm, it fed off Cormac's emotions. Wind beat against the house, sent leaves and twigs to strike walls and skitter across the roof.

Interesting, that. The barrier would keep *him* out, and any spellcraft, but it wasn't blocking natural effects of the storm. Cormac shifted into raven form, landed on a branch of the large cedar outside the front gate as a clap of thunder rocked the neighborhood.

● ○ ●

By the time Thia had closed all the drapes on the first floor, she had almost convinced herself that her fear, while springing from a...well, a complete freak-out, really...was reasonable. Most single women would refrain from walking alone at night, regardless of whether they'd had a psychic warn of impending danger and then received a supposedly magical relic from a great-aunt who was doing a good impression of having vanished off the face of the earth. Not to mention how that same great-aunt had also warned of danger, and the relic in question was tucked in Thia's jacket pocket. In light of all that, she thought she was doing pretty well.

At the ring of the doorbell, she jumped, squeaking in alarm.

Okay, so, maybe not all that well. Grabbing onto the frayed ends of her courage, she peeked through the door's lead glass inset. Not Doctor Who and his TARDIS or a bunch of druids or even a banshee, but Madame Demetka. Strange, yes, but harmless. Thia undid the deadbolt and pulled open the door.

The links of the safety chain she had neglected to unhook snapped taut and the door rebounded, slipping out of her grasp to slam shut in Madame Demetka's startled face.

"Thia? Thia! Is trouble?" A tremendous pounding began. "Open, please, I beg you!"

"Sorry!" Thia fumbled with the chain. "I wasn't expecting anyone so I—" Pulling open the door, she nearly got a fist in the eye.

Madame Demetka swiftly lowered her hand. "You are safe?"

"The chain was...stuck." She arranged a smile. "What can I do for you, M—"

Madame Demetka made a shushing motion, her red-tipped fingers glinting in the porch light. "My guides, they tell me I must communicate with you." She shuddered dramatically. "Do you not feel it? A storm, it is coming."

Thia looked beyond her to where branches shifted against the moonlit silver and black of thick clouds. Forecast or not, it smelled like rain.

"Not that storm." Madame Demetka cocked her head, like a dog listening to a distant sound. "Though it is part of it, I think. Yes. Somehow...part of it."

Thia shivered, tucked her hands beneath her arms. "It's late, Madame Demetka. What was it you—" Two sharp hand-claps cut her off.

"We must communicate. I tell you this already."

Thia frowned. "Wait, what? You want to do a reading? With me?"

"Of course with you. The guides, they insist."

"Now really isn't the best time." To say the least. "How about tomorrow—at the store?"

"No." Madame Demetka reached out, grabbed Thia's arm in a grip just shy of painful. "Please to be now. Here. Is no joke I make to you, *miri mora*. Is life and death."

Thia noticed it then: the tightness around the other woman's mouth. The slight tremor in her grip. The fear-widened eyes.

"Okay," she said and, taking a step back, pulled Madame Demetka inside

CHAPTER 6

Lightning momentarily brightened the candlelit room. The great boom of thunder that followed shook the house, rattling glass. Thia looked around with apprehension. If one of the candles fell over, it could start a—

"Attend please."

Guiltily, Thia jerked her attention back to the Tarot cards being laid facedown on the table. The gold stars on their blue backs gleamed, the flickering light letting them do a fair impression of a twinkle.

So much of a Tarot reading depended on focus, attitude and circumstance...which did not bode well for her. Her focus was lacking, her attitude was questionable—to believe or not to believe? And her environment was downright disturbing, a veritable checklist of spooky. Storm raging outside, check. Closed drapes and candlelight, check. Occult activity at the dining table, check.

And then, of course, there was Madame Demetka.

Immediately after seating herself across the table, she had reached into her giant bag of tricks (source of the two dozen white candles currently teasing the house's smoke detectors) and withdrawn a bulky satin turban to place upon her head.

With the slightest movement, its spray of purple ostrich feathers cast out bits of fluff. Thia watched as one drifted too close to the candles at the end of the table and—*pfft*—turned to ash.

The quiet night Thia had promised herself had become a macabre, flammable carnival act.

"He is close," Madame Demetka said almost absently as she placed the last card.

"Who?"

"Hm? Oh. I do not know. Let us proceed, yes?" She set the undealt cards aside. "We have asked my guides to kindly explain what it is they so insistently try to tell me." Her eyes closed and she lifted her hands as if in supplication.

Thia waited.

She had just about given up when Madame Demetka's eyes snapped open.

"*Hadza!* We will see now the results." She turned over the first card, the Raider-Waite illustration of a lady seated on a throne. Thia didn't know the meaning, but it looked fairly innocuous. Quickly, Madame Demetka turned over the rest of the spread. "Hm."

Thia followed her gaze to Death and the Devil. The artistic representations of them, anyway. With impeccable timing, another powerful clap of thunder rattled the house.

"How did we do?" she asked with forced lightness.

Madame Demetka looked up from the cards. Glints of candle flame danced across the surface of her dark eyes. "The trouble that was coming is already upon you."

A chill skittered down Thia's spine.

With a thick, artificial nail, Madame Demetka tapped the Queen of Swords. "Your life is structured. Logical. But there is trouble—see?" She pointed to thick clouds painted on the background. In front of them, high above a copse of wind-whipped trees, flew a lone, black bird.

Madame Demetka's finger moved to the most infamous card. Depicted as a skeleton clad in a suit of armor, Death rode a white horse and carried a black flag adorned with a single white rose. Beneath the horse's hooves, lay the body of a man. A woman and children stood nearby, weeping.

Madame Demetka tapped the image. "Usually, this is not to be taken literally. Most times, it represents transformation. Out with the old, in with the new."

Thia nodded, relaxing by degrees. She'd known that much already, but it was nice to be reminded.

"Except in this case," Madame Demetka said. "In this case, the guides say it is both."

"What?"

The storm, again with excellent timing, released a brilliant flash of lightning. The explosion of thunder sounded almost directly overhead, and the house shimmied, wood creaking ominously. Candles wobbled, sputtered.

"Death?" Thia's voice was uncontrollably shrill. "Whose death?"

"This is the cause." Madame Demetka tapped on the Devil's card.

A mopey-faced, pudgy beast, he didn't look all that fearsome to Thia. The fingers of his right hand formed what she thought of as the "live long and prosper" sign from Star Trek. Below the pedestal he sat upon were a man and woman—also horned—with chains about their necks.

"Again," Madame Demetka said, "not usually to be taken literally."

Thia prepared herself for the catch. "But in this case?"

"Also in this case. Look for greed. And entrapment." She pointed to the man in chains. "Lust."

"Oh. Okay."

Madame Demetka stabbed a fingernail toward the Wheel of Fortune card. "Events were set in motion long ago. This changing of the order, it is meant. From long ago. It is meant." She closed her eyes and began to murmur. Talking with her guides, Thia assumed, more than a little impatient.

Eventually, Madame Demetka's eyes opened and, sorrowfully, she rested her finger on the next card, that of the High Priestess. A woman sat between two pillars—one white, one black. Upon her head rested an odd sort of crown, while a crescent moon lay at her feet. "You recognize her, *miri mora?* A wise woman. Learned. Intuitive and understanding."

"Lettie." A tight ball of fear formed deep in Thia's chest. "That's Lettie."

Madame Demetka nodded, her dark eyes moist with unshed tears. "I am heart-sickened with sadness. Our brave Lettie, she is no longer with us."

"What?" Thia's fear exploded, shooting out fiery shards of panic. "No. That's not—She can't....No."

The feathers swayed as Madame Demetka slowly shook her head. "They are very clear in this, my guides," she said. "About other things, not so much. But this? This they know. They tell me very plainly."

"No." Thia pressed a shaking hand to her mouth. This was too bizarre. Vague warnings, a strange crystal sphere, and now this.

When had her life become like a bad dream?

"People don't learn of someone's death from Tarot cards," she said, lowering her hand. "They get phone calls."

Something heavy struck the porch, then rolled along it. A potted plant toppled by the wind, she figured.

Madame Demetka paled, her eyes fluttering shut.

Thia started to reach out, but then thought better of it, not wanting to startle. "Are you all right?"

"You must go with what was given."

"I'm sorry?"

Madame Demetka opened her eyes and pulled over the

card for the Five of Wands, where a bunch of tunic-wearing youths struck at one another with long, leafy sticks. "Rapid changes and conflicts. There is much competition over the same thing. Immediate travel is warranted. They do not tell me where, except that it is the origin of the gift." She picked up the next card and, her lips pursed, clucked her tongue.

"They do not tell me much about this, either." She pushed it across the table to Thia.

A dark-haired knight, his sword held high, rode a charging horse. Below his armor, he wore a tunic patterned with large black birds.

"An overbearing man with a troublesome temper," Madame Demetka said grimly, and again closed her eyes, myriad expressions flitting across her face. Prolonged seconds passed before she opened them and glared ceiling-ward. A shake of her head sent out a flurry of feather bits. "Piffle! You taunt me with nonsense. A young man who is ancient, whose loyalty belongs to another, yet only to himself. The power to do great right and great wrong. Riddles! Silly riddles, you give me." She jabbed an accusing finger in the direction of the chandelier, then lowered it. Her shoulders slumped.

"Madame Demetka?"

"I'm sorry, sugar," she said with a distinctly Southern drawl. She removed her turban, set it on the table. "This is a train wreck."

"Madame Demetka?" Thia heard herself repeating, but she already knew. Gone was the flamboyance, the zany.

"Sally," the woman corrected. She picked up the Knight of Cups. "See this here, in reversed position? It means overactive imagination. Deception. Playing with emotions." She picked up another. "And this one here, representin' support available to you? King of Cups, also reversed. That's a con man." She flung them down onto the earlier cards in the spread and then stared at the next.

Thia struggled to process what had happened. Madame Demetka had vanished, replaced by Sally Wilson. Was this schizophrenia? Or simple truth—the dropping of artifice to reveal the person beneath?

Sally pulled over the image of a naked woman pouring water into a pond. "At least your goals are encouraging. The Star. She's all about your Higher Self. Inspiration, self-acceptance. Peace after upset and turmoil. That's not the outcome," she clarified, dampening Thia's surge of hope. "I told you, those are only your goals. This here is the outcome."

Thia stared at the card that completed the reading. A man and woman fell from a burning tower as a jagged bolt of lighting struck and toppled its large golden crown. Clouds and flames filled the sky.

"That"—she cleared her dry throat—"looks bad."

"Maybe. Maybe not." Sally's hands moved up and down as if weighing two objects. "Sometimes destruction is good, like cleaning house. Getting rid of all the stuff you don't need anymore, or that might be harming you. Then again, sometimes destruction is just destruction."

She shrugged and then began gathering the cards. "None of this is set in stone. Stone." Her gaze shot to the ceiling. "Power. Power in the stone. Freed...by blood. Yours."

Thia's breath caught. How could she know about the—wait, what had she said about, "My blood?"

Sally blinked as if startled awake. "What was that, sugar?"

"You said something about power and blood." Thia's hands tingled with the memory of holding the Stone. "Mine."

"Did I?" Frowning, Sally shook her head. "Nope. Drawing a blank." She reassembled the Tarot deck. Cleaning up.

"Can you ask? Your guides, I mean?"

A horrendous gust of wind slammed into the front of the house. The cards fell from Sally's hands, spilling out across the table. Hurriedly, she swept them up, her motions unsteady. "I need to be going, sugar. I've done all I can. I'm sorry."

"Please," Thia said, leaning forward. "It's important."

"It's all important." Sally wrapped the cards in a white cloth. "Everything the cards said."

"But I don't understand what it means."

"That doesn't make it any less true."

Thia clenched her teeth against saying something she might regret. Anxiety was making her short-tempered. Psychic or self-deluded charlatan, Sally-Demetka meant well here. She didn't mean to come off like Yoda at his most frustratingly cryptic. Thia blew out a breath. "But what about the Stone? What did you mean when you said—"

"I don't know what I said, sugar. That's the way of it sometimes. And my guides aren't talking, except to tell me it's time to go." She stuck the wrapped Tarot deck inside her turban, then pushed back from the table to stand. "I really am sorry. But if one thing came through loud and clear, it's that either Lettie set something in motion, or her death did. And now trouble has its eyes on you."

Lightning cracked, followed by a foundation-rocking boom. Sally nodded, retrieving her tote bag from where it hung on the back of the chair. "Forces are at work," she said with a tip of her chin toward the drape-covered windows behind Thia. "And it's gonna get bad."

"This is all just symbolism, though, isn't it?" Thia said, feeling as if she were grasping at straws as she followed the other woman the short distance to the door. "I mean, really. It's only ideas and metaphors."

"You'd be a fool to believe that, Thia McDaniel. And you don't strike me as a fool."

Maybe not, but Thia certainly felt like one. She looked back at the table, the white candles fighting to hold off the dark.

Hardly any time had passed since she had opened the box from Lettie and tried to talk to her. She should allow for at least another day of anxiety-ridden silence before believing there might be any truth to all this.

Shouldn't she?

What would she do if she didn't hear from Lettie by morning? Call hospitals in London? Scotland? What if Lettie was in serious trouble? What if she needed help?

"What am I supposed to do?"

"Oh, *darlingk*." Cloak wrapped securely about her, Madame Demetka laid a sympathetic hand on Thia's arm. "You must do what you do. That is the blessing of fate. We must all go where we are going, whether or not the path is clear."

Thia could have cried. Yesterday, everything had been fine, hadn't it? Today was a nightmare. An inescapable, worsening nightmare. She unlatched the door only to pause, her hand on the knob. "We must go where we are going?"

Madame Demetka beamed, clapped her hands. "Exactly so, yes."

Exactly, *no*. It would be crazy for Thia to even consider it. Absolutely crazy. "How would I ever explain it?" she asked, more to herself.

Sally gave her a sympathetic smile. "Blame the guides, sugar. It always works for me."

● ○ ●

The door to Leticia's house opened and Cormac, perched out of sight in the cedar, stilled the winds. Twigs and gravel that would have pelted the house dropped abruptly to the ground. Dried leaves drifted aimlessly as, beneath the thick clouds, the night became calm and silent.

Thia's clownish guest hesitated in the doorway. Anticipation was like a choking hand around Cormac's throat. *Move,* he wanted to shout. *Go away.* She remained motionless, her robust frame blocking his view of the woman whose uneasy voice said, "What's the matter, Madame Demetka?"

Patience, already stretched finer than a spider's thread, snapped. At Cormac's signal, wind swirled to tangle with the interloper's patchwork cloak. *Demetka.* Her struggles drew her away from the door. It was the best Cormac could do, what with the property's wards.

And it would have been enough, had it not been for Thia. Instead of remaining in place, where his view of her would no longer be blocked, she dove into the billowing fabric in a misguided rescue attempt. "Come back inside," he heard her shout, followed by a muffled, entertainingly maddened, "Oh, good grief!"

He chuckled low in his throat and again calmed the winds. As the cloak's material settled, Thia worked herself free. The Demetka woman glared skyward and made an odd series of gestures. It looked vaguely obscene, though he assumed that wasn't the intent. More likely, she believed them to have some sort of "mystical import."

Much as he would like to, he couldn't write Demetka off as entirely harmless. Fraudsters had been known to manage a bit of genuine craft. The most bumbling novice could get lucky. The world was vast; its magic systems, varied. Those unfamiliar gestures of hers might have merit.

Thia placed a hand on Demetka's arm. Although Cormac couldn't make out her soft words, their intention was clear. She still wanted her guest to return to the house.

The reality of his situation struck hard. He had no strategy. No knowledge of this new foe, of her capabilities, her threat. He had flung himself halfway around the world with nothing but the vague notion to find out if she knew anything about the relic—and if she had it, to take it from her.

Thia McDaniel was nothing to him,. She had nothing on his centuries of experience. She was entirely human. He was half *Sidhe* and mercilessly tutored in The Arts, dark and otherwise. And yet he continued to sit like a boy with a crush, all tangled thoughts and knotted insides, no clue how to get the girl.

His luck took a turn for the better when Demetka, rejecting Thia's persistent invitation, lumbered down the porch steps.

Thia accompanied her to the gate, stepped ahead to open it. Cormac tensed.

If only she would continue through.

But she didn't. Demetka moved past her and onto the sidewalk, a comical example of superstition in action. One hand resumed the suggestive motions while the other clutched at the ample array of charms hung about her neck. Amethysts, a pentagram or two, a bit of Earth Mother paraphernalia, and assorted silver, New Age gewgaws. Maybe he *could* write her off.

Cormac considered his options. If Thia thought the woman to be in danger, she might run out to try to help. Or she might just as easily remain behind the barrier and try to work from there—or worse, lock herself in the house and summon help from another source: Anyone from powerful locals to police. Either of which, this being the States, might be armed with more than magic.

His life expectancy might be longer than average, but he was no more immune to a well-placed bullet than anyone else. The decision made itself. He could risk nothing until Thia was alone and guaranteed to stay that way.

He let Demetka pass without incident, watched along with Thia as she walked away, alternately gesturing and swatting at blowing leaves. She stumbled several steps when her clothes became tangled around her legs (something Cormac might've had a little influence in). Recovering, she shouted a few coarse words in what he identified as Romany despite the peculiar accent. She turned the corner, out of sight.

Finally, Cormac had his chance.

●　○　●

"Excuse me."

Thia whirled, her hand pressed over her pounding heart like that of some sort of Gothic victim-to-be. A man stood on the sidewalk some distance away, hardly more than shadow beside the towering lilac at the corner of the yard. She took an instinctive step back.

"I didn't mean to startle you," he said, and sounded sincere enough about it, she supposed. Even so, she felt her earlier irrational fears return, and with them, the urge to run. But the picket fence offered some protection. It wasn't high—or even particularly sturdy—but it meant she could give him a measure of trust. Besides, on any night before tonight, she wouldn't have thought twice about his motives or her safety.

"You didn't," she lied out of kindness, pitching her voice above a loud rush of wind. Her hair plastered itself across her face. By the time she fought it back, the man stood outside the gate, directly before her.

The light from the house illuminated him clearly, though it tinted his features a bit orange. Because of the downward tilt of his head, his eyes remained in shadow. He was around her father's age—mid-sixties—and more plump than she had first thought. The extra pounds gave his face a softness which spoke of inactivity. He looked non-threatening. Harmless. She relaxed slightly.

"Good. Very good," he said, taking a small step forward. Closing the distance with the gate between them. "Because, you see, I was hoping you could help me."

The light hit his eyes then, and Thia felt an almost physical impact, like being struck by a rogue wave at the beach. The exact color was impossible to discern, but that didn't make them any less remarkable. A dark ring around a lighter band, and then the black of the pupil itself, absolute and so very deep. If she were to surrender to the pull and dive in, would she ever touch bottom?

She blinked, startled by where her thoughts were taking

her. Since when did she find older, portly men attractive?

Since this one, apparently.

"What seems to be the trouble?" she asked him, and then had to grab the gate to brace herself against a hard gust of wind.

He glanced down at her hands on the pickets before giving her a plaintive look. "My car battery died. I wonder if I might use your phone?"

Simple enough. She dug into her pocket.

"Thank you," he said softly. "You're a lifesaver."

"Sure." She held out her phone, her arm extended over the fence.

He grabbed her wrist, yanked her forward against the gate. The phone fell from her hand. His grip was strong. Cruel.

"What are you doing?" she exclaimed, resisting.

Of course he didn't reply. He was too busy taking hold of her free arm so as to prevent her belated attempt to punch his face. His guileless, false, hateful face. If she survived, she and her instincts were going to have a long talk.

"Let go," she shrieked, compounding her folly. She braced her feet and pulled against him. He had weight on his side, but she had leverage on hers. And neighbors.

Taking a deep breath—not easy to do while being impaled on white pickets—she began to shout, "Fire! Fire!"

"Dammit, Thia," he said, the use of her name an additional shock.

She shouted again, as per the advice of a self-defense class taken years ago. No one would answer a cry for help, the instructor had insisted. Fire worked better. At the time, Thia had thought it wrong to lure potential rescuers with false advertising. Now she didn't give a damn. If getting help meant making people think the neighborhood was about to go up in flames, so be it.

The man pulled again, succeeded in dragging Thia's torso

over the fence. Wood scored her skin through her sweater. Her frantic wriggling only served to dig the points in deeper. Her feet scrambled, desperately seeking a toehold, a way to anchor herself while she continued to shout.

A torrent of freezing rain crashed down, soaking her in an instant. Stunned, she felt herself yanked forward another few inches. Her pendant slipped out to dangle, tapping against her chin.

Where the hell were the neighbors?

For the first time, it occurred to her that she might not win. She fought harder, screamed louder, gasping, sucking in water and strands of wet hair, then spitting them out. A drowning woman screaming fire. No wonder no one was coming.

The man began to mutter—strange words, guttural yet oddly lyrical. She couldn't *not* look up at him, at his eyes...his eyes. Such a beautiful, luminous blue.

"No!" she shrieked, conscious of a strange warmth creeping through her body. Strange...yet pleasant, which made it even more alarming. She reached deep inside herself, gathering strength, as conscious thought began to sink beneath a rising tide of crazed, instinctive action.

A berserker rage.

A fight to the death.

Her pendant flashed a bright white light, blinding her as what felt like fire coursed down her arms. The man released her with a shout. Her upper body dropped painfully onto the fence points. When her vision cleared a few seconds later, she found it filled with white painted boards. The outside of the gate, less than an inch from her upside-down face.

Had the man fallen? Oh, who cared? He wasn't holding her, that's all that mattered. Thia quickly righted herself and then, stumbling on the uneven stones of the entry walk, ran like hell toward the house.

She slammed the door, leaned her weight against it while she engaged the locks and hooked the safety chain with violently shaking hands. Terror screamed for her to keep moving. Call the police. Hide. Brace the door. Collapse. Find a weapon. Any and all of the above, all at once.

She held herself still, listening to the storm and her rapid, traumatized breathing and...*nothing.* No sound of the man running across the porch or pounding on her door. No sound of him breaking a window.

No sound of him at all.

She peered through the door's glass inset and immediately wished she hadn't. He stood outside her garden gate. A trim, shadowy figure. Watching. Waiting.

She reached into her pocket...and then remembered. Her phone had dropped. He had it.

Afraid to show herself through the windows, Thia dropped to her hands and knees and began to do her best imitation of a commando-crawl toward the house phone.

● ○ ●

That really could have gone better, Cormac considered, and examined his hands. Where they had been in contact with Thia was red and blistered and stung like hell. He held them out, palms up, and gritted his teeth as cold rain washed over his skin, drawing out the heat.

Although she clearly was not one, she wore the protection charm of a Brigantium novitiate. Had he Leticia to thank for that? Or was there some other, more troubling reason?

He balled his hands into tight fists, ignored the sting. As his emotions flowed into the storm, the winds raged, flinging sleet against the house. Lightning exploded directly overhead. Thia was undoubtedly contacting someone for help—exactly what he had wanted to avoid.

Forget *better.* That couldn't have gone *worse.*

Cormac shifted to raven-form and, lifting the spell that had prevented the neighborhood from hearing Thia's inexplicable shouts of "fire," returned to the tree.

● ○ ●

Her name, Thia remembered abruptly. He knew her name.

That changed everything.

Crouched on the floor, water dripping from her hair and clothes, she set the phone back on its cradle. It took her a few tries, she was trembling so badly. Adrenaline and terror and cold. She was soaked to the skin—the least of her problems.

Police would mean questions and, especially in a town like Granite Springs, attention.

Questions Thia could not answer, and attention Lettie had warned against.

She crawled across the oriental carpet to the front window, to one side where the curtains were gathered. She used them as cover to look out.

The sidewalk was deserted. As was what could be seen of the yard...and neighborhood. If he *had* gone, she knew it was only a matter of time. He would not stay gone.

He would find a way to get inside.

And so Thia could not stay. Could not simply wait for him to come after her. But the thought of leaving felt just as foolish. He might be out back, by the garage, ready to grab her when she went for the car.

"What a mess," she said, and hated how her voice was little more than a traumatized whisper.

When she said it again, her voice was stronger. More angry. And she followed it up with a phrase even Stefanie couldn't have smudged clean.

CHAPTER 7

"You're sure you don't mind such an early checkout?" Kendra asked again, unlocking the room door.

Thia had met the hotel's newly promoted director several times before through Abby; the two were good friends. When Thia had called the front desk to beg for a last-minute room, Kendra had come on the line to contradict the clerk who had been politely explaining there was no vacancy.

"Early is perfect," Thia replied. "I've got the first flight out." Or would have once she booked a ticket.

Kendra turned, a look of concern on her heart-shaped face. "This doesn't sound like a pleasure trip."

"No. It's a—well, I'm not exactly sure what it is."

"Oh, I'm sorry." Kendra preceded her into the room and began turning on lights. "Nothing too serious, I hope."

A short hallway opened into an enormous, lavishly appointed suite. Thia stopped, stunned. "Oh, no, this is way too much. I-I just needed a room."

Abby's friend drew brocade drapes across a window at the far end of a sunken lounge area. "This is a *room*." She flashed a grin before bending to pick up a remote control which she then aimed at a fireplace. Flames whooshed to life, crackling merrily. "It just happens to be a really big one. Besides, it's all we've got. Halloween, Christmas, and Easter, we're always booked. You're lucky."

Thia knew she was, not only to have a place to stay but to have reached it without incident. The crazed dash to her garage, near-dive into Lettie's car, and six-block race to the hotel's parking garage would be adrenaline-seared onto her memory forever. "But the rate you gave me can't be right— not for something like this."

Kendra laughed and, apparently satisfied all was in order with the miniature refrigerator, closed its mahogany-paneled door. "I gave you the 'good friend and local businesswoman discount.' Director's prerogative." She shrugged. "This was going to sit empty all night, anyway. The next occupant wants in at ten tomorrow, and the seven a.m. checkout we need for that was too hard a sell."

"You won't get in trouble?"

"Are you kidding? Murphy will love it," she said, referring to the hotel's owner. Her green eyes alight, her normally melodic voice dropped and took on a faint Irish lilt. "Money may not make the world go round, but it surely makes for a smoother ride," she proclaimed.

Despite everything, the impersonation made Thia laugh. She had never so much as glimpsed its subject, but had heard enough from both Kendra and Abby to understand Murphy was more business than man. "He actually said that?"

"And meant it." Grinning, Kendra reached for the backpack slung over Thia's shoulder.

Too tired to protest, Thia let her take both it and the wheeled suitcase, then trailed her into the bedroom. The bed was enormous—as big, at least, as the whole of Lettie's guest room. "Thank you. For everything. I really owe you one."

"Nonsense." Kendra set the luggage beside a large armoire,

then gave the room a quick once-over.

The giant bed had already been turned down; a plate of fruit and chocolate set on the nightstand. Thia's mouth watered. Her dinner had amounted to a granola bar while she packed.

Kendra finished closing another set of curtains. "I'm happy to help—as I keep telling you—and from the looks of it, you need quite a bit." Gone was the joking tone.

When she turned from the window, she subjected Thia to the same scrutiny she had given the suite. "There *is* more to this than you told me, isn't there? I'd imagine boarding up a broken window in this storm would be awful, but you look wrecked. What's going on? You can tell me, you know."

Guilt renewed itself at the reminder of the excuse Thia had given. The outright lie for why she'd needed a place to stay: a broken window leaking cold into the bedroom. Such a flimsy explanation, too, since one damaged room wouldn't make the entire house uninhabitable.

"No, that's it," she lied. Again. "Plus the things I need to go straighten out, of course. Really, it's noth—"

Kendra's phone beeped softly and Thia gratefully shut up.

"Speak of the devil," Kendra said, after looking at the phone's screen. "Murphy. Probably wants to go over the preparations for tomorrow's arrivals. Again." She gave Thia a quick hug, then moved toward the door. "I hope everything works out. And please tell me if there's anything I can do. As far as your stay tonight, Eric is working the desk and he's great. He can set you up with a ride in the morning if you'd like to—wait, that's perfect," she interrupted herself. "Keep your car here, leave the keys and your return flight details with him, and I can come pick you up at the airport when you get back."

"Oh, no, that's too—"

"Say yes or I'll take away your basket of Garden of Paradise goodies."

"Yes," Thia said instantly. The locally-made bath products

were luxurious in the extreme—and priced accordingly. Well out of her budget. Her chilled skin tingled in anticipation, and Thia playfully waved Kendra away. "You'd better go now. Work to do."

"I'm going, I'm go—Oh, but I should warn you," Kendra said, suddenly serious, and Thia braced for the worst. "We get mostly VIPs in this suite, so there are some...unusual touches. Probably nothing you haven't seen, but I don't want you to be too weirded out."

Thia nearly laughed with relief. "After the day I've had it'll take more than a pair of fuzzy handcuffs to upset me." A few weeks back, over dinner and drinks with Abby, Kendra had entertained them with tales from her previous hotel jobs—one guest in particular had wanted to give her husband a very special 40th Anniversary.

"I never should have mentioned those," Kendra said with a rueful shake of her head. And a grin. "But—fortunately or unfortunately—that's not what I meant." She stepped into the hall. "Sleep well. I hope everything works out. And, like I said, let me know if there's anything I can do. Anything at all."

"Thanks. I really appreciate it. And this," Thia said, indicating the suite. "Now please go—I've got bath products to use up and edible underwear to track down."

She closed the door to the sound of Kendra's laughter, then engaged both security locks.

Minutes later, Thia was wrapped in one of the Landmark's plush robes. Her rain-soaked clothes hung on the towel warmer in a room that resembled a spa. She wanted nothing more than to let the jacuzzi tub banish the chill of cold and fear and the ache of abused muscles. Instead, she found herself staring at the cloth-wrapped Stone she had taken from her jacket pocket. Such a small thing to cause such trouble, but she had no doubt it was the heart of it all.

"Oh, Lettie. What have you gotten me into?"

Yielding to temptation, she lifted a portion of the white cloth, touched the crystal's cool surface. A current of heat shot up her finger, thrummed up her arm. She jerked her hand away and tried to shake out the buzz. So much for hoping the first time had been her imagination...or a fluke.

What had Madame Demetka—or Sally, as she'd been at the time—meant about power being freed by blood? Thia rolled tense shoulders. What the hell had *anything* meant in that reading? The only "clear" thing had been Lettie's death, and she refused to accept that part.

Lettie was not dead. In trouble, certainly. But she couldn't possibly be dead.

Thia opened the bedroom closet to reveal a huge, walk-in affair that was completely wasted on her. Even if she had brought more than a few items of clothing, it was pointless to unpack them. No, what she sought was an in-room safe—and she found *two*. Identical and positioned side by side next to a built-in shoe rack, all their knobs and dials made them look like something out of a high-tech heist movie.

Choosing the one on the right, she put the Stone, its cloth again tightly wrapped, on the top shelf. It looked so comical there, a tiny bundle in an otherwise empty Fort Knox. She shut the door.

On the laminated card that explained how to program the trio of lock mechanisms, she found what had to be one of the unusual touches Kendra had alluded to. Steps one through five were straightforward enough, all about choosing codes and programming the keypad. Step six was the outlier, suggesting that if the Guest would like to perform a standard warding, supplies were located in the cabinet next to the minibar.

Magic rituals for VIPs at the Landmark? Yesterday, Thia would have laughed it off as being just one more example of Granite Spring's whimsy. Not tonight. Tonight it made her feel like the last to arrive at the party.

Or, rather, to wake up to it. Apparently, it had been going

on all around her but she hadn't noticed. Or thought to look?

She had always known that there were people who believed in magic, and that some of them—like Lettie—believed they could actually perform it.

Her time at Eclectica had led her to realize there were more believers than she'd thought, but she still hadn't considered whether there was anything *to* those beliefs beyond normal, physical effects. Any meditative activity could bring about calm and healing. The fact that a "magic" potion produced certain results—easing a headache, clearing an infection—wasn't magic; it was herbal science. Not that she necessarily *disbelieved* in magic, she didn't necessarily believe in it, either.

Ever since Thia had arrived in Granite Springs, Lettie had been trying to teach her spellwork of some kind or another, undaunted by what she described as Thia's "stubborn grip on conventional reality."

A few days before leaving on her trip, Lettie had shown how to "replenish the protections" set up around the house and garden. Warding, she'd called it—the same process the Landmark was recommending. Thia had watched, fascinated yet wary, as her great-aunt had described how to visualize layers and patterns of color in the mind's eye and form them into some sort of barrier to keep bad things away. It had all seemed so bizarre, Thia hadn't even tried. But Lettie had committed fully, and afterwards Thia had to admit the place had felt... cleaner. Safer. Although that could have very well been imagined, couldn't it? Simply a matter of suggestion?

Was belief the key? Could that make the difference between imagination and reality?

It didn't matter here, as far as warding the room-safe was concerned. Thia couldn't remember enough to even *hope* of performing such a thing—which she wasn't sure she wanted to do, anyway. Call it stubbornness, call it fear, but she wasn't ready to relinquish her grip on conventional reality. She didn't want to. It was what she knew.

Though she *was* curious. And, since it couldn't hurt to look—and maybe she'd find something useful, after all—she went into the main room to check out the supply cupboard.

It was crammed with a surprisingly familiar array of bottles, herb bundles, bowls, and other miscellany. Every item, with a few brand differences, was something Eclectica carried. A pricing list had been propped between a Tibetan singing bowl and a jar of powdered mugwort. Thia gaped at the outrageous mark-up, more than triple the wholesale cost.

"Two hundred bucks for Tara Water?"

She hoped even a VIP with money to throw around knew better than to throw it *that* way. Eclectica offered it for fifty. She closed the cupboard. What a scam.

She got her laptop from her suitcase, took it to the couch. Abused muscles and scraped flesh pulled and shifted as she lowered herself, tried to find the least uncomfortable position while her computer powered up.

She missed her iPhone.

Rain pelted the window panes. Somewhere beyond, in the quaint, friendly town she had come to love, was a man who wanted to hurt her. She hadn't seen any sign of him since the attack, but that didn't mean he was not out there, waiting. Her pulse picked up speed, her anxiety rising with it, and she glanced around the room.

She knew she was alone. She felt as foolish as when she had been a kid, triple-checking empty swimming pools for sharks. (The *Jaws* franchise hadn't done her childhood any favors.) Hotel security was excellent—fit for popstars, Kendra had joked. Closed-circuit cameras, alarmed doors, security guards ready to respond at a moment's notice. Thia could see phones had been placed throughout the suite itself, even in the bath.

She was alone, but not isolated.

Safe, even if she didn't feel it.

Once the computer connected to the complimentary Wi-Fi,

Thia went to a travel site and entered a search for flights to London.

Tears welled, blurring the screen. She hastily wiped them away. Lettie couldn't be dead. She just couldn't.

From a list of carriers all offering the same astronomical price, Thia picked the one with the earliest departure—five o'clock in the evening out of San Francisco. But after giving her payment details, she hesitated. Was she really going to drop everything and race off to...to what? This was a busy time for Eclectica. She would be leaving Abby short-staffed and in charge of the online sales, responsible for procedures Thia hadn't had a chance to fully explain. And what about Lettie's house? Sure, the mail wouldn't be a problem, going to Eclectica as it was, but what about the newspaper? She'd have to call in a stop-order from the airport in the morning— except she no longer had her cell phone; the man did.

He could break into Lettie's house while Thia was away. God, he could be breaking into it at that very moment. She should call the police...and tell them what? Nothing, if she were to follow Lettie's instruction.

She ran both hands through her tangled hair, tugged on it as she stared at the screen, one click away from commitment. Maybe she needed commitment of a different kind—the kind that included a straitjacket and a padded room.

Crazy or not, though, she couldn't stay in Granite Springs. With that man after her, if she continued to follow Lettie's insistent direction, Thia would endanger everyone there. She had to hope that when she left, so did he.

What if he didn't? Would he go after her friends and family if he couldn't find her?

He had her iPhone with all her contacts, emails, photos— her *life*. Not to mention her bank and credit card details. She had reported it stolen before leaving Lettie's and initiated a complete wipe using its link to her cloud account, but what if that hadn't been in time?

She needed to warn everyone. Her whole family. All of her friends. But how, when she couldn't really tell them anything? What if it resulted in *more* danger?

"Dammit, Lettie," she whispered. "What the hell have you done?"

Thia hit the return key, completing the transaction. That was that. She was going to London. And, much as she hated the idea, she hoped trouble would follow.

Better her than those she cared about.

• o •

An obviously pissed-off local stood at the entrance to the hotel bar long enough to make his intention clear before he began to wend his way over to where Cormac was seated.

Cormac cursed himself for having made it so easy.

Thanks to the parking garage's somewhat lax wards, he had placed a tracking spell on Thia's car in case she decided to leave in the night. He should have trusted in it and made himself scarce.

He hadn't.

With Thia beyond his reach in the "Guests Only" area (as enforced by physical means and protection wards); and with his attempt to become one of those Guests having ended in a politely efficient, "Sorry, fully booked," he had positioned himself at a table with a clear view of the lobby elevator and stairs.

It had been vastly frustrating to be inactive while, internally, all was in turmoil, but better by far than standing out in the storm he hadn't quite relinquished. From what the night clerk had said, there wasn't a room available for miles. Apparently, All Hallows in Granite Springs was quite the thing.

Now, because Cormac had lingered, he had *this* to contend with—an angry stranger who radiated fury and power, both barely controlled. And, damn. To go by the obsequious nods given by the bar staff, he was in good position to wield that power. Head of security, perhaps. Definitely some position of authority.

Whatever he was precisely, he took his time, strolling an indirect path past table after table of martini-toting patrons. He put Cormac in mind of a blue shark: all calm disinterest until the strike. Though his attention was seemingly elsewhere, he was observing, assessing, attuned to any possible weakness. Anything that might signify prey.

Two could play at that game.

Burying his unease deep, Cormac leaned back against the trendy booth's red velvet, stretched his arms across the top, and smiled his cockiest, most irritating smile.

A flash of temper was quickly hidden beneath a mask of unconcern that rivaled Cormac's own. The eyes that looked out from behind that mask, however, glowed in silent threat.

The gentle clinking of glasses, the low murmurs of conversation, the downtempo music from the stereo system, even the sounds of the rain beating on the plate glass windows seemed to fade as Cormac again called upon his Sight. With less than three feet between him and the man, more details revealed themselves...and were not encouraging. The power the man held was old, a good deal older than Cormac's own, and carried the resonance of the *Sidhe*.

Odd, that, since he would have sworn the guy was entirely human.

"You're not expected," the man said tightly. There was a slight rasp to his voice along with a trace of Irish. "Nor are you welcome. Take your storm and go."

"More than happy to," Cormac said, maintaining his smile with effort. "After I get what I came for."

"And just what might that be?" The man held up his hand. "Before you tell me that's none of my business, *báeth*, let me assure you it is." At his small gesture, the tabletop candle guttered and went out.

"As to that." Cormac snapped his fingers. The candle flared back to life. "I can assure you it isn't."

A wave of the man's hand, and the candle vanished, crystal holder and all.

Damnad. If Cormac hadn't been keeping such a tight rein on his reactions, that would have made him sit up straight. To manipulate fire was one thing. Solid matter was quite another.

"Many guests are expected this All-Hallows," the man said, sliding into the booth opposite. His rasp had become more pronounced. "Interference will not be permitted. Do yourself a favor and forget whatever it is you plan here. You're out of your depth."

"I couldn't care less about your holiday plans here." Cormac lifted his pint glass, took a swallow of ale. The microbrew was a good one, but at the moment, anxiety soured the taste.

"*You* may not." The man's brown eyes glowed bronze with lethal power. "But what of Idris Cathmor?"

Cormac failed to hide his surprise.

The man laughed. It was not a merry sound. "Come now... Cormac, isn't it? Did you not think you'd be recognized? You look a bit like her, you know. The eyes." With a quick check to make sure no one else was watching, he materialized a pint identical to Cormac's and lifted it in toast. "To your mother. Ever the life of the party."

Cormac's hand tightened on his glass but he did not lift it. "Seen her, have you?"

"A few times, in the course of business."

"Recently?"

"Aye. Recent enough."

To Cormac's knowledge, his mother hadn't set foot outside the Otherworld since she had bought her way back in. Whoever this guy was, he had more going on than simple hotel work. Not just anyone had dealings on both sides. Black marketeers did, mostly. Or mercenaries.

"Your father and I had business, too, as luck would have it. *His* luck more than mine." The man's smile went from amused to something nasty. "You might know of it. A bit of a dispute over the Achill Bell?"

Cormac's blood froze. Oh, yes. He knew about that.

He wished he didn't.

A mere boy at the time, he hadn't been involved at the start of the struggle for ownership of the cursed thing; but Idris had made sure Cormac had been present at the culmination. And for months afterward, Cormac had been afraid to sleep for the dreaming. Silly, that. His mind had proved perfectly capable of replaying it all when he was awake.

Idris and his followers had been particularly vicious that night. Spiteful in their triumph and convinced that retribution could be had through rage and pain and blood, they had reveled in the worst of their natures. For Cormac, hardly out of leading strings, it had been his introduction to true terror.

Even now, he pressed the flat of his hands upon the table, unconsciously using the old oak to soothe.

He had been silent too long. The man was watching him, his glowing eyes narrowed. Speculative. As if he knew.

Cormac swallowed, his throat dry. He could use the ale but didn't trust his hands to be steady enough. His voice came out as rough as the man's. "There were no survivors."

"One." The man held out his arm, pushed the sleeve up to expose the wide leather cuff at his wrist. "Declan Murphy, I'm called now."

Cormac stared at the tooled leather and froze while memory superimposed itself over the present. Idris had called the man Murchada. Anglicized from the Gaelic as "Murphy." The last captive, stripped and bound to rough willow planks. Already covered in gore, he had been unrecognizable even before the first fall of the axe. After the third, Cormac had run, uncaring of the consequences, hardly aware of where his feet would take him.

It was only natural he had assumed the man had died.

"That was a long time ago," Cormac managed, his tongue thick. Idris's people had found him days later, wandering the fells. "It has nothing to do with me."

"There is no statute of limitations on vengeance," Murphy said, both forearms resting on the table. More power gleamed in his eyes. "And it could have plenty to do with you. For all he took from me and mine, Cathmor deserves to lose his only son."

"He does," Cormac agreed, and was gratified to see surprise cross Murphy's face. "But it would only matter if he cared."

"You do his dirty work. He'd feel the loss of that, to be sure. His favorite errand-boy."

Cormac was not as certain, but that wasn't the sort of thing one admitted. Instead, he let some of his own power show and leaned back, once again the picture of confidence. Sometimes, the picture was enough to win the game. "Let me finish my business here, and I'll get you the bell."

Bribery didn't hurt, either.

"*You'll* get me the Achill Bell." Murphy arched a scornful brow. "Suppose you tell me how Idris is just going to let you do that."

"The old man currently has other interests." It held enough truth to serve. Cormac wasn't thinking ahead. If he didn't get Idris what he wanted before Samhain, a promise made here wouldn't matter. Nothing would.

"Lie to me," Murphy said, "and I will hunt you down and do what was done to me." He rotated his wrist, calling attention to the leather cuff—as if Cormac needed a reminder. "You'll do no harm at this hotel. You'll not so much as think about it. Or the consequences will be the same."

"Agreed, so long as you and anyone associated with you do

nothing to interfere with me," Cormac said. "In exchange, I'll see the Achill Bell returned to you."

"When?"

"Once my current obligation is fulfilled."

"When?" Murphy repeated, and touched the cuff.

Cormac forced his jaw to unclench. "Three months."

"Two."

Dàirich. Cormac's mind raced. He had a good idea where the bell was kept, and if Idris considered the loss necessary for getting the relic, then he might—

"Agreed." Cormac extended his hand.

Murphy clasped it. "Agreed."

Both men tensed as twin spikes of energy melded and then were reabsorbed, binding the deal in the Old Way. Should either of them break their word, the consequences would be severe. So would the pain, thanks to the bit of magic now lodged in them both. A bit like a shock collar on a dog, Cormac thought wryly. A little thing to keep them both honest, when that was the last thing either wanted to be.

Murphy released his hand and stood. "Finish your pint and get the hell out."

Thunder rumbled and a gust of wind sent rain to batter the windows. Cormac's smile was wry as he raised his glass. "*Slainte mhath.*"

"*Slainte mhor*—until you bring me the damned bell." Murphy walked away. No lazy, indirect path for him this time. He walked quickly, straight for the lobby.

Before the doorway, he encountered an annoyed-looking red-head—the same woman who had escorted Thia upstairs. Radiating quite a bit of power herself, she pointed to her watch.

After they walked out of sight, Cormac settled back in the booth and prepared to nurse his ale till closing time. After all, nothing had been said about how *long* he took to finish.

When the waitress walked past a few minutes later, giving him a playfully inviting glance, he reconsidered his options. She had been coming on to him, albeit subtly, since he'd sat down. Maybe he should take her up on it.

Forgetting his intention to nurse his drink, he took a long swallow, then set the glass down with a hard thunk. He could have resolved this back at Leticia's house. He knew that. Once he'd gotten hold of Thia's arm outside the barrier, he could have had her. But he had hesitated at the violence, and tried not to hurt her. Not too much, at any rate. And what did he get for it? Her pendant had tried to fry his synapses and nearly burned off the skin of his palms.

"Can I get you anything more?" The waitress stood across from him. She leaned over to set a replacement candle on the table—and gave a good view of her...offerings. And her name tag.

"Sherry," Cormac drawled, his gaze leisurely rising to her face. Normally he did this with more finesse, but he couldn't dredge up the enthusiasm. What was the point? They both knew how this would play out.

Straightening, she made eye contact. Her answer was easy to read—although Cormac had yet to ask the question.

"What time do you get off?"

She grinned. "I love your accent."

Morrigan's mercy. He was getting too old for this.

"I was supposed to meet a friend of my sister's," he said, and laid his hand over hers on the table. "She checked in earlier. I said I'd show her around."

"Yeah?"

He watched her pupils dilate as his thumb stroked the back of her hand. "I'm in luck, though, since she hasn't showed up. I'd much rather go with you."

She grinned.

She was making this so easy. He flicked a glance at the lobby entrance before leaning forward and tightening his grip. "I should hate to think she wandered down later and, not finding me, got herself into some sort of trouble. My sister says she's a bit flighty. Doesn't do well in strange places."

"Oh, it's perfectly safe here," Sherry said, then frowned. "Usually. It is pretty close to Halloween. Things can get kind of, well, you know. Strange." She shrugged.

"Exactly right. So I was thinking, maybe you know someone on the staff here who could keep an eye out for her?"

She nodded immediately. "Sure. Eric. He's the night clerk. He owes me."

"Brilliant." Releasing her hand, Cormac took a pen from his jacket. He wrote his mobile number on a coaster. "Could you give him this? That way he can call if he sees her. I imagine she's settled in for the night, but this way, I don't have to worry."

"And I'll get your undivided attention," Sherry said, teasing.

"Absolutely."

She tucked the coaster into her apron pocket. "My shift ends in an hour, but I think I can get off early."

"This really is my lucky night," he said, almost meaning it, but not for the reasons she thought. "I'll meet you outside, shall I?"

CHAPTER 8

Feeling the sharp impatience of the line of people behind her in the plane's narrow aisle, Thia double-checked the seat number with her boarding pass. Tempers had already been frayed by an hour-long delay whose origins had been blamed simply on "weather." Since the skies above San Francisco were clear, that was hard to believe...and she didn't think many did.

The man seated on the outside of the row hadn't so much as looked up from his copy of *Finnegan's Wake,* let alone make an effort to adjust his legs so Thia could shimmy past him to her window seat.

Her backpack made that maneuver hopeless, anyway. She struggled out of it, winced as last night's bruises and scrapes reasserted themselves and the Stone, cloth-wrapped though it was, pressed painfully against her sternum. Not for the first time, she wondered if she wasn't being a bit paranoid by carting it around in her bra. Yet after the attack, even her pants pocket had seemed too accessible.

Thank goodness she hadn't been picked to go through a full-body scan. Not that there was anything wrong with carrying a crystal sphere in one's bra, but it certainly was odd. Where there was oddity, there could be suspicion. Suspicion brought attention.

Should she have kept it in her pocket after all?

This was what Thia had been doing all day: second-guessing herself. She was making herself crazy with it. She hefted the backpack—which, naturally, with everyone watching, had become a too-heavy, ungainly mass. A desperate shove barely got it to the lip of the bin. Straps and nylon ties dangled, writhing against her face like living, fighting things while she tried to adjust her grip to try again. Her arms were already burning. Was she really so out of shape?

"Come on, lady," grumbled someone to her right. The line continued to build. Her fault.

You could help, she nearly suggested to the grumbler. Teeth gritted, she gave her pack another hard shove. A plastic clasp swung down to bounce against her nose but otherwise nothing budged. How could a few spare clothes and toiletries weigh so much? It felt as if she'd packed a boulder. Sweat broke out on her face as her arms began to tremble, and with a kind of dawning horror, she understood she had become that passenger: The one who, through stupidity or ineptitude or a disastrous combination of both, couldn't manage her own luggage.

But everything had gone smoothly this morning with the other plane. The smaller plane. She'd had no trouble getting her backpack into its bin there. She shoved again. It was like pushing against a wall.

"Lady, would you just—"

"Thank you, yes. I'm trying." The frayed ends of her temper flared, sizzled. Her fellow passenger had every right to be annoyed—they all did—but he didn't have to make it worse. He didn't have to stand so close, practically looming over her, and make her feel like a fool.

She couldn't see him clearly, not with the angle and so many straps hanging in her face, but he sounded big. She bet he could lift her backpack—and her—into the bin with one giant hand.

Since shoving wasn't getting anyone anywhere, Thia pulled instead, thinking to take the pack with her and deal with the bin later. If not past the still-oblivious Joyce Reader to her window seat, than anywhere down the aisle where she could step out of the way. But the damn thing proved to be stuck that way too.

"It's caught on something," she said, a little desperately, conscious of shuffling taking place beside her. The angry man, she assumed, going to complain to an attendant. "I'm really sorry. I can't seem to—" The back of her neck prickled, her only warning before someone new stepped up behind, his chest a light pressure against her back. She jerked in surprise as heat shot down her spine.

Her backpack popped free.

Deft hands grabbed it, stopped it before it could land on her face.

"Got you." Close at her ear. Soft with a light accent. Scottish? Northern English? Not enough words to know for sure.

She glanced over her shoulder, but with him almost directly behind her, she couldn't catch more than a glimpse of his jaw (firm and clean-shaven) and hair (short-cropped and dark).

He lifted her backpack as if it weighed nothing at all, slid it easily into the bin.

"Thanks." She lowered her useless hands. When this whole thing was over, she promised herself she would join a gym.

Her cheeks had gone hot. Embarrassment...and an added element which she attributed to her emotional vulnerability and his cologne. Although subtle, the latter was having a not-so-subtle effect. She had always scoffed at the implied (and often bizarre) promises of fragrance ads—but given the way her brain was fuzzing and her nerves were singing, it seemed there might be some truth to them after all. This was an alluring, woodsy scent with a hint of spice, somehow both simple and complex. It was also...familiar?

"Any time," came his reply, the breath of it light and warm on Thia's neck.

She suppressed a shiver. He stepped back, releasing her, and the belated identification came. Oak moss and clove. Of course she found the scent familiar. Eclectica sold quite a lot of each. Good for protection, she remembered, turning to face him. Protection, strength, luck, and—

Her polite smile froze on her face, her intended words all but forgotten when she looked straight into two very intense, surprisingly wary eyes. Eyes that held all the color and fascination of a stormy sea.

This, she thought distantly. *This* was trouble.

More trouble, even, than attempted muggings and missing relatives and mysterious crystal spheres tucked into ill-fitting sports bras. More, because despite all that—despite *herself*—this was the kind of trouble Thia longed for. The rush and whirl of attraction. The awakening of everything that had lain dormant, frozen in the aftermath of a broken engagement (though, as she had realized uncomfortably some time later, *not* a broken heart). This was exactly what she had craved and circumstance had denied. What terrible, ironic timing that it should present itself now.

The left corner of the man's precisely defined lips pulled the slightest bit upwards in the barest suggestion of a smile while a dark brow arched, drawing her attention from—good grief, she had been staring.

And now she was blushing. Perfect. "Sorry. You must think I'm ridiculous."

He laughed—a fleeting, nearly soundless huff—and inclined his head. "Not at all. I think you're—"

"Don't got all day, you two," the angry man cut in. He hadn't gone far, after all. And Thia had been right—he was built like a linebacker. After shooting her a particularly hostile glare, he pushed past her rescuer, knocking him into her. She stumbled backward only to hit the arm of the aisle seat at knee level.

"Oh." It was a silly sound, she knew, even as she made it. Just as she knew it was silly to flail her arms. Her balance was lost. No matter what she did, she was going to fall.

Only she didn't. Before Thia could drop onto the Joyce Reader, before she could so much as encroach on his personal space, her rescuer rescued her again. He reached out, gripped her outstretched arms, and yanked her forward to then steady her against him.

She blinked, startled to still be upright, not to mention in a kind of embrace. She was unaccountably aware of the fabric between them, the feel of his stylishly-casual canvas jacket through the cotton of her shirt, the chenille of her sweater. He was only an inch or so taller than her. Not so much slender as athletically trim. And his eyes, that intriguing mix of blues and grays, were so close she couldn't possibly look away.

Not that she wanted to.

"Saved again," she said because she had to say *something*. What an asinine impression she was making: the staring, blushing damsel in distress, unable to lift her own luggage or stand on her own feet.

"Any time," he repeated. This time, his tone was unmistakably wry.

She laughed. "I'm not usually so—" She broke off when he took a sudden, awkward step into her as the rest of the crowd pushed past him in the aisle. She braced herself against the jostling. Braced him as well, though she could feel him trying to take the brunt of it.

"You're not usually so...." the man prompted, clearly finding amusement in their situation. Both of them held captive until people stopped coming up against them.

"Self-absorbed." It wasn't what Thia had begun to say— *clumsy* had been her original thought—but this was no less true. Thanks to her time at golf camp, where her utter lack of skill had made her an obvious target for pranks and ridicule, she rarely got so caught up in something to the exclusion of all else.

"We're clear," she said moments later, when the last of the line moved on. His weight shifted, and she took a step to the side, attempting to extricate herself. Reluctantly. "I should take my seat—and let you find yours."

"Ah, but I already have." His hold tightened, a brief, almost possessive clutch of her arms, before he let go to gesture to the row. *Her* row. "It's right here."

"I'm sorry?"

"No need to apologize," he returned playfully. "It's not your mistake. It's his." Without warning, he snatched *Finnegan's Wake* from its reader's hands.

The man in question looked up, his fuzzy-white-caterpillar brows furrowing above narrowed green eyes. He held out his hand for the book. "I beg your pardon."

"And well you should, good sir." The book's thief moved it further out of reach, held behind his back while he leaned in to say almost conspiratorially, "Though I can understand the motivation. With her in the one beside it, that's the best seat on the plane." He gave Thia a wink before straightening. "I'd consider stealing it myself—if I had to."

She frowned, unsure what he was up to or that she could support it.

His lips curved, the mischievous sparkle in his eyes giving him a boyish appearance. It was hard not to be charmed by it, by him. But she tried. She really did.

"You're being absurd, young man, and I resent your implications." The now *former* Reader punched the call button on his armrest, the soft chime sounding throughout the cabin. "Return my book and apologize, then kindly take your seat. You're disrupting the flight." A sharp gesture indicated the many faces turned their way. People had nothing to do but watch now that they had found their places.

"I can't very well do that, with you in it," was the reply. But the book was held out, on offer.

It was quickly snapped up. "For the last time, this is *not* your seat."

"This is easy enough to clear up," Thia suggested, carefully neutral. "What do your tickets say?"

"Oh, of course you'd take his side." Anger flooded the older man's cheeks with red as he pulled his boarding pass from the back of his book. He held it out, tapped the print. "It quite plainly says thirty-six...G?" Surprise muddled his expression.

"That's an easy mistake to make," Thia said, because it *was,* which was why she had double checked her own ticket earlier. She pointed to the row markings. "This isn't thirty-six G," she said kindly. "This is thirty-six C."

● ○ ●

"I don't understand." The man's bewilderment was priceless.

Thia's wasn't bad, either, and Cormac couldn't recall the last time he'd had such fun. "It seems you belong back there," he said, gesturing.

"No, no." The gull blinked, looking from the ticket in his hand to the sign posted above the seat. "This can't be. I made sure they matched, and they did. The numbers matched."

"Ah, of course they did," Cormac said, deliberately patronizing. Inside, he was laughing. Because they *had* matched—up until a moment ago when, behind his back, he'd located the ticket in the book and used an elementary spell to swap the numbers with those of his own seating assignment.

So far no one, Thia included, appeared to have noticed the small use of magic. With any luck, the same could be said of the stewardess come to resolve the dispute. Petite and blonde, she eased past Thia and beamed up at him, her expression coy, not suspicious. It was about time something went his way.

"What seems to be the trouble?" she asked.

"A bit of a mix-up." He gave her a charming smile. It was entirely false, but he noted how Thia bristled—and Cormac found himself holding back a genuine one. Already didn't like him flirting with anyone else, did she? Brilliant. "I think we've got it sorted."

"I'm in the wrong row," the man said dazedly, getting to his feet. "But it should be right."

Graciously, Cormac stepped aside to give him room. "These things happen."

"Not to me, they don't." Looking lost, the man handed his ticket to the stewardess. After a quick check, she gently took his arm to guide him towards the rear of the plane. The look she sent Cormac over her shoulder was unmistakably inviting, and he returned it. One never knew what might prove useful.

"Excuse me," Thia said sharply, and without waiting for his response, she slid past him into the row.

Warm, lithe, soft. The feel of her, that one quick brush, was enough to make him forget all about petite blondes.

It was enough to make him forget *himself.*

He needed to stay focused on the right things. The relic and what Idris would do if Cormac failed to get it. He should most certainly *not* get caught up in how Thia McDaniel made him want to smile or how much he wanted to touch her again.

With deliberate ease, he took his seat. Next to him, Thia's head was tilted down, her hands adjusting the belt she had fastened across her lap. He could do this. He could remain detached, he assured himself, even as his pulse ratcheted up again.

He should have had the waitress last night after all, instead of spelling her to sleep straight after she had let him into her flat. Maybe if he'd had more than a restless night alone on an uncomfortable futon, he wouldn't be so susceptible today, so aware of Thia not as a target but as a woman.

Or maybe not, Cormac reconsidered, feeling the threat of unsteadiness in his hands as he pulled his own safety belt taut. There was more at work here than physical attraction. There was a quality about her, so foreign to his experience that of course it would fascinate, drawing him like a moth to light.

Innocence.

Throughout the day, he had watched her. Studied how she interacted with people, how she approached different situations. Despite her underlying anxiety, she had done it all with an openness, a genuineness, that at first he had judged as horrendously naïve. Perhaps it was, but it was also a gift to him, of sorts: a tool he could use. Thia McDaniel trusted people.

And, after the thing with her backpack (another spell of his she had apparently not detected), she now trusted *him*. He had worried she might not. Since he hadn't wanted to risk the larger use of magic, he had not glamoured himself. If Leticia had described him at all, or if Thia had seen him when he had followed her from Eclectica...well, here he was. The souvenir t-shirt and designer scout jacket he'd purchased at the terminal's shops could hardly be considered a disguise.

His eyes were the biggest risk, regardless. His presence on Main Street could be explained; Granite Springs was, after all, a tourist destination. But if Thia recognized the eyes of the man who had tried to carry her off last night, he was sunk. She hadn't seemed to, so far.

He set a hand lightly on the gentle warmth of her shoulder, withdrew it when she looked over. "You wouldn't happen to have any chewing gum, would you? I forgot to buy some. For the pressure change." He pointed to his ear.

A sequence of emotions—surprise to curiosity to concern to dismay—flitted across her face before he'd finished speaking. She was an astonishingly easy read.

"Sorry, no," she said. Concern again, to regret, and, with a roll of her eyes, exasperation. "I forgot too. After five hours in the terminal, you'd think I'd be better prepared."

She was a pageant of expression. Her face, her voice, her gestures. It was all there, out in the open.

Or was it? Did she show the truth, or only what she wanted him to see? It was in his nature to distrust, to find the worst in everyone. But, try as he might, he couldn't find it in her. He could see no lies, no artifice.

"Maybe the crew has some for sale," she said. "Or maybe there's some in here." She took up one of the gift bags the airline had placed in each seat pocket.

As she began to search through it, Cormac worked a quick spell, a modern twist on one he'd learned early in childhood. It was more involved than the others done on the plane, more liable to be detected, but harmless in nature and thus likely to be ignored. Indeed, no one looked his way, not even Thia, as she continued to rummage.

He had performed the spell for a woman back then too, he recalled abruptly. Girl, rather. A bright, cheerful little thing he had wanted to...well, he'd been all of eight. He had wanted to make a friend, and summoning a bit of candy floss had seemed a better way to go about it than tugging her hair like he'd seen the other boys do. Guilt was a knife's twist in his chest. He should never have done it. Should never have paid her any attention at all.

"Bingo." From deep in the bag, Thia pulled out the pack of gum Cormac had summoned there. "It's our lucky day."

He tried to return her smile but couldn't shake the memory of the other time, the other girl. The magic hadn't been over-looked then. Inside Fiends Fell, nothing he had done had ever been overlooked. But because he had hoped that time would be different, innocence had been lost. Not his, not by that point. But every scrap of hers.

"Would you like one?" Thia asked, jarring him out of his thoughts. She held up a piece of Trebor gum. "Save you the trouble of digging out your own?"

Summoning his own, more like.

"That's lovely. Thank you." This time, his attempt at a smile felt more successful.

● ○ ●

Oh, man, was he trouble, Thia thought again, and dropped the shiny pellet of gum onto his palm. It was a good thing he didn't smile like that more often.

But where was the harm, really? For the next nine, incredibly long hours, she was going to be stuck on a plane. Until she got to Lettie's house, there was nothing she could do, no help she could give, no question she could hope to get answered. When the alternative was to worry herself into insanity, why not let herself be distracted by a charming, incredibly attractive man?

She put the gum in her mouth and bit down—with instant regret. Spearmint flavor potent enough to peel paint flooded her mouth and seared her sinuses. She gasped, blinked away tears.

She heard that short, almost soundless laugh, then, "Strong, is it?"

She cleared her throat, wheezed a faint, "Oh, not too bad."

The man looked far too innocent as he tossed his piece into his mouth. Suspicious, she watched closely as he chewed. His expression didn't change, but she knew. His eyes gave him away—too amused by half.

"You could have warned me," she said crossly, then ruined it by laughing.

"I could have. Forgive me?"

"This time." And easily, she realized. Far too easily. Normally, she hated being teased.

The cabin shifted, rocking slightly. A bell chimed, heralding the preflight announcements. This was it. The plane slowly backed away from the gate, and Thia fought a resurgence of nerves. The animated safety video that played on the small console set into the seat before her made them worse with its graphic portrayal of impromptu water landings and sudden drops in cabin pressure.

Another bell chimed, followed by the captain's instruction that the crew please take their seats. As they did so, Thia felt a light touch, quickly withdrawn, on her arm.

"I'm sorry if the gum isn't to your liking."

"No, it's all right." She stuffed the pack, which she had been crushing unconsciously in her hand, into the laughably small storage pouch below the video console. "It was a surprise, that's all. Came on a little strong there at first." Wondering if he'd make the connection to his own behavior, she watched his eyes. "But I think I could like it. Quite a bit, actually."

The blue-gray seemed to darken as his pupils widened.

There. Hiding her smile, she returned her attention to the window.

The plane switched direction, moving forward.

When it began a deceptively lazy turn onto the runway, Thia felt a sudden pang of loss. Life as she knew it was shifting, changing. From here on out, there would be no going back.

● ○ ●

With a great, shuddering rumble, the plane accelerated down the runway. Beside Cormac, Thia tensed and closed her eyes. He was surprised the ends of the armrests didn't crumble to dust under the force of her grip.

The plane tilted, abruptly pulling free of the ground. After a sickening drop, it shot upwards, airborne and shuddering. He risked a look out the window, noted the ground was farther away and at a much different angle than he'd expected. Thia's face had lost all color.

He suspected the same could be said of his own. He gave up

on the view and let his head drop back against the seat, the forces of gravity and thrust impossible to fight. And to what end? He let his own eyes close, didn't stop his hand when it moved to the armrest. His palm settled atop the back of Thia's hand, his fingers covering hers.

The spark was no less startling for Cormac's being prepared for it. Given his body's other responses toward her, of course he had expected *some* reaction. He also expected, like the gum's flavor, that the intensity would soon fade into something manageable.

Only, it didn't. It spread. Though Thia's hand had twitched at the initial charge, she hadn't pulled away; and where skin touched skin, the warmth continued to flicker, soon easing its way in, following the trail of nerves up Cormac's arm to his shoulder, his chest. Sinking into muscle and bone.

This was beyond a spark of attraction: this was energy exchange. Cormac often did a version of it with the natural world. It was a means of replenishing power when he hadn't the time (or patience) to wait for the energy to replenish itself. Streams, meadows, mountains, oceans—all held energy. Living things *could* be used, and he had, but it was a far riskier prospect. With animals, especially, it was too easy to misjudge and take too much. They so often didn't know their own limits. Never had Cormac attempted it with another person.

Not out of concern for them but for himself. The act was too personal. Too intimate, really, along with demanding a certain vulnerability. He would never willingly give anyone that kind of power—literal power—over him.

And he hadn't, had he? He had not chosen this. It had simply happened. Or had *Thia* done it...inadvertently? Intentionally? With his body so relaxed, soaking up much needed strength like a sponge, it was difficult to think, difficult to move. But move he did, fighting his growing lethargy and gravity's pull in order to open his eyes and turn his head.

Beside him, Thia was not as pale as before. Otherwise,

nothing appeared to have changed—her face was still drawn with fear; her eyes, squeezed tightly shut—as if her greatest concern was still the plane's attempt to fly. Did she not feel what was happening between them?

Engaging his Sight, Cormac looked down at their hands. Energy currents of glowing white skittered across his skin to disappear beneath the cuff of his jacket. There were no such currents running along Thia.

His breath caught. She wasn't taking from him, only giving. If she had started this, he couldn't see the sense of it. She gained nothing and risked everything.

Through the connection, he could cause her immeasurable pain and she would be hard-pressed to do anything against it. He could *kill* her. If she still wore the Brigantium's pendant, he doubted it could defend her if he acted quickly enough.

As a last resort, if she wouldn't give him what he needed, he had thought to enthrall her. Could he use *this* against her instead? Maybe if he were to twist it so that—No. He wasn't thinking clearly. Whatever Cormac could do to Thia through the connection, she could do to him.

Panic had him end it. Like closing a door or flipping a switch. Cormac refused the connection and the current shut off. The suddenness of it left him reeling—though some of that might have been relief. She hadn't gotten to him.

If such had been her intention. He still didn't know. Was she an innocent or was she everything he feared? His wits were scrambled. Scrambling. It was impossible to think with the energy still swirling through him, not yet fully absorbed, and the thrice-damned plane threatening to shake itself apart in the fight to reach cruising altitude.

Panels and cupboards rattled, engines roared. The cabin rocked, unpredictably tilting left, then right. A pressure built in Cormac's head, pushed against his chest. How could they not be high enough? And yet the plane kept climbing higher, struggling harder, as if it would break free of the world itself and hurtle them all into space—or die trying. Cormac drew in a strangled, raw breath. He missed the ground. He should never have left the ground.

Beneath his, Thia's turned over and she twined her fingers with his. He had forgotten. He'd cut the connection, but he hadn't moved his hand. She held it now, tightly. Her skin was damp and a little cold. "You may have noticed," she said, "I hate flying." Her eyes remained closed, but she smiled slightly. Ruefully.

"I may have," he allowed. What was it about her that made him want to smile—to laugh, even—despite himself?

"Hm. Yeah. Thank you, for this." Her grip tightened, calling attention to their linked hands. Her tone was wry. "I'm—well, I'm glad it's you, here. I don't think the James Joyce Reader would be so considerate."

"Is that what I'm being? Considerate?" His thumb brushed the side of her wrist, stroking the soft skin there. He shut his eyes. "Maybe I'm just softening you up. Maybe I've some nefarious plan in mind, and I'm the last person you should be seated with. Maybe...maybe you trust too easily, and the *last* thing I'm being is considerate." Heart pounding, he pulled his hand away, crossed his arms over his chest. He could feel Thia watching him, doubtless puzzled by his behavior. She couldn't be more puzzled than he.

The plane leveled. The roar of the engines dimmed to a low rumble. The shaking stopped. A chime sounded. Something clattered behind Cormac. He opened his eyes, leaned out to see a stewardess pushing a large metal cart in the aisle. Good. He could use a drink. He turned back to Thia. "May I buy you a—"

Her eyes were closed, her head tipped back. She had put on headphones. Her entertainment console showed she was listening to "Relaxing Classics." She might as well have hung a do-not-disturb sign.

CHAPTER 9

Britways Flight 52
29 October

When Thia had asked for the vegetarian meal in order to avoid any concerns over economy-meal meats, she'd never imagined that she might be sabotaging her dessert. Puzzled, she looked from the miniaturized arrangement of yellowish cheese currently sweating on her dinner tray to the untouched apple tart on her neighbor's. (He had ordered the beef.) What possible objection could Britways imagine a vegetarian would have against fruit? Oh, hell—egg. Dammit.

No leg room, armrests like cement on seats that barely reclined, music channels corrupted by static...but Thia had no one to blame but herself for the lack of dessert.

"Would you like it?"

She startled at the unexpected sound of his voice. She and her seatmate had not spoken since takeoff almost an hour earlier. She had been too uncomfortable after their—well, she wasn't sure how to describe what had happened, even though she'd been unable to think of little else since.

Not for lack of trying. Yet no matter how many times it replayed in her mind, she hadn't been able to figure out what had come over her.

Oh, sure, she had identified the cause of her panic: anxiety, pure and simple. It was what had happened after that didn't make sense. Thia had held many hands in her life, under a lot of different circumstances and motivations, and never had it been like that.

She had wondered if he had felt it too, that strange, tingling warmth. And, beneath the strangeness, a sense of rightness. That was the truly alarming part, how *right* it had felt. To her, anyway. Maybe to him as well, considering the upsetting things he had said following. After that, she had sought to distance herself.

In retrospect, she wondered if that was exactly what he had been going for.

Fine with her. More than fine. Acting on an attraction was one thing. Getting in deep with someone was complicated, and she needed another complication in her life like...like she needed a magical crystal sphere stuck in her bra.

"The tart," the man said, bringing Thia's mind back to the present. And his offer. "Would you...?"

"You don't want it?" For the first time since dinner had been plunked onto their trays, she looked at him directly. In the light of his entertainment screen, his eyes were a deep, inviting Caribbean blue. How easy it would be to just dive in.

"Consider it yours." He set the small plate on her tray. And smiled.

It was like a push, that smile, right up to a cliff's edge. Warm, azure water sparkled below. Tempting. Beckoning.

With effort, she held herself back. "Thanks. I appreciate it."

"My pleasure."

She took up her fork, and then noticed that he hadn't done much more than peel back the foil of his dinner entrée and tear a chunk off the dinner roll. She hesitated. "You're sure you don't want some? We could split it."

"I'm fine."

Unconvinced but too hungry to argue, she dug in. Some

pasta and a few vegetables after a day of nothing but lattes was not going to get her through to breakfast.

The outer inch of crust refused to give, but the middle sank easily. Too easily. She withdrew a gooey lump.

"Wait," the man said, before she could lift it to her mouth. "There must be other options. Let me have them bring you something else."

She gave him her best dry tone. "Your first time in Economy, is it?"

He blinked. "What makes you say that?"

She grinned, amused by how he could look simultaneously surprised and wary. She should have known, given the quality of his clothes, the cut of his hair. So perfectly casual—the same kind of artful disarray presented in fashion magazines. This probably *was* his first time in cattle class.

"Even if there is a third choice, chances are it'll be worse," Thia said, then studied the blob on her fork. It smelled like what it was purported to be, which put it well ahead of the slices of cheese. "I think this might be okay. Really."

He remained silent while she lifted the fork to her mouth and nibbled.

Tart, quickly followed by a syrupy-sweetness. She took in the whole bite. Chewed, tentatively at first. Swallowed. "It's quite good, actually," she said, amazed. "Are you sure you don't want any?"

"No, please. Enjoy." His expression inscrutable, he lifted his wine in a toast. "To bravery, in its many forms."

She had finished off her wine before she realized that not much else would accompany it into her stomach to sop up the alcohol. Maybe that was why she felt a bit muddled. She shook her head, forked up another bite. "Not bravery. More like foolishness. I seem to have plenty of that."

"Don't we all." He finished his glass, set it aside.

Immediately, a flawlessly coiffed-and-complected attendant

stopped at their row and flashed the man a brilliant smile. "Coffee?"

"Yes, please." Thia responded, handing over her cup.

Darting admiring glances at the man, the attendant placed it on a hand-held tray and poured. "Cream? Sugar?"

"Both. Thanks," Thia said, and then watched the attendant held out the tray. Not to her, of course.

The man removed cup, sugars, and cream. "Thanks, love."

Beaming, the attendant moved on.

With what Thia had come to recognize as his laugh—that lone, nearly soundless huff—the man offered her the cup. *Her* cup. And looked damn smug about it.

"Thanks. *Love.*" Intentionally, she let her fingers graze his.

His expression blanked.

It was what she had wanted—to wipe the smugness off his face. But she hadn't been prepared for her own reaction. For the spark that had flared upon contact. It took effort to keep her motions steady as she set the cup down on her tray table and took up her fork.

He recovered quickly, with another laugh and the flash of a smile, which Thia caught out of the corner of her eye as she chewed.

Two packets of sugar and a tub of cream were set beside her cup, and she felt his shoulder press against hers. She swallowed, held herself still when he leaned in, his mouth nearly brushing her ear.

"Any time." A caress of breath and sound.

She suppressed a shiver and her eyes closed of their own volition. When they opened again, he was turned away, busy signaling another attendant.

"Tea?" The young woman asked. Different height, different hair color, same level of flirtation on her part. Same level of flattered amusement on his.

Thia poured sugar and cream into her coffee, stirred it with the little plastic stick provided, and wondered why she was annoyed. What did it matter if women—herself included—were inclined to throw themselves at the man? So what if he always reciprocated? She should see it as a good thing, a sign that whatever "rightness" she felt was all in her imagination, and that the reality was simple physical attraction. She didn't want complications, she reminded herself. She should feel relief...instead of irrational, jaw-clenching possessiveness.

She tapped the stick on the rim of the cup, set it aside. If she were smart, she'd finish the apple tart and her coffee and try to sleep, no matter how unattainable that felt. She should ask the attendant to send the other one back with decaf.

But she didn't say a word, not until the woman had gone.

"I'm Thia," she then said. She picked up her coffee. "Thia McDaniel."

The man cast her a brief look before tearing open a packet of honey. When he had stirred every last drop into his tea without answering, Thia assumed he wasn't going to—and wondered why.

Finally, he took up his tea and sat back, angling himself to face her as much as space and the seat allowed. His gaze oddly intent, he said simply, "Cormac."

No last name offered. Nothing unusual in that, by itself. But there *was* something strange. Almost as if he expected to be recognized. Oh, goodness—was he someone famous? That would certainly account for the fawning attendants.

But this was Economy, of all places. Celebrities flew first class or private, didn't they? Plus, no one had asked for his autograph.

And as for his watching her intently...well, she had misinterpreted, that's all. He was just showing interest. In her. Again.

Her throat suddenly dry, she cleared it, but ignored her coffee. The way her pulse was speeding, no more caffeine for her. Not for a good long while.

"You're going home—to Scotland, is it?" Her best guess on his accent.

"Mmm," Cormac said, taking a sip of tea. He cocked his head as he lowered the cup. "Thereabouts. And you? Business or pleasure?"

If it were not for his bemused expression, she might have suspected he was making fun of her trite attempts at conversation—and rightly so. Normally, she was better at this.

"Neither, I'm afraid." Her insides performed a somersault that had nothing to do with steadily increasing turbulence. "Someone in the family may have—that is, she may not be well."

"I'm sorry." Sympathy softened his tone. "You're very close with your...." The question trailed into another sip of tea, his gaze never leaving hers.

The cabin lights lowered in preparation for the long night, robbing all but the glowing entertainment screens of color. Even the rich blue of Cormac's irises leached to gray.

"My great-aunt," Thia supplied truthfully, abruptly tired of lying. "We were—*are* close. At least, I thought so. Now I'm not sure I know much about her at all." It hurt, to know she had been so ignorant, so blind to so many things.

"Yet your great-aunt asks you to go all the way to London, and you go. That's very kind."

"No. I mean, she didn't. I haven't been able to—" She caught herself, recalling Lettie's warnings. And, although Thia didn't see the point—she and Cormac were strangers and would remain so—she hedged. "It's a surprise."

"A bit risky, wouldn't you say?"

"I hope not. I really hope not." She clutched at her coffee, took a long, reassuring drink.

"Something *is* wrong, then," Cormac said gently, eyes wide with concern.

Too late, Thia realized how bleak she had sounded.

"The elderly can be so frail." Cormac took the cup from her, set it down to take her hand. The contact sparked, kick-starting the tingling warmth. "An illness, is it?"

"Oh, no, she's not ill—I don't think so. I don't really know how she is, or even if she's—" To Thia's horror, she felt her eyes fill with tears. She ducked her head, but there was no stopping the flow. What she'd been avoiding for almost a full day was happening.

She tugged free of Cormac's grasp to fumble with the latch of her seat belt.

"Here."

A neatly folded cloth was held in front of her face. A handkerchief. A *linen* handkerchief. She waved it away. "I'll ruin it."

"Please. I have more." Cormac's kindness was making it harder.

"No, really," she said, desperate. "I'll just get some tissues from the restroom." And pull herself together in private.

The plane dropped. Not violently, but several passengers cried out and Thia's instinctive twitch sent the gathered tears streaming down her cheeks. Frantically, she brushed at them as the plane climbed, seeking its original altitude.

It leveled quickly enough but continued to shudder. A bell chimed.

"Ladies and gentleman, the captain has now turned on the safety belt sign," came the announcement. "As you may have noticed, we have encountered some turbulence." That got a smattering of strained laughs. "It looks like it may continue for awhile longer, and we ask that you please remain in your seats. Thank you."

So much for privacy, Thia thought, and tightened the belt across her hips.

Cormac, though, was clearly trying to give her what little privacy he could. The picture of calm, he studiously ignored her, seemingly content to drink his tea and watch the people who had been caught out of their seats struggle back to them while the plane dipped and swayed.

On Thia's tray table sat the gift of his handkerchief.

● ○ ●

At the edge of his vision, Cormac saw Thia carefully dry her eyes with his handkerchief and then tuck it into her sweater pocket. Though he hadn't had time to work any spell into the fabric, he felt pleased with himself, more certain than ever that she was in this up to her neck—if not in over her pretty head. For the first time in days, he had everything under control.

Including, in a way, the plane.

Because a vulnerable person tended to let slip all sorts of useful things, Cormac had quickly called over the turbulence they'd been destined to hit shortly, anyway. A relatively simple matter that shouldn't get him in too much trouble should it be traced back to him, and it kept Thia beside him. That it had also served to pull her away from her sadness was of little consequence.

Cormac reclined his seat and, because nearness and touch had proved to be effective ways of keeping her unbalanced, he let his body gravitate towards hers, their shoulders nearly touching.

"I'm sorry to have upset you," he lied.

Her self-deprecating laugh surprised him.

He turned, found her looking perfectly composed, if weary. Purple crescents sat like bruises below her hazel eyes.

"That's easy to do this week," she said, her lips curved in a small smile. "I'm the one who should apologize. I've had a long day."

"And I keep chatting, when you could be getting some rest."

"Oh, no." Fine-boned hands waved away his words. "I don't

think I could sleep. Especially not through this."

They were in the heart of the turbulence now, the plane's fixtures rattling as it labored.

"I doubt I'll be able to sleep, either," he said, putting a bit of suggestion in his voice. He raised his cup, watched her gaze track the motion to his lips. Pursing them, he blew—ostensibly cooling the tea—before letting it into his mouth. Her own lips parted slightly; her gaze lifted to meet his, drifted to his throat when he swallowed. He set the cup down. Though the lighting was low, he could read the signs well enough: Uncertainty and, more importantly, interest.

The turbulence had her again white-knuckling the armrest. Cormac made sure that his inner protections were in place and then laid his hand over hers.

Her eyes widened at the contact and its predictable spark, and in them he thought he saw the same confusion he felt. He ignored his own as irrelevant and considered how best to use hers.

Slowly, lightly, Cormac stroked his thumb across the delicate underside of Thia's wrist, felt her pulse jump, speeding beneath the pad of his thumb. That his own leapt in response was another irrelevancy. He leaned in with a practiced smile. "We'll have to find something else to do, then, won't we?"

Her shocked expression was unaccountably endearing. "I'm not...that is, I'm not sure this is—"

"I am," he interrupted quietly, and took her hand in his. Without breaking eye contact, he drew it toward his mouth, let his lips graze the skin of her knuckles. "I'm sure."

She shivered, and he turned over her hand, pressed a kiss to her palm. Her muscles tensed as if she might pull away, but instead she leaned closer. Her pupils were dilated; her cheeks, slightly flushed.

He had her.

Careful not to rush, when everything in him demanded he

do just that, he used his free hand to lightly trace the gentle slope of her cheek. Brushed his thumb across her closed lips. They parted, allowing her breath to flutter across Cormac's skin, and he gritted his teeth as instinct threatened to throw strategy all to hell.

● ○ ●

"Will you be in London long?" he asked quietly, so close that Thia could feel the words drift across her skin. Could smell the honeyed tea on his breath.

"No. Not long." Her gaze on his mouth, she licked her own lips in anticipation. Angled her head as she moved closer still.

"What a shame. It's a grand city." His hand cupped her face, his thumb drawing slow, light circles at her temple. "You'll be staying with Letic—with Lettie?"

"Yes. At least, I think so." Was he not going to kiss her? She looked up into his eyes, two pools of stunning, luminous blue, like cobalt lit from within.

She frowned. They hadn't been quite that color before, had they?

He said something.

"Sorry. I missed that." She wasn't even sure he had spoken English.

He smiled. "You did, yes."

Between the wine, the lulling caress of his thumb, and the blue, blue, blue of his eyes, Thia was finding it impossible to concentrate.

"Are you—" Her thoughts scattered. She tried again. "Are you going to...tell me what it...was?"

"No." Cormac laughed again, a mere breath. So strange that such a small thing could make her feel so good. "What might you do in London?"

"I have no idea." Did he, or did he not, want to kiss her?

Cormac studied her a moment. "I'm beginning to believe

you don't." He sounded surprised.

She could look at him for hours.

Forever, maybe.

Wouldn't that be wonderful, she thought (if the current muddle of Thia's consciousness could be credited with such coherence). Everything was drifty, as light and elusive as dust motes in a ray of afternoon sun. She could just sit and look at him for—

"Thia?"

Her name. Cormac had said her name and it sounded lovely, almost like a lullaby. The reality of the plane slipped away, leaving only the glow of his hypnotic gaze and the delicious heat making its way up her arm to spread through her chest. Like before, during take-off...only different. Flowing *in* this time, not out, from the point of contact. What was it about Cormac that there should be this...this *this*. She was babbling. In her own head, she was babbling.

"Thia, why go to London?"

Hypnotic. The word repeated, a distant warning—an alarm, telling her to wake up. But she couldn't, any more than she could stop the words from leaving her mouth: "Lettie. I need to find Lettie. She hasn't answered my calls, and a psychic told me she was dead. I can't let myself believe it. I can't. But she sent me a—a note."

She shouldn't tell him, but it was so hard not to and she was so tired. So very tired.

"Lettie sent me a note. It said...it said the Stone...." Thia shook her head, helpless. "I shouldn't be saying these things."

"It's all right," Cormac assured her, his voice soothing. But his grip had tightened and his eyes, so intense in the near-dark, appeared cold.

She had seen eyes like his before, she realized with an odd detachment. Last night, at her fence. The attack.

"The note," Cormac said, leaning in. "Tell me. What did the

note say?"

"I can't." Thia tried to pull her arm away, but it would not move. *She* couldn't move. "Please," she said in a whisper rough with panic. "I can't tell you. I can't tell anyone."

Heat flared high on her chest where her pendant lay against her skin. Painless to her, but she watched Cormac flinch. His expression hardened. And his eyes...*glowed?* Thia blinked, fighting to keep her own open. She was so tired. Too tired, even, to feel afraid.

But just a moment ago, she had, hadn't she?

She could no longer remember. She fought a brief, losing battle against a yawn. Sleep had taken hold and was pulling her under.

"Thia. The note." Cormac's insistent voice seemed to come from far away. "What did Leticia—what did Lettie say in the note? Something about a stone? Please, you need to help me. What stone?"

"Your eyes," Thia said, fascinated. Her head, too heavy for her to support, fell back against the seat. Her vision blurred. Something was wrong about this. About his questions. About *him*.

Heat—her pendant—flared again and with a grunt, Cormac released her arm. She had hurt him? No...her pendant had. Like with the man the night before. The man with his eyes. Cormac's eyes. Or was it the other way around? Did he have the man's eyes?

She wasn't making sense, even to herself.

"I'm sorry. I'm falling asleep," she said, her words slurring as her eyelids dropped and she slid into a dreamless dark.

CHAPTER 10

Britways Flight 52
29 October

With Thia asleep and Cormac no longer touching her, the pendant stopped emitting pulses of *wanfýr.* He turned, expecting to have attracted some attention, but as he looked around the darkened cabin, it seemed that no one had noticed the flashes of blue energy.

Flashes, he realized, that were not dissimilar to those from personal entertainment screens. He rolled tension out of his shoulders.

If not for the connection Cormac had established before he'd begun the enthrallment, things could have gotten quite messy. As it was, he had been able to slip a couple of spells beneath the pendant's notice even while it worked to fend him off.

The first was a sleep spell to knock out Thia's panic and, he hoped, the pendant's automatic response. The second was a memory spell to make her forget whatever had caused the panic in the first place.

Had it been the enthrallment? He had just begun when her mood had gone from willing to frightened and the pendant had started doing its best again to cook his hand. Higher-level *Sidhe* magic had never been his strong suit, so it was possible he had slipped up, done something to alarm her. When done right, the victim remained unaware of danger.

The way she had been looking at him, though, made him wonder. So intent. So shocked. And directly in the eyes. Had she recognized him, connected him with the man outside her house?

It was just as well he had clouded her memory; if she *had* put two and two together, she wouldn't remember it when she woke.

He stood, stepped into the aisle. The section's passengers had either succumbed to the dark, monotonous rumbling of the flight or were fixated on whatever entertainment they'd chosen on their screens. There wasn't an attendant in sight.

With a glance at Thia, still sleeping peacefully, Cormac took her pack from the overhead bin and carried it to the lavatory.

The door secured, he set the pack on the sink. There were no wards on it, no protection at all beyond two run-of-the-mill travel locks. He made quick work of those—and quick work of searching. The pack held nothing of value.

Oh, certainly the digital camera was worth some money, as were a few silver baubles wrapped in a silk scarf (two rings and some bracelets, modern and devoid of magic). But clearly the pack served to hold what could not easily be replaced should the airline misplace Thia's checked luggage, plus some backup items. Cormac refolded a shirt, returned it to its place atop several pairs of socks and an interesting bra and panty set.

Interesting. That was a wholly inadequate description of the artful scraps of black satin and lace. His gut tightened. Under the rumpled practicality of her current clothes, did she wear something similar?

It didn't matter, he reminded himself and snapped the locks in place. Shouldering the pack, he returned to his seat.

She hadn't moved, not even a little. Her head remained at what looked to be an uncomfortable angle on the seat-back. Her breathing was deep. Regular. Cormac replaced her pack in the bin and, from the reserves stacked beside it, took down two blankets and one of the travesties the airline dared to call pillows. Then, settled once more beside her, he considered his next action.

Had he allowed enough time for her pendant to calm?

Thia's breath passed softly through her bow-shaped lips, a bit of drool collecting at one corner. He shouldn't want her, he thought, at a loss. He shouldn't.

He slid a careful hand behind her head, his fingers spearing through the warm silk of her hair. The pendant didn't react. Cormac could not say the same for himself. He forced a slow, deep breath into the tightness of his lungs, willed himself to relax before, lifting gently, he set the "pillow" behind Thia's head. Not that he cared, but she would be more comfortable now—or at least would suffer less upon waking.

His fingers grazed her cheek as he withdrew his hand. She murmured something, her lips curving into a faint smile that made his chest ache.

He unfastened her safety belt. Should anyone happen along, or should Thia awaken despite the spell, Cormac shook out the blankets, laid them at the ready over her knees.

Anticipation was the enemy. He clenched and unclenched his hands until he knew they could be steady, and then with skills honed over centuries, he set about picking her pockets, starting with the large button-closured one at her thigh.

A return ticket she had stashed there showed she planned to stay no more than two weeks. A passport with an astonishingly bad photo revealed she hadn't traveled outside the US (legally, anyway) in five years. A crinkled, heavily taped postal wrapper showed that Leticia had somehow mailed a parcel from Inverness when Cormac knew her to have been holed up in Kirkwall. And a letter, written in bold, clear script, proved he had been right about where Leticia had sent the relic.

Relief crashed down like water from a fall and he closed his eyes, dizzy with it. Ah, *Morrigan's mercy.* He had been right.

The Stone of Shadows. He had not known it by name—not known, even, that it was some kind of stone. Crystal, he could safely assume, given the amount of power it was reputed to hold. Cormac opened his eyes to reread the letter.

It made no specific mention of him, which was puzzling. More so was the implied mistrust of the Brigantium, though that explained much of Leticia's odd, solitary behavior in the past weeks. What had brought it about, he wondered— and when? He returned everything to the cargo pocket and continued the search.

Her upper pockets proved to be a wasted effort, containing nothing even remotely stone-like. She might not have it with her. She might have left it at the hotel for safekeeping or, as Leticia had, sent it to someone else.

But he found no evidence of anything like that, either. Not in her wallet, with her driver's license (its photo even worse than her passport's) and collection of twenty-dollar bills. Not in her slim case of business cards. Her two sweater pockets held only the pack of Trebor gum and his handkerchief.

There was nothing for it. He had to risk closer contact. He took in a shaky breath, blew it out slowly. Kept a stranglehold on his calm, even as an image of black satin and lace flashed through his mind.

Drawing the blankets up to Thia's hips as cover, he leaned over her, so close he couldn't help but breathe in the subtle, clean scent of her, feel the warmth she radiated. It only got worse when, after a quick glances around the cabin and at her sleeping face, he lifted the bottom hems of her sweater and shirt and slid a hand inside.

As soon as his fingers touched the smooth skin of her belly, her pendant flashed.

Blue light. Painful electrical shock.

Jaw clenched, Cormac quickly moved his hand along first

one side of Thia's waist and then the other, feeling only the elastic band of her knickers. No secret travel belt. Nothing taped to her skin.

Flash after flash of blue, ever brighter, as shock after shock grew stronger. Sweat beaded on his brow.

Cormac sent his hand higher, up Thia's ribs to meet another elastic band—her bra. Not satin and lace, this one. No, this was a thick, uniform expanse that clung too tightly to admit his searching fingers.

He closed his eyes against the searing flashes of light and cupped a breast. Round. Plump. *Perfect,* although he was in no state to enjoy it. He could hardly think through the pain, his heart beating an erratic, too-fast rhythm.

Frantic, he sought the cleft, where she might have hidden the relic...except there *was* no cleft. No cleavage at all, only taut, impervious fabric.

A sports bra, Cormac recognized dimly, barely hanging onto consciousness. A fucking sports bra. He would have cried, if he wasn't working so hard to merely draw breath. Under the assault of electricity, his heart began to falter.

But he could feel something in there, something unnatural and hard between the softness of breasts, and so he persisted. Awash in agony, his whole body trembling, losing strength, he struggled to get at whatever was under the damn fabric of her damned—

Something struck the back of Cormac's head, multiplying the stars he was already seeing. He wrenched his hand out from under Thia's shirt and whirled to face the attack.

Loss of contact with her meant no more electrocution. The pounding of his heart steadied. He could breathe again. His eyes quickly adjusted to the cabin's dim light and focused on the man seated across the aisle.

"I don't care what you two get up to over there," the man was saying in a furious, slightly slurred whisper, "but cut it out with that damn light. You'll wake the wife, and *she'll* care about that, I tell you. She'll care a helluva lot. About this too." He indicated the miniature bottles of Jim Beam on his tray table. Another—unopened—lay at Cormac's feet, which explained what had hit his head. "I'm only s'posed to have *one*."

Cormac nodded weakly. Swallowed. His throat felt burned and all he wanted to do was close his eyes, he was so drained.

At the sound of footsteps, he nearly groaned. The attendant who had relocated his seat's original occupant approached, clearly furious. This wouldn't be about a thrown liquor bottle. It wouldn't be about flashes of light, either.

"What seems to be the trouble here?" she asked quietly, and the pointed look she gave Cormac was confirmation enough. She knew what had been behind it all, and who was to blame.

"Some damn flashlight or something," the man across the aisle said, drawing her attention. "Thought it would wake my wife the hell up."

She laid a hand on his shoulder in a gesture of comfort. "I apologize, sir. I'm sure it won't happen again."

"Better not," he grumbled, though his expression had softened, his eyes closing. By the time the attendant lifted her hand, he was snoring.

She knelt beside Cormac, braced both hands on the armrest. In the dim light, her eyes glowed a faint bronze. "There are two air marshals on board, not to mention several attendants like myself who would be more than happy to assist you to another seat. But that won't be necessary, will it?"

"No." Cormac forced the word past his irritation.

"Excellent. Ms. McDaniel strikes me as a nice person, the sort who would be worried to wake and find her companion— no matter *who* he was—had vanished. And we wouldn't want to worry her, would we." Her eyes flashed, anger mixing with the power.

"No," he said. "We would not."

"Nor would we want her to experience any trouble after we land—which is why airport security will be keeping a close watch throughout. And why I've already had your photo sent to the proper authorities. It seems you're flying under a false passport...*Cormac.*" She smiled at the discomfort he'd failed to hide. "There's quite a queue of people who would like to speak with you once we arrive. You will, of course, make yourself available to them."

He managed a cool, "Of course."

The attendant's mouth tightened. Rightly, she didn't trust him. "They'll await you at the gate. Should you try to—"

"Is that wise?" Cormac asked innocently, and then shrugged. "It could cause a bit of a stir, even if such a welcome were to proceed without...incident."

"At Customs, then." The attendant stood, only to then lean in close. Threateningly. "You will be watched every moment. Don't even *think* to try anything."

Cormac said nothing. Damn her and her threats. Damn the situation for giving him no choice but to acquiesce to them. And damn Thia's pendant. Damn that most of all.

"Let me help you with these, sir," the attendant said in a more public voice. Reaching over him, she took hold of the blankets and drew them up to Thia's chin. "How considerate you are, thinking of your friend's comfort."

Cormac's jaw clenched so hard, he wondered that his teeth didn't crack.

The attendant finished tucking the blankets beneath Thia's shoulders and then fastened the safety belt. "Sleep sound and safe, here undisturbed," she murmured as her fingers traced invisible patterns. "Beneath blankets soft and, now, secured."

With a quick pulse of power, the spell engaged. The woman straightened, flashed Cormac a smile that did not reach the glowing bronze of her eyes. "Have a nice night," she said, then walked confidently away.

Cormac glared at the blankets—and the protection wards revealed by his Sight. They weren't much, nothing he couldn't break in an hour or two, even with his strength as diminished as it was.

But not without the attendant sensing the interference and calling in reinforcements.

The flight was a total loss and now enormous complications awaited in the airport itself. Beside him, Thia slept on, her alluring vulnerability nothing more than an illusion, thanks to the attendant's interference. Tension threatened to crush him.

He was exhausted physically and mentally. Emotionally, too, whether he willingly acknowledged that or not. A few seconds more and he would have had the relic, he was sure. Instead, it tormented him, so close yet so thoroughly out of reach.

He could wake her, he supposed, and continue the game of seduction. He needn't use magic to do that. But he was too furious to trust himself. Thia McDaniel had a way of making him forget. His intentions became clouded around her. *With* her.

So he would let her sleep until he could think straight, until he could be trusted to do not what he wanted but what was necessary.

He picked up the bottle from the floor, twisted off the cap. Bourbon whiskey. Not his favorite, but he was past caring.

● ○ ●

The Landmark Hotel
Granite Springs, Oregon

Abby Collins entered through the front doors, waved at the night clerk before she headed up the curved stairs to meet Kendra. She really hoped *he* wouldn't be there. The last thing tonight needed was an encounter with the Landmark Hotel's infuriating owner.

Eclectica had been jam-packed with customers all day, and

nothing—absolutely nothing—had gone smoothly.

Abby knew she made a fine manager, knew the employees worked just as well for her as they did for Lettie. The issue was Eclectica itself. In Thia's unexpected absence, the store had thrown a bit of a tantrum. Keys to display cases were not where they should have been—and then *with* the keys, locks were reluctant to budge. Stock that had been set aside for a customer to pick up had been found back out on the sales floor. The music system had frequently glitched: freezing, skipping, or, worse, repeating a few notes ad nauseum when staff was busy with customers and inclined to think someone else would deal with it...thus prolonging the torture.

Perhaps worst of all, the espresso machine in the café had stopped working after lunch, leaving Abby without even the hope of a mocha to carry her through the afternoon.

It was well after midnight now, she had barely made a dent in her Sabbat preparations, and had no doubt that tomorrow would be no better than today.

She definitely did *not* want to run into The Man Who Shall Not Be Named Lest It Encourage Him to Appear.

"I don't know how you can stand to work for him," she said in lieu of greeting to Kendra in the second floor ballroom.

Intent on a mirror hung high on the wall, her friend ignored the comment to instead ask, "Does that look uneven to you?"

Abby studied the leafy garland draped over the ornate gilt frame. "I don't know. I'm so tired my eyes are crossing."

"Me too." With a frustrated sigh, Kendra turned to face her. "I know why *I'm* not home in bed. Why aren't you?"

"I'm in charge of the altar wreath this season and needed to gather a few things." She patted the bag at her side, making the dried leaves rustle.

She could get some ideas from what Kendra had done to the place, Abby thought, taking a look around. The broom centerpieces were a particularly nice touch. She ran a finger along a table runner's velvet edge. "But I don't think I could sleep even if I didn't have five thousand things to do before Samhain. I'm worried about Thia. I think she's in trouble."

"Have you called her cell?"

"Straight to voicemail."

"Well." Kendra made a small shrug. "She went to take care of some family stuff, right? That means she went back east. Factor in the time difference and it's no stretch to figure she turned her phone off before going to bed."

"I suppose."

Kendra sighed. "You don't think that's what she did."

"No. I want to, but I don't. Something isn't right. I haven't been able to reach Lettie, either. She's in the UK on one of her buying trips. I'm wondering now if that isn't where Thia went—not to her family back east but to wherever Lettie is." Abby made a helpless gesture. If only her so-called gift could be more specific. "I can't help thinking they're in danger." She suspected Eclectica had been trying to indicate as much, too.

"Danger?"

"I know it sounds ridiculous. Of all people, they're the least likely to get into trouble. Especially Thia." Of any sort. "But yesterday, I got the feeling she was hiding something."

"When I checked her into the suite last night, she did seem stressed, but—"

"Hold on, what? She stayed here? Why?" Abby was stunned. When she and Thia had spoken, which they had done several times by phone through the day, Thia had never mentioned it.

Had that been Abby's fault, monopolizing the time with all her questions about the online ordering system—or had Thia deliberately avoided talking about anything personal?

"Thia told me that the storm broke a window at the house," Kendra said. "She boarded it up but said the cold was leaking in. What? What is it?"

Abby was frowning. "It's odd, that's all. She gets something from Lettie, says it's nothing—and you *know* whatever Lettie sends is never 'nothing.' Then she acts jumpy and strange the rest of the day, the storm blows into town—"

"The unnatural storm," Kendra broke in, and Abby felt the bloom of her friend's concern like shot of cold at the base of her skull. She resisted the urge to rub her neck.

"Exactly. Then, in the midst of this *unnatural* storm, rather than asking to stay with me, she checks herself into a hotel—before taking off right before Halloween. 'Family stuff' just doesn't cut it."

"I should have pushed her about it," Kendra said, sounding stricken. "I should have made her tell me what was going on."

"The same goes for me." Along with worry, guilt had plagued Abby all evening.

Kendra paced a few steps, stopped. "Okay. What's done is done. What are we going to do *now?*" The look she leveled at Abby was steely with resolve.

"Find out where she and Lettie have gone."

Kendra nodded. "I'll make some calls. In the morning," she amended, and Abby followed her gaze to the clock set above the far door.

She stifled a groan. Tomorrow—no, *today* was going to feel very, very long. She said as much.

"Big time," Kendra agreed. "Now get out of here before Murphy comes in and you two get into one of your things. We finally got the chandelier back from the shop."

Abby looked up at the object in question as a flush crept into her cheeks. "He started it."

"Uh-huh."

● ○ ●

Britways Flight 52

Gradually, Thia became aware of a persistent noise, a sort of

rushing roar. Like a vacuum cleaner. Or leaf blower, maybe...
accompanied by an annoying vibration and a seriously funky
smell. Rancid butter and, maybe, eggs? She opened eyes that
felt as dry and scratchy as her throat. And, after several hard
blinks against the unmistakable morning light, she managed
to make sense of where she was.

An airplane.

To London.

Shit. She pulled her hands from beneath two blankets only
to feel disoriented again. She stared at the wafer-thin sheets
of linty fuzz. When had she put them on? And how had she
gotten *two?*

An attendant must have come by, Thia decided, recalling
light touches and subtle perfume.

No, not perfume. Cologne. A very particular cologne. Her
heart stuttered and then pounded, sending a surge of blood
to her brain.

Fully awake at last, she turned her head.

"Morning," Cormac greeted smoothly, looking flawless and
alert.

"Morning," she croaked, feeling anything but.

A hand to her head confirmed that her hair had gone crazy
in the night. Smushed in the back, clumped here and there,
frizzed everywhere. Her eyes were crusty and she suspected
she had drooled, so there was a good chance that her face was
crusty too.

Embarrassed, she ran one hand over it while the other dug
in a pocket for a clip to put up her hair.

"They brought your breakfast," Cormac said when she had
finished. He pointed to a plastic-wrapped lump on Thia's tray.
"They tell me it's a sausage and egg bagel."

She frowned, dubious. "It doesn't smell like sausage and
egg. It smells like a mistake." Across the aisle, a man stuffed a
last bite into his mouth with fingers shiny with grease. Thia's

stomach lurched and she quickly looked away. "I'll just have coffee."

"Good choice."

Cormac, she noted, hadn't touched his "breakfast," either. Next to it sat a half-empty cup of what she assumed was tea, which meant the attendants had already made their rounds.

She was searching for the call button when she felt him go still beside her. His eyes were closed, his face tense. She laid a hand on his sleeve. "Is something wrong?"

"Not at all." He opened his eyes, all amusement once more.

Before she could puzzle that out, an attendant came rushing down the aisle to stop at their row.

The young woman's face, despite the make-up, was flushed; her breathing, fast. She held a small tray. On it was a single, steaming cup. "Coffee?"

"Oh, fantastic, thank you," Thia said, impressed that anyone on the crew had noticed she had awakened, let alone bothered to bring her anything. "Is it possible to get some cream and sugar?" The tray held *only* the cup.

"Already added."

"Really?" Thia took the cup and, indeed, the coffee was a milky light brown. "Thank you. How did you know?"

"No matter," the attendant said pleasantly, and collected the unopened breakfasts. Turning to Cormac, her expression soured. "Next time, use the call button," she told him, then left.

Too interested in the coffee to wonder about that, Thia took a hearty swallow. And nearly moaned. "Oh, wow, that's good." Settling back, she closed her eyes and let the caffeine work its magic. She held the cup beneath her nose to better breathe in the aroma.

"I'm not addicted," she said a moment later.

"Of course not."

She smiled at his wry tone. "Okay. Maybe just a little."

He chuckled, and Thia took another long swallow, not sure which warmed her more.

In preparation for the approach to Heathrow, attendants moved through the cabin. Trash and rented headphones were collected; customs forms were given. Had Thia recently been on a farm? No. Was she bringing agricultural products? *If only,* she thought as her stomach rumbled.

After writing Lettie's address as her place of stay, it dawned on Thia that she didn't have any idea where in all of London that was, let alone how to get to it.

"Problem?" Cormac asked, pen poised over his own form.

"I'm an idiot, that's all. I didn't print out directions to my great-aunt's before I left." She pointed to the address. "I don't suppose you know where this is? I'd like to avoid taking a cab, but if I don't know where I'm going...." She shrugged.

He leaned in, making light contact as he read. Then, "You're in luck. I know the area well."

"Really? That's—"

The plane banked sharply, beginning the landing, and Thia lost her balance to fall solidly against Cormac.

"Sorry," she managed before sensation overwhelmed her.

Mine.

Quickly, she righted herself...or was righted by a nudge from Cormac. She was too shaken to know for sure.

"—near the British Museum," he was saying pleasantly, as if nothing had happened. "The Piccadilly Line goes right by it. The Underground," he explained at her questioning look. "Pick up a map or check the posted ones before you leave the Russell Square Station. You should be able to find it within a few blocks. No need to worry."

"Great." That sounded easy enough. As for what she would do after that, she still had no idea. "Thanks."

His mouth curved. "Any time."

She smiled at the joking recall of their flirtation the night before—but was too caught up in her nerves to do more. He returned to filling out his form, leaving her to stare out the window, her thoughts speeding along with the plane.

Mine? Where had *that* come from? And why did he have to smell so good?

The plane drew closer and closer to a landscape that shifted from a patchwork of fields to industrial complexes that Thia ought to have expected with such a great metropolitan area but had not. The wheels touched down, bounced...hit again.

When they stayed down and the brakes engaged, rapidly slowing the plane, several cheers went up amidst a flurry of applause. Thia joined in. Even with her apprehensions about what lay ahead, it was wonderful to be on the ground.

"We made it," she said as they taxied toward the gate.

"That we did."

The plane rocked to a gentle stop. Seat belts were flung off and people—Cormac included—stood and opened overhead bins. The chime that gave permission sounded while Cormac was already holding out Thia's backpack for her to put on. She stood, hunching so as not to bash her head on the bin, and shrugged into the straps. He settled the weight on her back, and she then turned, wondering how many times more she'd end up telling him, "Thanks."

Tension gripped her. She was in *London*. She was really doing this. The Stone felt especially heavy against her chest.

The doors of the plane hissed open and life surged. People filed out of their rows, eager to return to the world.

Cormac stepped into the aisle. "Ladies first," he said with a teasing bow.

Aware of the line forming behind them, Thia didn't linger, and made sure to stay close on the heels of the person ahead—just as she felt Cormac, behind, was doing with her.

They would soon part ways.

Her memories after dinner were fuzzy, thanks to the wine,

but she remembered well enough that they had nearly kissed. She also knew that the unanswered question of that would bother her for a long time to come—and how ridiculous was that, really? Of all the unanswered questions plaguing her at the moment, "how a kiss might have been" ought to rank as least important. Maybe it only felt so vital because, unlike the rest, this answer was within reach.

If she dared.

But come on, could she? Could she really?

Hardly hearing the chorus of thanks and farewells from the flight crew gathered at the door, Thia stepped off the plane and into the claustrophobic gangway. Things were suddenly moving very fast, and she felt entirely unprepared.

She was about to carry a purportedly valuable relic through British Customs. Good lord—was she *smuggling?* She hadn't thought. What if there was an alert out on the Stone? Some sort of watch list for magical (and possibly stolen) antiquities?

Lost in an internal fog, she let Cormac take her arm and guide her through a maze of corridors involving sudden turns and inexplicable changes of direction. All around her, people chatted excitedly but she heard none of it.

Would Customs discover the Stone?

She should have a ready explanation, something that didn't make her sound crazy or seem at all suspicious—in other words, nothing of what Lettie had told her. Something like... how it was just an object used during meditation. Just a little thing her great-aunt had sent.

That Thia happened to carry wrapped up in her bra.

"This way," Cormac said and took her down another narrow corridor. They were moving at a good clip, keeping pace with the crowd.

If she were arrested, what would she do? What *could* she do? Would she be considered an international criminal? Did that mean being put on a plane to be arrested and tried in the US, or would she be put in a British jail, tried in a British court?

Cormac brought Thia to a stop outside a huge, cordoned maze. At its finish were the Customs officials, each one grim-faced, looking as if they could see through Thia in an instant. Well over a hundred people already waited before them, with more and more on the way.

"Doing all right there?" Cormac asked when Thia remained frozen. His eyes, not far from her own, seemed to hold genuine concern. He wasn't much taller than her own five-eight. She hadn't noticed that until now.

Kissing him would be easy.

"Sure." Her grin felt stiff. "Of course."

"You'll be fine." He gave her arm a reassuring squeeze before letting go. "I'm that way. Yours is over there." He pointed to the roped division between the two sections—one for those with British passports; one for those without.

With hardly anyone lining up in Cormac's destined area, he would be through in no time, whereas the line in Thia's was growing exponentially. Unless she and Cormac happened to meet at the baggage claim, she realized with a pang, this was goodbye.

"I had a—I really enjoyed talking with you." Thia hurriedly got out her wallet and pen, scribbled her personal email on her business card. Held it out.

He blinked, clearly startled, but took it. Read it over. "I... uh, I... Well." He slipped the card into an inside jacket pocket and gave her a surprisingly shy smile. "Thia. Thank you."

Because such unexpected vulnerability made Cormac look absolutely adorable, because Thia would never see him again, she stepped forward, grabbed his jacket.

"Any time," she said, and kissed him.

Talk about trouble. She had meant it to be a quick, playful peck, but she didn't pull away. She forgot about either quick or playful as Cormac's lips parted, moving on hers, and his hands came up. Thia's eyes closed as his fingers threaded through her hair, pressed against her scalp, held her as the kiss intensified. He tasted of honeyed tea, a fascinating contradiction of bitter and sweet.

"Thia." His whispered breath was warm on her skin.

"Yes."

Cormac's mouth covered hers again, no longer asking but demanding. Thia might have moaned—just a little—wanting more. *Needing* more.

She released his lapels so her hands could travel the breadth of his chest and up over his shoulders. *Perfect.* His height, his form, how he made her feel...everything about him was perfect. Thia's every nerve thrilled, alive with sensation as his hold tightened and he stepped into her, or she into him, so they stood chest to chest, hip to hip. Her mouth opened as his angled, sought. Their breaths rasped, mingling—

"Oy, get a room, mate." Laughter followed.

A lot of laughter.

Thia took a hasty step back, opened her eyes. It was like being awakened from a deep sleep, having one reality ripped away as another forced itself upon her.

Cormac, looking as shaken as she felt, stood some distance away, as if he had also retreated. Around them, a sizable crowd had grown, faces showing a range of opinions—shock, envy, disgust—and Thia blushed.

Either that or her cheeks had caught fire.

With the show over, their audience quickly broke up, most heading in the direction Thia herself needed to go...but she remained motionless. She didn't think her legs would work just yet. Cormac, too, seemed rooted to the spot. His eyes, in the harsh light of the fluorescents, were so intensely blue that they seemed to glow.

"Well, um...Okay." Thia didn't know what to say. Whatever had compelled her to do that? And in public, no less. She was afraid the answer was simple, if a bit unflattering: lust. She was also afraid she really, really wanted to do it again.

Cormac continued to stare.

"Um...See you," she said lamely and with an equally foolish wave, she turned and headed for Customs.

See you? She couldn't have sounded more ridiculous if she'd tried.

● ○ ●

Cormac watched Thia enter the Customs area. He continued to watch even after she was swallowed by the snaking crowd and he could catch only a glimpse or two of her at a curve or through a gap created when someone momentarily failed to keep pace with the queue.

He was aware of her card as if it lay directly upon his skin, jacket lining and shirt be damned.

She wanted to see him again.

Or maintain contact, at the least. She hadn't *said* as much but it had been implied. She had enjoyed talking with him, she'd said. And had written out her email. Not her business email—that was already on the card—but her own.

And then she had kissed him. In full view of everyone.

Cormac let out a long, tremulous breath. Something jittery and unfamiliar twisted through him, leaving him as addled and nervous as the schoolboy he had never had the chance to be. The schoolboy experiencing his first crush, knowing for the first time that the girl he liked did, in fact, like him back.

She hadn't wanted to say goodbye, hadn't wanted to leave. Hadn't wanted to leave *him*.

And he was going to use it against her, possibly destroy her in the process.

When the men approached, striding too easily through the chaotic bustle of international arrivals, Cormac adopted a nonchalant stance, hands at his sides. In his mind he reached out to the charmed glass hidden in Leticia's attic. It was far, a good fifteen miles or more. Not impossible, but nowhere near ideal.

Better, though, than what the alternative was shaping up to be: a public fight with magic and guns.

"Only four?" Cormac asked lightly as the men surrounded him. Their dark suits and military bearing proclaimed them to be some kind of security team—as did the guns beneath their jackets—but they wore no identification, no badges. Nothing to indicate to what agency they belonged.

The man in charge had sandy-blond hair styled less severely than the buzz cuts of the other three. He held up a thin silver disk. An old florin, or two-shillings coin, it looked like.

"Come with us quietly, or I'll bind you with this," he said. Oddly, no power glowed in his eyes.

"*You* will?" Cormac felt the internal click of his connection with the attic glass snapping into place. He began readying the location spell. "I very much doubt it."

"You won't come quietly?" The man took a step forward, the coin held out like a talisman.

The other men tensed. "Just do it, Tremayne," one said.

Below that impatience lay fear. It emanated from all three subordinates—along with several of the passersby that quickly skirted the area—but not the man with the coin. Tremayne. No doubt he believed it gave him control.

Cormac almost felt sorry for the man. "Done this a lot, have you? Bound someone's powers in silver?" His own spell was nearly ready.

Anger blazed in the man's narrowed eyes, but still no power. No magic whatsoever. Whoever had put him up to this had done him a great disservice.

"Dozens," Tremayne said tightly, and Cormac couldn't help but grin at the bold lie.

"Of course. Well, then." He lifted his hands in a mockery of surrender. "Best get on with it."

Insecurity flickered across Tremayne's face, but he took a step closer, thrust out the coin. Dull silver, worn with use and time. "*Adstringito argentum*."

Cormac winced. "Not that it matters, but your pronunciation is atrocious."

Tremayne frowned, glanced from Cormac to the coin.

"Did it not work?" asked the man on the left. "Thought you said it was foolproof."

"She told me it was," Tremayne said, and then tried again. "*Adstringito argentum*."

Cormac could feel the other men moving in. The one to the right had his hand inside his jacket.

Time to go.

"Give the Brigantium my best," Cormac drawled. The Latin had been a dead giveaway, although to expect someone with no skill to pull off such a high-level feat was clumsy of them. And since when did they employ armed security? He'd have to ponder that later.

With the flick of a mental switch, he released the spell held in his mind. The airport vanished—or so it seemed from Cormac's point of view. The four agents likely had a different impression.

CHAPTER 11

Unable to move quickly enough, Thia felt the automated rod of the station turnstile slam into the back of her thighs. She staggered forward, nearly tripping over her wheeled suitcase. She hadn't had a chance to extend the handle, so she was carrying it rather than being able to wheel; it bumped against her legs as she kept pace with the stream of people exiting the station. And suddenly, before she could get her bearings, she was outside on a bustling, rain-slicked sidewalk.

Buffeted by a damp, slightly gritty wind, she lurched over to a flower stand set up against the station's exterior— relievedly outside the flow of pedestrians—and took her first breath of fresh air in two days. Her first breath of London air, ever.

She coughed as it burned her lungs, coated her tongue with exhaust from cars that were surely going too fast for such a narrow, crowded street. The noise of wet tires, engines, and foot-traffic conversation resounded between brick buildings. The sky above was a deep, spotless blue.

For a terrible moment, Thia felt completely adrift, overwhelmed by the sum of a multitude of tiny differences. The sidewalk was made of cement, but instead of familiar rigid slabs, this was an arrangement of tiles that shifted under the impact of hurried feet. Cars were glossy and had four wheels, yet their designs were more compact, sleeker. And, of course, they were driven on the wrong side.

People were different, too, in a way that had nothing to do with nationality and everything to do with style. Suits were everywhere. Gray suits, with pants for the men and tailored skirts for the women. Gray suits with pastel shirts. Gray suits with patent leather shoes.

It had obviously rained not long before, yet there was hardly an overcoat or windbreaker to be seen. Instead, scarves were wrapped around necks and umbrellas of varying lengths were clutched like batons or tapped like canes. Thia looked down at her hip-length jacket, creased from its time in her backpack; her wrinkled cargo pants; her scuffed sneakers. To write the word "tourist" on her forehead would be redundant. Even without her luggage, she couldn't be taken for anything other than what she was: someone entirely out of place.

With an internal shrug, she then committed the ultimate but inevitable sin of the foreigner. She pulled out a map.

Fortunately, it was at least discreet, in the form of a book only slightly larger than her hand. Shelf after shelf of them—London A to Z—had lined Heathrow's exit in what might have been a heavy-handed sales push but felt also like a godsend. The pages detailed every street, no matter how small, in the entire metropolitan area, while the back cover presented a layout of the Tube system. She had taken the Piccadilly Line, as Cormac had advised, and used her time on it to plot a route from the station to Lettie's street.

Angling the book so as to correspond with her position, she traced her finger along the lines. Her first target was less than an inch away. She ducked her head to the left and peered through a mass of discounted calla lilies to see a formidable iron fence at the end of the long block.

She extended her suitcase's handle and then, gathering her courage, merged onto the sidewalk like a vehicle entering a freeway. Specifically, she decided, a motor home towing a trailer: Cumbersome and with limited visibility.

The pace was swift. The number of pedestrians restricted Thia's chances of changing lanes and left her no safe braking distance. People came up swiftly from behind to pass and then cut sharply in front of her. Her suitcase wheels caught the edges of paving blocks so many times that she gave up altogether and carried it—without attempting to lower the tow handle. Even a moment's pause risked a collision.

Caught up in the flow, Thia was swept past her destination before she even understood what had happened. The corner she had needed to cross was already a half block behind her, but she had no choice but to keep going, wending her way to the outer edge of the sidewalk where she found space to turn around.

With speeding cars too close for comfort beside her, she backtracked to her intended crossing, where yellow glass globes flashed on top of posts. Before she had finished reading the warning to "look left," thoughtfully painted on the sidewalk, all four lanes of traffic had stopped. She waved her awed thanks to the waiting drivers and hurried across.

Inside Russell Square Gardens, there weren't many people. She walked at her own pace, dragging her suitcase through murky puddles and soggy piles of brown leaves. Horse chestnuts, much larger than the ones in Granite Springs, dotted the worn paths. To prevent her thoughts from straying where they had wanted to go for the past hour on the Underground (namely, anything to do with Cormac) she concentrated on her surroundings.

It didn't help. Even if her mind could forget for a time, her body could not. He was imprinted on her skin. Her lips. She cringed. Had she really done that? With a man she barely knew, and in the middle of one of the world's busiest airports?

By the time Thia had exited the square's northwesterly exit, her shoulders ached and her back was numb—an unwelcome reminder of her promise to return to the gym. Though, really, some of this could be blamed on the luggage itself. Hurried packing was not thoughtful, weight-conscious packing.

She confirmed her location with the help of a hodgepodge of narrow signs stuck on a single post. The British Museum was behind her, the Underground to the right, a train station ahead...which meant so was the street she needed.

One more busy intersection under her belt and she was on her way down a quiet street lined with tall, once-white buildings. Residential, and quaintly so. Most had planter boxes beneath their windows, but due to the season, those were empty or contained only scraggly remnants.

The only cars Thia saw were parked, silent and empty, along the curbs. Soon the puckety-puckety-puckety of her suitcase's wheels and the rubber-softened impacts of her sneakers were the only sounds to be heard. The rush of traffic had faded, and then dropped out altogether as she wound her way to the place that Lettie, up until the time she had relocated to Granite Springs, had called home.

Tall and immaculately white buildings with gleaming black doors faced a central, fenced garden. The sidewalks were level and pristine, not a leaf or a speck of gum to be found. Even the gutters were impossibly clean.

The back of her neck prickled.

She stopped, looked around with a vague sense of alarm, yet the block appeared as deserted as ever. Deserted and almost eerily quiet. She resumed her walk, moving more quickly than before. Three houses...two...one. Lettie's was identical to all the rest, down to the waist-high iron fence before it.

The knob turned easily, and Thia pushed open the gate, its hinges letting out a faint creak. She dragged her suitcase through, let the gate clatter shut behind her as she crossed the bare flagstones. There was area enough for a small garden but there wasn't so much as a single planter. Not even out-of-season window boxes. Leaving her suitcase, she jogged up a set of steps, her focus already on the doorbell.

She jammed her finger on the illuminated button. Muted chimes sounded deep within the building. In keeping with its neighbors, curtains were drawn across windows, preventing anyone from seeing in.

After the chimes fell silent, the only sounds Thia could hear were her own. Anxious breathing. Anxious pulse. She rang the bell again. The door's brass knocker—a dragon's head with a thick ring gripped between its jaws—watched her impassively.

"Please be home," she whispered, increasingly desperate.

Not a single curtain twitched behind the glass panes.

Thia lifted the cold ring of the knocker, brought it down with a resounding metallic thunk. When that was followed by the sharp snap of a lock being released, her heart nearly leapt into her throat. She felt an ecstatic hug building, fed by a river of fear and joyful relief.

But it was not Lettie who opened the door. It was an elderly gentleman dressed in a black three-piece suit complete with bow tie and boutonnière.

Lettie had a butler? Or might he be a—Thia's mind balked, and yet it wasn't inconceivable that her great-aunt might have a...gentleman friend. Although, surely, wouldn't Lettie have mentioned him?

"Good afternoon." The man's voice sounded like the gate's hinges, creaky and faint. Bent nearly double as he was, he appeared to be speaking to his patent leather shoes. "May I help you?"

"Hello." Thia spoke to the back of his head with its white, thoroughly pomaded hair. "I'm looking for Leticia McDaniel. Is she here?"

"Oh-ho! You're a Yank," he exclaimed, and began to shuffle about, altering his position until he could look up at her. The wrinkles of his face lifted into a denture-revealing grin while a bony finger gestured to the suitcase at the base of the steps. "Best not leave that there, love." With a wink, he executed a wobbly turn and tottered into the house.

Thia was obviously meant to follow, but she couldn't move. He had Cormac's eyes. The very same mix of muted grays and sparkling blues. The very same mischievous glint. Or so she would've sworn.

It must be a British trait.

"Well, come in, young lady. Come in," he called, waving an impatient hand from some distance down a long, rather dark hallway.

By the time Thia retrieved her suitcase, set it and her backpack neatly to one side in the entry, and closed the door, the man was nowhere in sight. She stood alone for a moment more, looking down the shadowed hall. She didn't need to be told that Lettie was not home. Her great-aunt's absence was palpable, a mournful weight of silence and unmistakable loss.

Tears threatened. Despite the unanswered phone calls and messages, despite Madame Demetka's and even Lettie's own words, Thia had hoped to find her here, to have her welcome her with a hug and a grin and tell her everything was going to be all right.

"Well, where are you then, missy? There's not much to gawk at by the door," the man called from a room to the left of the stairs at the end of the hall. "Come, now. Let's get you settled and I'll fix us a lovely cup of tea."

Thia sniffed, wiped her eyes. Just because Lettie wasn't at home, that didn't mean she was...gone. She could well be in Scotland. Thia was being fanciful, attributing her own worries to the house's atmosphere.

She entered a shade-drawn room that was doing a shocking impression of a ransacked library. Piles of books sat beside empty or disarranged shelves; decorative items like vases and statuettes were set in haphazard groups; large sheets of brown paper and pieces of bubble-wrap were everywhere, piled on surfaces and scattered on the floor.

Fear coiled in Thia's chest. "What's happened? Is Lettie all right? Has she been here? I tried calling, but—"

The man cackled and looked up from where was clearing space on one of two sofas. "Now, now. It's no good working yourself into a state, missy. Why don't you have a seat and I'll fetch our tea." He shuffled toward her, his gnarled hands outstretched, to herd her away from the doorway.

She held her ground. "I don't want any tea. Thank you," she added, aware that terror was making her brusque. She didn't mean to be rude. "Tell me what's happened here. Please. Is Lettie all right? Where is she?"

"So many questions," the man chided, a smile in his blue-gray eyes. "And we really don't have time."

Again, Thia was struck with a sense of familiarity. She took a couple steps back, wanting to increase the distance between them.

He followed, and she began to feel the sharp prickle of panic along her spine. "I believe you have something for me," he said, his tone filled with a gentleness she didn't trust.

"Something for you?" Thia's hand crept up to her pendant. The metal, warm beneath her fingertips, soothed. She still felt that she might be in serious trouble, but the panic receded.

A frown clouded the old man's face, then was gone. His lips drew back to reveal straight, white teeth. She thought it was intended to be a friendly smile. It failed.

"Our dear Lettie placed something in your keeping," he told her. "You may give it to me now."

He reached out his hand and she watched, shocked, as the wrinkled skin smoothed. Age spots faded. Arthritic knuckles shrank. The man took a step forward, his pale, youthful hand moving closer.

She was dreaming, she thought, unable to look away from that hand. This had to be a dream. A nightmare. And as proof, just like in others she'd had, no matter how much she urged her feet to move, they would not.

"Give me the Stone, Thia. I won't ask again." Cormac's voice broke through the buzzing in her ears.

She wrenched her gaze from his hand to find herself looking at the man she had hoped to meet again—but not like this. Not at all like this.

"Where—" Thia cleared her dry throat. "Where did the old man go?" She knew it was a stupid question, but logic was having a hard time in the face of this new, irrevocable reality.

Cormac made a soft clicking sound with his tongue. "Thia, please. Hell, I thought you were onto me from the start, the way you stood like a statue at the door."

All she could manage was a weak, "I don't understand."

People couldn't look like one thing one moment and something entirely different the next. Not without make-up. Not without wigs and prosthetics and tricks of light.

Cormac's hand remained inches from her, its palm upturned in demand while his hard, blue gaze bored into her and made it doubly impossible to think. But she continued to try...and his earlier words about the Stone, finally sank in.

All along, that's what he had wanted from her.

Only that.

Thia began to take small backward steps in subtle retreat. Cormac matched her, maintaining the arm's-length distance between them, a predator stalking his prey.

Her eyes searched for a clear escape route but found none. Too many obstacles lay between her and the door. Even when she pulled out chairs and began knocking over anything and everything she could in attempts to obstruct his way through the narrow paths between furnishings and stacks of books, he kept up with her.

"Where is Lettie?" she asked, anger beginning to override fear. "What did you do to her?"

Cormac blinked, clearly perplexed.

Surprised by that reaction, Thia bumped into something—the back of a Victorian-era sofa—and in two quick strides, Cormac was there, trapping her against it.

"I didn't do anything to Leticia," he said earnestly. His arms bracketed Thia's waist, his hands gripping the carved wood of the sofa's frame.

Thia arched away from him. Beneath the awkward pressure of the Stone, her heart pounded, caught between previous attraction and present threat. Instead of doing any number of self-defense moves, she did nothing. Transfixed and curious, she didn't so much as flinch when he raised a hand to her face. His fingers traced her cheek, her jaw. Lifted her chin. Their gazes locked, and she felt her eyes widen. His—it looked like his irises were glowing.

"*Do kridjo, mo anatla,*" he whispered.

Thia's pendant flared, hot on her skin, and Cormac flinched. The pendant? Had the pendant somehow caused that?

"Your heart, my breath," he said, his voice tight with what might have been pain. His irises were definitely glowing. A brilliant, cobalt blue.

Tendrils of need began curling through Thia, and Cormac smiled as if he knew. His gaze drifted to her mouth and, as in the airport, Thia forgot herself. There was only Cormac and her own want. Overwhelmed by instinct—dangerous, foolish impulse—she took hold of his coat and pulled him closer.

He smelled so good, felt so warm. She moved her hands to the back of his head, drew him to her mouth. He tensed beneath her hands, almost like a resistance, then gave in on a low, grateful sound. Lips and tongues tangled, his demands meeting her own. He tasted still of honeyed tea, and smelled of sun-dappled forests and dark spices. Emotions mixed, mingled in the space around them.

Desire. Need. Loneliness. Comfort. Despair.

Behind Thia's closed eyes, a wall of brilliant color shattered into tiny fragments that flashed and danced like crimson and violet fireflies. Beyond where the wall had been, something waited, calling to her. Urgent, yet...afraid? All she had to do was reach for it. Reach for it, and it would be hers.

From far away, she heard a gasp—Cormac's, maybe, but it might well have been hers. She was pushed forcefully backward. She fell against the hard frame of the sofa and, leaning heavily against it, her legs too wobbly to provide support, she waited while her vision cleared. The beautiful lights dimmed to blues and greens, faded until only the shards in Cormac's eyes remained. Then they, too, dulled, leaving his irises a cold, emotionless gray. He stood some distance from her. His hands were at his sides; his expression, unreadable.

Here was her chance. Straightening, she prepared to run.

CHAPTER 12

The doorbell rang. Thia froze in stunned indecision.

"Tell them nothing." Cormac's voice was a furious hiss as he stepped in, grabbed Thia's wrists when she would've pushed him away. "Give them nothing, understand? *Nothing.*" His grip tightened painfully, making new bruises upon the old, and then he was gone.

Thia blinked. Stared. No wave of a magic wand, no puff of smoke. Just...Cormac there, then Cormac gone. Thia's hand reached out, tentatively sweeping where he should have been. She felt only air, slightly warmer than the rest.

The doorbell rang again, followed by insistent knocks. She looked blankly around the room, tried to think with a brain suddenly turned to sludge. This was not her house. She didn't have to answer. If she wanted, she could curl up in a ball and try to pretend none of the past few minutes had happened.

She wanted to. Oh, she wanted to. But maybe whoever was outside knew something about Lettie. Or Cormac. Or whatever the hell was going on. She lurched from the room.

Maybe this was a nervous breakdown. She touched numb fingers to her still-tingling lips. Maybe she would wake up any second and find herself back on the plane—or better yet, safe in Lettie's guest bed in Granite Springs.

When she had gotten halfway down the hall, the pounding stopped. So did she, to listen. She waited but heard nothing. They had given up. She took a relieved, grateful breath—only to let it out in a shriek when the door burst open and two figures, silhouettes against the afternoon sun, rushed in.

Thia yelled, pivoted to run, and immediately smacked into a wall that shouldn't have been there. Strong arms wrapped around her, held her against...*not* a wall. A man. He was big— tall enough that the side of Thia's face hit the middle of his chest. He smelled like Armani and probably wore the clothes too; the material her face was pressed into felt moneyed.

The constricting hold tightened and she yelped, terror and rage in one convenient, pained sound as her panic intensified. With Cormac, she had failed to react. This time, she didn't hesitate.

"Fire!" She lashed out, sucked in another breath of luxury-product-tinged air. "Fire! Fire!" Before she could strike at the Wall's vulnerable bits, a second attacker grabbed her wrists, immobilizing her arms entirely. She shouted again while her kick connected solidly with shins both in front and behind. The grunts resulting from the latter were distinctly feminine, which explained the searing pain in Thia's lower arms: Fingernails. Whoever this woman was, she fought dirty.

After a moment or two of frantic wriggling, kicking, and stomping, Thia recognized that the crescent-shaped pains in her arms were the whole of it. She wasn't being held so tightly that she couldn't breathe—just enough that she couldn't pull away. She wasn't being whacked on the head, or pummeled in the kidneys, or any other violence that would've been simple to perform since there was a third person yet to join the fray.

"Miss McDaniel? Perhaps we might have a word?"

Thia stilled. The nails withdrew from her arms.

"Maybe," she said into the Wall's coat. His grip relaxed; she stepped quickly back, bumped up against a slim table. A vase of dried flowers rocked close to the edge. She managed to still it with an unsteady hand, her focus never leaving the three intruders.

Wall was big, well over six feet and with an athlete's build of wide shoulders, broad chest, and trim waist. His suit was indeed a designer product, and had been tailored and draped to perfection. His face was magazine-perfect as well, making it almost *too* handsome. But his expression was shy—bashful, even, as if he knew how overwhelming the sight of him could be, and he felt a bit guilty about it. His hands hung loosely at his sides, open and non-threatening. An identically photo-ready woman posed similarly beside him, but with the feel of those fingernails fresh in Thia's mind, "non-threatening" was not so easy a sell.

Taken together, they made quite a picture with their molasses-dark hair and classic, bold features, and Thia was all too conscious of how rumpled and travel-gritty she was.

"You *are* Althia McDaniel, yes? Leticia's grandniece?"

The voice was the one Thia had heard during her frenzy and belonged to the man standing in the entryway. He had at least twenty years on his companions. Gray hair stood out from his head in confused tufts.

"Thia," she corrected automatically, still braced to defend herself. Just because it appeared she had misjudged the threat level here, it didn't mean she actually had. The man in Granite Springs had appeared harmless right up until he had grabbed her—and he had also known her name. And then there was Cormac, of course. She had misjudged him, too. On so many levels. She adjusted her stance, asked, "You know Lettie?"

"We thought that we did." The older man's pewter-colored eyes were anything but friendly. "Circumstances, however, suggest otherwise."

"Perhaps we might go into the parlor?" the woman asked in a honeyed contralto. Her gesture indicated the room Thia had just left. "You look as if you could use a seat, Miss McDaniel. I'm afraid we've given you quite a shock."

They didn't know the half of it, Thia thought, and remained where she was. "Now might be a good time to tell me what you're doing here."

"Looking for you," came the woman's easy reply.

"Me?" Thia moved her hand surreptitiously toward the vase. Not a great means of defense, but she could work with it if she had to. "Why would you be looking for me? How would you even know I was here? I only just—"

"We were alerted to your arrival," explained the older man. "Customs then informed us that you intended to stay here with Leticia."

"But how did you know I was *here*—inside, now?"

"There was evidence of someone having been welcomed through the wards."

"Wards?" Thia looked at the others' faces for signs that they thought the older man was talking nonsense. There weren't any. "What wards?"

"The protections placed around the house." said Wall. As an explanation, it fell short of the mark.

Thia let the subject drop, adding it to the growing list of things to be considered later. "So, when I didn't answer, you figured you should break in?"

"The door was unlocked," the woman pointed out.

"And in any case we have a keys." Wall jingled a set before returning them to his trouser pocket.

Thia's discomfort increased. It seemed *she* was the intruder.

"Really," the woman said, "I think we'd be more comfortable in the sitting room."

The hallway was cramped, with little room to maneuver and few viable weapons. Thia would have better luck, potentially, in the ransacked...sitting room, as it had been called. "Sure," she acquiesced.

"Wonderful," the woman said. She and Wall smiled brightly, a tooth-whitening ad come to life, and led the way.

Thia followed. "You haven't said why you were looking for me."

The pewter-eyed man walked beside her. "I'm Eben Trimble. Perhaps Leticia mentioned me?"

Thia shook her head. "Sorry. I don't think so. Should she have?"

"I suppose not." He indicated the others. "My assistants. Matthew and Cassandra Swinton."

Twins. Of course. That Thia hadn't realized it straight off was proof how overloaded her brain was. "Nice to meet you," she said, hoping that after all this it would be.

They flashed identical grins, then entered the sitting room. It had been in bad enough shape before the encounter with Cormac. Now it looked as if a tornado had hit.

"Brigid's mercy," Eben exclaimed, and the three rushed over to the area near the sofa, where Thia had watched Cormac do the impossible.

"It was like this when I got here. Mostly." Thia bypassed the seating area to stand near the fireplace. More specifically, the set of fireplace tools. "I had a little...accident with some of the books. And chairs."

Why she was doing as Cormac had asked—covering for him—she had no idea.

They weren't even listening.

"He's been here." Cassandra cast a bewildered look at her brother.

He looked decidedly grim. "Recently."

"How recent?" Eben's back was to Thia but she could hear his displeasure clearly enough.

"Ten minutes. At most."

They *knew?* Thia set a casual hand on the shaft of one of

the tools. The poker, she hoped, and risked a quick look to confirm. The dustpan or stubby little broom wouldn't do her much good.

With his assistants speaking quietly of relative temperature and something like "negative transfer of energy," Eben glared across the room at Thia. "The barriers are intact," he said, as if in accusation.

Her grip tightened on the poker. "Excuse me?"

"They're crafted to admit family, as was Leticia's will. You let him in." He took a step toward her. "You let Cormac into this house."

"No, I didn't. *He* let *me* in."

Eben continued to walk toward her, closing the distance. Like Cormac had. Thia took up the poker.

"He did," she insisted. "Looking like a decrepit old butler, he opened the door and invited me in. Then he made a bunch of demands and—and *poofed* away when you got here."

Eben had stopped but continued to glare.

"You haven't answered *any* of my questions," Thia went on, feeling the ragged edge of control. "I don't know what you want with me, or how you think you know about whatever might have happened *there*"—she waggled the poker at the sofa, where Matthew and Cassandra were still in discussion. "But as far as I know, you're breaking and entering, key or not, and I should call the police. Which I'd be happy to do."

Ignoring her, Eben returned to the twins. "Search the house. Quickly. He must have a focus inside. Find it."

"No, wait. Stop." Thia said to no effect as Cassandra headed out into the hall. With an apologetic look, Matthew followed. "I mean it," she insisted, but felt foolish. "I'll call the police."

"And I meant what I said, Miss McDaniel." Eben said as he reached into his suit pocket.

Thia tensed, her breath locked in her chest. But what Eben pulled out wasn't a gun, wasn't a weapon of any kind. It was just a crystal on a thin silver chain. A pendulum, the same sort Eclectica offered for sale.

"My assistants and I have permission to be here," Eben said. The clear crystal caught the light, swayed as he dangled it above the spot where Cormac had stood. "You do not. Whom do you think the police would arrest?"

"I'm Lettie's grandniece. I'm here for her."

"Yet *she* is not here. Nor did she give you leave to enter. An intruder did that, as you yourself admitted." Eben knelt, putting the crystal closer to the carpet. Studied the motions.

Thia had seen dowsing before—had even tried it herself for fun at the store but without success. Eben was having much better luck, and she wondered what could cause the crystal to twitch like a fish on a line beneath his motionless hand.

Whatever it was, it had him looking up at her with narrowed eyes.

A blush heating her cheeks, Thia looked away. He couldn't know *exactly* what had happened there. Could he?

Her gaze wandered over a tumbled pile of books, an overturned chair. A row of empty shelves. Some of the disarray was her fault, but not the worst of it. She lowered the poker, letting its point rest on the well-worn floor. "Where is Lettie? Something has happened to her. Happened *here,* by the looks of things. Please. Won't you tell me what's going on?"

Eben returned the pendulum to his pocket and slowly got to his feet. "You'll need to come with us"—he raised a hand when she began to protest—"to a safe place. There, *and only there,* Miss McDaniel, may you receive answers. This location has been compromised. Perhaps irreparably."

Thia shook her head. "I'm not going anywhere. Not until I know Lettie is okay."

Eben seemed to weigh whether she was something other than what she was: A confused, traumatized woman teetering between anger and fear. Finally, he clasped his hands behind his back, having apparently reached a conclusion—and not a particularly comfortable one, by his expression. He cleared his throat. "I'm sorry to say Leticia died sometime in the last week."

"No." The room spun. Thia leaned on the poker for support. Madame Demetka had been right. How could that be? How could cards—wait. "That can't be. Someone would have told us. Her family. We'd have been notified."

"That's not how we do things."

"I don't understand. I don't understand any of this." Dizzy, Thia righted the nearest chair, a fragile looking thing, and sat. It made some worrisome noises as it shimmied a bit, but held. "Of course we'd have to be told. We're her family."

"She was murdered by the man who let you into this house," Eben said as if she hadn't spoken. "It's imperative we leave as soon as whatever he used to get past the wards is destroyed."

He said more, but Thia couldn't hear it over the roaring in her ears. Lettie was dead. *Murdered.* And Thia had laughed with the man who had done it. She had embraced him. *Kissed* him. Disgust, hard and unforgiving, lodged in her throat. She scrubbed a hand across her lips. If only she had sandpaper. Acid. *Anything* to remove the lingering feel of his mouth on hers. His hands on her body.

Her hands on his. Thia choked back a cry. Even if she *could* rid herself of the phantom sensations, the remembered feel of him, the worst of it would still remain. She had lusted after Lettie's murderer.

"He looked like an old man and then he didn't," she said stupidly, barely noticing that she spoke over whatever Eben had been saying. "He stood right there, and then...he didn't. How could he do that? How could anyone do that?"

"Cormac has many talents, Miss McDaniel." Eben gave the hallway an impatient glance. "Which is why we need to go somewhere more secure."

"How—how did it happen? Lettie, I mean. You're...you're absolutely sure it was Cormac?"

"Without doubt." Eben frowned at his watch, again glanced at the doorway. "We believe she was stabbed."

"Stabbed." Thia felt decidedly sick. *Oh, Lettie.* So full of life, and so thin, so frail, in her old age. "How could anyone—why would anyone do that?" But she already knew the answer. The Stone. He'd wanted the Stone. Everything else between them had been a lie. She fought the intense burn of betrayal.

He had killed Lettie for it, and somehow knew Thia had it. Would he have killed her?

She stared down at the poker, clutched so tightly her hand was aching. She had come to help Lettie, and to *get* help *from* Lettie. She was too late on both counts...and in way over her head. She couldn't get through this on her own. But to keep Lettie's advice, that was exactly how Thia needed to remain: on her own.

"I'll need to talk to the police, or whoever is in charge of the investigation," she said, and watched Eben's expression shift back to one of suspicion. "Is that you? You still haven't told me who you are, or what gives you the right to come into Lettie's home." She looked around the ransacked room, saw the mess in a new light. "*You* did this."

Not Cormac as she had assumed. Eben's infuriatingly casual shrug confirmed she had the right of it now.

"Standard procedure where a member is concerned," Eben said. "Anything of import has been taken for study. Items of no interest to us will, of course, be returned. The police have not been involved. Nor will they be." He gave her a pointed look. "As you may or may not know, Leticia was a prominent member of our organization. It is for us to see justice done."

Rapid footsteps heralded his assistants' return. Matthew burst into the room, the neck of an empty soda bottle pinched between two fingers. "Found them, sir."

His sister was only a few steps behind. Cradled on her palm was a tiny glass sphere. It looked like a "shooter" from a set of marbles, clear with yellow and green streaks in the center, but from Eben's reaction it was more than a child's toy. Another Stone? Without a word, he took both items to the fireplace and then flung them against the interior bricks.

The bottle shattered easily. The marble ricocheted, bouncing and rolling its way to a stop against Thia's shoe. Definitely a marble, now sporting a series of cracks and powdery craters.

Eben picked it up, tossed it in among the bottle remnants and artificial logs, then ignited gas flames with the flick of a switch. "It won't melt them, of course. But it will render them useless." His assistants nodded, intent on the wreckage.

"Who *are* you people?" Three heads turned Thia's way. "And what in the world are you doing?"

Eben gave her a quizzical look before shutting off the fire. "You can't expect any of us to believe you're as ignorant as all that, Miss McDaniel, sitting as you are with Leticia's old novitiate pendant about your neck." As Eben stepped close, Matthew and Cassandra moved to stand in the doorway. To block it? Thia readied the poker lying across her lap.

"You resemble her quite strongly, you know," Eben told her. "It would be ridiculous to think you didn't inherit any of her gifts as well. That *is* why she gave it to you, is it not?" His fingers reached for Thia's throat—or rather, she hoped, for the pendant she wore.

Before she might find out, she stood, held the poker out like a sword to keep him back. "She gave it to me when I was a kid. For my birthday. A present. As for inheriting *gifts,* I don't know what you're talking about. I don't understand any of this." She waved the poker around rather wildly.

Once again, Eben leveled his flat, gray stare at her, as if by scowling at her fiercely enough, she might blurt out whatever it was that he wished to hear. Instead, Thia clamped her mouth shut and scowled back. In the hush of the room, the low, irregular clicks and clangs of the fireplace's cooling grate were inordinately loud.

He broke the moment with a sound of annoyance. "There are others who will better know how to answer, Miss McDaniel. At length and—as I've already said—in safety." He gestured toward the hall, as if she should precede him out.

"Do I have a choice?"

"Perhaps not in the way you would wish."

Thia considered the situation. Sure, she had an iron poker, but any fight would be three on one. Problem enough before then considering that the three might have skills beyond the one's imagining. Might? More like probably. Before she could change her mind, she lowered the poker. "Let's go, then."

Matthew gave her a small smile of approval before turning and walking into the hall. When Thia would have followed, his sister laid a hand on her arm, halting her. "You won't need this." Cassandra's other hand took hold of the poker.

Reluctantly, Thia let go.

"Brilliant," Cassandra said with a smile to match. She leaned the poker against the wall and then shifted her hold on Thia's arm to something more casual. "You're right to trust us," she said, and began leading Thia down the hall. Eben followed, his steps the loudest on the polished boards and thin carpets of the empty house.

Something too fresh, too raw to be called grief screamed at Thia to be set loose, but she couldn't allow it, couldn't yet allow herself to mourn, to regret. She had to remain focused, alert to anything and everything.

Cassandra released her to open the door, and Thia walked outside to the narrow stoop.

Parked at the curb was a luxury model car, its black paint and tinted windows especially glossy in the afternoon sun. It was the only vehicle on the block. No sign of Cormac—or any other person, for that matter. Thia supposed she should have found it comforting. Instead, it felt odd.

"I'll get your things, Ms. McDaniel," Matthew called from the house. She turned to see him take up her luggage.

Comprehension was slow to arrive. "We won't be back?"

"Not until it's safe, no. I'm sorry."

"Oh." She didn't ask when he thought that might be. She didn't think she'd like the answer.

"Everything will become clear soon enough," he said kindly, shouldering her backpack. "You'll see."

"Yes, you'll see," Cassandra agreed, returning to Thia's side. Together they walked down the steps. "Everything will soon be made right."

With Lettie dead, Thia couldn't think how that would ever be. She exited the barren yard, watched the car's rear doors swing open. Mysteriously, as it turned out, since the car was empty, and Matthew and Eben were back at the house steps. Remote control, maybe? Pretty fancy, if it was.

"In we go," Cassandra urged, going around to the other side.

Thia climbed in. The door closed quickly and with a muted click—the lock engaging. Cassandra slid gracefully in from the other side. That door shut quickly and locked, too, without any apparent remote control device.

Instinct had Thia going for the door handle, only to find the move blocked by Cassandra's arm as she reached over to grab Thia's seat belt.

"Better put this on," she told Thia, and handed her the buckle. "Eben is a frightful driver."

Thia fastened herself in but kept her fingers near the release. Not that she would use it. What choice did she have but to go along? Lettie wasn't in London, or Inverness, or anywhere else. Lettie was beyond helping and beyond help. Thia had come too late. Tears flooded her eyes.

Automatically, she reached into her pocket for the handkerchief. Her fingers touched the smooth linen and stilled. She had forgotten, momentarily, what Cormac had done.

Her tears vanished, burned away by shame and a growing fury. A gift from Lettie's killer. She yanked her hand from her pocket, rubbed it along her pant leg.

"I'd like to see the bastard get through that," Cassandra said suddenly. With a flick of well-manicured fingers, she indicated where Eben and Matthew stood by Lettie's closed door. With their hands tracing shapes in the air, they looked to be having a highly demonstrative discussion.

Thia had seen it before. Something like it, anyway, and it wasn't conversation. "That works?" she asked, and regretted the incredulity in her voice.

"You're acquainted with warding?" Cassandra's expression had taken on an odd intensity.

Thia shrugged. "Not really. Lettie said she put protection wards around her house and Eclectica. She had me watch her do something to the ones at the house before she left, but I didn't really know what was going on."

"She didn't teach you to do them yourself? What a shame." Cassandra settled back on the plush seat. "Leticia was said to be one of the best in the art."

Guilt stabbed deep. Thia should have paid better attention.

To so many things, it seemed.

"This must be so overwhelming." Cassandra set a hand on Thia's knee. The gesture of a sympathetic adult to a child, although they could not be far apart in age. "It was the same when Matthew's and my training began. So much was beyond our understanding. We know so much now. I hope my brother and I can be of help to you, Thia—may I call you Thia?"

"Thank you. Sure," Thia said, and felt the hand leave her knee. Her gaze drifted to the windows of Lettie's house. The vacancy their curtains concealed called to her, resonated with her own sense of loss. Could a building, one which had known a person's presence for so many years, mourn the permanent absence of it?

"I do hope you'll call me Cassie," the woman said, oblivious to the odd turn Thia's attention had taken. "It isn't strictly protocol, but it seems nicer, right? And I'm sure my brother would like you to call him Matt, of course."

"Of course," Thia said absently, still commiserating with the abandoned house. So many rooms, all filled with the sorrow of Lettie's absence.

The front doors of the car opened. As the two men climbed in, the motor came to life. Remote control for sure, but how? Sensors? The doors closed while the men belted themselves in.

When Eben unexpectedly whipped the car away from the curb, Thia's shoulder smacked against the paneling.

"Told you," Cassandra whispered in her ear. "Terrible driver."

The car accelerated through empty residential streets with Thia watching through a tear-misted blur. In no time at all, they were among the traffic speeding around Russell Square.

The shrouded Stone sat heavy on her chest. Grief, however painful, she might eventually handle. The Stone, she feared, was something else entirely. She had been counting on Lettie's explanations. After everything, Thia still had only the note's cryptic warnings. And Cormac's threat.

The foreign sights and sounds of London zipped by outside the car windows, the vibrancy of it all such a contrast to the mood inside, where silence squeezed like an ill-fitting jacket.

● ○ ●

With one of the park's vicious holly bushes for cover, Cormac watched as Thia was escorted to the waiting black sedan. He had presumed the Brigantium would monitor the barrier and thus know the instant Thia entered the house, but he hadn't expected them to arrive so quickly. At this time of day, a drive from headquarters should have taken at least forty minutes.

Something must have alerted them beforehand.

British Customs? Cormac hated to think the Brigantium's reach extended that far, but it tracked. After Thia's phone call the other night, they must have assumed she was involved—and Thia had put Leticia's address on the Customs form. Easy enough, once the Brigantium learned she was at Heathrow, to send people where they knew she would go, long before she had so much as set foot on the Piccadilly Line.

"*Amadán,*" he muttered when a shift of position resulted in yet another set of holly leaf scratches. He touched fingers to his stinging cheek but couldn't risk a healing spell. Not with the Brigantium so close and clearly on alert. He had felt the destruction of his foci. They were onto him.

Whether that was because of anything Thia had told them, Cormac couldn't determine from appearances. Her face was drawn, her motions awkward on the way to the car. A woman in shock. They wouldn't have needed a coercion spell to get her to go with them. After what had happened in the sitting room, he figured she would willingly go with anyone but him.

But had she given them the Stone?

He watched her duck into the sedan's rear seat. Out of his reach when only ten minutes before she had been so close. There weren't enough curses vile enough to suit.

The first incantation had triggered the pendant but not so much as to be a threat. By the second, Thia had been hooked, her soul opening, his for the taking. Yet he had hesitated, surprised by the ease—hell, eagerness—of her surrender. And that had cost him everything. When he should have been the one to initiate, she had kissed him. And he had been the one enthralled.

His throat closed tight with panic. *Enthralled.* Having never experienced it before, he didn't know for certain...but what else could that have been? He had felt the pull, the need to reach out, not to take but to give. He had felt the warmth of her, the waking of a need that went beyond any he had known before. In that moment, he had forgotten himself, forgotten everything but the woman in his arms and how she made him feel—

He shook off the memories, getting new scratches in the process. How he had felt *then* wasn't important. Wasn't real. It had been the enthrallment at work, bespelling him. Somehow he'd had enough presence of mind to understand that and had been able to step back, but not soon enough.

What he felt as the sedan pulled away with Thia inside was confirmation of that. As if a rope had been wrapped around his chest and tied to the car, the constrictive pull increasing with distance, urging him to give in and follow.

Had Thia known what she was doing? He had thought her an innocent. But, then, he'd also believed that only a *leanan sidhe* could perform that particular enthrallment spell.

A spell that he had no idea how to unravel and no time to find out. The Stone took precedence. He could only hope—a bitter chuckle welled up—to get Idris what he wanted before the thrall took complete hold. When it did, Cormac would think only of Thia. Would live only for her. Die for her.

If he killed her, would the spell unravel on its own? Or would her death be his undoing as well? He was not as versed in his heritage as he ought to be. Even if Idris had not forbidden it, Cormac's admitted resentment made studying anything related to that side of the family distasteful. They wanted nothing to do with him? Fine. He wanted nothing to do with them, either.

A mistake, it seemed. One of many.

The sedan accelerated down the street, turned the corner toward Russell Square. Heedless of damage to flesh and cloth, Cormac scrambled out of the holly to take to the air in raven form. He would follow, though he could guess the destination well enough: the Brigantium's primary building on Waterloo Place, where he hadn't a hope in *ifrinn* of getting at either Thia or the Stone.

CHAPTER 13

The car slowed to a stop before a square, architectural gem of a building that did nothing to put Thia at ease. Quite the opposite. When they had said *headquarters,* for whatever reason she had pictured something bland. Dull gray cement with tinted windows, like the modern buildings seen on the way. But this building with its carved filigrees and gleaming white facade was anything but bland. This was magnificent. Three stories of grandiose perfection.

Were those crystal chandeliers she saw shining through the windows?

At the top of a tall set of steps, two majestic doors awaited beneath a portico reminiscent of a small Greek or Roman temple: columns with detailed capitals topped by a peaked roof, all in white. While Cassie stepped out, a symphony of grace and elegant clothing, Thia fumbled with her seat belt's release. She was not ready for this, whatever this was.

Her door opened and, suddenly cooperative, the seat belt popped free. She frowned at it, wondering.

"Don't worry." Matt leaned down to smile at her through the opening. He offered his hand. "You're safe here."

After a pause, Thia accepted the assistance. "Thanks."

Although she felt unsteady on her feet, she quickly pulled her hand back. It felt important that she stand on her own. Even if the deadening effects of shock had her wishing for someone to lean on.

"You aren't alone anymore, Thia," Matt told her, as if he'd read her thoughts. From her face, no doubt, and easily since she had neglected to hide them.

Cassie laughed suddenly, drawing his attention. The change in his expression was marked, and alarming. At the other side of the car, his sister chatted with man in a dark suit. Something in the latter's stance, the rigidity of his shoulders, made Thia think armed forces.

With Cassie's smile continuing to sparkle, he reached out, tucked a strand of her hair behind her ear, and then slid into the driver's seat. She closed the door for him. Matt crossed to her as the car drove away. Whatever he said then made her smile vanish. She rolled her eyes, shrugged. The car rounded the corner.

"Where is my luggage going?" Thia asked, causing the twins to turn to her.

"We'd best get inside." Matt indicated where Eben waited at the entrance atop the steps, its doors open. Another dark-suited man with military bearing stood by him. Private security? Government agency? Thia had given up asking questions on the ride over, since every answer had been the same: a polite version of "not now."

She climbed the steps. Without her luggage, she could no longer pretend she hadn't given herself over to these people entirely. Ah, shit. What if they searched her?

But, really, would it be so bad if they found the Stone? She had a terrible feeling Lettie would say yes.

Thia paused at the threshold. Maybe this was a bad idea. She was about to back away when Eben placed a firm hand on her elbow. Right. If she did refuse, what would that get her?

A bird squawked, startling in its unexpectedness, and Eben's grip tightened. Thia flinched.

The squawks continued, louder and more frantic. Curiosity had her look over her shoulder for the source. She guessed a kind of crow, but before she could locate it, Eben pulled her across the threshold. "Deal with that," he ordered someone behind him.

Deal with what, the *bird?* As she was taken into the opulent hall, Thia glanced back to where the twins remained by the open door. They held a cell phone between them, as if using it on speaker. Thia faced forward again so as to not trip. "What's the matter?" she asked Eben.

He said nothing. She hadn't really expected him to. Anyway, she told herself, the silence served to let her appreciate her surroundings—and, even under the circumstances, there was much to appreciate.

Marble floors caught reflections like water did on a windless day. Faceted crystals suspended from chandeliers and wall sconces winked like thousands of captured stars. Dark wood furnishings, their polish rivaling that of the floors, held everything from truly ancient-looking busts to vases full of vibrant flowers. She breathed in their soft scents, felt herself relax by degrees. Maybe Lettie had been mistaken?

A life-sized statue caught Thia's eye, and she slowed despite Eben's hold. The subject looked to have been cast in bronze mid-motion, the spear in her one-handed grip raised in either triumph or threat. She wore a breastplate over a simple tunic, another reminiscence of ancient Rome and Greece. What had been carved on the armored plate, however, struck closer to home. The distorted face of an old woman with fangs and overlarge eyes matched the one on Thia's pendant.

Eben made a frustrated noise, tugged Thia back to speed. They climbed a wide staircase to an equally luxurious floor, then turned down a hallway crowded with silent people with harried expressions. They nodded respectfully to Eben when he passed by. Thia, they mostly ignored.

Eben stopped outside a closed room marked with a brass plaque. Before she could read it, the door opened and she was drawn inside. Only then did Eben release her arm.

A thin-faced woman of indeterminate age scrutinized Thia from behind a neatly kept desk. Receptionist and gatekeeper, guarding another closed room just beyond. In this one, a sofa and several chairs placed around a thickly piled Oriental rug formed a waiting area. On a low table, reading materials—not magazines, but various academic-looking journals—lay in precise lines.

"Mr. Trimble, you are expected," the gatekeeper informed Eben, and pressed a button on a small console.

He walked past her desk to knock twice on the door, then fling it open without bothering to wait for a response. "Miss McDaniel," he said, and gestured for Thia to precede him.

Resolved to *not* be nervous—or at least to not show it—she entered the inner sanctum. The door clicked shut. Compared to the preceding room, this one was surprisingly small. Or maybe the monumental (and monumentally cluttered) desk only made it seem so.

A man sat behind it, facing the door; a woman, beside. Both stared owlishly at Thia. Behind them, three narrow windows overlooked a park of autumn-toned grass interrupted by lines of bare trees and a few intersecting paths. In warmer months, it would be quite a view, she imagined; green and lush, full of people and activity.

Eben unhooked the ties that held back a heavy set of drapes. They swept across the windows, covering them and blocking the light entirely. A chandelier brightened to compensate for the loss.

Thia was vaguely aware that books and a wide variety of objects—pottery, carved figures of stone and tarnished metal, framed photographs of groups of people—filled wall-to-wall shelves. Her focus remained on the man centered at the desk. Thick brows frowned above icy blue eyes made unnaturally large by the lenses of glasses that were slightly askew.

"A raven was heard in the vicinity," Eben said, sitting on the unoccupied side of the desk. Bizarrely, the others seemed to take his statement as both a sensible greeting and cause for alarm.

The woman shifted in her seat, her widened eyes looking toward the covered windows, while the man turned on Eben with an angry, "Was it him?"

"Most likely."

"Hell and damn. That bast—"

"Arthur," chided the woman. She turned friendly gray eyes Thia's way. "Please have a seat, dear." With a graceful wave of her hand, she indicated the vacant chair in front of the desk.

Thia sat.

"This is Arthur Barnstable." The woman said of the angry man. "Head of our Society here. I am Beatrice Meriwether. I don't suppose Leticia ever mentioned us in—"

Eben raised an interruptive hand. "Cormac was inside the home. With Ms. McDaniel."

While Beatrice paled, Arthur's face went red—the emotion behind it clear in his voice. "Why were we not notified?"

"I did what needed doing," Eben answered smoothly, then proceeded to give his version of the events.

When he finished, Beatrice looked sympathetically at Thia. "Oh, my dear. Some tea would be welcome, I should think." She reached to depress a button on a console similar to the one used by the receptionist. "Tea, please," she said and then sat back, looking at Thia once more with kindness. "Are you all right, dear? He didn't hurt you?"

"No. He didn't hurt me," Thia said...starting things off with what was less than the truth. He hadn't hurt her, physically. Emotionally? Different story.

"He threatened," Thia said carefully. "He wanted me to tell him what I knew about—about things. But there wasn't time for much. I mean, we weren't together there very long before Mr. Trimble and the Swintons arrived and he, um...left. *Poof.*" She lifted her hands, palms up. Empty. "He was there, and then he wasn't."

"Relocated," Eben broke in. "But the energy remnants were off the charts. Far too much for a simple relocation."

The look Thia received from Arthur was stony. "Would you care to explain?"

"Me?" She blinked. "What could *I* possibly explain?"

"How Cormac got into the house, for one," Eben said.

"We've been over this." Thia's hold on her temper slipped. She didn't care if some of their distrust was justified. She was tired, she was grieving—she'd had enough.

"I've only been in this country for a few hours," she said, her voice rising. "A man greets me at my great-aunt's door and lets me inside. The doorbell rings and he disappears *literally* before I can blink and you guys come barging in, scare me half to death, and then tell me that man murdered Lettie and I'm in danger. You refuse to answer *any* of my perfectly reasonable questions unless I come here with you." She stood, her energy too much to remain seated. She splayed her arms. "So here I am, and instead of answers, I'm getting accusations. If that's how this is going to be, I think I'd rather just—"

"Sit down, Ms. McDaniel. Please," Arthur added when she remained standing.

"You're very like her." Beatrice's tone was wistful. "Leticia was a fixture here for so many years. She and I never became friends, exactly—she was much older, of course. But she was a constant. For so many of us. We're all so terribly saddened by her passing." She gestured to the chair. "Please bear with us. It may be that we are as lost in this as you."

Thia sat.

"Thank you, dear."

Thia shrugged, not wanting to dwell. "How did it happen? All Mr. Trimble said was that the man I met on the"—she corrected herself—"in Lettie's house had killed her. And that she had been...stabbed."

"It's under investigation." Arthur adjusted his glasses. "As is the reason for it. We're hoping you can help."

"I was promised answers," Thia repeated, but with caution. "For one, you say it's being investigated, fine—but by whom? You? I don't know who you are."

Red blotches bloomed on Eben's cheeks. "I must insist that respect is shown for—"

"Leticia told you nothing about us?" Beatrice inquired.

"Mr. Trimble asked the same thing," Thia told her. "And the answer is still no."

After a moment of uncomfortable scrutiny, Beatrice let out a breath. "I believe you, dear."

It was a start, at least. The men continued to look skeptical.

A soft tap sounded on the door. Arthur pressed a console button. "Come."

The gatekeeper entered, pushing a fancy wooden cart laden with a silver urn, china cups, and several plates of sandwiches and pastries. "Shall I pour, Mr. Barnstable?"

"I'll do it, thank you, Phelps," Beatrice said, and the cart was rolled to her side. Silence reigned until Phelps had exited, the door shut silently behind her.

"You must forgive our reticence, Miss McDaniel," Arthur offered stiffly. Bone china clinked as Beatrice began to arrange cups and saucers. "Secrecy has been—will always be—first and foremost. Given the situation and the evidence you bear, we were naturally concerned that Leticia had broken that pact."

"Evidence?" Thia went cold when, by way of answering, he pointed to her chest. Oh, God. *He knew.* Somehow, he knew she had the Stone. Her hand crept up to her chest.

And encountered the cool metal of her pendant. She hadn't yet put it back under her sweater.

"Leticia's novitiate medal," Arthur said, nodding. "Presented upon commencement of her study. Made obsolete upon her final initiation, but, nevertheless, not something to be given away."

He *didn't* know. He had been talking about—pointing at—the pendant, not the Stone. Thia let her hand drop, felt her chest relax enough to allow for a full breath.

"Cream and sugar, dear?"

She turned to find Beatrice watching her with interest. A little too much interest. Thia wondered what she might have revealed in her expressions. "No, thank you. Black is fine."

Beatrice filled a cup from the urn, held it out on a saucer.

Gratefully, Thia took it, then concentrated on not rattling it in her anxious grip. "So, all of this...you're what, some kind of secret society?"

"Of sorts, yes." Arthur accepted his cup and saucer, set it on the desk blotter. "We began as a gentleman's club over two hundred years ago. The Society of Brigantium, dedicated to study and higher learning with an emphasis on mythology and folklore of the British Isles. Over time, members began to make practical use of their knowledge. For the good of all. Noble motivations, but necessity forced them to work in secret."

He pushed his glasses up from where they had slid on his nose. "It was eventually discovered that others existed whose motives were not noble at all. Others who threatened the order of things. Cormac, for one." He took a sip of tea then abruptly set the cup down. "Bea, you forgot the lemon."

"What? Oh, my. So I did." She passed him a thin slice. "How careless."

Thia tried to clarify, "Others *like* Cormac, you mean."

"No," Eben fielded while Arthur's tea was repaired. "He

means Cormac."

"In the Eighteenth Century?" Thia shook her head. "I'm sorry, you lost me."

"No, dear," Beatrice said. "You're following just fine. We don't know the exact date of Cormac's birth, but there are mentions of him in records as early as the Eighteenth Century. As the son of a *Sidhe,* such longevity is to be expected."

"Son of a—" Thia caught herself before saying it. *Sidhe.* Death-bringers and soul-stealers. Screaming wild women.

Shape shifters. Able to change his appearance at will? Logic, once her friend, turned traitor. Worse than if it had deserted her completely, it whispered to her instead, telling her that if one apparent impossibility were found to be true, so could another. And another. And another. If beings from the Otherworld and magic were real, could illustrated cards actually tell the future? After all, Madame Demetka had been right about Lettie.

Thia felt her thoughts tumble one over the other, never to be right-side-up again, as things said during the Tarot reading, nonsensical at the time, began to make a disturbing kind of sense.

Destruction—the condition of Lettie's London home (and, potentially, Thia's sanity).

An overbearing man both young and old—Cormac, with his youthful appearance and, apparently, substantial age.

She shuddered. If the *Sidhe* existed, did the Cailleach? Could the Stone be everything Lettie claimed?

"Are you all right, dear?" Beatrice's concerned inquiry pulled Thia out of her speedy fall into madness. "Have some more tea."

"S-sure. Fine." Throat dry, she took a gulp. Swallowed.

"Heard of them, have you?" Above the bent silver frames of his glasses, halfway down his nose once more, Arthur's eyes were slits of mistrust.

Thia set cup and saucer aside with a faint clatter. "I've been working in Lettie's store," she said, skirting the truth, "so I've heard a little about a lot of things. I just never—I mean, it's hard to believe they're real."

"But true," Beatrice said.

"There *can* be truth," Eben corrected. "There can also be a lot of nonsense."

Somehow that made Thia feel a little better. "Is that what you do? Sort through the nonsense for what's true? And keep things from getting into the wrong hands? Like a police force."

"In very basic terms." Arthur sipped his tea.

A police force for mysticism and folklore. The idea sounded ridiculous...but where there was great danger, of course there needed to be regulation. The general, unaware public especially would need protecting.

Weapons or whatever other potentially harmful things (such as, say, crystal spheres imbued with the power of a goddess) would need to be kept out of the wrong hands.

"I know Lettie traveled a lot in the past," Thia said, "before opening Eclectica." And had continued to do so after, in order to search out new merchandise—or so she had claimed. "Was that for you? Even after she came to Granite Springs?"

She looked around the room, finally taking into account the objects on the shelves. Artifacts, more like. Museum-quality. "Even then was she working for—I'm sorry, what did you say you were called, again?"

"The Brigantium, for short." Arthur set down his cup. "It's easier for Whitehall. Though they'd doubtless prefer a set of initials."

"The government," Beatrice put in at Thia's blank look. "We deal with them—unofficially and in a purely advisory capacity, of course—from time to time."

"Lettie worked with the British government?"

"Hardly," Eben scoffed. "She claimed no interest in politics or current events. Too caught up in her own pursuits. That shop of hers is nothing to do with us."

Beatrice sighed quietly. "She lived two lives in that regard, ever since she declared herself mostly retired from her work here. Her shop became her primary focus, but if she came across something of value, she passed it along. Sometimes this meant she acted as a broker for items of interest. Other times, she merely gave information. It was a situation which worked well"—she gave Eben a hard look—"well *enough*, until this."

"Right." He plowed his fingers through his hair, leaving it even more chaotic than before. "Until now, it was fine for her to break protocol, fine not to tell the appropriate people exactly what she was doing. If she had, she would never have been allowed to be off on her own for so long. She wouldn't have gotten herself killed in Brigid-knows-where."

"Sorry?" Thia asked. "She was killed where?"

"A turn of phrase," Beatrice explained. "We don't know the location, only that it was likely in Scotland." She frowned into her cup. Sighed. "We didn't so much as suspect anything untoward had happened until one of our members, Quentin, had a vision. Afterward, we tried to reach Leticia. Couldn't."

Thia sat up. "That's all? So you don't really know she's dead. She could be okay. She could be hiding somewhere." The surge of unexpected hope was painful. And short-lived.

"There is no doubt. Not for us." Arthur's tone brooked no argument. "Leticia is dead."

"We conducted a ritual for confirmation," Beatrice said. "One which has never been wrong. It was quite clear."

"On that matter, at least," Eben grumbled, and the three exchanged a look.

"How do you know who killed her," Thia asked, "if you don't even know where it happened?"

"Quentin saw him do it."

"In a dream." Thia couldn't help but sound dubious.

"Vision. Yes."

"And you just accepted that as fact?"

Beatrice inclined her head. "Of course."

"The boy has his...issues, I grant you," Arthur supplied, "but his Sight is never wrong."

"What, exactly, did he see?" Thia's throat was tight. "Please. I'd—I need to know."

Looking like grim statues, no one spoke.

"Did she suffer?" Thia pressed. "At least tell me if—"

"Quentin believes it was quick," Beatrice said. "At night, at an isolated place near the sea. The only clear image, he says, was of Cormac. Watching at the moment of death." She looked down at her hands, clasped in her lap. Her knuckles were white.

Arthur cleared his throat. "Leticia, to our knowledge, was after an important relic. A thing which someone like Cormac would easily kill to possess." Thia worked to hide her surprise. They didn't know what the Stone was?

"Cormac has it, then?" she asked while doing her best to ignore the cloth-covered weight lodged between her breasts. "The thing Lettie was after?"

"Relic. And, no, it doesn't appear so," Arthur said, with a glance at Eben, who nodded grimly. "Not if he was in Leticia's house this afternoon. He would have no reason to be there if he already has what he wants."

"Then why kill her?" Thia asked. "If he didn't get the relic from Lettie, and she had it—or at least knew where it might be—wouldn't he need her alive?"

Unless he'd been certain where he would be able to find it.

"He made a mistake," Arthur snapped. "Acted out of anger. Who could say? He's not infallible, just a damned menace." His hand came down sharply on his desk, rattling cup and saucer.

Beatrice cringed. "Do be careful, dear."

"What? Oh." He looked contrite. "Apologies, Bea. I know how much you care for the set."

She nodded and then looked over at Thia to ask, "Have you heard of Idris Cathmor?"

"No."

"You're certain?" Eben demanded.

"Absolutely." Thia wasn't great with names, but she wouldn't forget one like that.

Beatrice prepared a second cup of tea for herself. "He was a powerful sorcerer until, oh, what was it, Eben—just over a century ago?" At his grumbled affirmation, she continued. "Long before that, he made a bargain with a young *leanan sidhe* stranded this side of the Otherworld. In exchange for passage across, she gave him a son. Cormac."

"*Leanan*—" Thia broke off, avoiding the word again. "Those are the ones who take people's souls through…uh, seduction?"

"Exactly so."

And didn't *that* shed a horrible new light on things. She felt the blood drain from her face.

"The *leanan sidhe* lure someone, usually by inciting feelings of lust. They then create a link that enables them to draw off the energy of the person's soul. Death is inevitable."

"Good lord." If Thia's soul were draining away, she would feel it, though, wouldn't she? Because she didn't think she felt anything like that. But how would she know? What *did* that feel like, anyway? She should ask….but she couldn't. She was afraid to.

"Eben is quite right to call Cormac a menace," Arthur said, barely audible to Thia over the pounding of her own heart. So loud, so frantic, it was a wonder no one else heard.

"And he's devoted to Idris," Beatrice added. "A man with an insatiable lust for power."

"His father is still alive, too?" This was crazy.

"Oh, yes. Although our sources tell us he is very weak and with hardly any followers at all."

"Unless he gets the relic," Eben said. "Then he may well be able to take up where he left off. Which, according to records, would rival anyone else we've got. Combined."

"And that would be bad," Thia said.

Arthur peered at her over his glasses. "That would be very bad."

"Disastrous," said Eben.

"Mountains would crumble?" she asked wryly. She couldn't help thinking they were laying it on a bit thick.

Arthur and Beatrice looked to Eben, who shrugged. "The evidence is apocryphal, but, yes. In 1502, we believe he came close. Up near Kendall, that was."

Beatrice leaned in. "Wasn't there also the time with the—"

Thia didn't want to know. "So, this Idris Cathmor needs the relic. And Cormac is trying to get it so Idris can be powerful again and go back to doing...whatever it is he wants to get back to doing."

"Precisely," Beatrice said.

"Okay." Thia's pulse re-accelerated in anticipation of what she next had to ask. They might lie, which wouldn't be any help at all, but she needed to at least *try* to find out what they knew. Or didn't know. She made her best attempt at simple curiosity. "So, what sort of thing is it, this relic?"

By the uniform disappointment shown on the others' faces, it appeared they had been hoping that *she* would be the one to tell *them*.

"Unfortunately," Eben grumbled, "since your Leticia chose not to pass along her discoveries in this, we have no idea. Not what it looks like. Not what it does. She might have known all that and more—what it was for, how it came to be, what it might mean. But because she concealed her actions, because she ignored basic—"

"Eben," Arthur warned, but only succeeded in becoming the target of the other man's ire.

"Dammit," Eben said with a frustrated sweep of his hands, "Idris is but one part of this. Neither of you are considering the Cailleach herself. Before she left the world, she put much of her power into this unknown thing and gave it to whatever followers remained. Could they access it? There's no evidence of that, so why do it? Why bother—unless she couldn't take the power with her and plans to reclaim it." He rubbed a hand down his reddened face. "Thanks to Leticia's actions, we're playing catchup regarding her death and in locating the relic, when we might ought to be preparing for the Cailleach's return."

Thia was ready to cower in dread, but Arthur was scornful. "Hardly anyone worships her now, Eben," he said. "She has no reason to return, even if it were possible."

"Why wouldn't it be? Nothing we have is clear on where she went. The Otherworld? It would have been mentioned by name." Eben banged the heel of his hand on the arm of his chair. "This should be included in our investigation. It's ludicrous that we continue to ignore the possibility—"

"No," Arthur nearly shouted. "What is ludicrous is the idea that Leticia was killed by a vengeful Celtic deity looking for the rest of her powers. That *would* have been noticed. She has no followers," Arthur emphasized. "And neither Leticia, Cormac, nor Idris would be interested in initiating her return. Idris, especially."

"There must be a way for someone else to access the power," said Beatrice. "That's the only reason Idris would bother. And *that* is what deserves priority, Eben, not your worry about the return of the Cailleach. More tea, anyone?"

Thia didn't add her cup to those passed across the desk. She was jittery enough without loading up on caffeine. Rubbing her temple, where a headache lurked, she said, "So...Cormac killed Lettie for a mysterious relic she'd found, but because nothing apocalyptic has happened since, and also because he broke into her house today, you figure he doesn't have it. But you're sure Lettie did have it, at some point, because he killed her."

"Correct," Arthur said.

"So, where is it?"

At their distressed looks, Thia felt a weight lift from her chest. Figuratively speaking, anyway—the Stone's real weight remained where it was. But they didn't know that. They didn't seem to so much as suspect.

"We hoped you knew." Beatrice set Arthur's second tea on the desk. He made no move to take it.

"There must be something in Leticia's papers," Eben said quietly. "I'll assign more people. Requisition some diviners."

Thia pressed her lips together, forced herself to remember Lettie's warnings. These seemed like good people—not necessarily likable, as of yet, but certainly not bad. And clearly, Idris and Cormac could not be allowed anywhere near the Stone. The Brigantium could do a much better job with that than Thia could, alone.

But Lettie hadn't sent the Stone to them. She—a previously well-trusted member of the Brigantium—had sent it to Thia, her grandniece who had no idea how to deal with any of this stuff.

Arthur's sigh was deep enough to ruffle papers on his desk. "Regardless, Miss McDaniel, you are not safe. The novitiate pendant is some security, but not nearly enough if Cormac has you in his sights." He looked to Beatrice, who nodded; then to Eben, who did the same. "Right. That's decided, then. You will remain with us, Miss McDaniel. You may yet prove valuable to the investigation, and we can protect you."

Whether Thia trusted the Brigantium or not, she didn't see she had a choice.

CHAPTER 14

Covent Garden, London
30 October

"**I**t isn't much, I'm afraid," Matt said, and pushed open the scarred door. Given the state of the lobby and hallways they had just walked through, Thia was not surprised to find similar wear-and-tear here. The room's carpet was a thread-bare eighties-era orange; the walls, a smoker's white—namely, mottled beige and tan. It didn't *smell* smoky, at least, thanks to strong odors of must and chemical cleaners. Thia stepped inside.

A three count took her to the sole window, where she then turned to watch Matt enter with her luggage. What with the furnishings taking up most space, little enough remained for one person, let alone two. She pressed herself against a blocky wardrobe, careful not to brush up against a hissing radiator.

Matt set her things on the twin bed's sagging mattress and then returned to the door. "The bath is at the end of the hall. Shared, of course, but I shouldn't think that will be much of a bother. We've very few guests at the moment."

Thia nodded abstractedly. The numbing, disorienting cloud that had enveloped her since her encounter with Cormac and the unarguable news of Lettie's death had grown so thick she could barely see. Maybe that was why everything seemed so drab.

Turning, she lifted the sheer window curtain. The outside view didn't help to orient her. For a moment, she thought the glass had frosted over, but it was grime. She managed to make out the hazy form of the adjacent building. More old brick and curtained windows. She sighed.

"I'm sorry we can't offer better," Matt said gently.

Thia let the curtains drop, turned to see him grimace at the stained and threadbare carpet. Blobs of something—candle wax, possibly—speckled the area near the bedside table. The Brigantium's headquarters might be glorious but *this* place of theirs left a lot to be desired.

Although, since their offer of protection felt like a kind of imprisonment, she supposed things could have been worse. They could have escorted her to a dungeon or locked her in a tower.

"It's fine," she said.

"It's not," Matt countered, chuckling. "But it's secure."

She couldn't argue with that.

Back at headquarters, Thia's acceptance of protection had brought the meeting to an abrupt end; and while Arthur had made several phone calls, she had tried to get herself a place in the investigation—or at least within the information flow. She wasn't sure she had succeeded. But that only meant she'd try again, and would keep trying until she knew what to do with the Stone and saw that Lettie would have justice.

After Arthur had finished making arrangements, Matt had come to take Thia to what they called their "safe house."

She had anticipated another drive through London but had gotten instead a circuitous walk through hallways and down long sets of stairs followed by a lengthy elevator descent and another walk—this time through an underground passageway. By the end of it, she had no idea where she was in relation to anywhere else.

After a corresponding elevator ascent she'd arrived at what

appeared to be the lobby of a dilapidated hotel. She sat in a central waiting area while Matt had gone to pick up her room key and already-delivered luggage from a reception desk. Two sets of doors there led to a busy street. Next to them sat a man in a rumpled suit, his lazy slouch belied by his watchful eyes. The cord that trailed from his ear to the inside of his jacket hadn't looked like it belonged to a music player. He was no guest, Thia had determined, waiting for a taxi or friends.

"I imagine you'd like some time to yourself," Matt said now, jarring her back to the present. She took the room key and small card he held out.

"My mobile number is on there," he said of the card. "And, if we may, Cassie and I would like to invite you to dinner." He smiled. "Nothing fancy, but it seems a shame for you to spend your first night in London cooped up here."

It hit Thia again how protection was a kind of prison. But it wasn't necessarily the Brigantium keeping her from going out on her own; it was Cormac and the danger he presented.

It was also the Stone. Her own safety concerns aside, Thia couldn't put it at risk. And until she thought of something better than to carry it in her bra, then wherever she was, it would be, too.

"We won't let him near you," Matt promised, interpreting her silence. "You'll be safe with us."

Did she believe him? She wanted to. And she did *not* want to be someone who always distrusted others. Who constantly second-guessed. Who couldn't trust *herself.* She forced a smile up through her exhaustion. "Dinner sounds wonderful, thank you. Count me in."

Matt beamed. "Brilliant. We'll come by at six, if that's all right?"

"Sure." It's not like she had other plans.

"Wonderful. Until then." Blinding her with a full-wattage grin, Matt stepped into the hall and shut the door.

With that, the last of Thia's energy vanished, and she barely managed to lock the deadbolt before staggering the two feet to the bed. Sprawled face down on its scratchy cotton duvet, she sank into a sleep so deep that the stale scent of laundry detergent couldn't reach her.

● ○ ●

Pall Mall, London

For all of its difficulties, London provided innumerable places to hide, particularly for a raven. City folk—even those who should know better—rarely paid attention to birds.

Cormac stretched his wings and sidled closer to the chimney, where he then tucked himself deeper in shadow and resumed his watch. There had been no sign of Thia since she had gone into the Brigantium's headquarters hours ago. Hours Cormac had wasted.

Hours in which she could have given them the relic.

Was she still inside? What if she had slipped out some other door while Cormac had been circling the perimeter? Worse, there could be truth to the rumors of subterranean access.

How could he possibly track her then?

A vision of Thia, smiling, teasing, flashed through his mind, bringing with it the phantom sensations of her lips, the smell of her skin. The welcoming feel of her.

These flashes of memories, the sense of loss he had been enduring since they had parted were likely the first symptoms of the thrall.

Slate roof tiles began to tremble—the external effects of his internal state—and dust and other debris swirled around his feet. Squawking, he tamped down his unruly emotions. The rage, the fear. Gradually, the debris settled, the tiles stilled. But it cost him. He couldn't keep everything bottled up, not for long, in this form.

Nor could he afford to wait any longer.

With a hop and a flap of wings, he took flight. Another look around the building couldn't hurt. Perhaps he'd missed something. It was a large, complicated structure, after all. There had to be a weakness somewhere.

Yet, deplorably, during Cormac's repeated search the only weaknesses he sensed were his own.

● ○ ●

Covent Garden, London

A strange sound roused her. An oddly sonorous tone and not unpleasant...but disturbing all the same...eventually.

Thia's eyelids cracked open.

Strange room to go with the strange sound. Drool glued her cheek to a rough pillowcase. Slim pillow. Musty. She peeled it from her face and blinked, her lids scraping like sandpaper over her dry eyes.

Safe house. London. Cormac.

Lettie.

Thia's head snapped up, the rest of her body scrambling. A phone on the bedside table was ringing. Had been for some time. She lunged for it.

"Hello?" It took two attempts for her to get the word out, and even then it was unrecognizable. Her mouth and throat had more cotton batting than the pillow.

Though, really, that wasn't saying much.

The voice that came over the line held an intimidating level of energy. "Hi, Thia—it's Cassie. Are you ready to go? Matt and I are in the lobby."

Thia swung her legs off the bed to sit up, confused from too little sleep and sudden waking. Ready? Of course she wasn't ready.

"I'm sorry...I'm, uh, running a bit late."

Her free hand rubbed first at one eye then the other, *almost* clearing her vision. According to her watch, it was five after six. She had slept for two hours? She'd only meant to lie down for a little while. She cleared her throat. "I'll be just a couple of minutes."

"Certainly," Cassie chirped. "See you soon."

"Okay. Great." After hanging up, Thia immediately sprang to her feet—and then had to shift the Stone from where it had lodged uncomfortably against her right breast. No time to consider a safer location than her bra. No time to change out of her messy, long-inhabited clothes, either. But Matt had said "nothing fancy," hadn't he?

Yeah. He had also worn a tailored designer suit to work.

Thia grabbed her jacket, scooped up the room's key, then stepped into the hallway. The door seemed the kind to lock automatically, but she checked after closing it to make sure and then dropped the key into her cargo pocket.

Okay, so how did she get to the lobby?

Her memories of walking from the elevator were faint, but luckily enough, the hall ended at a closed door only a few feet from her own. To go left was the only option.

Soon enough, her sluggish brain began to recognize things she had passed before. An end table with the vase of artificial flowers. A long stretch of numbered doors and framed prints depicting hunting scenes. The restroom. Oh, thank God, the restroom. She darted inside, eyed the deep, old-fashioned tub with longing as she made a beeline for the toilet.

At the elevator a short time later, Thia tried to forget what she'd seen in the over-the-sink mirror when she had washed her hands. It had been her worst suspicions confirmed: lank hair, wan complexion, dark circles under her eyes.

"Sometimes, Thia," she muttered as the door to the elevator rattled open, "ignorance is bliss."

"Isn't it just?" agreed a man's wry, cultured voice.

She froze. She didn't know the voice, but Cormac had fooled her before. And whoever this was, he stood in the deepest shadow of an already dark interior. As had been the case when she'd ridden up, the overhead light wasn't working.

She could see the man's build well enough—slim frame, maybe six feet if he weren't leaning on a cane. He wore a dark, probably black, knee-length coat, and a long white scarf. Black leather gloves. Ambient light from the hall allowed her to make out sharp features and wary eyes. Their irises were a startling light gray.

Not Cormac's eyes.

"I assure you, I don't bite," the stranger said.

The safe house was protected, Thia reminded herself. She was being paranoid...and rude. Quickly, she stepped into the narrow compartment. The doors shut, leaving the illuminated lobby button as the only source of light.

"I'm sorry," Thia said as the car began its slow, shaky descent. "It's been a long day. A long, strange day."

"We have a lot of those." He shifted his weight. "You'll get used to it eventually."

"Is that a promise?"

He laughed, a rusty, brief bark of sound, and tilted his head. Studying her, it seemed, and Thia wondered what he might possibly see in the near-dark. To her, he was barely more than a silhouette.

"It's a matter of survival," he said a moment later, in answer to her question.

The elevator lurched to a stop, rocking violently, and the stranger swayed. Thia reached out to steady him with a hand on his shoulder.

"Are you all right?" she asked in concern. Beneath his coat— cashmere, her fingers informed her—the man felt too thin.

The doors opened.

"Better than I was," he said, exiting ahead of her. His gait was uneven but surprisingly quick. Thia was soon left behind. The man's hair, which she had mistaken for dark blond, was a mix of silvery grays. Premature ones, since she didn't think he was much older than thirty-five.

"Good luck, Thia," the stranger said without looking back, and pushed open the main doors.

"Thanks," she called after him. "You too."

Matt and Cassie approached from the seating area.

"Sorry I'm late," Thia said. "Should I change clothes? You said nothing fancy, but—"

"You look fine." Matt gave her an appreciative smile.

Before she could call him out on the blatant flattery, she was lost in Cassie's enthusiastic embrace.

"I'm so glad you agreed to come," the latter gushed, placing two kisses in the air near Thia's cheeks. Then, quickly linking her arm with Thia's, she began to lead her toward the doors.

Matt had gone over to say something to the rumpled man, still slouched at his post.

Cassie gave Thia's arm a quick squeeze. "How do you know Quentin?"

Thia nearly stumbled. That was Quentin? The man who'd had a vision of Lettie's death?

"We rode down the elevator together," she said.

"Oh, of course." Her voice lowered, Cassie added, "Such a shame, really, what happened to him in th—"

"Cass," Matt scolded, catching up with them to hold open the door.

"I'm sure Thia doesn't mind a bit of gossip." Cassie grinned impishly as they stepped out. "You don't, do you?"

Thia shrugged, her concern elsewhere. There were a lot of people outside. Any one of them could be Cormac. A cold, damp wind wrapped around her. Cars zoomed by, their headlights turned on against the impending dark.

"We're walking?" she asked, edgy. She didn't know whether to feel grateful for the twin's close proximity...or trapped.

"It's not far," Matt said, sounding amused. "We thought you might enjoy a spot of local color."

"*We* did not," Cassie corrected, rolling her eyes. "But I tired of arguing my more elitist sentiments. My brother—goodness knows why—loves the place. Though how he even found it, I have to wonder."

After several turns and crossings that traded wide, straight streets for narrow, twisting ones, Thia also began to wonder.

Crowds for isolation was another component of the trade. With no other sounds to interfere, their footsteps sounded far too loud, a bold announcement of their progress.

The buildings in this area were older than a century if not two, with chipped bricks and cracked, high-set windows. The doorways were shadowed; the cobbles in the street, battered. This was the essential London, timeless and timeworn.

"It's no secret, this pub," Matt said, stepping back so they could walk single-file beneath a length of scaffolding. Cassie led the way, forced to relinquish Thia's arm. "It only seems hard to find because of the route we're taking. I want to be sure we aren't followed."

They cleared the scaffolding and he came up beside Thia to place a light hand on her back. The paving was in bad shape, making walking tricky, so she couldn't fault him for wanting to be helpful, but all the herding touches were beginning to grate.

"About Quentin," Cassie said, dropping back to take Thia's other side. "There was an accident not that long ago. He and several others were attempting a complex spell—no one will say what, exactly—and it all went horribly wrong. Quentin was fortunate to survive. None of the others did."

"How awful," Thia said, conscious of how inadequate words could be. "What happened?"

"I overheard Beatrice speaking of it once." Like a cat given cream, Cassie fairly purred. "Apparently, they tapped into the

Otherworld—or something like it, at any rate—and couldn't stop the energy transfer."

Energy? Thia had expected to hear someone had gotten an ingredient wrong in a potion or a fire got out of hand. Something tangible. Something understandable.

Cassie was nodding. "The result was a massive energy shift. Much more than any of them could handle. When Beatrice found them, she summoned help, of course, but it was too late."

"For all but Quentin," Matt amended.

"Technically, no." The look she shot her brother was smug. "I heard he was brought back. I suspect that's when he gained his particular Sight."

Turning a corner, they left the darkened streets for a better lit, more populated area. Trees lined the sidewalks. Small shops (including two liquor stores) did brisk business.

"What do you mean by 'sight'?" Thia asked, as Matt's hand pressed more firmly onto her back, encouraging her to keep moving when she might have preferred to stop for a moment and get her bearings—physical as well as emotional.

"It differs, depending on the person," he explained. "For some, like Quentin, it's visions of past events. More commonly, it's an ability to see or at least sense magic in its various forms. Protections wards, a spell being invoked, that sort of thing."

Matt stopped at a door. Its stained glass insert was a garish jumble of colors—along with a fist-sized patch of cardboard held on by black tape. According to the faded wooden sign overhead, they had arrived at The Seven Brewers.

"After you," he told Thia with a grin and opened the door.

Noise immediately slammed into her and she took an automatic step back. Laughter, boisterous talk, clinking glassware, chairs scraping on a wooden floor. It all seemed way too loud and as disorienting as a kick to the head. She entered with reluctance, immersing herself in air that felt like putty, nearly solid with heat and humidity and reeking of *eau du* stale beer. Grease, carried in the steam from fried food, quickly slicked her skin. People were standing shoulder-to-shoulder in the aisles. Every booth, stool, and seat was occupied. Thia stopped, unsure where to go.

"Let's grab a table," Cassie yelled in her ear.

"How?" Thia yelled back.

"You'll see." With a wink, she pulled her into the crowd. As they moved through the barely-parting masses, Thia caught sight of Matt making his way to the bar where rows of people were stacked three deep.

"Here we go," Cassie said in triumph. They had arrived at the lone booth at the far end of the room just as its occupants were getting up to leave. As they put on coats, Cassie eased around them to slide onto the bench seat.

Thia followed, sank into an upholstery-covered pit caused by broken springs. On the table top, glasses and plates were stacked alarmingly high. Wadded up paper napkins soaked up spills and condensation while a cardboard coaster for Toady's Ale drooped wetly off the edge.

"I don't know what Matt sees in this place," Cassie said, and lifted a hand to catch the attention of a harried server.

The young man rushed over immediately to load dishes into a plastic tub and swipe a grungy cloth across the table's worn surface. After giving Cassie a nod, he exited through a nearby swinging door. Matt arrived soon after to set down three wineglasses of pale liquid. He shrugged out of his coat and then straddled the padded stool to Thia's left.

"What do you think?" he asked her, giving Cassie his coat to stick in the wide niche above the bench.

"It definitely has character," Thia said, and added her jacket to the pile.

"You hate it." He pushed a glass in her direction. "We could go somewhere else if you—"

"No, no—it's fine. Really." Thia laughed when Cassie gave her a look like she was insane. She picked up her drink, sniffed it. "What's this?"

"Mead," Cassie said, and Thia took a sip.

Smooth, honeyed liquid coated her tongue, slid gently down her throat to finish with a pleasant tang.

"I'm sorry," Matt said, looking chagrined. "We always order mead, and I didn't think. I can go get you something else."

"Please don't," she told him. "It's nice. Refreshing." Like a summer garden after a rain shower.

"Oh, good." His expression relaxed. "Cheers, then."

They all clinked glasses and drank.

Settling back against the worn seat, Thia read a placard that listed various pub meals. Cheese-and-chips, chili-cheese-and-chips, fish-and-chips, or just chips. A fitting metaphor for her life: the appearance of choice with an overriding element of inevitability.

Ah, well. Decision made, she set the menu down. The twins cut off their muted discussion of the décor.

"Find something?" Cassie looked dubious.

"Fish and chips." Not a daring a decision, but given the way things were going, this was not the time to gamble on chili-cheese.

"Good choice," Matt said, getting to his feet. "I'll have that as well. Cassie?"

His sister waved a hand. "Sit down. Here he comes." The now-familiar server was headed their way.

"Watch yourself, Cass," Matt said with an irritation Thia didn't understand.

Cassie merely laughed, then flashed a smile at the server. "Three fish and chips," she told the young man and, after he'd left, said, "It's harmless, Matt. And so easy."

"It could call attention. *That* isn't harmless."

Cassie leaned back with a pout, took a sip of her drink.

Thia thought about the ease at which they got a table; the rapid clearing of the dishes; the quick service. She looked at the numbers of people unable to find seats, the tabletops in desperate need of bussing.

She turned to Cassie. "How did you do it?"

The woman's honeyed eyes lit with amusement. "A little persuasion spell. Certainly nothing to get upset about." She shot her brother a look.

Thia took a big swallow of mead. Since arriving at Eclectica, she had met a lot of people who claimed or merely hoped to use "magic," whether in the form of little tokens purported to bring luck or ward off trouble, or Tarot cards to predict the future, or herbal mixtures to bring things like true love and good midterm grades. Not until yesterday had Thia thought anything of it, let alone been concerned that such means could be used to manipulate people.

She should have.

"I did it with this." Cassie reached under the collar of her blouse to pull out a delicate silver chain.

Thia's breath caught. The pendant on the chain was a perfect match to her own.

"Every apprentice has one," Cassie said, tucking hers away again.

"And it can make people do things?"

"Yes and no." Matt set down his mead. "They're given out to apprentices—to protect us during our studies, mainly. But they can also augment certain learned skills."

"The protection benefit is automatic," Cassie said. "Other aspects require knowledge and experience. You couldn't use yours to persuade anyone of anything tonight. But perhaps, with training, you might. It's a very simple spell."

"What would I have to do?" The question left Thia's mouth

before she could think to stop it. Normally, the idea of...this was a form of mind control they were talking about, wasn't it? Normally she would find that repellent. But if it meant the difference between dying a violent death at Cormac's hand or living peacefully ever after, she'd take it.

But only for defense. Not for frivolous things like prompt service in a busy pub.

"You would have to join us," Matt said, looking grave. "The Brigantium, that is."

"I know it seems sudden and perhaps extreme," Cassie put in. "But it's so dangerous to go on your own. Consider what happened with Quentin."

Conversation paused while plates of fish and chips were set before them, followed by bottles of ketchup and malt vinegar.

"We don't want to scare you," Matt said after the server left. "But it's only fair you understand the situation." He bit into a piece of battered fish. Grease ran down his fingers.

"I'm not sure that's possible." Thia took up a slice of deep fried potato liberally dusted with salt, stuffed it in her mouth, and chewed. *Oh, man.* She swallowed, reached for another. Her stomach, blithely unconcerned with things like fat content and lack of nutritional value, rejoiced.

Cassie daintily dissected her meal with a bent-tined fork. "That's why we wanted to meet with you tonight. Away from the others." She impaled a small portion of fish. "Sometimes they let protocol interfere with what's best."

"And you don't?" Thia asked, sprinkling vinegar all over her plate.

The twins smiled. "Not always."

● ○ ●

Pall Mall, London

"You met her?" Arthur's tone held the sharpness of a man interrupted. A block of peat shifted on the nearby fire and sent up tiny sparks.

"Thia, yes. That was the plan, was it not?" Quentin lowered himself into the armchair opposite, laid his cane across his lap. "She's an innocent. Someone who needs to be protected, not thrown to the wolves."

From behind him, Beatrice tutted and then moved to stand in front of the hearth. "So melodramatic, dear. It doesn't suit you."

Quentin glared. "Nevertheless. Thia McDaniel should not be involved in this."

"But she *is* involved." Much too keenly, Beatrice eyed him. "You were to determine how much. What did you find?"

"She knows more than she's saying. And less than you fear."

Arthur thumped the side table, jostling his brandy snifter. "We don't have time for your games. Not tonight."

"Of course," Quentin returned, surprised to find himself growing angry. "Wouldn't want to disturb your Courvoisier, now, would we? You are aware, then, that she has left the safe house?"

"Accompanied by the Swintons," Arthur responded. "She's perfectly safe."

"She's *bait*. And you don't even know what it is you hope to trap."

"Of course we do," countered Beatrice. "We hope to draw Cormac out."

Quentin focused on her. "Really? Are you certain that's all?"

Even in the low light, made amber by the fire, he could see how her face paled.

Arthur's eyes narrowed behind his glasses lenses. "Say it, then. Without the riddles."

"It doesn't work that way." Even so, Quentin let his focus go soft on the flames eagerly licking at blocks of old earth while he recalled his encounter with Thia. He was barely aware of speaking. "Danger. Nothing as it appears. Secrets. Secrets and shadows. Trouble...for everyone." He blinked, shook off the inky sensations. "She shouldn't be outside the safe house."

Beatrice, to her small credit, looked worried. Arthur merely frowned and said, "It can't be helped. We need to gain her trust—which won't happen if she feels she's a prisoner. The Swintons will befriend her. Make her feel comfortable. Then she will tell us what more she knows."

"Perhaps," Quentin acknowledged with a shrug. And then very casually dropped a bomb. "She has the relic, I suspect."

Beatrice's sharp intake of breath was drowned out by Arthur's exclamation.

"Impossible." He looked like he wanted to thump the table again. "The search of her luggage yielded nothing. No residual energies. *Nothing.* We have people headed to Granite Springs to search Leticia's house there, but—"

"How very Orwellian of you, Arthur, and within a foreign country to boot," Quentin drawled, his lips curling in distaste. "Next, will you search *her?*"

Arthur waved that away. "Can you swear she has it?"

"No." Not entirely a lie. "I had only two brief and separate impressions. An object that has become something to fear... and concealment."

"Damn."

"Those qualities could refer to Leticia's pendant," Beatrice argued. She sounded tired. "Thia seemed stunned to learn it was anything other than a bit of jewelry." She shook her head. "It's not enough, Arthur."

"I know that, Bea," he grumbled, picking up his brandy. "I can't risk losing her goodwill and cooperation by forcing her to undergo a search. Not without absolute certainty." He swore again, setting the glass down with a dangerous clunk. Precious liquid sloshed, bruising.

Beatrice set a hand on his shoulder. "We'll keep an eye on her—even let her feel a part of things—and win her trust. For her safety, and for ours. That's all we can do. For the moment." She arched a brow at Quentin.

What, did she think he was withholding information? To what end? Once, perhaps, but no more. He had thought that she, of all people, understood.

"We cannot stoop to Cormac's level," she said, her hand still on Arthur's shoulder. "We cannot simply take what we want. If we do, we are no better than Idris and his ilk. We would deserve to fail."

Quentin commended himself for not inquiring when the leopard had changed her spots.

"I have no desire to see us become like our enemies, Bea," Arthur said, and gave her hand a pat. "We will not seek out violence. But that doesn't mean it can be avoided. We must do whatever is necessary to protect order."

"Of course. We can do no less." She shot Quentin a dark look. "Each and every one of us."

CHAPTER 15

"Let me make sure I understand," Thia said after a drink from her second (possibly third) glass of mead. "The Brigantium thinks I'm involved in Lettie's murder?"

Her voice was too loud now that most of the patrons had gone. Several heads turned in her direction. Out of the corner of her eye, she saw Cassie do something with her fingers that resulted in the heads turning away again.

"Why would they think that?" Thia asked, no less outraged, but quieter. "How could anyone think that?"

Matt laid a warm hand on her wrist. "No, no. No one thinks you were in any way responsible."

"No one is accusing you of anything," Cassie said gently.

"I should hope not." Thia set her glass clumsily on the table. (Definitely her third.)

"But perhaps there is something you know—something that might help us bring Leticia's killer to justice?" The probing light in Cassie's eyes suggested the question was not as casual as her tone implied, and Thia felt her pulse spike.

Since Matt hadn't yet removed his hand from her wrist, he might have felt it as well. Using a wayward strand of hair as an excuse, Thia removed herself from his grasp, adjusted her hair clip.

How much did she dare admit? How much did they already know? "There *might* be something," she allowed. This whole evening could be a trick, as she had considered several times already. Ply the suspect with drink, make her comfortable, pretend friendship—all of it just another infuriating attempt at manipulation.

Had Lettie lived her life like this, always uncertain of everyone's motives? How awful.

Thia reached into her pocket, pulled out the folded brown wrapping. Her fingers shook as she spread it out on the table.

"Lettie mailed me a package this week." The sentence was barely finished before Matt and Cassie reached to touch the wrinkled paper. Thia pointed to the postal mark, though by their shocked faces, she figured they'd already noted it. "On October nineteenth, she must have been in Inverness. You didn't know?"

Cassie's mouth pressed into a thin line as she ran her fingers across Lettie's writing. Well, technically the tape that Lettie had laid over her writing.

"We didn't." Matt pulled his hands back. "No one has been able to find out where she went after Edinburgh. This is—"

"What was inside?" Cassie jerked her hands back.

"A paperweight." Thia gave the same lie she had told Abby. "Lettie was always sending me stuff like that. Little souvenirs of her travels."

"Did she say anything? In a note, perhaps?" Matt asked.

"Only that she hoped I was well, that the store was running okay. That sort of thing," Thia said as anxiety quickly cleared away the alcohol in her system. The twins were watching her much too intently. "She didn't even let me know she was in Scotland. See?" She pointed to the return address in London. "At first, I'd thought she'd sent this from here."

"Do you have it with you? The note?" Cassie held out an

expectant hand.

"Sorry, no," Thia said, then dove headfirst into another lie. "I didn't think to keep it."

The hand withdrew. "Yet you kept the postal wrap?"

"It had her address." Thia plastered on a self-deprecating smile. "Saved me the trouble of finding my address book."

Cassie looked ready to question but Matt intervened with, "May I borrow this? Since you no longer need her address?"

"Sure." If she had another option, Thia couldn't see it.

"This might be our first big break." Matt folded the tape-laden paper, tucked it into his jacket pocket.

"What will you do with it?"

"We have people adept at all sorts of divinations."

Not quite the forensics-based television montage Thia had imagined: gloved hands, tweezers, miscellaneous vials, and all-purpose blue light.

"And psychics," Cassie added. "They might be able to sense Lettie's feelings at the time—maybe even what she did before or after handling the paper."

"That's amazing," Thia said, uncomfortable. She'd thought the Brigantium would get little more than the location and some useless fingerprints. But then, she'd thought they would be using science.

Matt got to his feet. "I should take this in right away."

Figuring they would all go, Thia reached for her jacket.

"No, no. Finish your drink. Cassie can see you back."

"Hang on," Thia objected. "I can't just sit in that safe house and wait for updates." Especially since she couldn't be sure they would give her any. "Please. Isn't there something I can do?"

Matt held her gaze for a strange, silent moment and then, "I'll speak with Eben. It won't make a difference for tonight, I'm afraid. But tomorrow, maybe." He glanced at Cassie. "I'll do my best."

"Thank you." Once more, Thia felt the unexpected threat of tears. "Lettie...she meant a lot to me."

Sympathy warmed his brown eyes. "Of course. I'll—well, I'll see you soon. Tomorrow, I mean." He shook his head, looking chagrined. Tried again. "I'll see you tomorrow."

Thia laughed. "Okay. Thanks again."

"Yes, thank you, Matt. Off you go," Cassie said, with more than a little exasperation.

He inclined his head, turned away to then walk past a line of tables whose chairs had been overturned and set on top in preparation for closing. The pub held a new tension, an urgency Thia blamed on the hour. Conversations, few and far between, were hushed; the faces of the participants, anxious. The wall clock showed it was nearly eleven. Likely everyone felt pushed to finish before they were told to go altogether.

● ○ ●

A Short Time Later

Keeping a cautious distance from the two women, Cormac followed them into the thickening fog. Sounds carried easily in the damp, still air, and he took care to be silent. Their route from the pub was taking them in the general direction of the Strand with its busy nightlife and plentiful taxis, but first they had to wend their way through the rougher, darker streets of Covent Garden.

What was the woman from the Brigantium thinking, taking Thia out alone?

It was as if they wanted trouble. And perhaps they did— perhaps this was all to lure him into the open. To what end? What could she and Thia possibly do against him?

So little of this night made sense. For starters, there was the shoddy choice of pub. Aside from its questionable food and sanitation, the Seven Brewers had no wards. Maybe its owners could not afford to be particular about their patronage—or, more troubling, maybe they didn't *want* to be.

Seated at the bar, Cormac had nursed a glass of execrable scotch and noted several known black marketeers among the markedly disreputable crowd—and those were those who had gone undisguised. He had detected a number of glamours in use: no way of knowing whom they concealed.

He had employed one, himself.

But the point was, the pair from the Brigantium couldn't *not* understand how dangerous a place that pub was. Just as this one, now, had to recognize how foolhardy it was for two women to be in such a neighborhood as this so late at night. And that was without taking into account Cormac's known and very particular interest, and what they knew was at stake. The Brigantium couldn't possibly think one apprentice-level girl was enough protection.

Her giant of a brother had left with the postal wrapper. Had he also gone to fetch reinforcements? *Was* this a trap?

It had been too easy to find Thia's location at that hotel in Soho. Her luggage, taken from the Brigantium's headquarters in plain sight and then loaded into a black sedan—Cormac had thought it careless at the time, but hadn't given it much consideration beyond that. He'd been too intent on keeping the sedan in sight.

He thought differently now, and wondered again if he wasn't playing right into their hands. But what could the Brigantium want with him? He had nothing that—

A sharp prickling at the back of his neck was his only warning before three hooded figures emerged from the thick bank of fog at the intersection ahead. He had been right about being a target. Quickly, he weighed his options: fight or flight.

Yet instead of charging into the alley toward Cormac, the three men surrounded the women.

This was a trap, all right—but not for him.

One hooded man made a slashing movement with his arm, and Cormac felt a surge of dread. But it was not Thia who crumpled to the ground. It was the other woman. Thia was yelling. Something profane and about...fire?

Heavy, sluggish with relief, Cormac forced himself to think, to move. He darted forward, concealed himself behind trash bins and stacks of crates and cardboard.

He couldn't say what weapon the attacker had used, magical or otherwise. Nor did he sense any energy residue—though, granted, it was hard to sense anything through the maelstrom of his emotions. As soon as he rescued Thia, he promised himself, he'd make her give him the relic and undo whatever she had done to his enthrallment spell. And then he'd make her regret making him care.

That was Cormac's last clear thought before Thia's panicked, furious shriek pushed him beyond reason.

A large man stood behind her, holding her against him his chest with his thick arms wrapped around her. She was lifted, her arms pinned, as the other men tried to take hold of her wildly kicking legs.

Coming up from behind, Cormac went for the one holding Thia. He breathed in the stench of incense embedded in the man's heavy cloak.

"Fucking hell, Jim," one yelled at Thia's captor. "Knock her out, would you? We haven't got all night."

"Shut it! Don't you think I'm trying?" Jim yelled back, and did something that caused Thia to cry out.

Instinct. And rage. With both hands, Cormac grabbed the man's head, gave it a vicious twist. Bone snapped. As the limp body dropped, Cormac wrapped his arms around Thia, much as the dead man had done.

"What the fuck?" The two remaining attackers stared—the one who had spoken, at Cormac; the other, at the body of their comrade. Shock held them immobile, but it would not last long.

Cormac had to get Thia and the relic—assuming she still had it—someplace safe.

Home. He could take her home. Silently, he readied the spell. He had only ever used it with himself, but if he held onto her, and she to him, it ought to work. Had to work.

"Thia," he said. "I'm going to—" Instead of relaxing upon hearing his voice, she fought harder.

"Fire," she shrieked again. "Fire!"

Peculiar woman.

"Stop. Thia, stop." He gave her a little shake. "Please. I'm here to help."

"You're a liar," she shouted, kicking. "A murderer! Let go of me!" Her pendant flared, sending out a razor-sharp wave of energy.

He stumbled. "Thia, stop. Let me—damnation!" Her heel had connected with his knee. "You'll pay for that," he ground out, adjusting his hold, tightening it. Sharp nails clawed at his hands.

"No, you'll pay, you bastard." Her voice was thick with fury. "For Lettie. For Cassie. Everything!"

Energy summoned by her pendant struck again, so strong that Cormac's vision blacked. His legs threatened to buckle.

This was not going to work.

"Run," he spoke into her ear. And, opening his arms, let her go. She didn't fight him on *that,* at least. The instant her feet touched the ground, she raced back the way she had come, shouting. The foggy night quickly hid her from view.

The remaining men knelt by the body. Cormac was nearly recovered from the pendant's effects. This would present no challenge at all.

"Who's next?" he asked with soft menace.

The two men looked up, their hoods falling back to reveal

pale, young faces. Fear was much more evident in one than the other, and made for an easy choice.

"So be it," Cormac said, and let power show in his eyes.

Energy flowed to his upturned hands, forming two hovering spheres. One glowed white; the other blue—incapacitating *wanfýr* and deadly *wælfýr,* respectively.

Cormac lifted his hands, got ready to send the lethal sphere toward the man on the right: the stronger of the two. The frightened man on the left would get a reprieve...contingent upon how well he answered questions.

"Wait, please," that one begged while both began to stand— only to collapse like puppets with their strings cut.

Both of them dead before they hit the ground.

Power crackling between his fingers, Cormac braced for an assault. Reached out with his Sight.

He sensed nothing, but he had sensed nothing before the men had been struck down, either.

What could do that? Or, more importantly, who? Maybe once Cormac could have listed a fair number. Not anymore. He couldn't think of one.

Yet, clearly, there was at least that.

Seconds passed, silent and still, until gradually Cormac let the energy at his hands dissipate. The attack was over.

Or perhaps it had merely returned its focus to Thia, who was currently running around on her own. He tamped down his initial alarm; with her pendant, she could do a fair bit of damage to anyone who—

But it had not acted against these three men. It had only acted against Cormac.

He took off at a run, tracking the faint sound of Thia's voice, her continued cries of "fire." Curious, that. But it meant he could locate her, so he wasn't about to complain.

His breath plumed visibly in the chill air as he tracked her haphazard course. His throat burned; his chest, too, after only a short while. The long weeks had taken a toll. Mentally and physically, he was off his game.

Much necessary information had died with the three men. Who had ordered the attack? What powers had been used to do it? How they had known to target Thia and been able to get through her pendant's defenses?

Whoever had was ruthless, obviously. And formidable.

Nearly wheezing, he at last saw Thia ahead, a silhouette in the fog as she ran towards the Strand's bright lights.

Cormac's less than silent approach would be masked by the carrying sounds of boisterous, drunken conversations and rumble of cars packed bumper to bumper. But once she got to the main thoroughfare, she would be lost to him. Again. It would be too public.

As he ran, he gathered energy at his palm—a sphere of *wanfýr.* If he struck her unaware, maybe the pendant wouldn't have time to react.

The energy at his hand glowed white. Ready. So near to the busy street, with its dodgy food vendors, the air was thick with the scent of frying onions and unidentifiable meat. He had to do this now.

Slowing to a stop, he took aim. His vision suddenly blurred, wavered,; in a violent motion, he used his free arm to wipe away the sweat running into his eyes. Thia was nearly at the corner. Blinking rapidly, he aimed again. Guilt sat heavily on his shoulders.

"I'm sorry," he said, too low to be heard, and flung the ball of energy at Thia's back. It would only stun—knock her out, ideally—but it would hurt. For hours, potentially, without intervention. And Thia was human. Fragile. He cringed as the white sphere neared her.

"Thia, watch out!" someone bellowed, and Cormac swore as the oaf from the Brigantium rounded the corner to pull Thia out of harm's way and throw a *fýr*-ball of his own.

It struck Cormac's and the two energies scattered with a blinding crackle of sparks.

"Matt? What's—"

"Thia, get behind me," ordered the overlarge, interfering man. To his credit, when Thia didn't react quickly enough, he stepped in front of her. Protecting. Lethal *wælfýr* glowed at his right hand.

Cormac smiled, crafted one to match.

"Matt? What's going—oh." Peering out from behind her rescuer, Thia looked directly at Cormac.

He couldn't risk it, not with the chance she might get hit.

"Matt." Still looking at Cormac, Thia tugged on the other man's sleeve. "Cassie is hurt. We need to go back."

When the man looked to her Cormac had the distraction he needed. He hurled the *fýr*-ball a safe distance behind and to the left of them. It hit a metal skiff filled with construction debris and set off another explosion of sparks. Both turned at the noise, and Cormac ducked into a nearby alcove, well out of sight. Leaning back against the cold bricks, he prepared to make his next move.

"Matt?"

"Cassie!"

Cormac cautiously looked out, watched Thia and Matt rush to the woman walking unsteadily in from the Strand. With a cry of relief, the brother scooped up his sister. She rested her head on his shoulder, held out a trembling hand to Thia, who grabbed hold with a breathless, "Cassie, thank God. Are you all right?"

"Yes. I'm so sorry." The other woman's voice was shaky. "It was all my fault...back there. I'm so sorry."

Screeching tires drew Cormac's attention to where a black sedan had managed to insert itself in the queue of taxis along the sidewalk. Amidst a barrage of horn-blasts and profanity, two men got out of the back and walked directly to Thia's cozy little group. Though they held themselves still, their eyes swept the area.

Warriors cloaked in dark suits and ties.

Efficient, Cormac had no doubt, and deadly. The potential, the power to kill, came off them in brittle, cold waves. Not magic, but *guns.* A glimpse of a shoulder holster confirmed but didn't make it any less shocking.

A man ushered Thia none too gently to the sedan, its motor idling. "Where are we going?" she asked. "What is all this?"

Cormac had broken cover, taking steps toward her before he realized. He stopped. Heads turned in his direction. He only cared that Thia's was among them. *Don't go with them,* he wanted to say, but her expression robbed him of his voice. Loathing. *Hatred,* even, though he could hardly believe it. He took an unsteady step back, surprisingly affected.

Anger, he might have expected from her. He hadn't treated her well, after all. But hatred? He had *helped* her. And missed several opportunities because of his concern.

What was it she had said while her pendant had been doing its best to fry him—something about his being a liar? And a murderer. And how he would pay for Lettie and Cassie.

Cormac could (grudgingly) understand her mistaking what had happened with Cassie and the alley attack. But why had she mentioned Leticia?

Matt turned from settling his sister in the backseat of the car and grabbed hold of Thia's other arm.

"There! He's there," one of the men shouted. More cars, coming from all directions, braked sharply to block multiple lanes of traffic and expel their business-suited occupants onto the street.

Incredulity held Cormac in place. Forget security team, this was an armed force. And, as its men approached with guns drawn, he had to accept the night's inevitable outcome.

Warnings were shouted, inconsequential things about not

making a move. Fine—he needn't move to make his escape. As the men neared, Cormac's gaze returned to Thia.

What did she think he'd done to Leticia?

"Another time," he promised, and activated the spell. In a moment, he was well out of harm's way on a rooftop farther down the Strand.

● ○ ●

As Thia continued to stare at the spot Cormac had just been, she felt a sharp tug on the arm not currently gripped by the James Bond-type man. She turned, hardly trusting her eyes, to find Matt looking down at her.

"We need to go," he said, and then as if the necessity was somehow unclear, "Now."

Thia nodded, too stupefied with shock to do otherwise, and the other man immediately released her arm. Matt lead her to the waiting car, where several men guarded its open doors. The motor was already running.

People had attacked her. *Cormac* had attacked her.

Again.

"Watch yourself," Matt warned, and placed a light hand on her head as she ducked into the back seat. Cassie was already there, sitting with her legs pulled up and her head on her knees, face hidden from view. For too many horrible minutes, Thia had thought the other woman had been killed. Had been almost certain that she would be too.

"Heythrop," Matt said as he got into the front passenger seat. The doors slammed shut. With a quick shift of gears, the driver sent the car squealing into traffic.

His leather-gloved hands worked the wheel, swerving in and out of lanes with ever increasing speed. The back of his head, the line of his shoulders, looked vaguely familiar.

"How are you?" Matt asked, turning in his seat. His hand reached into his jacket pocket to pull out a phone.

Thia was about to respond when Cassie, without lifting her head, murmured, "I'm fine."

Thia's cheeks warmed. Of course Matt wasn't asking about her. She hadn't been knocked unconscious and abandoned in a dank alley.

"You are not fine, dammit," Matt argued. "I *felt* it. I was looking for you—I couldn't tell where you were. Of all the foolish things, Cass. You could have been killed."

Cassie's head came up. "I wasn't expecting Cormac to have help, that's all. I could have handled him." Bitterness laced her words. Her head dropped again to her knees.

City light strobed across Matt's face as the car zoomed onto a relatively empty motorway. His attention shifted to Thia. "You're not hurt?"

She didn't know how to answer. Places on her arms burned, bruised to the bone. Her chest ached from being squeezed. Her back was tight, the muscles angered during the contortions made while fighting off the men. Her legs, not used to flat-out runs down cobblestone streets—any kind of streets, really—felt like rubber. And she'd already been sore from the fence-attack.

"No, I'm okay," she said. It might have been more convincing if it hadn't come out all shaky and weak. But aches and minor pains were one thing: She was over her head in a situation she didn't understand and she was scared beyond measure.

"You did great," Matt said. Reaching beneath the seat, he pulled out a blanket and held it out to her.

She took it. The fleece was soft and delicate, a luxury to her cold hands. "Thanks, I—"

"For Cassie, if you would. I have to call this in."

"Oh, sure. Of course."

He'd already turned away, his phone held to his ear.

She unfolded the blanket, draped it carefully over the young woman's shoulders.

"I'm sorry." Cassie's manicured hands crept out to grab the blanket's edge. She kept her face down on her knees.

"No harm done." Thia tucked her own hands in her lap to warm them. She was doing a lot of lying. More, it felt like, in the past three days than in her entire life.

"Hello, sir," Matt said into his glowing phone. "Yes, they're both safe. We're with Tremayne. Yes. I thought it best." He proceeded to give an account of the night's events—what he knew of them, anyway.

Thia watched road signs flash by. None of the city names were familiar, nor those of the roads. This was not her country. She had no friends here.

Cassie shifted position, lowering her feet to the floor and leaning back in her seat. Within moments, the quiet sound of deep, easy breathing reached Thia's ears.

She envied the ability to sleep. The adrenaline that had surged during the attack was draining, leaving her exhausted, and yet her mind refused to calm.

I'm here to help.

For a moment, with Cormac's arms wrapped around her and his words a rough whisper against her skin, she had believed. It had been all she could do not to relax against him, as if he were safety personified. She would have gone anywhere with him, let him do anything.

She was such a fool.

● ○ ●

With a distinct sense of *déjà vu,* Cormac had watched the Brigantium's car cut a swath through the Strand's congested traffic. The sudden pricking of the summons then took him by surprise; before he could ask for a postponement, he was inside Idris's chambers, dirrectly before the dais. The break in tradition did not bode well.

Cormac had a disconcerted moment to note that the room

was darker than usual, the orbs on the walls hardly glowing, before the weaponized force of Idris's anger slammed into his midsection and doubled him over.

Another blast struck like an uppercut to the jaw. His teeth clicked together and he stumbled back. He tasted blood, felt it trickle down his chin.

Regaining his balance if not quite his breath, he forced his spine to straighten.

"Hello, *Athair.*" With feigned nonchalance, he pulled out a handkerchief, dabbed at his mouth. "I'm afraid you've caught me at a crucial point in—" He broke off with a hiss as streaks of light tore across his chest and left white-hot pain in their wake. He felt his skin open, the welling blood quickly pulling the silk of his shirt into gashes masked by the black of his coat. Later he'd find there were five, like claw marks, crossing from left collarbone to right hip.

Cormac gritted his teeth, used a minor spell to damp down the stinging burn. Full healing would have to wait. With all he had yet to do tonight, he couldn't expend too much energy here.

"I had it, *Athair,*" he said, his voice carefully regulated. "The relic. I could have—"

«*But you didn't.*»

A fiery slash down Cormac's left arm stopped his protest. He dropped to his knees, the impact of bone on cold marble reverberating through his legs, up his spine, as the paltry numbing spell dissolved. He bent forward, dizzy, to place his hands on the smooth floor. Solid. Cold.

"She was too protected," he managed to grind out, working to control shameful tremors. He had to get a hold of himself or Idris would be encouraged to do worse. Ride the pain. This was but one moment in a lifetime.

"The Brigantium came," he continued. "A great many men, all with guns. I was about to follow her."

Instead, he was here wasting time and energy while all traces of Thia and the Stone were potentially lost.

«Excuses.»

A blow from behind sent Cormac sprawling. His cheekbone struck the marble of the bottom step. Light exploded behind his eyes. Someone moaned—him, most likely—and he tried to push himself up. His left hand slid, wet with blood, and he went down on his injured arm.

Perhaps he could stay down a moment longer, he mused distantly, adrift in the pain. He took a breath, tried to anchor himself. Stale incense tickled his nose, triggered a memory of Thia's attacker. The man had reeked of the very same blend.

Odd, that.

How was it the same scent also lingered in Idris's chamber? Come to think of it, why did Idris show no concern over the mention of the Brigantium's armed men? Cormac had found their existence shocking; Idris, living as he did in complete isolation, should have been surprised at the very least. Of course, he might have simply done an excellent job of concealing it.

And yet...curiosity would have been natural. Idris had not asked a single follow-up question.

«You disappoint me.»

Break over, Cormac got slowly to his feet.

CHAPTER 16

Near Heythrop, England
31 October

Thia awakened to the thump and scrape of wiper blades across rain-drenched glass; the same sounds which had lulled her to sleep some unknown time before. She rubbed her eyes, tried to get them to focus. The dashboard clock read twenty minutes to one. So, nearly an hour of sleep. It hadn't done much good, unfortunately. Fatigue remained wrapped around her like strips of cloth around a mummy.

Paper rustled—Matt unfolding a map. He gave a hushed direction to the driver, who nodded and then slowed the car into a left-hand turn. As Thia had drifted into her nap, she had figured out why he looked so familiar; she had seen him outside the Brigantium. He was the man who'd made Cassie laugh and driven away with Thia's luggage.

Beside her, Cassie slept on. Thia turned to look out the side window. Her reflection confronted her, pale and transparent against the blackness outside that she assumed was countryside. Water, sparkling with the faint light of the car's interior, streaked across the glass. Stand-ins, Thia supposed, for the tears she couldn't afford to shed.

Lettie was truly gone.

Gravel crunched wetly as the car negotiated a winding, rutted road. Thia couldn't make out much detail beyond the scope of the headlights. Rain-slicked stone walls. Thick tree trunks with low, overhanging branches made skeletal by the autumnal fall. Even as the heater pumped hot, dry air through the vents, she thought she could smell decayed leaves.

London's metropolis was far behind. So was Thia's luggage. She could hardly whine about unavailable pajamas and socks, though, considering that these people had saved her life. The Stone was the most important thing, and she still had that, its weight both comfort and burden. She wanted to hold it in her hand or, even more, put it up to her eye and watch the shift of light and shadow, to try to remember the joy she had first felt instead of this overwhelming grief and fear.

Angling himself in his seat, Matt told her, "We should be there soon." His face was entirely shadowed. The glow from the dashboard instruments tinted the tips of his hair blue. "I shouldn't have left the two of you alone. I wasn't thinking of anything but taking that paper to be examined. So stupid of me. I might as well have handed you to Cormac on a platter."

Thia leaned toward him, kept her voice just above a whisper so as not to wake Cassie. "You couldn't have known he would find us." She touched his arm briefly in reassurance. Before she could pull away, he took her hand up in his own.

"Your skin is like ice." He chaffed her fingers. The contact felt awkward. "You should have said. There's probably another blanket in the boot. We could—"

"No, no." Gently, Thia extricated her hand. "Thank you, though. I'm more scared than cold."

"I know I said this before—and look what happened—but we *will* keep you safe. I swear it. No one expected anything like that attack. Cormac has always worked alone."

The driver made a scornful noise. "Then how was it the old lady saw him watching her while the knife slid into her back? Sorry," he added, meeting Thia's horrified gaze in the mirror. "They didn't tell you the details, I take it."

"No. We had not," Matt said tightly. "We didn't want to be cruel, Tremayne."

The driver made the noise again. "The truth can be, that's right enough. But sometimes cruelty is exactly what's needed." His voice was tight. Bitter. "Not my place to argue."

"It isn't, no."

The condescension in Matt's tone surprised Thia but not, apparently, Tremayne. The portion of his mouth she could see lifted wryly and he said, "It isn't my place, either, to suggest you're all lucky not to have been killed tonight over nothing more than a blinding bit of stupidity."

Thia's cheeks burned. He was right. She'd known she was in danger, a target of sorts, even if she didn't understand why— or the nature of the danger itself.

She had a better idea now, and wouldn't let herself get taken by surprise or be so vulnerable again. Somehow.

Cassie's voice was startling. "I do hope you aren't accusing me of being stupid, Max."

"Ah, sweetheart. You wound me," Tremayne said easily. "You know I'd never dare."

"Good." Cassie smiled. "I should hope—"

"Which means you should've known better."

The smile vanished. "As should you, Max. How dare—"

"Yes, that's quite enough, Tremayne," Matt warned, though it wasn't the driver's temper that had flared, but Cassie's. Thia could practically feel it rolling off the woman in cold waves.

"We didn't mean to wake you, Cass," her brother continued peaceably. "How are you feeling?"

"Fine."

After several seconds of uncomfortable silence, Thia voiced something that had been bothering her for hours. "I'm sorry I ran, Cassie. I was trying to get help. I didn't know what else to do."

"You did exactly right," Cassie said, waving it off. "I'm glad you got away."

"Thank you." Thia's guilt would not be so easily dismissed, but she'd work on it. She looked to Matt, still turned to face them. "How did you know something was wrong?"

"I felt when Cassie was hurt." He reached out to his sister, who clasped his hand.

"We have a connection, you see," she told Thia. "One of the gifts of twins."

"And one of the curses," Matt added with a chuckle.

Cassie pouted and playfully dropped his hand. "It is true there can be times when too much of a connection can be... inconvenient." She gave Tremayne a speaking glance, but as his attention was on the road, Thia didn't think he caught it.

"You felt what was happening?" she asked Matt.

"More or less."

"How did you know *where* she was?"

"Mobile phone," the siblings answered at once. And laughed at Thia's groan over her own stupidity. So tangled up in the unusual, she had overlooked the obvious.

"I called Matt when I woke," Cassie said. "We arranged a meeting place on the Strand."

"It was sheer luck that had you and I meeting there," Matt told Thia.

"And the cars?"

"We were tracking their phones," Tremayne answered her, but it was to Cassie he looked in the mirror. "Standard procedure for a Level Three alarm."

"You called it in?" Cassie asked Matt, who then shrugged.

"No alternative," he explained. "At that point, there was no knowing what the bastard was going to do."

"Nothing, in the end." Cassie sounded bitter.

"That's interesting in itself, isn't it?" Thia asked.

The interior was not so dark that she missed the pointed looks directed her way. She shrugged. "Why would he kill his own men? If that's who those guys were."

Matt's phone call at the start of the drive had brought the news that all three attackers lay dead at the scene. Two from unknown causes; one from a broken neck.

"Perhaps they were his father's men," Matt suggested. "And Cormac wants the relic for himself."

"The whole thing could have been staged." Cassie leaned forward excitedly. "Think about it. He saves you, Thia, from a violent attack—and by doing so, gains your trust."

"I'm not that easy," she insisted. But she almost had been. Her first reaction to Cormac's appearance, to his touch, had been dangerously simple-minded. She'd quickly come to her senses, yes, but it hadn't been easy.

"No, you're no fool," Cassie said, and patted Thia's knee. "Cormac underestimated you."

"When he grabbed me," Thia said, "it seemed to hurt him. Not just my kicking. It was as if something moved through me. Kind of like, I don't know, an energy? Tingly and hot. The pendant got really hot too, and flashed a bright light." It had done that when the man had grabbed her at the fence. And in Lettie's parlor. And...on the plane. She frowned, the memory vague.

"That's how you know it's working," Matt said.

"So it *did* do something to Cormac?"

"Most assuredly. When defending against a physical assault, the pendant can draw energy from the wearer and direct it at an attacker. Or attackers. Apparently it feels like an electrical shock to them. Quite painful."

Thia couldn't help feeling glad of it. For what Cormac had done to Lettie, he deserved all that and more.

"But when the others grabbed me, nothing happened."

"Nothing at all?" Tremayne was watching her intently in the

mirror—too intently, she thought, for safe driving.

"The only thing fighting them was me."

"You're certain of this?" Doubt filled Cassie's voice. "With everything that was going on, you're certain the pendant was not engaged?"

Instinct supplied an immediate answer: No. But if Thia had learned one thing over the past few days, it was how wrong her instincts could be. So, she considered the speed of the attack, the terror she'd felt. In the midst of all that, might she have failed to notice the pendant's activity?

"I don't know," she admitted.

"Here we are." Tremayne brought the car to a stop in front of an enormous wrought iron gate.

Thia's nerves jangled. Not that she wanted to keep riding in the car all night, but it had become familiar. Whatever lay beyond the gate was yet another unknown.

With heavy drops of rain pounding on the roof and streaking through the beams of the headlights, Tremayne rolled down his window to slide a card along a slot in a stone post. Cold wind whipped through the car and Thia shivered, crossed her arms for warmth. Gears rumbled as metal squealed, sliding along a track. The gates eased open.

Tremayne closed his window and moved the car forward.

After several minutes of slow driving through what looked to be thick woodland, bright lights broke through the watery dark. A building the length of a city block, its every window aglow, lay at the end of a circular drive.

They called this a "safe house?" Safe *manor* house, more like.

As the car pulled up before the main entrance, a man and woman emerged. That they were elderly was all Thia could tell before they opened two massive, black and yellow striped umbrellas, obscuring their heads and shoulders. They hurried forward, looking like two shiny mushrooms.

Thia undid her seat belt. The opening of her door flooded

her vision with the bright yellow of one of the mushroom's raincoats.

"Quickly, quickly, before you catch your death," its wearer instructed and reached out a yellow gloved hand. Thia let it snag her wrist and pull her under the umbrella's shelter. With rain pummeling the plastic, she was hustled up wet steps and into the dry, warm building.

Her head swam, slow to adjust to the new surroundings, and she was having difficulty processing her escort's constant chatter. Not a mushroom at all, she thought dimly, but a bird. A canary-woman.

Her name was Mirabel Crisp, the woman announced in the midst of pointing out partridge-eye marble and counting off the number of visits from Queen Victoria.

In sharp contrast, the man (introduced by Mrs. Crisp as her husband, Elias) was tall and thin and—so far—silent. As he hung coats on and placed umbrellas in an elaborate stand, Mrs. Crisp continued to chatter, her fingers fluttering over her white hair and gauzy yellow dress, setting both to rights.

Matt, with Cassie leaning on his arm, closed the door. The sounds of rain and wind were immediately muted. "Thia," he said, leaving Cassie with Mr. Crisp. "Before you're shown to your room, I'd like you to take this." He held out something small and shiny. A charm.

After a moment's hesitation, Thia took it. A jagged letter R had been engraved on an otherwise plain silver disk. It was a runic symbol, she knew well enough from Eclectica's similar items, but couldn't recall what it was meant to represent. The edges were rough. Whoever had crafted it wasn't very skilled.

Matt was watching her. Waiting. She forced a smile. He had given her a gift. Tiredness was making her rude. "Thank you. It's…What does it mean?"

"Here. I'll help you put it on." He stepped behind her and before she understood his intent, he had lifted her hair. His fingers found her necklace's clasp, unhooked it.

She shivered as his skin brushed hers.

"Sorry," he said, and she felt her necklace lift. "My hands are cold." He reached over her shoulder, and she handed him the new charm. It soon slid down the chain to clink lightly against the other, larger pendant.

"With this on," he said, "if there's trouble, all you have to do is think of Cassie or me. We'll know and come running."

Secured once more, the chain settled against Thia's nape. For such a little thing, the new charm added a lot of weight.

Matt gave her shoulders a squeeze and then stepped back.

"You think something might happen tonight? Here?" Thia asked, turning to face him—and the others, all watching her.

"Of course not," Mrs. Crisp said cheerfully. In a face lined with age and laughter, her eyes were small and bright. Both Crisps were probably in their eighties. "Nothing will happen here. We're extremely well protected. I'm sure the young man simply wants to make you feel additionally so." She gave Thia a knowing wink.

Matt paled, stammering, "I didn't mean—that is, I—"

Smothering a laugh, Cassie nudged him in the ribs. "Come on, Mattie. I'm asleep on my feet, and we've still got a lot to do. Starting with that phone call to Eben. Goodnight, Thia. See you in the morning, all right?"

"Right. Thanks."

Mr. Crisp ushered the twins into what looked to be an office. It seemed Thia's very long day was coming to an abrupt end.

"Let's get you into your room and a nice, hot bath," Mrs. Crisp said, bustling her toward a grand set of stairs. "You've had quite a time of it, I hear, and nothing is better for a body than a good soak, I always say."

"A bath would be wonderful." Thia struggled to keep pace. Really, if it hadn't been for the promise of the bath, she'd have been happy to bed down right there on the stairs.

Mrs. Crisp, on the other hand, was a whirlwind of energy. Conducting a lively architectural tour, her hands never stilled. They flitted over furnishings, pointed out numerous *objets d'art*, and straightened paintings. Thia tried to attend to the accompanying flow of words but couldn't. The information simply washed over her, everything from the intricacies of how a particular carpet had been chosen to what the advent of electricity had meant for the wallpaper.

Two flights of stairs and a long corridor later, they arrived at what was to be her room. Mrs. Crisp flung open the door.

Vines covered everything. Artistically speaking...if that was the right word for it. In a decorating scheme run amok, ivy leaves swirled across thick carpets while still more covered the large bed's butter yellow comforter and matching canopy. Jasmine twined over the wallpaper in a riotous maze of green, yellow and white. Everything from the fireplace's elaborate mantle to the knick-knacks atop it—even the furniture inlays and carvings—had a vine motif.

The attached bath had not been spared, either, Thia saw when she was led into it. Even the enormous claw footed tub had been painted with leaves.

That didn't stop her from wanting to get in. Both long and deep, it would allow her to fully submerge. She could soak away all her aches and allow her concerns to float away.

"You needn't worry about a thing," Mrs. Crisp was saying. Her rapid fingers drifted from a plush terrycloth robe hung beside the tub to an array of bath salts set on a nearby shelf. "Your luggage should arrive by morning, and there's a nightgown in the wardrobe. If you need anything else—something from the kitchen, or a hair dryer and such—the bell pull is to the right of the bed. When you're in it," she added with a light laugh. "Otherwise, you'll find the pull on the left."

Thia forced exhausted muscles to smile.

"You're safe now," her cheerful hostess went on, re-arranging the items on the shelf above the pedestal sink. Toothbrush.

Paste. Water glass. Tiny, carved soaps in a wicker basket.

"Thank you, Mrs. Crisp. I think I can—"

"Do call me Mirabel. But, of course, you must be tired, and here I am, nattering on." In a flurry of yellow chiffon, she returned to the bedroom. "Extra wards have been placed on windows and doors, so don't you worry about that, either." She exited into the hall, shut the door behind her with a secure click. A silent moment later, she called through, "Breakfast is at eight. Pleasant dreams."

Thia took a deep breath, allowed herself a few seconds of stillness and relative quiet before she opened the taps. After a brief squeal, water thundered down on the cast iron. She adjusted the temperature, set the plug, and then left the tub to fill. At the hallway door, she edged the back of a wooden chair beneath the already-locked handle. The precaution felt a bit foolish and wouldn't hold off a determined invader...but might alert her to the presence of a sneaky one.

Back in the bathroom, to keep the Stone from rolling free of its shielding cloth, Thia nestled it among the carved soaps in their basket. One of the bottles of salts with its decorative sprig of dried flowers caught her eye. She took it up, pulled out the cork stopper. Sniffed. Lavender... sage...chamomile... and something citrusy. Bergamot, probably. Brisk yet sweet, promising to both cleanse and soothe. She sprinkled a liberal amount into the rising water and the drifting steam instantly took up the scents. She breathed deep, drawing them in.

Tense and strained muscles complained as she undressed. Bruises of various ages mottled her skin, reminders of everything she had been through in the past...with the time change, she had lost track of the hours and was too tired to attempt a calculation. Easier, maybe, to track the physical marks. Marks of red and purple left by fence pickets and a stranger's hands. Marks from her encounter in Lettie's hallway. Faint red and yellow splotches from Matt's fingers on her arms. Angry red crescents from Cassie's nails. And, most recent, marks left by another stranger, cloaked in black.

Thia would never forget that sound, the dull pop.

One moment he had been crushing her and she had been afraid for her life. The next moment, he'd been...gone. In the most total and unalterable sense of the word.

She removed the rest of her too-long-worn travel clothes— sighed audibly at the sports bra's long-awaited unclasping— and then lowered herself into the fragrant water. Almost too warm, but it would reach perfection soon enough. A terry-cloth pad at the rear of the tub cushioned her spine, and she let her head drop back. Water, rising steadily, lapped at her collarbone. She nudged the taps closed with her toes.

With the pipes gone silent, she could hear the rapid beat of the rain upon the room's tiny window set high in the thick, tiled wall. She pressed wet hands to her face, succumbed to a moment of panic. *What was she to do?*

Cormac would not stop until he had the Stone. Thia could not possibly keep it safe on her own. These people, with their magic and their weapons...she should hand it over to them before anyone else got hurt.

Killed.

But these were Lettie's people, and she hadn't trusted it to their keeping. No, she'd had entrusted it to Thia.

"Why, Lettie? Why me and not them?"

A drop of water fell from the faucet, plopped into the bath, as the storm continued outside.

Suddenly all was silent darkness and Thia felt herself slipping—moving through space and picking up speed. Vertigo? Fainting? But her eyes were open, weren't they, and she was conscious, was she not? She was able to think, so...yes? But she couldn't see a thing, couldn't *feel* a thing except the awful sensation of motion. She must have fallen asleep—not safe to do in a bath—and was dreaming. She struggled to wake.

CHAPTER 17

Icy darkness. Massive, dizzying headache.

Thia sucked in a startled breath and nearly gagged. The air was thick and pungent and left a metallic taste in her mouth. The bones of her back and pelvis pressed uncomfortably on a hard, cold surface. Very cold.

She couldn't see.

Not due to blindness, she realized with what would prove to be short-lived relief, when her eyes began to adjust to the extreme dark.

There must have been a power outage. The manor house was old. The storm was violent.

But why was she on the floor? Had she slipped getting out of the tub? And *what* was that godawful smell? Like the worst sort of incense. Musky, bitter, and suffocating.

Thia began to sit up but then stopped, belatedly confused by the specific feel of the floor. Smooth as glass and wet. The wet she understood—bathwater soaked her hair, slicked her skin. Of course the floor would be wet. But smooth?

The bathroom's floor was made up of small white and green tiles. She should have been feeling ridges. Grout. And, if she had fallen by the tub, she should be feeling the plush rug laid

there and—she moved her hands over the flawless surface—
her discarded clothes.

Lifting her head, she saw globes of light floating—no, set
along walls too distant for the dimensions of the bathroom.
She squinted, strained in the dim, flickering light. The walls
looked to be made of stone.

This was not the bathroom. This wasn't any room she had
been in before in her life.

She was still asleep, she realized with new alarm. In the tub.
She could drown. She needed to wake up.

Why wasn't she waking up?

She sat up abruptly, her heart pounding. There was nothing
to worry about, she told herself. She would try again to wake
up, this time it would work, and everything would be fine. All
she had to do was focus, tell herself to...Belatedly, her mind
registered sounds from a short distance away. The faint in and
out of breath. She was not alone.

She held herself almost painfully still. And waited.

No change occurred that might indicate her presence had
been noted. Cautiously, she looked left, toward the sounds.

Barely more than a silhouette, the man knelt but a few feet
away. His head was bowed, obscuring his face in shadow, but
she knew him. Of course. She'd have been more surprised if
her mind *hadn't* placed Cormac somewhere in this nightmare.
She pressed a hand to her chest and took a relieved breath.

Too bad she hadn't brought her clothes into the dream. Or
at least a big towel. She was soaking wet and the room was
awfully cold.

Wait...clothes.

She looked down.

Oh, no.

She tucked into a protective ball, arms hugging legs to body,
head down. The pendant and new charm settled between her
breasts as mortification bloomed hot on her cheeks.

One set of cheeks, anyway. The other set, equally bare, were freezing, pressed as they were to the ice-cold floor.

Naked, every inch of her.

At least this proved she was asleep. She'd had similar stress dreams in college, night after night imagining herself arriving at lectures and exams without any clothes. A classic manifestation of anxiety.

Yet this felt *awfully* real.

She squeezed her eyes shut and recalled all the assurances of safety she had been given. Popping naked into a room with Cormac was *not* safe. Not even close.

She'd sort that out later. Nightmare or reality, failed protections or not, she would not just sit—naked, for God's sake—and wait for bad things to happen.

She took hold of the new silver charm and thought emphatically of Matt and Cassie. If it worked like it was supposed to, they would know she was in trouble and...well, she didn't know what might happen next. Matt had said they'd "come running," but run to where? Where *was* she?

If this was a dream, that didn't matter. In a dream, all that mattered was imagination. She could make anything happen if she tried.

«Have you recalled the proper respect, boy? Or shall I continue the lesson?»

The unfamiliar voice boomed inside Thia's head and she bit back a startled cry as the words continued to swarm inside her skull like trapped, angry bees. Who had spoken—and how?

Cormac exhaled something like a sigh, and Thia worked to hug into a tighter, impossible-to-notice ball. Maybe she could imagine herself invisible.

"I meant no disrespect, *Athair*," Cormac said tonelessly and, thankfully, aloud. "There were things tonight which felt...not as they should. I did not mean to imply—"

«It is no concern of yours, culén.»

An electric-like buzz lifted the fine hairs on Thia's skin. The floor began to tremble, the strange lights on the walls glowing brighter, rattling in their holders. It was getting much easier to see—and to be seen. She needed to move, to hide. Immediately. But where could she go? And how would she get there? Movement was bound to attract the attention she had been lucky (so far) to avoid.

"Of course, *Athair*," Cormac said. "Yet the men tonight—such actions carry too many risks. They threaten everything."

"You dare to make me repeat myself?"

The stranger's rough, enraged voice was outside Thia's head that time, coming from the darkness at the top of a grand, marble platform. The base of it wasn't far, she judged in the ever-brightening light.

It would have to do.

She scurried the few feet to her right to huddle beside it, well out of sight of the very angry, very terrifying man at its summit.

Cormac was another problem altogether. Thia looked over, felt her panicked heart leap into her throat. He was staring right at her, his eyes wide with...shock? At her nudity, no doubt.

His mouth had dropped open. He closed it, only to open it again on a croak of sound.

«Cat got your tongue, whelp?»

She watched as he blinked—hard—and shook his head as if trying to clear it. And, when he again met her gaze, she made a silent plea with every fiber of her being that he not give her away.

Silly of her, she knew. He was no friend.

"W-we—" He swallowed, cleared his throat. "We have a—a bargain, *Athair*."

«I am well aware,» the man snarled as the room stopped rumbling and shaking. *«I had thought perhaps you had forgotten.»*

Thia's mind raced. Cormac hadn't yet mentioned her, but she couldn't count on that continuing. Couldn't count on him for anything.

She needed a plan. Running was probably the only option, but a bad one. Assuming she could get her freezing muscles to work, she could barely see the edges of the room let alone any exits. And, say she managed to find one, there was no telling where it might lead.

«I am not blind to your motives, boy. Even if you may be.»

With a pained grunt, Cormac fell forward onto his hands and—because Thia's instincts seemed to be kinder than they were smart—she automatically reached toward him. Against her skin, her pendant warmed and began to glow. *Shit.* She grabbed it, held it in a tight fist to try to block the light.

«Answer me, boy. I know you haven't passed out yet.»

"No, *Athair.*" Cormac spoke slowly. Tiredly. As he began to push himself up on shaky arms, Thia felt another unwelcome rush of pity.

The heat of her pendant increased as the light brightened, seeping through the cracks between her clenched fingers.

«Is someone here?»

Thia held her breath, watched something like fear flicker across Cormac's face only to be quickly masked. She didn't have time to consider the odd reaction; the pendant seemed to be attracting the enraged man's attention.

She didn't know how, since the seeping light wasn't all that bright so as to reach the top of the platform and from such a location, unless the man stood at the edge and looked directly down. She might've preferred to believe that was what he was doing rather than the bizarre alternative: that he could sense her presence somehow by the—what had the twins said? The energy the pendant was sending out.

Thia undid the clasp, gathered the necklace in her fist. If she had to, she'd throw it. She'd rather not, since she didn't think her chances without its protection were good at all. But she would be ready if she had to.

Cormac cleared his throat and Thia knew her time was up. She figured to run left, away from the platform. It would take her past Cormac, but if she went wide, she could avoid him. Terror and desperation would give her speed, she told herself. Plus, if she did this right, surprise would be on her side.

She shifted into a crouch, heard Cormac's slow inhale, his heavy sigh.

Push off and run in five. Four.

"*Athair, I—*"

Three. Two.

"—see no one."

Thia stopped herself mid-launch. She dropped back down, met Cormac's unreadable gaze.

I'm here to help, he'd said during the attack in the alley. She hadn't understood him then any better than she did now.

"You are certain?" came the voice from the platform.

The room lurched, sending Thia off-balance. She fell hard on her hands, slammed the necklace against the floor.

Cormac had resumed his initial posture—on his knees; head bowed—but there was a new tension to it. A brittle rigidity. At his sides, his hands were clenched so tightly they shook.

It was then that Thia noticed the blood.

Dark and glistening, the liquid red wended its way through the white lace of Cormac's shirt cuff to trickle down his hand and drip onto the glossy black floor.

He was hurt.

The remark about his not having passed out made sudden sense, and Thia found herself scanning the surface of his coat for evidence of wounds. She found none: the material was too dark—just as the floor was too dark, too glossy for her to be able to make out how much blood he might have already lost.

She must have made some sort of sound because Cormac's head snapped up, something ominous in his expression. He started to say something.

But before he got a word out, Thia was flying backwards, away from him, away from everything. She heard a scream, an anguished sound that cut off abruptly along with every other in the absolute dark.

Unable to see, unable to hear, she continued, impossibly, to hurtle through the air, her muscles braced for impact.

An impact that didn't and didn't and didn't come.

No room could be this large, she thought—right before being surrounded by cold liquid. Water rushed into her nose and ears, turned her reflexive shout into a choked gurgle. She sat up, spluttering, coughing. Dragged wet hair away from her face and blinked cool, perfumed water from her eyes.

The bath. Pedestal sink. Painted tiles. Clothes—her clothes, exactly as she had left them, strewn across the floor. Rain, blown by howling gusts of wind, struck like fistfuls of gravel on the windowpane.

Thia scrambled out of the tub, splashing water over everything in her rush to the soap basket. The Stone was exactly as she'd left it, but she picked it up anyway, needing to hold it, to feel it even through the silk wrapping. *Safe.* Holding it between her cupped hands, she took several deep, thankful breaths. It was safe. And so, apparently, was she.

Relief had her muscles going weak.

Careful of the now-slick floor tiles, she dripped her way to the robe on the door, put it on without toweling off. She was shaking, her teeth beginning to chatter.

She looked at the tub, its water sloshing gently against the sides. The room looked like a water bomb had gone off.

What had happened here, really?

She had fallen asleep, obviously. And then, during her nightmare, she'd slid underwater. The shock of it must have woken her—and thank God for that.

Slipping the Stone into one of the robe's deep pockets, she eased the door open a crack and peered out. Bright light, busy décor. No evidence of lurking horrors. Chair in place at the door to the hall.

She darted across the wide room to the bed, quickly buried herself beneath soft sheets and a voluptuous down comforter. A ragged sigh escaped as she snuggled, warming at last.

None of it had been real. Not the danger, not the terrifying voice. Not the agonized, heart-wrenching scream.

● ○ ●

So much blood. Broad streaks and smudges, like strokes from an enthusiastic brush, spread out from a congealing pool at the base of the dais. A masterful commemoration of anguish and power.

«*You failed. The girl did not carry the relic.*»

The Sorcerer's voice was strong, heavy with the same power that filled the chamber with light. The Chosen bowed deeply. They would not move again until given permission. They had not done well tonight.

«*And you risked alerting not only your comrades but my halfling son. Do not be so bold again.*»

In silent apology, they crossed their arms over their chests. They had seen an opportunity and taken it without thorough consideration of potential outcomes.

Yet it still might have worked had they had been able to get through the extra protections the old woman had placed on Thia's door.

«*It was enlightening, however. They are drawn to one another. Such vulnerability is an unexpected gift.*» Idris Cathmor's amusement left as quickly as it had come. «*Collect that before it goes to waste.*»

They began to circle the crimson pool, the hems of their robes smearing its outline. At their murmured command, the blood lifted, rushing to form a spiraling coil between them. One word, one gesture, sent it twisting through the air to fill a shallow onyx font.

"What of the rest, my lord?" they inquired, their voices as one.

«*Let it adorn you, as tonight you shall be made my Vessels.*»

The Chosen exchanged surprised looks, then let their eyes fill with what their mouths did not dare express: pride.

"As you wish, my lord."

They extended their hands toward one another as the blood changed course to encircle them. When their palms touched, it entered their robes, transformed into lustrous threads that quickly wove scarlet through the black.

«*Approach and be made ready.*»

Continuing to hold hands, they climbed the dais. No blood remained on the floor or steps. The fabric of their robes was already dry. As they neared the side of the Sorcerer's bed, they exchanged a look.

So much blood—surely almost a man's worth. But it could not have been. It was not yet time for the father to kill the son.

Not yet time. But soon.

They risked a smile.

CHAPTER 18

Thia hadn't meant to close her eyes but at some point in the night she must have, and her overtired body had seized the opportunity to send her right to sleep. Now she was late for breakfast and felt like her brain had been replaced with mush.

She hurried down another set of stairs. At least she had on fresh clothes, thanks to someone having placed her suitcase and backpack outside her door while she had slept so exhaustively. Beyond that, nothing more seemed to have happened. The chair had been exactly as she had placed it beneath the handle; the Stone had been in her robe pocket (all night, as evidenced by the indentation in her thigh); and she couldn't recall a single dream other than that awful nightmare during her bath. She didn't think she had so much as rolled over on the bed (again, as evidenced by the Stone-shaped dent).

At the bottom of the stairs, she found herself in the grand entry half-remembered from the night before. Polished wood gleamed in the morning sun. She didn't know where to go from here...but could hear faint clinks of metal on porcelain and low mumbles of distant conversation. She turned in their direction.

"Good morning, miss." A young woman in a classic maid's

uniform of black and white emerged from a doorway on the right and bobbed a curtsy. "If you would please follow me?"

"Oh, thank you, sure." She followed the girl down a bright hallway lined with vases of flowers. "I'm afraid I'm late."

The maid gave a polite smile. "Oh, no, miss. Not at all."

Thia checked her watch again, confused. It was nearly ten. "But I thought breakfast was at eight?" The sounds of activity grew louder, coming through an open door ahead.

"It is, miss. Usually." Another polite smile. "But the others only themselves arrived a little while ago."

"Oh, good"—wait—"others?" Thia had very much hoped to feel less adrift today. So far, that was not happening.

"Here we are, miss." At the doorway, the girl bobbed another curtsy.

Thia thanked her again and entered the room—and then had to pause. It was like being stabbed in the eyes with light. Glass-paneled doors and floor-to-ceiling windows let in all that the sun had to offer—which was quite a lot, surprisingly, after such a storm. It bounced between yellow walls, glinted off silver and glass.

"Good morning," she said, feeling out of place. She wasn't prepared for so many people. At least fifteen, seated at a long table laden with flower arrangements—and for the most part ignoring her. She recognized only four: Eben, at the far head of the table; Matt and Cassie to his right and left respectively; and, on Cassie's other side, Tremayne. He looked up then, as if aware of her notice, and she was struck anew by the alertness in his gaze, the tension in the way he held himself. She smiled tentatively. He returned his attention to his plate.

Cassie, looking to have recovered from her ordeal, flashed Thia a grin, and Matt turned from speaking to Eben. "Good morning," they chorused, and Matt gestured to a vacant place beside him.

"We saved you a seat," he said. "And there's plenty left on

the sideboard." An array of silver chafing dishes glinted.

"Thank you. It smells wonderful," Thia said, and went to take up a plate. She stuck with the familiar, avoiding a dish of what appeared to be pinto beans and another of baked fish complete with scales and eyes. She looked away before she could lose her appetite.

After filling a delicate china cup with coffee, she took the saved place beside Matt. He and Eben were again in conference while Cassie and Tremayne, although it was impossible to hear what was said, were openly flirting: mischievous looks, bodies leaned toward one another, arms nearly touching on the linen tablecloth.

The rest of the group glanced at Thia only briefly before they resumed their conversations. Introductions, apparently, would come later. She took a very welcome sip of coffee and nearly wept with joy. Easily the best thing she had tasted in days. Smooth, excellent quality, and potent. Almost instantly, her mental fog began to clear.

"I trust you slept well, Miss McDaniel?" Eben inquired, all polite reserve, and apparently done with Matt.

"Yes, thanks. I did," she replied in kind. She nodded at the picturesque view through the windows. "It's lovely here. Very peaceful."

A sweeping, autumn-browned meadow sparkled with left-over rain beneath a pale, clear sky. Some distance away, a soft blanket of mist covered the trunks of a large grove of trees. A flock of birds, tiny specks of black, flew up from the branches only to settle again. Crows or ravens, by their size.

Swallowing, Eben set down his glass of orange juice, dabbed at his mouth with a napkin. "Peaceful," he repeated, raising a skeptical brow. "Yes. Quite."

Thia slathered her toast with marmalade.

After an awkward pause, he said, "Last night's events make our course of action clear."

She stilled, bread halfway to her mouth. "Last night?"

"The attack." He seemed annoyed by having to clarify, but Thia was too relieved care. Her hand shook with it, forcing her to set the toast down. He had meant the events in London, not anything later.

Well, of course not. Nothing had happened later except a bad dream.

"We leave soon for Inverness," Eben continued, giving Thia a hard look. "I trust you have no objection to accompanying us?"

She nearly choked on her surprise along with her toast. "No, that's—" She coughed. Took a swig of coffee. "No objection at all. Thank you."

"Wonderful," Cassie said from across the table.

Attention back on his plate, Eben grunted and stabbed his fork into a thick slice of bacon.

"How are you?" Thia asked Cassie. "You're all right, after... everything?"

"Oh, yes. I feel better than ever, actually. All thanks to Mrs. Crisp."

Tremayne looked over, his brows raised.

"Mrs. Crisp," Cassie insisted coyly and then pretended to ignore him. "She left the most wonderful concoction for the bath. I felt quite transported."

Scrambled egg fell from Thia's raised fork. She retrieved it from the tablecloth, set it on the edge of her plate. "Really."

"Oh, yes."

Thia wondered at the word choice but couldn't bring herself to ask. That was definitely a blush on Cassie's cheeks, and Tremayne looked rather smug. Maybe it was lover's code and didn't mean she had literally been...transported. By a bath.

"Ten minutes, people," Eben announced. He set his napkin on his plate and stood. "Don't bother about your luggage, Ms. McDaniel. It will be brought down."

"Thank you." She took another bite of toast although her appetite was gone. A shame, really. The food was excellent.

Eben left and most everyone followed, leaving unfinished meals and crumpled napkins behind. Only Matt and Cassie stayed with Thia.

"Why have I been invited?" she asked. "Yesterday I was to stay in the London house—for safe-keeping. Other than our being attacked in the street, what changed?"

"Matt convinced Eben that you could be useful," Cassie said with pride.

"I said I would," he said with a shy smile. "At the pub, I said I'd talk to them about letting you be more involved. It didn't take much convincing."

"You don't look pleased," Cassie told Thia with a frown. "Is something wrong? Would you rather remain here?"

"You'll be perfectly safe with us." Matt laid a light hand on Thia's arm. "He won't get anywhere near you."

There was no question who *he* was. "How can you be sure?"

"He surprised us before. We're ready now." Cassie sounded confident. Maybe too confident.

Matt nodded solemnly. "Trust us. You'll be fine."

● ○ ●

The frantic calls of several ravens startled Cormac from his restless, chilled sleep. He jerked upright, the sudden move waking a host of dull aches. His breath plumed, joining the mist that had yet to clear with the day.

"Show me."

High in the trees there was a great rustle of feathers as the large conspiracy gathered its thoughts.

Soon came a chorus of squawks and a barrage of images—a dizzying array of the same subject seen from different points of view—and Cormac pressed his hands to his head.

"One," he demanded, and the internal assault ended, leaving

him with one clear vision of the estate. A literal bird's-eye view as one raven flew high above the treetops.

"Much better, thank you. Well done."

Several birds made a low, knocking call, and Cormac felt the pleasure they had taken from his praise.

The birds deserved it. Without their help along the way, he would never have tracked Thia from London. And, although he had nothing to offer but the novelty of the enterprise, they had willingly taken up watch throughout the night, allowing him much-needed rest in the ancient oak grove outside the Brigantium's property.

It had been a gamble to assume Thia had returned here after her appearance in Idris's chamber, but it had paid off.

"Theeea. Theaaaa," chattered one of the elder birds, playing with sounds from the memory Cormac had shared in order to identify her. More soon joined in, so that while he observed Thia through the flying raven's eyes, her name wove through the cold-stripped oaks. Individual threads of sound formed a tapestry, a kind of summoning cry.

"Theeea. Theaaa."

When she got into one of several cars idling in front of the house, Cormac broke the sight-connection. The raven cawed anxiously, its question a delicate prodding at the back of his mind.

"No, *caraid*. This I must do myself," Cormac said, pushing to his feet. His aches went from dull to sharp; he stumbled as exhaustion grayed the edges of his vision. Blindly, he reached out, fell against a broad tree trunk. He pressed his forehead against the rough bark, splayed his palms.

"Thank you," he managed, hoarse, as the ancient oak again lent strength. As it had done through the night.

Branches shook as some of the birds took flight. The ceaseless chant increased in volume. "Theeea! Theeea! Theeea!"

An image flashed, sent from above the manse: cars moving

through an open gate.

"Thia," said one raven, hopping on the frosted ground near Cormac's feet. Her dark eyes urged him to hurry. "Thia," she repeated and then took to the air. "Thia. Thia."

The ravens were going to help whether he asked for it or not.

"Silly birds," he muttered, while something warm, like a soft blanket, settled around his heart.

On a deep breath, he pulled away from the tree. Pain flared, but not nearly as sharp as before. He shifted forms and joined the ravens, still amusing themselves with Thia's name, as they followed the line of cars west.

● ○ ●

En Route to Inverness, Scotland

Thia hadn't imagined how agonizing it'd be to keep secrets of such magnitude. Having to carefully consider each and every word before speaking kept her at a distance from people—a distance she was not accustomed to maintaining. Usually, her days were filled with genial, open interactions. Friendly chats. Laughter.

For the thirty-minute drive to Coventry Airport, she had been placed in a car with strangers from the breakfast table. By the end of it, she had managed only to get their names. Her attempts at casual conversation had sailed on by, making her feel like a lone tennis player, serving to no one while a crowd looked on. It was a strangely public isolation.

When she had finally given up, her fellow passengers had begun animatedly talking amongst themselves. She had told herself it wasn't anything personal, that it was because they knew one another. They had a shared history together, as told in their comfortable manner, shared smiles and joking grimaces—of which she had no part.

Now, for the third time in as many days, Thia found herself looking through thick plexiglass at ground that was uncomfortably far below. With her legs stretched out to make the most of the amazing amount of room, her fingers played over the soft material of the armrests. There was something to be said for private planes, she supposed.

She turned to Matt, seated across the wide aisle, to ask: "Do you travel like this often?"

"Not often, no." He swiveled his seat to face her. His grin was boyish. "Brilliant, isn't it? It's usually reserved for people of Arthur and Beatrice's rank. You know, the higher-ups. Our lives aren't usually so eventful." His smile faded.

"What are they usually like, then?"

"It depends. Mostly we study, Cassie and I, to prepare for our initiations. And we assist Eben. Cataloging reports and documents, organizing the libraries and collections, helping someone else's research. That sort of thing. There can be a bit of security involved, policing stolen items and such, but that's rare." He shrugged. "It's usually a very academic life."

"And that's how you prefer it?" It was hard to picture him behind a desk or filing books on shelves.

"Not necessarily. Though I truly regret what brought this trip about. Leticia was an inspiration to so many of us."

"Really?" Sorrow awoke with a hard kick. "How so?"

"Her enthusiasm," Matt said immediately, his brown eyes bright like amber held up to the sun. "She was interested in anything. Everything. And because of it, she was able to make fascinating connections. Her work on the Vacomagi sites in the Cairngorms—in the etymology of the name alone—was revolutionary."

"Cairngorms?"

He nodded, clearly warming to the topic. "These days it refers to an entire mountain range, but really, it's one moun-tain. And not terribly far from Inverness, actually. We might fly right over it. Convention defines the name as 'gray stones,' but Leticia managed to show fairly soundly that it more likely refers to a large burial site." He leaned forward. "She found an alternative definition of the word 'gorm,' you see. Aside from 'gray,' it can also mean 'great' or 'illustrious.' And 'cairn,' of course, can mean 'burial chamber' or 'pile of stones.' Nothing has been found—yet," he added with a smile. "But nevertheless, her suggestion helped our understanding of a number of regional myths, some dealing with the creation of the land itself."

Lettie had talked about ancient ruins and burial sites she had visited in her lifetime of travel, but Thia couldn't recall having heard that particular name before or anything about a mountain range. Maybe it was a recent discovery, one which might have unearthed the Stone. "Might she have returned there, to the mountain? It's near Inverness, you said."

"Possibly. With her failure to file detailed reports, and with so many of her journals missing, we have no idea what she was doing, let alone where."

During the meeting in the director's office, Thia had been told the Brigantium was going through Lettie's field journals —books kept at her London home which held the details of her research and explorations. Many could not be found. Beatrice had suggested that Cormac had stolen them. Eben thought Lettie might have disposed of them herself in order to "cover her tracks."

Thia didn't know what to think.

"What is known about the relic itself?" She had asked these questions then in the office. She wanted to know if she'd get the same answers now. "Do you know what it looks like? Or what it's supposed to—I don't know—*do?*"

"No, no, and not much at all—to answer in reverse order. What we know—assume, rather—is that it was meant to be used by the Cailleach's followers after she left the world. A chosen representative, for instance, could wield the relic and channel the power it contained, augmenting any magic he or she might seek to perform. Qualities and subjects associated with the Cailleach in particular would come much easier."

"Like destruction."

"Exactly, yes. And, since she ruled in winter, those powers would be stronger during that time. Beginning in a few days on Samhain, coincidentally. Or not." Matt shifted in his seat. "Of immediate concern is that someone like Cormac—or, worse, Idris Cathmor—could take the relic's power into himself."

Thia frowned. "What, like, *absorb* it? The power could go *into* a person?" She had touched it. She had felt...something. Good grief, she was *carrying it around.*

"With the right ritual at the right time."

Thia relaxed slightly—she hadn't done any rituals. "What does the Brigantium want with it?"

"To keep it out of the wrong hands. We would study it, of course. But primarily, we'd safeguard it."

There was a reason Lettie had involved Thia and not the Brigantium. There was a reason she hadn't trusted them. But so far, Thia couldn't see it. "No one would try to access its power?"

"Not without merit," Matt answered. "We have strict guidelines when it comes to working with any artifact, let alone one of this nature. It involves a fairly lengthy approvals process."

"That's a yes, then."

"It's a possibility. And why not? If used wisely, such power could do great things."

She wondered what the man from the elevator might say about that. Quentin. Sometimes, despite the best intentions, things got out of control. Sometimes, the chance of calamity was greater than the potential benefit.

Maybe that was what Lettie had feared. That someday the Brigantium would play those odds. Thia could promise she wouldn't. She couldn't even get her pendant to work properly.

"You're awfully quiet," Matt said.

She pulled out her necklace. The two charms jingled. "I was

wondering what good will this be if I can't get it to work?"

He paled. "You tried to call us? You tried the new charm?"

During the nightmare, she had. Did that count?

But that wasn't what she meant. She shook her head. "The one from Lettie. I told you last night. It did something against Cormac but not the others. What am I doing wrong?"

"It detects threats on its own. There's no need for you to consciously do anything. It should pick up on energies around you as well as your own perceptions."

"Well, I certainly perceived a threat when those guys came out of nowhere, knocked Cassie down, and grabbed me," she said, caught somewhere between frustration and annoyance. "But it didn't react until Cormac grabbed me. After that, it went crazy." As it had later, during her dream, when she had reached out after Cormac had been dealt an unseen blow.

"I don't understand," Matt said after a moment. "It should have reacted at the start of the attack. As Cassie's had."

"Hers worked?" Not very well, Thia judged, given that Cassie had been knocked unconscious. "She didn't say anything last night, but maybe it didn't—"

"I'll speak with her again about it. She might not remember now. Her memories of the event are hazy, more so today than immediately afterward."

Thia could understand that. Her own memories were blurring, mixing with images and sensations from her dream to leave her utterly confused.

I'm here to help.

I see no one.

Something wasn't right. She knew it, felt it—could practically *hear* it, buzzing and crackling like an old electrical line.

If only she could figure out what it was.

CHAPTER 19

"Oh, aye. I remember the lass right enough," the elderly postmaster, Robert Mackintosh, said and gave Thia a twinkle-eyed smile.

"*Lass?*" Matt repeated.

"Aye. No more than twenty, I'd say she was. Excited, too, to be sending a parcel to the States."

"I don't understand." Thia touched a finger to the shipping wrapper spread out on the counter. "You're absolutely sure that's who mailed *this* package?"

"I am, aye. Most certain."

Thia believed him. So, then, why hadn't Lettie mailed the package herself? Matt seemed equally taken aback.

"This is really important, Mr. Mackintosh," she said, unconsciously smoothing the wrinkled paper. "My great-aunt is missing and we're afraid something terrible has happened. Can you think of anything that might help us? Do you know the—the lass, as you called her? Her name, maybe?"

"I'm sorry, I am, for your troubles. But I'd never seen her before that afternoon nor have I since. As to her name...well." His craggy brows lowered, shading sympathetic green eyes.

"I suppose I made some assumptions—let slide some things which maybe I oughtn't. But it seemed innocent, her intention to do a service while she was down from the islands. I never imagined she might be caught up in bad business."

"We don't know that she is," Thia reassured him, and then registered a detail: "Islands, you said—you know where she was from?"

"Oh, aye, lass. That I do. Orkney." He grinned. "There's no mistaking the island brogue, and she entered right after the Thurso coach went past." He indicated the window. "The station is down the street, there."

Thanks to Eclectica, Thia had heard of Orkney. The Norse and Celtic-themed jewelry made by a company based there was in high demand, and the islands' ruins and standing stones were the subjects of several popular coffee table books and posters. (No wonder, that; the images were striking. A great turf-covered mound on a flat, grassy plain. Thin, jagged stones reaching up to cloudy skies. A tiny, stone-lined entrance to a chamber built into a cliff high above a turbulent sea.)

"Come to Inverness to shop and have a bit of fun, some do," Mackintosh explained. "Less now, though, with the internet."

Thia caught Matt glancing at his watch. "I suspect you're right, sir," he said. "The girl was probably doing a favor for Miss McDaniel. Saw no harm in it."

"I'd feel better if I knew the lass was safe," Mackintosh responded.

"As would we all," Matt agreed. "Do you have closed-circuit cameras? If we had a photo of her, we'd have an easier time finding her."

Mackintosh chuckled. "Ah, no. Sorry, lad. We've no need for that sort of thing here. Not as of yet."

Thia was surprised, but maybe she shouldn't have been. Her impression of Inverness thus far was of a lovely city, calm and gentle even with the energetic rush of commerce around its

High Street. Despite hosting a number of chain stores and fast-food outlets, the old stone buildings managed to retain their character. There was a timelessness here and an underlying tranquility, no matter the difficulties the centuries had brought.

Mackintosh gave a rough description of the girl and then promised that on Orkney, she shouldn't be too hard to find. "She'd be telling all her friends about her adventure, wouldn't she?"

Later, after leaving the quiet post office for the noise and activity of High Street, Matt took out his cell phone. "Looks like we'll be going to Orkney," he told Thia, watching her as he placed a call. "The weather up there can get pretty rough. And cold."

"Worse than this?" Thia flipped up the collar of her jacket, jammed her hands into pockets. A blustery wind had picked up while they had been inside. Heavy clouds blocked the sun, threatened to soon fill the sky completely.

"Much worse." He held his phone to his ear. "We passed a place—one of those cheap souvenir shops, I'm afraid, but it had sweaters and scarves in the window. If you need warmer clothes, some gloves, maybe...." He shrugged, then, "Cassie. Yes, we're just finishing up." He began to relay what they had learned, and Thia scanned the nearby storefronts. The souvenir shop was easy to spot and, gesturing her intent to Matt, she jogged over to it.

● ○ ●

Inverness Airport, Scotland

Disguised to blend in with the white collar types currently milling about the regional airport's terminal, Cormac watched two sedans approach the jet on the tarmac. The Brigantium had finished its business, whatever it had been. He had arrived too late to have any hope of locating where they'd gone in the city.

Cormac had lost Thia's trail soon after the Brigantium's jet had taken off from Coventry. He had bribed an official there to reveal the destination and then taken a commercial flight to Inverness. That had put him about two hours behind. He had been considering how to proceed when he'd seen the Brigantium pilots rush out of the hangar, a crew of mechanics close at their heels to prepare the plane for another flight. Fairly confident, Cormac had chosen to wait with a sandwich and tea from the airport cafe.

Yet, now, Thia wasn't among the people getting out of the sedans that had pulled up outside the hangar. The oaf wasn't among them either—though his twin was. Speaking with the disheveled man who'd appeared to be in charge when Thia had been escorted from Leticia's house, the young woman pointed to her watch and then back toward the city.

Cormac felt it then, the intense shift in the air, the sudden change in pressure like the front of an impending storm.

An all-too-recognizable storm.

Shaken, he backed away from the window. The Brigantium had sensed the danger as well, its people gathering together in obvious concern, no doubt trying to predict how the threat would manifest and from which direction. They needn't bother. There could be no predicting Idris Cathmor.

Dread settled cold and leaden in Cormac's gut as he ducked behind a pillar, shifted his disguise to one of a security worker.

"*Athair,*" he said quietly, attempting to open a line of communication. "What is it you do here?"

No answer.

Cormac pushed through an authorized-personnel-only exit at the side of the terminal. Rain-flecked wind shoved hard, whipped through his hair, tugged at his open jacket. Angry black clouds converged overhead. He spied the rental car lot and ran for it.

He hadn't been able to figure out how—or why—Thia had

come to be in Idris's chamber last night. *Damnad.* For all he knew, she could be there again. Now. While Cormac had been foolishly watching the plane.

The rain increased, steadily building to a deluge as he ran. Thunder rumbled. An attack was imminent and he wanted no part of it. He darted through an opening in the lot's chain-link fence. Where he would go, how he could locate Thia—presuming Idris didn't already have her—he didn't know. Icy rain soaked his clothes, plastered them to his body.

He opened the door of a nondescript economy car, slid behind the wheel. A simple spell started the engine. No one bothered him when he sped out of the lot. The employees, sensibly, had all taken shelter from the storm.

Lightning crackled, striking a metal rod on the terminal's roof, and Cormac hoped the people inside had sense enough to keep well away from the windows. As he pulled onto the main road to the city, he felt the first glimmer of the attack, the first slip of the power's leash. Rain beat down, coating the windscreen despite the frantic swipes of the blades.

"Run," he murmured, sending the thought out. Not that it would do any good.

● ○ ●

There was a fire at the airport. Thia didn't want to believe her eyes, but there was no denying it. Even in the sheeting rain, thick smoke billowed.

"It looks like it's coming from near the—"A siren wailed some distance behind, building to a scream, and Matt pulled the car over to the side of the two-lane road. Soon a fire engine zoomed past, its wake buffeting their much smaller vehicle.

As the sound lessened, Thia heard beeping. Matt grabbed his phone, took the call. "Cassie," he said, "Cassie, slow down. What's—" His face lost all color. "No," he said. And a moment later, again. "No."

Thia watched the fire engine pull into the airport drive. The smoke roiled upward, dark and ominous, like a rippling tower thrust into the storm. Lightning snaked across the sky. She felt sick. What was it Madame Demetka had said about that card, the one with the tower? A getting rid of things. Cleaning house.

"How many?" Matt asked, barely audible over the raging storm. "All but—you're sure? Cass, are you sure?"

Thia sat forward, trying to see more of the airport than was possible given the distance. Flames reflected on the wet surroundings, but she couldn't locate their source. The engine turned, went out of view behind the terminal.

"Yes," Matt said dully. "I understand."

The shrill sounds of more sirens had Thia twisting to look through the rear window. Police cars—a lot of them—were headed their way, speeding toward what she suspected was a disaster.

"Take care," Matt told his sister and disconnected the call. He set down the phone, rubbed a hand over his face.

Thia watched the line of police cars race down the airport's drive.

"There's been an attack," Matt told her.

The smoke plume lightened, gray mixed with white. Smoke and steam. They were getting the fire out.

He cleared his throat, set his hands on the wheel. "We can't go there. It's not safe and there would be questions from the authorities. Too many questions. We can't afford a delay."

When he didn't continue, didn't even move, Thia asked the unavoidable. "What happened?"

He closed his eyes, pressed his lips together in a visible struggle for control. "Cormac," he said a moment later. "He took out the plane somehow. Cassie said it looked like lightning but wasn't. Then he went after the survivors."

"My God."

"Eben has been taken to hospital along with Tremayne—the

man who drove last night," he explained, as if Thia wouldn't know. "Cassie managed to escape into the terminal. She says she's only a little banged up. She's talking to police." He took a shaky breath, blew it out. "There were no other survivors. Two airport mechanics were killed in the explosion."

Thia heard him, vaguely. Moments from the breakfast, the ride to the plane, the arrival at Inverness, played in her head like a badly edited film. Witnessed moments of conversation. Smiles and quiet laughter. It seemed impossible that most of those voices, those lives were gone. She couldn't believe it... or that she had been so wrong about Cormac. It horrified her anew how charmed she had been by him. How irresistible she had found him. *I'm here to help.* Pleasure and longing. Bloody hands. Lies, told *for* her, told *to* her, all intermixed.

"Was Cormac—" Her throat closed unexpectedly. Killed, she had meant to say. *No other survivors.*

"Caught? No. He got away."

Thia rode out a roller coaster of emotion. Sorrow's steep plummet. Relief's quick rise. Self-disgust's stomach-churning drop. No matter what she knew of Cormac, she had trouble making her heart understand that he was not a person she should care about. He deserved hatred, or at least loathing. Nothing more.

"Cassie credits Tremayne with saving her life. For shielding her from what would have been a lethal strike." Matt rested his head on the steering wheel. "He's critical. Chances aren't good. Bloody awful, in fact."

"God." Thia thought of the confident, penetrating gaze that had met hers so often in the rear-view mirror. And Cassie. Poor Cassie. There had been something between the two of them. She must be going through hell, having to answer questions, to relive everything while the man she cared about was fighting for his life and not expected to survive.

So many dead. So many, and no time to mourn. Roughly, Thia wiped at the tracks tears had made on her cheeks, then pressed the heels of her hands against her eyes to block the rest. Later. She would let them all flow later. For those killed today. For Lettie. Thia pulled her hands away, dried them on her pant legs. "What do we do now?"

"We press on." Matt's eyes were moist, but determination hardened the line of his jaw. "Cassie has been in contact with Arthur. You and I are to go to our lodge in Glen Affric. She'll meet us there with reinforcements." He released the parking brake and scanned the road for traffic. "I suspect we'll be on our way to Orkney soon after." Executing a lurching u-turn, he headed the car back toward Inverness.

"The lodge is another safe house?"

"A very remote one, yes." Matt was driving fast. Too fast, considering the wet conditions. The rain was teeming down, making certain parts more river than road.

Maybe the speed was necessary, Thia thought, but when she checked the mirrors she saw only empty road. People under stress made poor drivers. She was about to suggest he slow down when he said, "The lodge is in the highlands. It's used more often these days as a retreat—a place of contemplation and study. But it works as a refuge as well. Highly secured." His hands clenched and unclenched on the wheel.

"It must be hard, leaving like this," she said.

"Especially leaving Cassie." He increased the wiper setting. "But she'll be all right. Security personnel are already on their way."

"Good. That's good," Thia said, then frowned. "Wouldn't it be better for us to wait for them as well?"

"Too conspicuous. Right now, we're hoping Cormac doesn't know where you are. The sooner we get you to the lodge, the better."

"Oh. Sure." She supposed that made sense. And accounted for the speed of his driving.

"We should be fine if we keep a low profile," he said. "No

more phone calls, no magic. Nothing that might be detected or traced."

"How far away is it?"

"An hour...maybe two in this weather. Into the mountains to the West."

No cars ahead on the road. She re-checked the side mirror. No cars behind. "Can you sense when Cormac is near?"

Matt's brows furrowed. "If he were manipulating energy—in other words, using magic—I would. It might depend on the intensity, but I think I can give fair warning if he or anyone else gets close."

"So if he disguised himself, you'd know him anyway?"

"I'd know someone was using a glamour, yes. I might not be certain it was him unless I saw his eyes. Cormac can't disguise them no matter what glamour he uses." Matt chuckled. "Not when he's a raven, either. Or so the rumor goes. No one has ever seen it."

"I'm sorry—raven?"

He shot her a look of surprise. "Did no one mention that? On top of being able to alter his appearance with spellcraft, he can take the form of a raven."

Right. Okay. Thia shut her eyes, rubbed both hands down her face. Cormac could turn into a raven. And no one had thought to mention that before now.

Well, of course they hadn't. She would have thought they were insane. She might still, once the greater shock of every-thing else wore off. Assuming it ever did.

"Except his eyes," she said, opening her own. She lowered her hands to her lap.

"Right—although, naturally, the shape and size transforms. It's only the color that doesn't."

Thia didn't understand how he could sound so blasé. A *bird*. Cormac could turn himself into a bird.

"You haven't sensed anything so far?" she asked a moment

later. Matt didn't appear too concerned about the threat of pursuit. He drove fast, yes; but unlike Thia, he hardly checked the mirrors.

"No. Nothing at all." He angled the car onto a ramp marked for the A96. What it led to resembled a smaller U. S. freeway: double lanes in both directions with a central cement divide. There was a fair amount of traffic which Matt, accelerating further, skillfully wove around.

Thia tried to get a look at the drivers as they passed, but even when she managed to catch a glimpse it didn't help. She couldn't see their eyes well enough at all.

"Relax," Matt told her, noticing. "Remember, the pendants can sense imminent threats."

She had forgotten again—probably because she hadn't had much luck with it on that front. "So...the others knew something was about to happen?"

"Yes. But couldn't do a thing about it."

"Not exactly a reason for me to relax."

He let out a quiet breath. "I suppose not."

They zipped through a traffic circle, took an offshoot that would avoid the city center. The rain had subsided to a tame drizzle, patches of clear sky visible in the distance.

Thia touched her pendant. The metal was merely warm—heated by her skin, not in response to danger. "Did you ask Cassie about hers? Did it react before the attack in the alley?"

Matt changed lanes to avoid cars slowed for an upcoming exit. "I did, yes. She said it had but things happened too fast."

"It *was* fast, that's for sure." Fast and terrifying. The cloaked men had appeared, Cassie had collapsed, and...hold on. Matt had said that he and Cassie could sense each other's strong emotions. She had just experienced a hugely traumatic event. Yet Matt hadn't expressed any alarm until he, like Thia, had seen the smoke.

What did that matter, Thia argued with herself. People had

died, another was most likely dying. How a purported psychic connection between twins did or didn't work was a ridiculous mental distraction.

"What will the victims' families be told?" Thia asked quietly. Families, like Lettie's, that might not know what their loved ones did for the Brigantium.

"It depends," Matt said after a time, no doubt aware of the need to tread carefully. "The director will take care of it as he sees fit, I suppose. He might hedge around the facts—a plane crash, for instance, while on assignment for a foundation. I can't imagine the Brigantium has had to deal with something so public and of this magnitude before."

The car drove onto a bridge across the River Ness, and Thia looked down at deep water made choppy by the storm. Had the famous monster swum here on its way in from the sea? Or was Nessie just another bit of make believe—a fabrication made up of misperceived reflections and shadows combined with fear, used to explain the unexplainable. She knew what her answer would have been a few days ago. Now, she wasn't sure.

"What about the mechanics?" Thia asked. "What will *their* families be told? This will make the news. Airport employees, emergency responders, passengers waiting in the terminal— people know this happened. Videos are probably already all over social media."

"Not if Arthur and Beatrice can help it."

They had crossed the bridge. The ancient city of Inverness was behind them; ahead were block after block of modern row houses nearly identical in their absence of character.

"Can they?" Thia asked, incredulous. "Help it, I mean. Can the Brigantium keep something like this quiet?"

"We're unknown to the general public, yes, but not to the government. Members have long advised the Privy Council, Royal Family, and every Prime Minister since Churchill. This will be taken care of."

"Covered up."

"Whatever is best."

"Best for whom?"

"For everyone." Matt switched off the windshield wipers. They had out-driven the rain. "Imagine the chaos if suddenly everyone learned how much of their folklore and nightmares exists. That's why *we* exist. To hold back the chaos."

"I'd rather know the truth."

"You aren't the norm. Trust me. Most people are content with not knowing." He gave her a smile that she supposed was meant to comfort.

It didn't. But she silently conceded he had a point. Would she want to know about dangers she could do nothing against?

What was she saying—she already did, and it was a horrible and untenable situation. So, she needed to make it tenable. She needed to find what she *could* do against the dangers.

"The alley attack was about me, right," she began, "because Cormac believes I know something vital about the relic. Why, then, would he attack the Brigantium at the airport? For all he knew, the relic could have been destroyed with the plane."

"It wasn't though, was it?" Matt darted her a look before he pulled the car into the right lane to pass a truck. Blue sky shone above, not a cloud in sight.

If Thia assured him that the relic was safe, she'd reveal she knew where it was. Anything else would be a lie. She couldn't do that either, so she asked instead of answered: "But how could Cormac have been sure it wouldn't be? Why would he go from wanting the relic to wanting everyone dead?"

Matt appeared to give that some thought before suggesting, "It could have started out as another kidnapping attempt. If he'd managed to learn of our flight plan, he could have gotten there ahead of our plane and observed our arrival. He would have known you went into town with us. If he believes you're in possession of the relic, he could have assumed you'd taken it with you. Then, when he saw the cars return, he initiated the attack—but didn't realize that ours was not among them."

"We would have been," Thia said, chilled. "I made us late."

"Thank goodness for tartan scarves and ill-fitting gloves."

Thia's intended quick stop in the souvenir store had taken longer than expected. The scarf had been easy. She had asked the clerk for the warmest one, he had asked her name, and within moments handed her a wool scarf in a red and green tartan—the Clan MacDonald, he'd told her. *Her* clan. She had been inordinately pleased. The gloves had been the problem, requiring the clerk to search in a newly arrived shipment for the right size.

That had put them fifteen minutes behind schedule.

"To blow up the plane, though," Thia said, still bewildered by the act. "Cassie said that happened first. That's seriously over the top for a kidnapping."

"A show of force. Or punishment for our keeping you from him." Matt shrugged. "He might've done it simply because he could. For all we know, he may consider killing a sport."

Thia felt sick. "He's done a lot of it?"

"Well...not that anyone can prove. Someone like him has ways of concealing his crimes. There's no evidence of Leticia's murder, after all."

Thia felt as if she were looking through a prism: the world was clear but skewed, its subjects misshapen and displaced. Pieces didn't fit as they should.

She had felt Cormac's anger. She had been victimized by his lies and manipulations. She knew he was someone who was capable of despicable, terrifying things. Yet her heart—

Thia gritted her teeth and stared blindly out at the passing countryside. Her heart was wrong, that's all.

CHAPTER 20

Glen Affric, Scotland
31 October

"It's not what I pictured," Thia told Matt as their car neared the lodge. Twice as long as its two-storeyed height, the multi-gabled building was at least three times the size of the cabin in the woods her imagination had conjured.

Unaccountably uneasy, she studied the surrounding pines. "I got that part right, anyway."

"There's a lake as well." Matt shut off the engine and flashed a smile. "Although here they call it a loch. It isn't far. You can see the trail." He pointed to where a gravel path cut across a brown, scraggly lawn to enter the trees.

After the talk of cover-ups and misinformation, she and he hadn't spoken much aside from casual remarks: an interesting sight or piece of historical trivia, the distance left to go. It had not been uncomfortable, but Thia longed for some time to herself. A walk through woods to a lake—loch—would have been a perfect opportunity...but not these woods or this loch. Not while she was under such threat. People had died today. Cormac had killed them.

Matt knocked on her window, startling her. She hadn't realized he had gotten out of the car.

"Sorry," she said. She stepped outside, the sack of gloves and scarf clutched to her chest, and shivered. It was even colder than it looked. The trees moaned, wind giving voice to their waving branches. Was it in welcome or warning?

The main door was not far, thankfully; Thia and Matt soon stood inside a dark, low-ceilinged anteroom. Behind its large counter, a middle-aged man with a pinched expression folded and set aside his newspaper before looking up to greet them with a curt nod. His hair had been ruthlessly slicked back, the color impossible to determine beneath an oily sheen. His brows were dark lines above light, unfriendly eyes.

Thia took a rare, instant dislike but made sure to keep her own expression pleasantly neutral.

"We're expected," Matt told him as they approached.

"Aye," the man said in a reedy voice. His hand whipped out to strike a bell on the counter. The shrill sourness of the note made Thia wince.

A door next to the stairs creaked open, and a tiny slip of a girl scurried out to stand by the newel post. She kept her head down, almost as if she were hiding. Or painfully shy.

"Clara will show you to your rooms," the man said.

The girl in question bobbed a curtsy, her hands clenched on the cotton of her apron, before starting up the stairs.

"After you," Matt told Thia, and she then moved to follow Clara. He trailed behind, jingling two keys.

"Bath and toilet are there," Clara said when they reached the landing.

No particular indication had accompanied the direction, so Thia had to look around, finally picking one narrow door out from the rest by its lack of a posted number.

Showing remarkable similarity to the man downstairs, Clara shot her a glare. "There's only the one. We're not fancy up here."

Thia felt the ends of her temper fray.

"Your room is at the end," she told Thia from halfway down the hall, and then gave Matt a pink-cheeked smile. "Yours is right here, sir."

Thia didn't wait around for whatever might come next.

It wasn't until her hand was on the knob of her room's door that she remembered her luggage had been on the plane. She now had nothing beyond what she wore or carried. Thinking to go talk to Matt, she turned around. He stood right behind her. She squeaked in surprise, stepped back to bang into the closed door.

"Sorry," he said but fought a smile. He held out a key. "You'll need this."

"Thanks." Thia took it, shifted the souvenir store's paper sack tucked beneath her arm. "I need to replace my clothes."

It took Matt a moment to comprehend. His smile vanished. "Our luggage. Goodness. I hadn't thought. Not with...well." He blew out a breath. "Not with everything."

"It's not important," she said, feeling guilty for thinking of personal comfort at such a time. "Maybe tomorrow in Orkney I could—"

"No, no. I'll tell Cassie. She'll take care of it."

Clothes shopping seemed a particularly awful thing to ask of a woman who had just endured a horrific tragedy.

"Not personally," Matt said, accurately reading Thia's face. "Cassie will get someone else to do it. That's what I meant."

"They'll know my size?"

"And what to replace. We have a list from when your—" He looked distinctly uncomfortable.

Right. "From when my luggage was searched. I assumed it would be." Thia opened the door, stepped into the room she had been assigned. It wouldn't win any decorating awards, but its single window offered a nice enough view. She went over to it.

The pines continued to moan, the dance of their branches even more dramatic than before. The dark water of the loch churned while a bank of clouds, lower and markedly denser than those already overhead, rolled into the squat valley. The top half of the left-side mountain was already obscured.

"I *am* sorry, Thia," Matt said from the doorway. "We didn't know you yet. Eben felt it a necessary precaution."

She couldn't take her gaze off the clouds. "If it's all right, I could really use some time to myself. I'm very tired," she added by way of explanation. A half-truth.

"Of course." Matt's voice was soft with understanding. "I'll be in my room should you need anything. And, if you like, the land line in the lobby should be safe to use."

"Oh, that's great. Thanks." But who could she call? Not her family. Not her friends, either. They'd all know something was wrong, and what could she say then? Nothing that wouldn't increase their worry and even put them in danger.

No. Much as Thia desperately wanted to, she couldn't call anyone.

"Thank you, Matt. For everything," she managed through the press of tears. She waited until she heard the door close before turning from the window. Sorrow crested like a wave. She flung herself onto the bed and buried her face in a pillow to muffle the sounds. Finally, she allowed herself to weep.

● ○ ●

What was the old man up to? Driving up the mountainside's rutted track, Cormac continued to replay events in his mind. And continued to fall well short of understanding. An attack such as that was tantamount to a declaration of war. Such a violent, public assault—at an airport, for Morrigan's sake— risked world-wide *and* Otherworld-wide attention. Idris had to understand that. He was isolated, not stupid.

Never stupid.

Smartphones were ubiquitous. Video of the aftermath and possibly the event itself would be all over the internet before morning. If it was found to be anything other than the freak lightning strike it appeared to be, defense agencies would be all over it. So would occult groups, dabblers, fanatics—*ifrinn*. It would be easier to list who wouldn't get involved.

Sweat trickled down Cormac's back to pool at the base of his spine. He had been running on fear since Idris's power had crashed down like floodwater through a burst dam. A single strike had destroyed the Brigantium's plane along with those unlucky enough to have been nearby.

It had also effectively destroyed Cormac's hopes—the ones he had tried so hard not to have.

He had misjudged everything with Idris.

Approaching another switchback, he downshifted, jammed the resistant lever into the slot. The car bucked in grinding protest.

"Don't tempt me," he muttered, releasing the clutch.

The motor settled into what he had come to know as its usual, teeth-rattling rhythm.

He rounded the curve, caught sight of the glen below. What looked to be an old hunting lodge sat near the northern end of a narrow loch. The storm he had tracked from Inverness—Idris's storm—stretched over the entire landscape.

● ○ ●

Thia exited the bathroom to find Matt coming up the stairs. She was less of a mess than she had been when she went in, but her eyes were still puffy from her crying jag.

If he noticed, he didn't comment. "I was just coming to get you. Cassie's here, and we've had some food prepared. I don't know about you, but I'm starving."

"I could eat," Thia said, but felt wrung out and not the least bit hungry. She walked beside Matt down the stairs. "How is she?"

"She's coping," he said after a moment. "It's been...difficult. For everyone, but for her especially. She won't admit it, but

I can tell."

At the base of the stairs, he directed her to a door across the lobby. The pinch-faced man was nowhere to be seen. Neither was Clara. Or anyone else, for that matter. The lodge was too quiet; felt too empty. Matt opened a door to reveal a large sitting room.

Thia preceded him inside. Numerous sofas and chairs were arranged to break the large space into smaller clusters more suited to conversation. Cassie sat in one that faced a smoke-stained hearth where flames eagerly consumed blocks of peat.

Thia hurried to her. "Cassie," she said and, bending, gave a gentle hug. "I'm so sorry."

"Thank you, Thia." She held herself stiffly, as if she took no comfort from the embrace, so Thia pulled away, sat on the adjacent sofa. The low table before it was laden with plates of finger sandwiches. To the left of Cassie's armchair, nearest the fire, was a serving cart laden with a large, dented urn and other tea supplies.

"It has been a difficult time. For so many of us," Cassie said, an echo of her brother's earlier words. "Eben was awake when I left, so at least there's that."

Matt shut and—if Thia wasn't mistaken—locked the door.

"He insisted that he be allowed to join us," Cassie went on, "but the hospital would prefer he remain under observation. I'm afraid Max is still critical. They've induced a coma." Her voice broke and she looked away, into the fire. "No one holds much hope." Cassie held a cup under the urn's spigot.

"I'm sorry," Thia said again, wishing she had more words. Better words.

Matt seated himself beside her on the sofa. "Their being so far from London is an additional complication." He took the tea Cassie offered. Sipped. "Lovely. Thank you, Cass."

"I'm told a team will be with them in a few hours," Cassie said. "They had to land in Aberdeen. Thia?" She held out a cup and saucer.

"Thank you." Not thirsty, Thia took it anyway.

"Cass means a team of healers," Matt explained. "They've been permitted to assist the hospital staff—within limits. No candles or incense in ICU. And no loud chanting, of course." He smiled wryly.

Thia supposed the attempt to lighten the mood was well intentioned, but it fell flat. She nudged a serving plate a few inches to the right, set down her unwanted tea.

Metal squeaked as Cassie used a set of tongs to serve herself from the array of sandwiches. Slick, gelatinous filling oozed from between slices of mangled white bread. "There's been a change of plan," she said.

Thia's apprehension spiked. "We're not going to Orkney?"

"Oh, no—of course we're going there." Cassie's smile was bright as she handed Thia the tongs. "Never fear about that."

"We'll be going tonight," Matt said around a bite of sandwich. "Cover of darkness."

The thought of more travel so soon hurt. Even Thia's bones were exhausted. "What about the reinforcements you talked about?" she asked, unable to hide her dismay. "The security personnel. We should wait for them, shouldn't we?"

"They'll meet us in Orkney," Cassie replied, relaxing back in her chair. "We'll be fine until then. As long as we maintain a low profile."

"You don't have to come with us," Matt said gently. "It's safe enough here."

Strangely—or not so strangely, since Thia's only company would be pinch-faced man and Clara—that thought appealed even less. "What about the drive? Is it safe for us to be on the road?"

"Absolutely," Matt said, "or we wouldn't consider it. Cormac has no way of knowing where we are or where we're going."

Thia put the tongs down unused. She needed to come clean.

People had been hurt—killed over the Stone. Would they be alive if she had been honest from the start? She could never know. Truthfully, she didn't want to. But if there was even the slightest chance she could prevent more deaths, shouldn't she take it?

Lettie, forgive me.

"Thia?" Matt laid his hand on her knee. "Are you all right?"

She took a deep breath around the lump of indecision in her throat, then said in a rush, "I have the relic. I'm sorry. I'm so sorry. I've had it all this time. Lettie sent it to me. She called it the Stone of Shadows."

Silence.

Then, "We thought as much," the twins chorused.

"You did?" Thia looked from one to the other. "Was it so obvious?"

Cassie laughed, which didn't help matters any, while Matt shook his head with an unconvincing, "No, no. Not at all."

Thia felt so humiliatingly naïve.

"It seemed likely, dear. That's all," Cassie said, and poured herself another cup of tea.

"You could have asked for it. Demanded it."

Matt put down his emptied plate. "Would you have given it over willingly?"

"No."

"Would you do so now?" Cassie's brown eyes were alight. An illusion, of course, caused by the particular angle of her head to the flames.

"It's not mine to give." That, at least, was something Thia knew with utter certainty. "Lettie entrusted it to me. Until I have reason to think she was wrong, I have to do as she asked. If I don't, I'd be failing her. I'd be failing myself."

The twins exchanged a perplexed glance and then, "Perhaps she was right," Cassie said with a graceful sweep of her hand.

"Sorry?"

"What were Leticia's reasons for sending it to you? Perhaps she was right." Cassie shrugged. "Or perhaps she was wrong. If you tell us, we can help you decide."

"I don't—I can't say." Thia looked from one sibling to the other. "She didn't explain."

Matt leaned toward her, his eyes alight as well. "May we see it?"

Thia leaned back. Away. And lied. "I don't have it. Not on me. But it's in a safe place."

"Here in the lodge?"

"Yes." She shifted uncomfortably.

"The Stone of Shadows, you said Leticia called it?" Cassie asked, leaning in like her brother. "What *is* it, precisely? What does it look like?"

After a slight hesitation, Thia described the Stone.

"A crystal orb," Matt said after she finished. "Quartz, by the sound of it. We should have known, Cass."

"Why?" Thia asked Matt while his sister, oddly abstracted, turned to look at the fire. "Why should you have thought anything in particular?"

"Quartz is an ideal medium, capable of holding a great deal of energy." He leaned back, grinning. "I can't wait to examine it. What a thrill."

Thia considered her experience with it. The feeling when she had touched the smooth surface, watched the glow and shift within. *Thrill.* Yes, that was one word for it.

"Well." Cassie again held out the serving tongs. "Eat up. We have a long drive ahead."

● ○ ●

His mind reeling, Cormac stumbled back against the side of the car he had parked on the mountain road. The particular shimmer of color in the wards around the lodge below clearly associated them with the Brigantium. The streaks of black, like inky fingerprints, just as clearly associated the wards with Idris.

What need did he have of Cormac if he already had *this?*

Was Cormac merely some sort of fallback?

Was his involvement nothing more than a loyalty test? If so, he had failed miserably. Several times over.

Cormac slid down to the gravel, rested his arms against his bent knees. His head tipped back against the car door. The price of failure in such a test would be...great. He closed his eyes on a heavy sigh, shut out the sight of the moving clouds above.

Was that how Thia had come to be in Idris's chamber last night? Idris had planned it all along? After she had gone, the old man had been vicious but silent, and Cormac had wrongly taken the latter to mean his lie had been believed.

Since the attack in the alley, Cormac had known that his father had people after Thia, and he had assumed they were somehow responsible for her arrival—and her departure. But he hadn't understood the scope of what that meant.

There was nothing in this for him anymore.

He sprang to his feet, prepared to flee to the one place of safety (albeit temporary) in order to think, to consider what options he might possibly have.

Home.

Yet he hesitated, looked up at the impending storm. Idris had let Cormac go last night, even knowing he had lied. And now, although his power was all around, Idris did nothing. It was if he still expected Cormac to fetch the relic.

Nothing made sense.

Not even Cormac's own mind.

Even here, instead of focusing on his survival, his thoughts strayed to Thia. The soft eagerness of her lips, the feel of her body against his. He had seen much of that body last night, but not enough. Not nearly enough for what he wanted.

Needed.

With a groan, Cormac forced his mind to clear. It was the enthrallment, he knew, muddying his usually crystalline sense of self-preservation.

At the sound of a car, he ran to the edge of the road. Below, the gray sedan Thia had arrived in was pulling away from the building, heading toward the drive that led to the main road. On the move so soon? He opened his car door, slid onto the seat as he triggered the ignition, then released the brake with a snap of his fingers.

With the cold engine threatening to stall, he popped clutch and stomped on the gas. The car shot forward, bucking and sputtering in a flurry of gravel.

CHAPTER 21

Thia braced herself against the sudden lurch when Matt changed lanes to pass a bus that had slowed to a crawl on the rural road. For the past three hours, they had been among a very few who dared to skirt the eastern edge of Scotland in the midst of a gale. The punishing rain had turned the car's roof into a metal drum, making conversation almost impossible; but in an effort to ease her nerves, Thia tried anyway.

"Is that the North Sea?" Frothy waves, barely visible even with the high-beams, crashed against jagged rocks that were much too close for comfort.

"Hm?" Cassie, in the front passenger seat, sounded relaxed to the point of disinterest. "Oh, I suppose it is, yes."

"How much farther do we need to go?"

"Another two hours yet, I'm afraid." Matt flicked the wipers onto a manic setting. Rainwater continued to flood the glass.

"You're sure?" Cassie no longer sounded disinterested. "Last time it only took—"

"It's a smaller ship than the ferries," Matt interjected. "Plus there's the weather."

"That's cutting things close, Matthew."

As usual, Thia felt out of the loop. "Are we expected

somewhere?" she asked, but was drowned out by the storm and Matt's curt, "I can't control storms, Cass, as you very well know. If *you* can, please have at it." Fighting a hard gust of wind, he angled the car back into the left lane.

"Do you think *he* is?"

"It's late October in Scotland," Matt said as if the question were not extremely odd. "Sometimes a storm is just a storm."

"Regardless, we'll need to lose him soon."

"Someone's following us?" Thia asked, alarmed. She twisted to look out the rear window. Sure enough, headlights wobbled some distance behind, their car's driver having as difficult a time as Matt was to stay in the lane. The bus was nowhere in sight.

"For the past hour," Cassie said with amazing unconcern.

Thia, on the other hand, felt a claustrophobic sort of panic. There were no turnouts, no side roads to take. Nothing but the ocean below on the right and towering cliff to the left. "Is it Cormac?"

"I can't tell," Cassie said. "How far to the harbor, Matt?"

"Eight miles. Roughly," he said through gritted teeth as the car shimmied along a curve.

"Right." Cassie's tone held an odd note of excitement. "No time like the present." She began a soft, sibilant chant.

"Remember that we need him alive," Matt said, taking the car around another sharp curve. "If it is him."

Thia's pulse raced. What were they thinking to do, attack? How? And with what chance of success? Cormac had blown up an *airplane*. What was a car in scale to that? "Can't we just try to outrun him and—"

"Quiet," Cassie snapped. "I need to concentrate."

Without warning, the air pressure changed. It was like being squeezed in a vise. A shrill whistle filled Thia's ears, like that of a boiler about to blow. She thought she might pass out.

A thunderous clap rocked the car and the pressure abruptly

lessened. The internal whistle cut off, replaced by an external roar. Not wind. Not ocean. Cassie turned to look back. Thia did the same, watched in awed disbelief as a great crack sliced through the road behind them, widening as asphalt and rock crumbled into a rapidly expanding trench.

The beams of the other car's headlights became visible as it rounded the blind curve, and fear kicked Thia hard in the chest.

"That ought to do it." Cassie sounded entirely pleased.

Matt took them through another tight turn, curving inland. Sheer rock blocked Thia's view to the rear.

Yet she maintained watch, straining to see even a glimmer of headlights in the darkness. There was only the red sheen of their own car's taillights reflected on rain-streaked glass.

● ○ ●

"Son of an Unseelie bitch."

Cormac swerved hard to avoid the massive gap in the road and slammed on the brakes. The car hit the guard rail, bending metal and knocking over a post before coming to a stop. The front wheels had left the tarmac; they rested now, somewhat precariously, on loose gravel and the now-crumpled guard rail. A wave crashed on rocks not far beyond. Foamy spray mixed with the rain sheeting across the windscreen.

Thankfully, Cormac hadn't been driving faster. He dropped back against the seat, let his hands unclench and slide down the wheel. The car was nearly perpendicular to the road. A foot or so more and he would be in the ocean. He put the car in park, set the emergency brake, but left the engine running.

So, they had known he was following them. And they had cut him off completely. This was the only road north through this uninhabited region. Either he'd have to backtrack, take a circuitous route and no doubt end up losing them completely, or he would have to change his mode of transport.

Flying was out, thanks to the bone-snapping wind.

Cormac swore again, softer this time, and reached for his phone. To think he had believed he wouldn't have to look at Holpnick's damned leyline map for a good, long time.

Another of so many ways he had been wrong lately.

His course plotted, he killed the car's engine. The wipers froze halfway through their arc. He left the lights on to give the bus fair warning and then, shoving open the door, stepped out into the icy-cold wet.

"Orkney, for fuckssake." Again, Orkney.

His teeth chattered. Rain had already found its way inside his coat. The leyline access point was only a few miles inland, but it would feel like twenty by the time he got there.

He began to run.

● ○ ●

Raigmore Hospital
Inverness, Scotland

The air affected Quentin the most, with its pervasive mix of cleaning chemicals and fear. Sound came a close second. The maddening, monotonous humming and clacking and beeping of lives balanced on a keen technological edge. He blotted at the sweat beading on his upper lip with the silk handkerchief from his jacket pocket, then replaced the cloth.

The slick, treacherous flooring universal to hospitals forced him to slow his pace, his cane both hindrance and resented help. He glanced at the nurse's station. The two women there were too intent on their tasks to pay him notice. He supposed they had become used to people coming and going from Bed Seven.

He stepped into the confined "room" and then turned back immediately to pull the curtain across the entrance and cast a quick spell. There could be no disruptions, or else Maxwell Tremayne wouldn't be the only one in trouble.

Relaxing his posture, Quentin limped to the bed. With no one to witness, there was no need for him to force his body to work smoothly. The man occupying the bed lacked the ability to process Quentin's graceless lurching and ungainly collapse onto the bedside chair.

The ventilator clacked and, with a soft hiss, forced a stream of air through the tube jutting from the inert man's mouth. Strips of tape held it in place. Wires and tubing were everywhere. Trailing down from under the gauze that swathed his head. Attached to a port inserted in his lower arm. Emerging from beneath the thin sheet used to cover him from toes to chest, the top of which was folded down in a precise line. No one would believe this man was merely asleep. No one slept this neatly.

Quentin tugged the leather glove from his right hand and stuffed it into his pocket. So far, he hadn't felt a thing from Tremayne. Nor, thankfully, anything from the other patients in the ward. He lowered his guard a little more.

Still nothing.

"Maxwell," he chided. "You're quite far, aren't you?"

Unsurprisingly, the security agent did not respond. But as Quentin well knew, that didn't mean the man could not hear or comprehend. He could be lying there, unable to move or speak, while the sounds of the machines slowly drove him mad and no one bothered to visit except to make demands. *Explain yourself. Wake, damn you. Do you have any idea what you've done?*

Not now. Quentin closed his eyes, blocked the sounds of the room as best he could. He was here for Tremayne's memories, not his own.

He took a deep, steadying breath and, eyes open, clasped Tremayne's arm.

"Pardon the intrusion," he said, and the world went black.

● ○ ●

John O'Groats, Scotland

Bracing herself against the relentless wind, Thia watched the ship—some sort of commercial fishing vessel—bob wildly at its moorings. Industrial lights mounted on an array of masts and cross-poles lit the small harbor bright as day. Two jetties of rough-hewn stones had been laid out like two sides of a triangle with the shore as the base. Only a narrow opening at the apex allowed access to the sea. Waves that failed to enter crashed angrily, spraying high in the air.

She wondered if Cormac had seen the break in the road in time.

Matt and Cassie were speaking with the captain down at the gangway. Even if Thia were closer, she doubted she'd be able to hear the discussion over the fall of rain on the raised hood of her borrowed slicker.

The captain shook his head, gestured emphatically toward the turbulent sea. Was he refusing to sail? Thia felt a measure of hopeful relief at the thought. She'd seen A Perfect Storm. She'd rather not experience it.

Clearly furious, Cassie yelled something, waving her arms, and Matt reached into his jacket. Thia took an apprehensive step back, but all he brought out was a thick stack of money. Ah. Of course. What else had she thought he might do?

The captain didn't look at all happy but he snatched up the cash quickly enough. Tucking it away in his waterproof coat, he stomped down the gangway. Immediately, men began to undo the ropes holding the ship at the dock.

"Thia! We're all set," Cassie shouted above the clanking of chains, the groan of metal against rubber bumpers.

Thia forced a smile. Forced herself to move. Despite the slicker's hood, rain pelted her face, ran into her eyes as she followed the twins up the swaying, slippery ramp to the ship. She had to rely on the ropes on either side for balance and couldn't help thinking this whole thing was a mistake. They should wait until the storm cleared. Or at least until the sun came up.

The engine sputtered and rattled to life as she stumbled the final steps to the deck. Matt reached out, took a steadying hold of her elbow.

"Thanks," she said, embarrassed. "And we haven't even left the dock."

He grinned. "You'll be all right. There's a lounge that's quite nice, considering. You can spend the whole time there, if you like." He began guiding her across the pitching deck.

"It's a North Sea trawler," Cassie said, close behind. "The captain assures us they go out in conditions like this all the time."

Given the obvious reluctance she'd witnessed, Thia doubted the captain had said any such thing.

The vibration of the deck increased and the ship's up and down motion took on a forward aspect. They were heading out.

Matt led Thia to the large metal hatch that served as the lounge's door. She helped him open it against the wind, then stepped over the raised threshold. The room was small, utilitarian, and almost entirely and quite nauseatingly beige. Beige paint, beige linoleum. A beige kitchenette took up one side while a beige table with beige padded seats filled the other. Anything that might move was bolted down. There were no windows.

Thia's anxiety level skyrocketed. And then the ship *really* began to move. She grabbed hold of one of the seat-backs as the rocking, rolling nightmare she had anticipated began.

"Make yourself comfortable," Matt said, looking in from the deck. He had to be joking. "Cassie and I are going to set up some protection around the ship. There should be some refreshments in the kitchen there."

He closed the door.

Thia dropped onto the seat she had been holding and willed herself not to be affected by the room's smell: an unfortunate mix of gasoline, cigarette smoke, and scorched grease. Bacon, she suspected. Queasy, she closed her eyes, breathed through her mouth.

Had Cormac stopped his car in time? She shouldn't care—should maybe even look on his death as justice for the lives he had taken.

But she worried.

● ○ ●

Near Stenness, Orkney

Cormac dropped out of the leyline into a muddle of fog and dark. His feet skidded wildly, the surface beneath them unexpectedly slick. Disorientation made him overcompensate and he landed flat on his face in muddy grass.

With something between a groan and a sigh, he raised his head, wiped silt from his mouth with the back of his hand.

Druid Fog surrounded him, thick and growing thicker still. It emanated from a point some distance ahead. He vaguely made out the outline of a nearby megalith—the Watchstone, official marker of the ancient Meginland crossroads. With that, even as the magical fog attempted to muddle his sense of direction, he knew Maes Howe lay just over a mile to the right, with the Stones of Stenness only yards distant.

He got to his feet. That way there, toward the source of the fog, lay the Ring of Brodgar. He made his way to the paved road on the north side of the Watchstone.

As he walked, lapping waves could be heard to his right and left; the presence of a loch on either side of the road adding to the directional confusion. He could assume the Druid Fog would mess with his phone's GPS; otherwise he would have gladly used it. Instead, he did his best to keep his mind fixed on the road itself. He knew from times before that it passed near the Ring. Simply putting one foot before the other, no matter how the fog's spell might tempt him to stray, gave him the best chance of getting there.

Time was something else the fog distorted. What felt like a few minutes could be hours in reality—while the reverse was also true. What felt like hours might be minutes.

During whatever the time was, he encountered no one else. The island population was sparse, and the night was, after all, Halloween. The absence of cars on the road wasn't necessarily Idris's doing, but it couldn't be ruled out.

Gradually the fog grew brighter, illuminated by something within, ahead. Cormac, aided by his Sight, could discern the rough silhouettes of people moving about, but couldn't gauge the distance. He slowed, left the road for the turf beside it so as to mute his steps. The fog thinned abruptly and he dropped to a crouch in the roadside ditch. Icy water shot through the lacing of his boots, soaking his feet in an instant.

That, unfortunately, was the least of his problems.

Men and women in black robes were unloading crates from the rear of a parked truck and then carrying them along a path leading away from the road. The fog quickly swallowed them, but Cormac had no doubt where that path led. Or to whom.

Idris's presence was like the dull, throbbing pain of a septic wound: undeniable and, if left unchecked, deadly.

Idris Cathmor, *here.* Along with a number of his followers and, given the crates, enough paraphernalia to perform the most complex of his pick of rituals. It didn't bode at all well for Thia.

It didn't bode well for anyone.

Keeping close watch on the activity at the truck, Cormac made a series of brief phone calls in order to get the number he wanted. The man himself picked up after only two rings.

"Who is this? How did you get this number?" Arthur

Barnstable demanded without preamble.

"Never mind that." Cormac kept as close to a whisper as possible. "Idris Cathmor has taken over the Ring of Brodgar. You need to send—"

"This is my private line."

"—people here, armed to the teeth."

"Dammit, who is this? Who gave you this number?"

"Your Miss Phelps," Cormac said. "Eventually." His nerves buzzed as someone with skill sought his identity. He allowed it, to a point, and in the background heard a woman's voice announce his name.

"By Brigid's Spear," Barnstable said. His choice in profanity would have been amusing in different circumstances. "If you did anything to—"

"She'll be fine," Cormac interrupted as static crackled. The connection was tenuous despite his signal-enhancement spell. See if he ever trusted Renaissance Faire merchants again.

"What kind of fool do you take me for?" Barnstable asked.

"A great one, if you don't listen to what—"

"You murdered nineteen of my people. Damn good people, along with Miss McDaniel and two innocent mech—"

"I had nothing to do with that." Cormac felt a sinking in his gut. This was worse than he'd thought. "And Thia McDaniel isn't dead—yet. She *will* be if you don't stop your people from bringing her here."

"What?"

"Tell the people with Thia to turn around. Don't let her get near the islands, let alone the Ring. If Idris can't get the Stone from her—"

"Miss McDaniel was killed at the plane along with everyone else. Killed by *you*. That you believe me stupid enough to fall for your lies is to heap insult upon—"

Cormac ended the call with a growl and barely kept himself

from bashing the phone against a rock. He took a deep breath instead. He should have known the Brigantium wouldn't trust him, but why would they blame him for what happened at the airport? He was almost afraid to imagine.

They thought Thia was dead? And the two people currently with her?

Dread and adrenaline made Cormac's hands unsteady as he scrolled through his phone's contact list for its newest entry.

Would the promise of revenge be enough?

He hadn't anything else to offer. Hell, he probably couldn't even hope to come through on the bargain they had already made.

He located the number only to hesitate under the weight of unexpected guilt. He shoved it off quickly enough. Idris had betrayed him first, after all. Many times over.

One way or another, this would be the last.

CHAPTER 22

Kendra moved the tip of her pen to the next item on her list. "I told Four C to use the rooftop garden if they needed to chant that late again. An apology, along with a gift basket, has been taken to those who might've been disturbed last night." She looked up in time to catch Murphy's curt nod, the one she'd come to take as approval. The world's most communicative boss, he was not.

"Is that all, then?" he asked with a not-so-subtle glance at his watch. They both had a million tasks to complete before sundown—when things would really get hectic. A function in every public room, private events in several of the suites, not to mention the special requirements of countless individual guests.

"A few more." She again consulted her list and then barely repressed a groan. She had been dreading this one. "The VIPs in the Titania Suite brought a yearling calf. They claim it's a pet, but...." Her expression made her opinion clear enough.

"Did no one explain the rules?"

Declan Murphy was hard to read and even harder to know, preferring to keep his employees—no matter how closely he might work with them—at considerable personal distance. In business, he could be ruthless and unforgiving. Kendra didn't know if he was the same in his personal life. It was entirely possible he didn't have one. He gave the impression of being incapable of warmth. On rare occasions when he did show emotion, it was invariably temper and invariably cold.

As it was now.

"A copy of hotel policy was included with their reservation documents," she said, feeling almost sorry for the bloodthirsty fools. "After housekeeping alerted me to the calf's presence, I spoke with their assistant"—she looked at her notes—"a Mr. Rosvald Black to remind them. Which is when I was assured that it was just a pet."

"You're thinking he's a liar," Murphy said, the musicality of his Irish accent somehow conveying more menace, not less.

"Yes."

Mouth pressed thin, Murphy reached across his desk, took a pen from its holder. Kendra watched, fascinated, while he wrote the man's name on a slip of paper, folded that a precise three times, and then tucked it beneath his watch's leather cuff. He returned the pen to its holder, leaned back against the padded back of his office chair. His expression was once again neutral.

As if he weren't planning to unleash hell on Rosvald Black and whoever employed him.

She took the deceptive calm as a signal to continue. "The caterers for the Wilson party need an extra hour to—" She broke off, hearing the door open behind her, and turned to see Abby rush in. Madame Demetka, of all people, followed in all of her kaftaned, turbaned glory.

Kendra sprang to her feet as her friend came to a breathless stop at Murphy's desk. Something was terribly wrong. Aside from knowing Abby would never willingly seek out Murphy's company, Kendra had never seen her so pale, so frantic. "Abby, what's the matter? Are you—"

"My dear Miss Collins, do sit down before you fall down,"

Murphy drawled, then grinned when Abby shot him a fierce glare.

"I'm fine," she snapped. But she sat, angling herself toward Kendra. "It's about—"

"All this way, we ran," Madame Demetka interrupted as she adjusted the fall of her many necklaces. "Timing is key."

"Was it, now." Murphy's wry tone earned him another one of Abby's glares. If he didn't take care, he was going to get himself another costly repair bill.

Kendra gave her friend a warning look before moving to close the door.

"Tell her, Madame Demetka" Abby said. "Tell her what you told me."

"Yes, do tell us," Murphy said, putting particular stress on the plural. "My office, and all that."

"I received a desperate communication from my guides. A cry for help on behalf of another."

"Oh, dear—has Timmy fallen down the well again?"

"Shut it, Murphy." If looks were lasers, Abby's would have fried him on the spot. "Please continue, Madame Demetka."

"Of course, yes." She took the remaining seat by the desk. "The night of the storm, I did a reading for Thia and told her many things. Troubling things. Ever since I have tried to make them clear in my mind. Finally I have luck. This afternoon, it became clear as daylight: Thia needs her friends to be in the office of the man who spoke with the storm, before it is called again." She looked at Kendra. "Is very good you were already here. Timing—"

"—is key," Kendra finished along with her, and then looked to Abby for translation help.

Her friend merely shrugged, incomprehension plain on her face.

Murphy, on the other hand, leaned forward, his lower arms on the desk. His dark eyes held an alarming glint. "You think

Cormac is going to—"

On the desk, his cell phone lit, vibrating. He glanced at the screen. One brow lifted, the clearest show of surprise Kendra had ever seen him make. "Congratulations," he told Madame Demetka. He took the call.

For what felt like an age, he listened, inscrutable.

Kendra's mind went over what Madame Demetka had said, and the name Murphy had mentioned in response—Cormac. She wondered who that was and what he might have to do with Thia. She couldn't hear so much as a syllable from the phone. Apparently neither could Abby or Madame Demetka, given their shared looks of frustrated curiosity.

"My pleasure," Murphy said at last, and his tone sent a chill down Kendra's back. He hung up, slipped the phone into his breast pocket. He then stood and, without explanation, took a set of keys from his top drawer.

Abby shot to her feet. "Well?"

He spoke as he crossed to the door. "How are your skills with the lines?"

Kendra flinched when he got close enough to reach past her and open the door. Energy radiated from him in low, jagged waves.

"Leylines?" she asked for clarification, following him out. "I do okay."

"Same here," Abby said, keeping pace as he led them across the lobby at a good clip. Her answer surprised Kendra; she suspected it wasn't entirely honest.

"We've got business out-of-house," Murphy called to Ben at the front desk.

The young clerk looked aghast. "But you'll be back tonight, won't you? I mean, Mr. Murphy, sir. You'll both be here for—"

"Renée can handle it," Kendra said, and prayed she was right. "Everything will be fine."

"But—"

"My part in this is finished," Madame Demetka called out, cutting off whatever Ben was about to say. Kendra stopped, turned. The psychic stood in the middle of the lobby, waved her kaftan's sleeve like a flag. "Best of the *baxt* be with you all. *Sastipe!*"

Having no idea what most of that meant, Kendra lifted her hand in return, then hurried to catch up to Abby and Murphy, already stepping into the elevator.

Murphy's phone was to his ear as he said, "Change of plans. Tell everyone to collect their gear and head for the Vale. We're for Scotland." He pressed a button on his key fob. His black Maserati chirruped in greeting. He pulled open its door. "I know, I know. Bloody miserable timing."

"What's going on?" Kendra asked Abby.

"He hasn't said." Abby yanked open the right-side door as Murphy slid into the driver's seat. "I guess we'll find out when we get there."

"Scotland." Kendra could hardly believe it. "What has this got to do with Thia?"

"Your guess is as good as mine." Abby collapsed the front passenger seat in order to climb in back. Kendra then righted it for herself. Murphy ended his call as she was settling in.

"What are we heading into?" she asked, fixing him with a look that never failed to cow a recalcitrant employee.

But he was employer, not employee; he fixed her one in return and then started the engine. "Battle, most like."

She kept her hand on the open door, using it like a bargaining chip. They wouldn't go anywhere until she closed it. "With?"

A muscle bunched at his jaw. "Idris Cathmor."

She frowned. "The sorcerer? I thought he was just a legend. Something to scare kids around the campfire."

"Oh, he's real all right." Murphy revved the engine.

"What are we stopping him from doing?"

"Killing your friend, for one."

Kendra yanked the door shut. "I'll need my weapons from home."

"Me too." Abby said from the back. There was a click as she fastened her seat belt. "It's on the way."

"I remember where you live, Collins." Murphy threw the car into reverse, stomped on the gas. With four hundred and forty horses under the hood, it was like being fired from a cannon.

Quick reflexes and a strong arm were all that kept Kendra from hitting the dash.

● ○ ●

Ring of Brodgar, Orkney

Cormac watched his phone's screen dim. *My pleasure*, Murphy had said. There would be one cavalry coming to the rescue, at any rate. Assuming it could arrive in time.

And then find its way through the Druid Fog.

Maybe his phone could be of help with that. There was no knowing if the Irishman had a way of tracking it, but better to assume he did and prepare for it than do nothing.

Cormac darted over to the drainage pipe at the end of the ditch, set his phone on top. Even with the boost from the Renaissance Faire spell, he couldn't count on it working from a closer location. The Ring's inherent power plus whatever magic Idris was working might generate enough interference to block the signal entirely.

So, regrettably, it was this or nothing. He did a quick spell to ensure the battery had enough to last the night—

With the icy tingles of the summons spreading out from the back of his neck, he knew his mistake. Of course Idris would be alert to any magic that took place within the fog. Cormac might as well have shot off a flare.

His body automatically answered the demand, materializing inside the Ring only a scant few inches from Idris.

Idris, standing on his own two feet.

Idris, smiling.

Cormac had barely a chance to register the danger before Idris reached out to grab him about the shoulders and pull him into a shocking embrace.

"*Athair,* what—" He gasped as a hot slice of pain, the burning invasion of poisonous metal, made his question irrelevant.

His arms were grabbed from behind, held to keep him from reaching for the blade. He struggled to clear the agony from his mind, gathered power to his hands.

Idris held a small amethyst sphere. Triumph gleamed in his amber-colored eyes. "*Àdòn forbind.*"

Cormac's powers drained.

When his knees buckled, the men holding his arms jerked him upright. Idris took hold of his chin, forced him to hold his gaze.

"You know well the price of betrayal, my son."

Cormac flinched but Idris held firm, nails digging in, eyes burning. "It will be the last thing you know."

● ○ ●

Inverness, Scotland

When the call to Arthur connected, Quentin set the phone in the dashboard cradle. "Extremely bad news, I'm afraid, old man. I've just—"

"We have been betrayed," interrupted his heretofore silent passenger.

"Eben?" Arthur's voice broadcast through the car speakers, rough with static. "What are you doing out of the hosp—"

"Did you not hear me?" Needlessly, Eben leaned toward the phone, raised his voice. "We have been *betrayed*. The people you sent are still in Inverness working over the events there, but Quentin and I are returning to London. We should be at the Aberdeen airport in..."

"Twenty minutes," Quentin supplied, accelerating onto the motorway.

"What? London? That is not—you're needed at—" The line hissed, Arthur's garbled words fading in and out.

"Cormac had nothing to do with the attack," Quentin tried. "Most likely nothing to do with Leticia's death, either."

"But your vision—"

"Manipulated."

The silence that followed made him think the call had been dropped. But then Arthur's voice returned with a stunned, "How is that possible?"

Excellent question. If only Quentin had an answer to it. His hands tightened on the wheel. "It shouldn't be."

While Arthur said nothing, Beatrice could be heard in the background, asking if he needed to sit down.

"The pendants, Arthur," Eben said, bringing up the second major issue. "The pendants don't do a damn thing when the threat comes from our own. We need to warn everyone, set up new measures of protection—"

"The bastard phoned not long ago. Cormac did," Arthur cut in. "Said Idris was at the Ring of Brodgar with his followers."

Eben lurched forward, straining the safety belt. "Dammit, we've had people observing his stronghold." He was nearly shouting. "Their reports have suggested nothing that—"

"Compromised." The speakers made Arthur's sigh sound like a gust of wind. "We must assume they were compromised."

CHAPTER 23

"**I**'m afraid we haven't been entirely honest," Matt said, continuing to speed the car through the pea-soup fog which seemed to cloak the entire island. It was no less thick the further they got from the harbor.

"No?" Thia ran a finger beneath her seatbelt in an attempt to get some slack. The damn thing was too tight.

"Neither of us enjoyed the deception, of course, but—"

"Speak for yourself," Cassie said. "*I* rather enjoyed it."

"We never meant you harm," Matt said, either not noticing or not caring how his sister's expression belied his words. "In the alley the other night you wouldn't have been hurt. They were only to take the relic."

"What?"

"Oh, dear. Did you not suspect?" Cassie laughed, shrill and malicious. "Not even a little?"

"After Cormac ruined things there," Matt continued, "we tried the transportation charm. The silver one I gave you. It was meant to be a surprise for Idris. Not very well planned, I admit, but it would have worked if—"

"—if you'd had the relic on you then," Cassie finished. "We should have crafted the charm for more intensive use. If the round trip hadn't exhausted the spell, I could've been saved all that trouble at the airport." One shoulder lifted, fell in a graceful shrug.

Thia struggled to process what was happening. What were they saying? That they had been working against her, working against the Brigantium this whole time? Her hand went to the charm Matt had given her. Useless now, apparently, and never intended to help. Her nightmare hadn't been a nightmare—not a sleeping one, anyway. It had been real? Matt and Cassie were claiming responsibility for it. And also for what had happened at the airport. "I—I thought Cormac was the one trying to get the Stone for Idris," she stammered.

"He was." Cassie's laugh was mocking. Shrill. "But after so many screw ups, can you blame us for stepping in? Honestly, with his reputation and what was at stake, we expected more from him."

"So did Idris," Matt said. "He's paying for it now, I assume."

"Idris is?"

Matt chuckled. "No."

Cormac, then. Thia tugged at the immovable seatbelt. "He survived what you did to the road?"

"Oh, yes." Cassie turned her smile on Thia. "But by now he probably wishes he hadn't."

"What do you mean?"

Ignoring her, Cassie turned frontward to point at something through the side window. "Look, Matt. There's where—"

"Cass." His tone held a warning. "This isn't the time."

"Don't be silly. Of course it is." She twisted around again as the car rounded a long, sloping curve. "That's where Leticia died."

Thia saw nothing but white. The fog had gotten so thick, she didn't know how Matt could see to drive. Or how Cassie could tell exactly where they were. Or how they could...Oh. Oh, *no*. Thia felt, more than heard, herself speak: "How do you know exactly? Did Cormac tell you?"

"Of course not. He had nothing to do with it."

A noise, high-pitched and awful began to sound inside Thia's head. Like something trapped was screaming to get out.

"It was a dark and stormy night," Cassie said dramatically, and then laughed. "Poor Leticia was on her way to a ship that would take her off the island. We crafted a glamour for Matt so he looked like Cormac—almost perfectly, too, but for the eyes. We hadn't known yet about that little detail. Even so, it was brilliant." Smug. She sounded so damned smug.

"Matt positioned himself just beyond the curve back there, and when Leticia came around it, there he was. She swerved, of course. Ended up in the ditch. She was so focused on him when she got out of her car, she didn't know I was there. She was wonderfully surprised, wasn't she, Matt, when my knife went into her back?"

The noise in Thia's head had built to a roar. She struggled with the seatbelt's clasp. It wouldn't unlatch. Intentionally? She struggled all the more.

"It was genius, that glamour," Cassie continued with awful glee. "Because Leticia believed she was seeing Cormac, we captured some of her memories and sent them to Quentin. He thought he had one of his visions." She grinned. "And then he alerted headquarters, setting everything in motion. With Cormac held to blame for it all. Oh, I *do* wish I'd seen Leticia's face when she realized how mistaken she'd been." Cassie leaned in, closing the distance.

Presenting an opportunity.

"She knew it was us in the end, you see. Right before she breathed her last, she knew, and I—"

Thia punched Cassie in the face. She would have done it again, too, never mind the pain in her hand, if her seatbelt hadn't then pulled impossibly tight. The breath left her lungs. She tried to take another. Couldn't. She couldn't breathe.

Flinging off her own belt, Cassie lunged with a feral hiss, her fingers like claws. Thia turned her face away, raised her hands protectively. Bright dots began to dance before her eyes. She was passing out.

"Enough!" Matt grabbed his sister's shoulder, pulled her back into her seat as he steered one-handed. "Cass, enough. You brought that on yourself."

Thia's seatbelt loosened enough so that she could breathe, and consciousness returned in an oxygenated rush. Cassie was glaring at her...with eyes that seemed to glow a reddish-gold. Thia blinked. Maybe consciousness had not returned after all. She blinked again.

Still glowing.

"Power," Cassie said. Something wet glistened on her lips. Blood, dark and colorless in the dashboard lights. Her lip was bleeding.

It was not enough, Thia thought, hatred pounding where her heart used to be. Nothing could ever be enough. "Why did you kill her? You didn't even know where the Stone was."

"We thought Cormac had it." Cassie's eyes flashed amber.

"Leticia suspected the Brigantium had become corrupted," Matt explained, slowing to make a left-hand turn. "It was only a matter of time before she traced that corruption back to us. With the right questions asked of the right people, she'd have found out her reports had been altered. Unfortunately for her, only a handful of people could have done that."

"Including the two of you."

His shoulders rose and fell with a heavy sigh. "I am sorry for her death, but it was unavoidable. Too soon, as it turned out, but it had to happen."

"Not the way I see it."

"No, I imagine not. Ah, here we are." He pulled the car to a stop behind some kind of freight truck and killed the engine.

He and Cassie got out, and Thia's stomach commenced a

series of somersaults that lasted through the automated— or more likely, magical—unlatching of her seat belt. Her door opened. She refused Matt's hand and climbed out.

Icy darts of water, drifting in eerily still air, stung her face. She shivered, thrust her hands in her pockets. Moisture was collecting on her skin, her hair. "Could I have my scarf and gloves, please?" The words were polite. Her tone was not.

Cassie smiled. "I'm afraid we forgot them."

Yeah, sure. Forgot them on purpose.

A short distance away, the land rose in a kind of grassy berm. The fog was too thick for her to see anything beyond.

"You'll only get lost," Cassie advised, correctly interpreting Thia's thoughts of running. "This is Druid Fog."

"It causes confusion," Matt explained. "Wander around long enough and you'll not know your own name." He took hold of Thia's right arm before she could step out of reach.

"What keeps you from getting lost?" she asked, planting her feet when he tried to pull her toward a path worn into the berm.

"We're supposed to be here." Cassie took hold of Thia's left arm, forcing her onward. Three abreast, they walked up the slope, the mist of their breaths merging with the fog.

"It's a shame you won't see the Ring on the approach," Matt said. "To see the stones rise from such a desolate landscape and pierce the sky is...well, it's striking."

The Ring of Brodgar, they had told her in the car. She had already known of it. Had even seen pictures. It was one of Orkney's most famous sites.

"According to Leticia's journals," Matt's informative lecture continued, "this is where the Stone of Shadows was created."

"I thought you said any relevant journals were missing."

"Missing as far as the Brigantium is concerned, yes."

"We took them, obviously," Cassie said, releasing Thia's arm to walk ahead down a narrow track. They had come upon a ditch, very wide and carpeted with scraggly, low-lying shrubs.

"Leticia had several with her when she died," Matt said, his grip remaining firm as he escorted Thia down the slope. "But it was easy enough to get them from her house as well, since we supervised the search of it." They walked across the flat bottom and up the other side. Sounds intensified within the fog. The crunch of gravel. The snap of a twig. The rasp of fabric.

Never had Thia felt so alone, so powerless. What could she do? Her normal life was filled with options, with choices, and she excelled at sorting through them. Whether to have the Angry Gnome's Daybook come up in a search for "children's books" on Eclectica's website even though it was shelved as general nonfiction. How to photograph and feature the hand-carved walking sticks to best effect. When and where to take her lunch and what to eat. The myriad choices she took for granted as people with stable, mostly contented lives might tend to do. Yet here, tonight, she could see only inevitability, could only move along a path of someone else's choosing.

It was exactly that, she realized: someone else's path. She had made the initial decision to come to London, to look for Lettie, to find answers. From then on, however, her actions had been the result of manipulation. As surely as Matt was doing now with his grip on her arm, he and Cassie had guided her to this moment.

They came up out of the ditch and, as if a curtain parted, out of the fog into clear, surprisingly warm air. Thia's steps faltered. She had seen pictures of the Ring of Brodgar. None of them compared to the reality.

The word "beautiful" came to mind but wasn't right. The ragged, mismatched stones were not at all beautiful, not even in consideration of the whole. Not beautiful: Amazing.

Thia was brought to an abrupt stop at a gap between two of the megaliths so that Cassie could trace patterns in the air.

"She's opening a space in the wards," Matt said, though Thia had already surmised as much.

The stone to her right topped her by several feet. The one to the left was even taller. Rough lichen-spotted slabs, both were broad across but of a depth no wider than Thia's palm. Together with at least twenty others, the Ring occupied an area about the size of a football field, if not larger. Several of the stones tilted at odd angles and, judging by the varied spacing, there were quite a few missing.

The overall effect was of a mouth of chipped, crooked and missing teeth. Not a smiling mouth, Thia thought, but not a snarling one, either. A neutral mouth, dormant...and empty. Not a single person stood inside. "Are we the first ones here?"

Matt smiled and then, urging Thia forward, followed Cassie through the gap. If coming out of the fog had been a curtain lifting, this was the flick of a switch. One moment the Ring was empty and dark; the next, a hive of activity illuminated by torches and bonfires.

Malevolence landed on Thia like a woolen blanket soaked in stagnant water. Leaden and foul, it wrapped around her, and she felt a bone-deep terror, a need to be anywhere else. When she balked, Matt simply firmed his hold, taking her inexorably toward the center of the Ring. The largest bonfire burned there, surrounded by people in black robes. She knew those robes. The attackers in the alley had worn the same.

There had to be a hundred people, all standing rapt while a tall figure dressed in red threw handfuls of something upon the flames. Whatever it was resulted in great expulsions of yellowed smoke and smelled like rot. The man was in profile to Thia, but his shockingly white hair hung so she couldn't see any of his face—for which she was grateful. The wrongness, the malevolence she felt originated with him. She really, really did not want to see him in more detail.

"Is that Idris?" she asked. She felt sick. Dizzy. These were the same scents, the same feelings as in her nightmare. The nightmare that had been real.

"Yes," Cassie said with reverence. "But we won't bother him with you just yet. Besides, there's someone who won't be at all glad to see you." Grinning like she'd made a great joke, she pointed to a form lying some distance from the altar. A man on his back, arms outstretched. Motionless. Thia couldn't see *his* features, either.

Other than a worn path around the inner perimeter of the Ring, the ground was covered with scrub grass and heather. Thia's foot snagged on a branch and she stumbled, wrenching her shoulder when Matt yanked it to keep her upright. Instinct and temper flared; Thia planted her feet, tugged against his hold while striking at him with her free hand.

"Don't be silly," he chided, outmaneuvering her increasingly frantic struggles. Holding both her wrists, he spun her around so her arms crossed her chest, and pulled her against him. It was the reverse of her position in their encounter in Lettie's hallway, and no less effective.

"Restrain her legs." Cassie's voice came from some distance away. Three robed men stood with her. At her command, two moved in and, despite Thia's violent efforts, succeeded in capturing her legs. They held them lifted, tight against them, so that between the two men and Matt, Thia's lower body hung suspended above the ground. Blood trickled from one man's nose. The other's left eye was swelling shut. Thia had gotten a few solid kicks in, at least.

Cassie walked up, clucked her tongue. "I've been wracking my brain, trying to think what I would do in your place." She patted Thia's cargo pocket. "Not anywhere so obvious, I'd say. But perhaps...." Quick as the strike of a viper, she poked Thia between the breasts, directly on the Stone. Her eyes lit with triumph. And power. They glowed as she took hold of Thia's sweater, thrust her hands beneath to root under the sports bra and pull out the Stone.

Thia's mind blanked on a combined rush of terror and rage. She didn't decide to scream like a wild creature—hell, like a banshee, maybe—or to thrash and strain against the men who held her. She didn't decide, she simply *did*. And, of course, it did no good.

"Take her."

She was vaguely aware that Cassie had spoken, and that the third man had come to take Matt's place. He succeeded in it, even as she bucked and twisted and tried to hit him with her head. She might as well have saved her energy.

"It's glorious," Cassie said, the reverence in her tone drawing Thia's attention. She held the Stone on her palm. "Look at it, Matthew. All that power."

Thia's mind cleared. She stilled. "It isn't for you."

Cassie flicked her hand. A dismissal. The three robed men began to walk, hauling Thia away. She resumed her struggles, fighting the men and her own increasingly panicked dread.

Some distance into the Ring, she was lowered to the ground. Pinned by a multitude of hands, she couldn't do much more than watch as ropes were wound around her wrists and ankles and then tied to thick metal stakes. Like a calf roping at a rodeo, it was over in seconds.

Without so much as a glance, the men hurried off, returning to the bonfire—and Idris, standing at it. His back was to her, so she still could not see his face. Behind him, three carved stones formed a massive table...or, rather, altar. Its top was littered with objects easily identifiable despite the distance: chalices, bowls, bundles of herbs, a wicked-looking knife on an elaborate stand.

Thia tugged at the ropes, found little give. "Shit."

"That's putting it lightly."

Foolish though it was, relief shuddered through her at the sound of Cormac's voice. She craned her head, saw boots and black-clad legs only a few inches to her right. Like her, ropes wrapped around his ankles, secured them to stakes. "You're a prisoner too?"

The answer obvious, he ignored the question. "They haven't hurt you."

"No. Not yet," she said, wriggling, adjusting, until she could twist her neck enough to see his face. His gaze was intense. And so very, very blue. The crushing tightness around Thia's chest eased a little. At the moment, it didn't matter who he was or what he had or hadn't done. It only mattered that he was here. She was not alone.

"How about you?" she asked, looking him over. "Are you—oh, God."

The knife's hilt was dark, nearly matching the black fabric of Cormac's coat. The blade was not visible at all, stuck deep into his abdomen, just left of center.

"H-how bad is it?" had to be the stupidest thing Thia had ever asked.

"Bad enough," Cormac replied, a ghost of wry amusement flickering across his face. He tipped his chin, indicating the knife. "Iron. A bit of overkill, that—pardon the pun. With my powers bound, I couldn't have done much against any blade."

She strained against the ropes holding her arms. Her wrists burned, the ropes abrading, then shredding her skin. "Do you know what they're planning? How long we have?"

Cormac looked beyond her in the direction of the central fire, his expression once again shuttered. But she could hear the tension in his voice clearly enough. "He wants the Stone's powers. The ritual requires a blood sacrifice."

"Yours?"

"I'm thinking yours, actually." He met her gaze. "So that I can watch."

Thia increased her rope efforts. Thanks to the slick of sweat and blood on her skin, she had made slight but encouraging progress at her left wrist. Cormac hadn't answered her second question, but she let that go. She was already working as fast as she could; knowing how much (or how little) time they had wouldn't help.

"I don't think it will be painful." Cormac said. "Not more than it need be. Idris won't care to waste time with anything but the basics."

The rope bit into the knuckled base of her thumb. Rotating her wrist, she

"He'll save that for me," Cormac continued absently. "Once he has the relic's power, he'll think he has all the time in the world. Maybe he will." His rueful laugh cut off with a pained curse.

She twisted her upper body, adding torque. The rope didn't budge...but *something* did. The stake. She stretched, managed to brush two fingertips across its rough metal. "Cormac."

"Still here."

It wasn't easy, but she ignored the sarcasm. "I think I can get my hand free. Can you keep watch? Warn me if anyone is looking." She felt the change. A predator going on alert.

"They're all focused on the fire," he said. "Idris is about to light the ferfaen wand."

"Ferfaen?" Thia twisted to her right, felt the burn in her left shoulder as she struggled to tilt the stake.

"You might know it as vervain or the Latin *herba sacra*. Used frequently in sacrifices. And as an aphrodisiac." He sounded breathless, his voice strained.

Rolling toward the stake, she lunged for it. Didn't make it. She adjusted position, got ready. "How are you doing?"

"I've got a fucking iron knife in the gut. How do you think I'm doing?"

She released a relieved breath—if he was sniping, he wasn't dying—and then rolled again, lunged again. Swore soundlessly when the binding on her right wrist refused to allow the inch she needed. Vaguely, she wondered if a person could pull their own shoulder out of socket. It certainly felt like she might. Would that be such a bad thing? It would get her the stake.

Ignoring the pain, she kept stretching. Trying. Her fingers touched metal. The first joints, then the second. Enough to hold on. With a muted cry of triumph, she began pulling the crude metal shaft out of the damp ground, slow inch by inch. Tears mixed with the sweat running down her face.

"Do you think you might hurry it along a bit?"

"Not helping," she ground out, muscles screaming. She was about to join them when the stake popped free. Her arm shot up, visible to all, before she regained control, jerked it down to something like her initial pose.

"Did anyone see?" she asked softly.

After a slight hesitation, "No. They're all watching Idris."

"Let's hope they stay that way." She didn't dare think it would be so easy. Both hands worked to free her right wrist. "You still doing all right?"

"Would you believe me if I said yes?"

"No." She shifted her hold, wiggled the stake like a loose tooth. "I've almost got it. Then I just—" She broke off at the start of chanting. A sickly sweet smell reached her nose.

"So it begins," Cormac said dully.

So many voices. So many people. And she thought to escape them? The second stake came out of the ground. Her feet were still secured but there was some play in the rope.

"Thia."

Something in Cormac's tone made her stop, look over. Firelight glinted on the sweat coating his face, flickered across his wide, grave eyes. "There's little time. Use the knife."

She knew enough about first aid to understand the wrongness of that. And, from his expression, she had to suspect he did too. "No."

He closed his eyes, his expression tightening. "There's no choice. For either of us." His eyes opened, unfathomably blue and, she thought, honest. "Thia. You have to."

"No." Trying not to attract attention, she pulled herself to within reach of the stake holding Cormac's left wrist. Once she freed it, he could free his right, and then they could both work to free their ankles. Somehow. Then they would run. Or more likely, he'd stagger while she tried to support him...and they would go...somewhere.

They were in so much trouble.

"It'll be fine," he told her. "Without the iron's interference, my powers could heal the wound."

Did Thia believe him? Not entirely. But she wanted to.

The stakes, still tethered to her wrists, dragged across the ground as she reached out, one hand grasping the knife's hilt, the other resting gently on Cormac's midriff, beside the blade. His coat was wet, saturated with blood, and warm. Too warm.

"If Idris succeeds, I'm dead anyway," he said, barely more than a whisper as Thia watched the hilt, felt the rise and fall of his breathing. "But you don't have to be. Please, Thia. I've enough on my conscience."

She closed her eyes, searched within herself for the right decision. All she felt was fear. "You can heal this?"

"Sure. Once the iron is out."

"With your powers."

"Exactly."

Something was off, but why would he lie? There was nothing to be gained by it except the danger of bleeding out. Before her hands could shake, before she could think better of it, Thia gripped the cold hilt and yanked. Cormac's head rocked back on a stifled groan as the knife pulled free.

Blood glistened on the jagged blade as more ran freely past the hand Thia pressed to the wound it left behind.

"I'm sorry. I'm so sorry." Dropping the knife, she used both hands to try to stem the terrifying flow.

● ○ ●

"It's not stopping," Thia said, bearing down mercilessly, and

Cormac struggled not to cry out. "Why isn't it stopping?"

His gut burned, the flames threatening to devour him. But he would remain conscious. He would do that much for her, at least.

Her hands lifted from him. The pain lessened enough for him to understand she was using the knife on *his* bindings, not her own.

"Dammit. *Dammit,* Thia." He used his newly-freed left hand to slap at her hands as they sawed at the ropes binding his right.

"Do something useful," she said, grabbing his hand mid-slap. She pushed it down to his wound. "Press hard."

Hot blood ran down his chilled side.

"This isn't healing," she said in a thin, urgent whisper. He could feel the trembling of her hands as they added pressure. Her face was pale, terrified.

He had never thought himself a coward until that moment, when he looked into hazel eyes full of fear...and had to look away. When Thia went back to freeing his other hand, he was too shaken to argue.

"Hold on," she said when finished. "I'll have to do my legs before I can reach yours. Don't move. Dammit, don't move!" She shoved his chest when he would have tried to rise.

She went to cut the ropes on her ankles, and he succeeded in sitting up. Too fast. His vision blacked, then filled with swirling dots. He lay back down. Or maybe he fell. He heard her mutter something that sounded like, "Stubborn fool."

By the time he could see again, Thia had freed herself and was quickly cutting through the last of his restraints.

"Okay," she said, her breath coming fast. With a look toward the figures circling the fire, she crouched over him and made short work of his coat and shirt to expose his abdomen. She cut a strip of fabric, folded it into a pad. "Let me in," she said, moving his hand so she could replace it with the makeshift compress. His vision grayed.

When it cleared, Thia was staring at her hand on the cloth. Blood seeped between her fingers, the cloth pad already wet with it. The look on her face, the wealth of emotion shown in her eyes astonished him. He had never thought...No one had ever...He hadn't known it was possible. "Thia."

"We need a way to keep this on," she said. "Can you hold it? I can make more strips, do something with the ropes."

Guilt swamped him, left him drowning in regret.

"Thia. *Muileach.*" He laid his hand over hers and watched understanding leach the hope from her very being.

"You lied?"

With his free hand, he found hers. Held it. So delicate, her hands, yet so very strong. Her grip was crushing. "Not a lie, no. My powers are bound," he reminded her gently. "If I still had them, I could heal."

Her gaze was haunted. "I didn't understand. When you said that before, about their being bound, I didn't understand." Tears pooled in her eyes. "I still don't. I don't understand any of this."

He hadn't known he could hurt this much.

It was just as well he would be dead soon. And, thanks to the increased rate of blood loss now that the knife had been removed, probably well before his father could make use of it. Not the triumph Cormac might've preferred, but it would do.

"Go," he urged. "Before they see you. They'll never find you in the fog." He tried to pull his hands from her grip.

She wouldn't let him. "They told me that you killed Lettie. I know you didn't. I'm sorry I believed them. You helped me in the alley. And in my nightmare—only it wasn't, it was real—when you *did* lie. For me." A tear ran down her cheek, and to Cormac's horror, he felt his own eyes threaten to fill. "Why did you do that?" she asked, squeezing his hands. "Why do you keep helping me?"

"I don't know," he said, more proof of cowardice. He didn't know because he didn't *want* to know.

He looked to the gathering around the central fire and this time, when he tried, Thia released his hands. "Everyone is focused on the ritual," he told her. "You have a weapon. Take it and go. There won't be a better chance—for either of us." His focus blurred. Swam. With effort, he brought it back to Thia, caught her on the third try.

She was removing her jacket. "I won't leave you," she said as his vision fuzzed, drifted again. He closed his eyes. When she didn't say more, he figured she had changed her mind and taken his direction.

They always left, he thought vaguely, and let his head drop to the grass. The mother Cormac had never known, his early tutors, his father's cook—the one who would fix him honeyed tea and let him sit by the kitchen fire. The alchemist who had come for a month and promised to take Cormac away with him. They always left. Everyone but Idris, who never let him go.

Though Cormac had encouraged it, and knew Thia had to do it, her leaving hurt worst of all. Maybe it was because he knew she hadn't wanted to. Maybe it was simply an effect of the enthrallment.

A nearby rending sound startled his eyes open. Thia knelt beside him, knife and jacket in hand. She hadn't left.

"*Damnad*, Thia, you need to—"

"Finish this bandage," she said resolutely and proceeded to slice strips off her jacket, "so we can both go. You helped me. Now it's my turn."

The chanting around the fire changed, jumping an octave as the tempo increased.

"*Muileach*, there's no time." He sat up, ignored the pain, the dizziness, to point to the perimeter. "If you're worried about the fog, don't be. I made calls. Murphy is bringing his people.

The Brigantium didn't believe me, but they'll probably send local forces, at least, to check things out. Someone will find you."

Thia's look was steely. "If they do, and I bring them here, could they help you?"

It was a risk, his answer. He didn't want her to return, but he figured whomever she encountered wouldn't permit it. He nodded. "Yes."

"You're lying again."

He swore vehemently, a string of curses in the old language, and then had to grab her wrists to keep her from pressing a fresh wad of fabric to the wound. "Thia, please. This is it."

Thickening smoke from the smoldering herbs was making it even harder to breathe. Soon very few within range would be thinking clearly.

"I won't leave you here," Thia insisted in a broken voice. But when Cormac released her wrists, she didn't come at him with the cloth.

"You have to."

Instead of leaving, she continued to look at him, so directly it was as if she thought to read his very soul. Ah, *ifrinn*. Too late, Cormac shut his eyes against the longing he hadn't the strength to hide. She had seen.

Feather-light, the tips of her fingers brushed his cheek. Her breath followed a moment later, and even though he braced himself, he tensed when her lips touched his. Her hands bracketed his head, held him in place.

As if he would pull away. With all that Cormac had left, he returned her kiss. She tasted so sweet.

She *was* sweet—and unexpectedly, uniquely formidable. His heart pounded, undoubtedly speeding along his end.

"Cormac." She whispered it against his mouth, quiet as air and full of longing. He felt himself falling, although he knew he hadn't moved. Color exploded behind his eyes. Shards of magenta and gold swirled and shattered, splintered into every imaginable hue. Thia's mouth lifted, ending the kiss, and her hands slowly drew away from his head.

Emptiness settled around him: The absence of her, genuine this time. The fireworks behind his eyes dimmed.

He had no explanation for those except as a component of the enthrallment. But that could only be initiated by a *leanan sidhe*, and he had done no such thing here. Not this time. Was it something Thia—no, he knew better now; she was exactly as she seemed when it came to magic and spellcraft. She had little knowledge and no practiced skills whatsoever.

If the kaleidoscopic colors weren't part of a spell this time, what did that mean for the time before? Was what he felt the result of a spell or...or was it simply...what it was.

"Damnad."

He lifted his head, found Thia already a good distance away, bent low over the ground in an admirable attempt at stealth. But she had a long, exposed way to go before the perimeter. No matter what she did, she made an easy target. With one hand pressed to his wound, Cormac lurched to his feet.

● ○ ●

Much as Thia hated it, her running away was the only chance they had. Cormac might be wrong to stay behind, but maybe he was too weak. He had lost a lot of blood. The sooner she left the Ring, the sooner she could find the help he seemed to believe wasn't far away.

She hoped that hadn't been another lie. It likely was, given Cormac's propensity for them. On the way in with Matt and Cassie, she hadn't seen anyone else at all.

Thia tripped, regained her footing only to lose it again. Her balance was off for being nearly doubled over, and the rock and heather-strewn terrain wasn't making things any easier. She had already fallen once and scratched her palms deeply enough to draw blood. She had dropped the knife then, too, and spent precious time locating it in the heather. She kept a tight grip on the hilt now with the blade pointed down in case she fell again.

Someone grabbed her from behind, lifted her off her feet. She kicked, tangled her legs with his, and momentum took them both forward. As they fell, she didn't think: she reacted. She positioned her arm so she could brace her hand against her side. She hit the ground hard, the man slamming down on her back. And impaling himself on the knife.

She felt the blade enter him; heard the crunch, the pop when it broke through cartilage and bone to pierce his chest. He cried out, a shocked, agonized sound.

She knew that voice. Knew that man.

Oh, God.

Matt. She had stabbed Matt.

His weight settled fully upon her, his muscles going slack as his breath rushed out, hot against her neck. She blocked the fear, fought the nausea to gather all her strength and shove against him, rolling him off. She scrambled to her feet, the knife bloody in her hand, and whirled to defend herself.

He lay on his back, staring at her with wide eyes. Frightened eyes. His mouth gaped. Pink froth bubbled at the corners of his lips. His chest heaved as he struggled to breathe. He was making liquid sounds. Sickening sounds.

Thia's stomach roiled. She had done this. She had stabbed a man who, up until a short time ago, she had considered a friend.

And now he was going to die.

Distantly, she became aware of raised voices. She began to turn toward them, but something hot struck her chest and sent her flying.

CHAPTER 24

**The Ring of Brodgar, Orkney
Samhain**

"*S*aigh!*" Cormac tackled the woman who had struck down Thia with *wanfýr.* He recalled her name after they hit the ground.

"Matthew!" Cassie continued to shriek her brother's name, her scattered focus allowing Cormac to pin her beneath him and wrap his hands around her throat. Idris bellowed, trying to maintain the ritual. At his command, three *thegnas* left the procession to go to where Matthew writhed on the ground. Thia lay some distance from there, unmoving.

Cassie bucked against Cormac's weight, raked nails across his cheek. He hissed, drew one hand back in a fist. The punch that followed left her unfazed. Unlike his, her powers were not bound. He leaned harder on her slim throat. Her face, already mottled with rage, darkened.

"My lord, we cannot staunch the bleeding," someone called out to Idris, and Cassie's eyes flashed gold. *Wælfýr* gathered at her hands.

«*Not yet, Cassandra! Do not kill him yet!*»

She flinched, no doubt hearing Idris's shout in her head as well as Cormac had,. Out of the corner of his eye, he saw his father moving swiftly to where the dying man lay. The three *thegnas* worked frantically, murmuring useless incantations.

The injury, anyone could tell, was mortal.

"It's no good, you know." He smiled down at Cassie. Hatred burned in her eyes...and made them startlingly familiar.

His father's eyes, set in another's face.

Either Cormac was hallucinating, closer to succumbing to blood loss than he realized, or—"Kin," he breathed, shocked witless.

His sister landed a blow that snapped his head back. A swift knee to his wound followed, and his muscles seized in agony. She dislodged him easily and ran toward her brother. Her other brother. Cormac lay on his side, struggling to catch his breath.

He had a sister. And a brother.

Damnad, he had been so grateful when finally, decades ago, Idris had granted him permission to leave Fiend's Fell and set up his own home. With that he had gained a measure of freedom—and made himself vulnerable to secrets. Cormac shuddered, pressed a hand to his abdomen where the velvet of his coat was saturated with blood.

He had been such a fool.

Cassie had reached Matthew. As she dropped to her knees, she brushed against Idris's robes. To Cormac's astonishment, instead of distancing himself, Idris laid a hand on her bowed head. Tenderness? From Idris Cathmor?

He looked to where Thia lay unmoving. She had been struck with *wanfýr,* not *wælfýr,* but there had been occasions where its lesser energy had resulted in death. Cormac forced himself to his feet.

"Thia. *Muileach,*" he called roughly, swaying. The warming spell on the Ring remained active, but he shivered with cold. "This isn't a g-good t-t-time for a n-nap."

After a breathless moment, he saw movement. She made a small sound—a sleeper awakening. Relief dizzied him. Or maybe that was exsanguination. "Th-that's right, Thia. Time to w-wake up," he urged, and began an awkward shamble to the altar.

Alive. The thought repeated with every difficult step. Thia was alive and, for the time being, overlooked.

The masses continued to circle the fire, their chant holding the nearly-completed ritual in place. The only thing missing was Thia's sacrifice, yet Idris remained by his daughter and fallen son and ignored all else.

Including Cormac.

He stumbled, nearly fell. Kept going. The altar was only a few feet away. He ran to it—ran *into* it, planted his hands on the cold, smooth onyx to keep himself upright. The top held a jumble of items: bowls, both empty and filled; an ornate goblet; Idris's favorite athame; containers of powders, herbs, liquids. And just there, the amethyst sphere that served to bind Cormac's powers. He lifted the polished crystal, felt the bind unravel.

His powers flowed from the sphere and into his hand. They traveled along his nerves, coursed through his blood, settled into his bones...in less time than it took him to breathe. The healing began, quickened by the potency of the location. Idris had chosen the Ring of Brodgar for good reason.

Although Cormac didn't know what it looked like, only that Cassie had placed it on the altar, the Stone was easy to locate using his Sight. Whatever had masked its presence when Thia had carried it was no longer in use. Within the dark sphere, trapped power buzzed like bees in a hive.

Warning and temptation. Such potential, like honey, could be deliciously sweet. And the stings, deadly.

"Here goes nothing," Cormac murmured, a kind of prayer.

● ○ ●

"Thia. Come on." Cormac's voice. "Wake up."

A metallic scent filled Thia's nostrils. Her hands felt sticky.

She opened her eyes to look...and remembered.

Blood.

Gagging, she tried to wipe it off on the scraggly grass.

So much blood.

"*Damnad,* Thia. Leave it." Cormac grabbed her hand, forced her to stop. "You need to go. Before they notice this is gone." He pressed something onto her palm, closed her fingers around it. She immediately recognized what it was. What he had returned to her.

Warmth shot up her arm, burnt away the bleary confusion in her aching head. She looked up, found Cormac's face only inches from hers. His face was so drawn, his gaze so intense, that she instinctively reached out to cup his beard-shadowed cheek. Her other hand, clutching the Stone, remained clasped in both of his. His eyes closed and, with an audible catch in his breath, he dropped his forehead to hers.

"Cormac, what—"

Abruptly, he pulled away, springing lithely to his feet.

There was no reason to lay low, she realized then. Everyone else was either madly orbiting the fire or kneeling by—Thia's stomach lurched. *Matt.* She hadn't meant to do that, to stab him. Yet she had put the knife in that position. Out of instinct or conscious thought, it didn't matter which. She had gripped a potentially lethal weapon with intent.

"Hurry." Cormac tugged her arm, helped her to stand. "I've got my powers back, so I'll do what I can to distract them while—"

"You aren't coming?"

"I have business with Idris," he said with startling viciousness. He dropped her hand, took off for the altar before she could object.

She would be a fool to follow him. She knew that. Knew the smart move—the only move—was to pick up where she left off before...before Matt.

Despite knowing that she had no choice, every step toward the edge of the Ring felt like hardest thing she had ever done in her life.

● ○ ●

Breathing hard, Cormac hid himself at the far side of the altar and watched Idris step away from the group clustered around his son.

Who had been the mother? A human, since the twins had no distinguishable Otherworld qualities, but had there been anything special to her? Had the aim been mere breeding...or something more? Had theirs been—Cormac nearly choked on the thought—a true family?

The double-edged blade of Idris's athame gleamed wicked and sharp. Cormac picked it up, wrapped his fingers around the smooth, ebony handle. A woman's anguished wail brought his head up in time to see Cassie struggling to pull an utterly limp Matthew into her arms.

Dead. Her brother, his half-brother. Idris's son.

Cormac looked to the latter, watched his attention lock on something in the distance: Thia, almost at the perimeter.

Protective magic glistened, a formidable boundary linking the stones, meant to keep unwanted visitors out and wanted prisoners in. Cormac felt a clutch of alarm.

There hadn't been any protection before. When had Idris crafted it? He'd been busy with the ritual, and then Matthew. He couldn't possibly have—no, of course he hadn't. He hadn't have needed to. The boundary had been there all along, but while Cormac's powers had been bound, *Cormac* had been unable to see the wards. And he had set Thia right at them.

To her death.

Cormac lurched into action, his heart pounding frantically as he ran. He called her name, screamed for her to stop, but she wasn't hearing him. He wasn't going to reach her in time.

No wonder no one had cared when he and Thia had gotten loose.

"Thia, stop! *Stop!*"

Something struck his back and sent him sprawling. *Wanfyr,* he identified when his mind cleared a second later. Scraggly heather pricked his skin. Grit peppered his face and hands. He had lost his grip on the athame. Gone. He didn't care. He heard people approaching—didn't care. Lifting his head, he sought Thia, saw her stopped a few feet from a broad stone. She stared at something in her hand.

"Thia, don't go through the—"

A kick to his back cut off his words and knocked him back down. Steel flashed near his right hand: the athame, not lost after all. He grabbed it, rolled, slashed at reaching hands as he leapt to his feet.

Three men, their hoods fallen back, faced him. At the fire, Idris culled several more, sending them after Thia. Cormac had to get to her before they did. Before she resumed her run toward a boundary strong enough to kill.

He slashed again, faked left and darted right. It might have worked, but a *fyr*-ball struck the ground ahead, forced him to make an awkward pivot. Another explosion threw twigs and dirt in his face. His eyes burned, teared. He dodged a tackle only to take a solid kick to his side. He staggered, tripped on something and fell, the breath whooshing out of his lungs even before someone planted a knee on his back. A hard boot came down on his hand, pinning it.

Cormac had thought to keep the recovery of his powers a secret, partly to cover up for the fact that the Stone had been removed from the altar. But he couldn't see a way around it now. Struggling to catch sight of Thia, he gathered energy.

She hadn't moved, seemingly transfixed by something held on her palm. It glowed, a bright, golden sphere.

Sudden comprehension froze the breath in Cormac's chest.

Idris roared, no doubt realizing the same: Matthew's death, unintentional though it was, had completed the ritual.

Cormac flung *wælfȳr* at the men holding him down. At such close range, it was impossible to miss. Freed, he pushed off in a dead run.

"Thia! Drop the Stone!" he screamed. "Drop it!"

● ○ ●

She didn't understand what was happening. With only a few feet between her and the perimeter, the Stone had heated in her hand. She'd looked down at it and been astonished to see dark patterns swirling beneath the blood-smeared surface.

It trembled suddenly, startling her so badly she would have dropped it had it not seemed to cling to her palm. The bloody smears sank into it to merge with the writhing shadows. The glossy, once-again pristine surface sparkled invitingly, like tea poured over ice on a hot summer's day, and began to glow.

Mine.

Shivering, she closed her hand, felt the call travel along her spine. The tremors increased and a clear, high-pitched tone sounded. Like that of a delicate bell.

Mine.

"Yes," she said, as if a question had been asked.

Or an offer made.

She looked up to see Cormac about to run her down. His mouth moved like he was shouting but all she could hear was the crystal as its initial, pleasant tone rose to an ear-splitting wail. Cormac wrapped his arms around her, took her down in a tackle as the Stone exploded.

Thia's vision blanked white and what felt like a thousand hot needles stabbed into her skin.

She didn't feel herself hit the perimeter path's hard-packed dirt with Cormac on top of her. The Cailleach's power was burning its way along every nerve, every fiber. Her muscles tensed, cramping. She tasted metal on her tongue. Her bones ignited.

Dimly, she wondered if she could change her answer.

● ○ ●

She didn't know how much time passed in agony. The clearing of her vision was a gradually thing, eventually presenting her with a ball of white on a black background. It didn't make much sense until she realized she lay on her back. She was seeing the full moon shining down on her from a starless sky.

Cormac's face moved to block her view. His eyes were wide, lit as if with a brilliant blue flame. As in the moment before he'd tackled her, his mouth shaped words she couldn't hear.

Her vision went out again as her entire body seized. Agony returned to sizzle and crackle through her bones. She couldn't stop shaking. A cry built but couldn't escape. She was going to die, electrocuted by a chunk of quartz. *Make it stop.* She would do anything to make it stop.

"*Muileach.*" Cormac's voice suddenly came through loud and clear. "Please, you have to let me help."

Yes, help, Thia thought, unable to speak. Help *now*. She felt herself drifting, seeking escape. Any escape at all.

Cormac's hand touched her cheek, and he sucked in a sharp breath. "I'm sorry," he said, and then lifted her. She'd thought she could not possibly hurt worse, but she had been wrong.

"We won't go far—just to where they can't see us," he said as she felt herself moving. The pressure in her chest built to a scream. "Shh. It's all right. You're all right."

She couldn't have disagreed more.

"Here. It's done." Horizontal motion became vertical and then stopped altogether.

She became aware of him, the feel of him, as pain receded. His arms were around her, holding her to his chest. Her head rested on his shoulder. Her forehead rested against his neck.

He was warm. Warm and so very dear.

Gradually, the sensation of razor-cuts lessened to pin-pricks. Long, stabby pins, but still. It was much easier to breathe. Shaking became trembling. She could almost think again.

● ○ ●

"That's better, isn't it," Cormac said, trying not to shift Thia too much when he leaned to one side, craned his neck to look beyond the monolith's edge to the mess inside the Ring. It looked like a bomb had gone off.

In a way, it had. When Thia had claimed the Stone's powers, a shock wave had struck down objects and people alike, blown out fires, shattered the boundary wards, and burned off the fog. Such was the strength of what she had taken into herself. Elemental energy, as potent as it was unpredictable.

Cormac slid back behind the stone. There was a little time, with everyone within the Ring currently incapacitated, either unconscious or moaning on the ground. "Ease into it," he told Thia. "Let it find its way."

"Hurts."

He stroked her hair, rested his cheek on its softness as he held her to him, the energy uniting them both. "I know it does, love. I know it does."

And he did. The same Otherworldly power that was trying to make a new home in her coursed through his body as well. The crucial difference was that he had Otherworldly blood. She didn't. Nor had she any experience with this sort of thing.

If he hadn't been close enough to hear the crystal's keening; if he hadn't gotten to her in time to mitigate the impact of the explosion; if she hadn't trusted him enough to accept his offer of help, allowing him to siphon off some of the power—

So many ifs. He tightened his hold, allowed her warmth, her soft strength, to soothe his fear. "*Muileach.*"

She made a plaintive sound. Not quite a moan, not quite a

cry.

It tore at him more fiercely than a scream.

"I'm sorry, *muileach*. I'm so, so sorry."

His Sight alerted him to increased movement inside the Ring. Idris was attempting to stand. Soon he would rouse his people and the hunt would commence.

Thia made a sleepy sound, nuzzled Cormac's neck.

"*Muileach*." He gave her a little shake. "Love. We need to get you away from here. Can you walk, or do I need to carry—"

"Cormac?" She sounded surprised. "I feel strange."

He could imagine. "Like something dances in your bones?"

He felt her nod.

"It should settle eventually."

"What did I do?"

He wondered how much of that was natural confusion and how much was memory loss. "You don't remember?"

She made a derisive snort. "I wish I could *forget*. No, I mean what the hell did I do? I was running and the Stone started going crazy. Glowing, absorbing blood, making noise—" She broke off with a shiver. Pressed more firmly against him.

"It's over now." Cormac tilted his head, let it rest against hers while he kept his Sight trained on the Ring. They had so little time, but he answered. "Matthew's death completed the ritual. He became the sacrifice. Because you were holding the Stone when it happened, you became the focus."

She was silent a long moment. Then, "The Cailleach's power is in *me* now?"

"Whatever of it had been bound within the relic, yes. Minus whatever went out in the explosion. Or into me."

She took a deep breath, then slowly let it out. "What does that mean? For me, I mean. Will it do things to me? Will I be able to do things with it?"

"I should think you'll have a lot of new abilities." As might he. There was no way to know, really, with new power.

Idris, along with Cassie, had moved to the altar. Their hands worked patterns in the air.

"The wards are being resurrected," Cormac said. "We need to go."

Thia looked beside them, at a gap between the stones. "Is that what those are? The colors shimmering between the— what?" She shifted, trying to get a look at his face. "What's the matter?"

He willed the sudden tension out of his body, maintained an easy expression. "That's what one looks like as it forms, yes."

"You've always seen them this way?"

"It's part of the Sight. An Otherworldly trait."

She settled back against him with a rueful laugh. "I can't believe I was worried about becoming an eccentric. I'm so far beyond that now."

Humor. She had the right to be frightened out of her mind, yet she was able to beat it back. And laugh about it.

To bravery, he thought, remembering his toast to her on the flight, and felt a catch in his chest. In its many forms.

"We need to get you away from here," he said again, and helped her to her feet.

She wobbled, her face drawn with exhaustion, then offered a small smile. "Where to?"

● ○ ●

"Allow me," Cormac said, and Thia squeaked in surprise when he scooped her up and ran.

At the outer ditch, a good distance from the stones, he set her on the slope, crouched down beside her.

"I don't think they saw us," she whispered, peeking over the rim. The colorful shimmers around the Ring had grown more saturated. Bolder. She blinked, still having trouble believing her eyes weren't playing tricks. Idris and Cassie continued to wave their hands around—making the wards. So, as colorful as the boundary was, it wasn't finished yet.

Cormac, studying her, radiated concern. "We could remain here awhile longer," he said, his voice pitched low, "give you more time to—"

"I'll be okay." When he moved like he would pick her up, she stopped him with a hand on his chest. "I can walk."

He arched a skeptical brow. "But can you run?"

Run? She felt like overcooked pasta. "Sure."

A corner of his mouth quirked. "You're a terrible liar." He moved toward her again. "Let's—" He stopped. A strange mix of emotions flashed across his face.

"Cormac?"

Regret. Right before he vanished, she thought she saw regret.

CHAPTER 25

The Ring of Brodgar, Orkney
Samhain

It took Thia a moment to realize that she wasn't shaking; the ground was. Shouts from all directions filled the air. She turned to the closest—behind—and found she was about to be overrun by a charging line of people. People brandishing a crazy assortment of weapons. Pikes and crossbows. Assault rifles. Pistols. Swords. Lots of swords, she noted, frozen.

Not that there was anywhere for her to go even if she *could* get her feet to move. People were coming at the Ring from every direction. There was no way to avoid them, no cover to take. The closest line charged down the far side of the ditch and she braced herself, cursed Cormac for abandoning her.

Just when she was sure she was about to be mowed down, she heard her name. "Thia! Thia, oh thank *Morrígu!*"

She turned and was promptly caught up in Kendra's fierce, embrace. Together they staggered, found their balance. Thia returned the hug, giving as good as she got—and then had to fend off an ill-timed rush of emotion.

"Thank God." Kendra shouted in Thia's ear while people thundered past. "We were so worried."

"What are you doing here?" Thia stepped back to get a good look. Kendra kept hold of her, as if fearing she'd fall. Maybe she would have. "Am I imagining you?"

"I came with Murphy. And Abby. We met some Society of Brigantium forces on the way. There's no time to explain," she said with an apologetic shake of her head. "I need to rejoin the others, and you need to get out of here. There's one of our vehicles, a van from a tour company, parked not far from here. The name McSweeny is on the side. The keys should be under the seat. Take it and go. Follow the signs to Stromness and wait in the lot by the harbor, okay? By the harbor. We'll find you when this is done. Gods, I'm so glad you're okay."

Thia was pulled into another hug before Abby's friend—no, her friend too, now—ran to catch up with the others.

"Wait," Thia called, chasing after. She was so sick of being left behind. "I want to help. I need to help." But Kendra was fast, and Thia faltered upon seeing what was happening inside the Ring.

Chaos, utter and nightmarish, and all she could think for a moment was that Cormac was somewhere at its heart. As was Abby, according to Kendra—who was no longer anywhere in sight. A few feet away, one of Idris's black-robed acolytes was run though by a pike and thrown to the ground by a man in a brown delivery-company uniform.

Throughout the Ring, a great battle raged. Men and women from both sides were swinging clubs, hacking at one another with swords, and most bizarre of all, flinging strange glowing spheres of blue or white. Some who fell got up to fight again. Some dragged themselves—or were dragged—away. Others remained as they had fallen, dying or already dead.

Cold horror rooted Thia to the spot. There was no plan to the fighting, no organization. Only violence. Shouts and cries of rage and agony; explosions of rock and other debris when the strange spheres missed their targets and struck ground instead; the sharp crack and echo of gunfire; the clash of steel. Patches of heather smoldered, clouding the recently-cleared air with acrid smoke.

Thia couldn't begin to think how to help. There had to be

something, but she only knew the very basics of self defense—
and shouts of "fire" would be utterly useless. She had power
but no knowledge.

A voice cried out to her left, where a middle-aged woman
in corduroy pants and a tweed blazer grappled with a robed
man. Thia ran, picked up a rock she spotted along the way.
Coming upon Idris's man from behind, she clubbed him on
the head.

She would never forget *that* sound, either. Or the way the
body went utterly limp and dropped.

The woman he had been fighting stared at Thia; and then
as shock gave way to gratitude, she smiled. Round and a bit
pudgy with pale skin creased with age, she reminded Thia of
a favorite school librarian. Beneath the tweed was an argyle
sweater. She had to be about sixty.

"Thank you, dear," the woman panted. "Oh, do look out."
Shoving Thia aside, she lifted her hands. Two white, glowing
spheres quickly formed above her palms. She flung them and
Thia whirled around, saw them strike the chests of two men
who had been charging with raised swords. They fell back,
crying out, to writhe on the ground.

"Come." The woman tugged Thia's arm. "Beatrice is looking
for you."

"She's here?"

The woman had already set off at a jog. Thia joined her.

Just past two Ring stones, a robed man was about to club a
man on the ground. The woman shouted a word that sounded
like Latin and threw another of those strange white spheres.
It struck the wooden club, blowing it apart. Flaming debris
ignited the man's robes. He shrieked, flailing in a wild panic
which only served to fan the flames.

"'Ta, Nell." The rescued man, grinning through his thick
white beard, rose to join them. He carried a staff. Something
at the tip—a large crystal?—glowed blue. "Damned nuisance,

this heather. Tripped me right up. You're Leticia's grandniece, eh?"

"Yes," Thia said, surprised by that. By so many things, really.

Taking the innermost position beside them as they jogged along the Ring's edge, he kept his arm raised as if to make a curtain of his cloak's sleeve. Blue velvet with yellow stars and crescent moons, the pattern was like something out of a children's book.

"It's protected," he said, noticing Thia's attention. "Guided by my will, it makes us invisible to most."

"Most?"

"No guarantees. Especially not with magic, as you'll learn. I'm Damian. Sorry to meet under such circumstances. You've already met Nell here, of course, from the Islands Branch."

"Brigantium?"

Nell's smile was sweet. "Of course, dear."

Thia saw Eben not far ahead, directing the construction of a barricade made from what appeared to be sheets of Plexiglas mounted on interlocking, metal frames. Behind it, Beatrice stood at the apex of a huddled group. Thick white smoke rose from their midst. Eben spoke into some sort of hand-held device, and the smoke plumed red. The outside of the Plexiglas clouded, turning an opaque white. As Thia passed behind it, she saw that the inside view remained clear.

"Thia, thank goodness," Beatrice greeted and then returned her attention to the group. She, like the others of the group, wore a white cloak shot with silver. The smoke came from a cauldron set atop a small folding table. It continued to billow red as they chanted.

"Let it be done," said Beatrice. A column of fire shot up, making people flinch (Thia among them). When the flames died down, the smoke was again white.

"Here we go," Nell murmured beside Thia as the ground's shaking increased. The standing stones themselves began to tremble, humming like giant tuning forks.

Where were Kendra and Abby? Where had Cormac gone? Terrified though Thia was, she couldn't stay behind the barricade. She couldn't do *nothing* while people she cared about were in danger. She turned to go.

Damian laid a firm hand on her shoulder. "Not now."

A new bank of fog poured out from the center of the Ring, rapidly enveloping the ongoing confusion. Those who weren't dressed in black robes ran for the barricade.

Not all of them made it. Those overtaken by the fog did not emerge. Rapid bursts of weapons-fire could be heard coming from within as flashes of color went off like lightning inside a cloud. The glow balls, Thia assumed, after one flew out to blow up a good-sized patch of earth in front of the barricade. Eben, standing near a narrow opening, waved people in from the field.

"How were you able to get here?" she asked Damian. "They told me no one could find their way in the fog."

"They didn't consider Quentin," he said proudly. "Got us all the way to Stenness before he lost his bearings. Your friends were already there. We were working with that Murphy fellow to track some sort of mobile phone signal when this place lit up like a beacon. And then that explosion blew the fog clear. Knocked out the wards, too, just like that." He snapped and a spark flared between his fingers, startling them both. "Sorry. I keep forgetting powers are heightened here."

"Thia, dear." Beatrice joined them. "I'm so relieved that you aren't—" Her expression hardened, her eyes like cold glass. "You have power."

Damian looked confused. "She didn't before?"

"I didn't mean for it to happen," Thia said.

"Didn't you?" Beatrice's accusation took Thia aback.

"No! Well...I mean, there was a moment when I accepted, but I didn't set out to—"

Thunder clapped overhead, jarring the ground.

"We can deal with it later"—Beatrice snagged Thia's wrist—"and make use of it now."

When she tried to dislodge the firm grip, Damian took hold of her other arm. "It'll be alright," he said.

They took her past the cauldron. The people who had stood around it had relocated to a few feet away. More had joined them, forming a large circle. One of the newcomers was Abby.

● ○ ●

He'd done it. Cormac had summoned a storm—on Samhain night, no less. On Orkney. At least he wasn't riding it. Not yet, at any rate, he thought grimly. Maybe news would be slow to reach the Otherworld and (assuming he survived) he laid low, it would all blow over...figuratively speaking. Better yet, maybe he could find a way to pin the whole of the blame on Idris. There were, after all, two storms forming overhead. As long as no one found out whose had come first, it might work.

He triggered another clap of thunder, gathered more rain while he dodged a series of *wælfȳr* flung by his half-sister. He sent one of his own as he dove to crouch behind one of the wider megaliths. With each explosion against it, cracks spread through the weathered flagstone. He'd have to abandon its cover soon. Preferably not until the winds arrived.

That his father would summon a storm to rival Cormac's was deliciously petty—and exactly what he'd counted on. The old man couldn't stand to think someone else could best him in anything. And with his concentration less and less on the fight on the ground and more on the clouds gathering overhead, Murphy and the Brigantium might be able to gain the advantage.

The truly thrilling part of it all was that Cormac was able to draw strength from the storm instead of expending his own. He had to think it was because of what he'd absorbed of the Cailleach's powers. Storms were one of her areas of expertise.

The Ring might have something to do with it as well.

He sent a fat bolt of lightning straight into the resurrected central fire. Flaming chunks of wood flew up amidst a shower of sparks. Unfortunately, Cassie's shriek was more outraged than pained. She lobbed another *fýr*-ball his way.

Cormac hoped Thia understood what had happened back at the henge, that she knew his leaving hadn't been his idea. But with only seconds between his sense of Idris's summons and the event itself, there'd been no time to explain.

More *wælfýr* struck the stone, blowing the top to bits and sending shards down on Cormac's head.

● ○ ●

"Abby," Thia said, and felt some of her nerves settle. "Who's minding the store?"

"We closed early." Abby's smile was mixed with relief and exasperation. Exasperation that quickly turned to shock. Her violet eyes widened. "What the hell have you done to yourself? Where'd you get all that power?"

"By meddling," Beatrice said as people moved to allow her to join the circle.

Damian guided Thia in beside her. "Will you let us use it? The power," he clarified at her blank look.

"Gladly, but I don't know how. I wish I did, but—"

No sooner had the words left Thia's mouth then she felt a tingle in her spine. It spread, moving out through her bones.

"Become part of our circle," Damian instructed, extending his hand. "We'll do the rest."

Thia clasped it; then, with her left, Beatrice's. The rest of the group—sixteen in all, including Abby—followed suit.

"Relax," Beatrice told Thia. "Let the energy flow out."

"Permanently?"

"No," was Damian's disappointing answer. "Once power is taken into ourselves, it becomes part of us. Think of it as a rechargeable battery. When power is used, the battery loses charge. Over time or with certain aids, it will recharge. Right now, we're hoping to harness what's in your battery, combine it with ours, and direct that at Idris."

"Okay," she told Damian, despite her confusion (and a good number of misgivings). She then tried to make it happen.

He chuckled. "Don't work so hard. Let it do what it will."

"Sorry. I'm not used to—"

Heat shot down Thia's arms, burning her palms. There was a collective gasp. She watched people startle, tensing, as the energy moved down the line.

"T-too much." The strained voice belonged to a man who stood directly across the circle. Abby, beside him, looked over with concern, asked him something too faint for Thia to hear.

It took her a moment to recognize him from the elevator. Quentin. His eyes, locked on hers, were glowing blue—the same sapphire blue as the strange, deadly spheres. The same blue she had seen in Cormac's eyes when he'd held her after the Stone exploded and she'd been unable to think past the pain. Had her eyes done that too? Glowed?

Quentin dropped to his knees, though he continued to hold hands with Abby and the white-cloaked man at his right. Even at a distance, Thia could see him breathing hard. "Shouldn't we stop?" she asked Beatrice.

"No."

"But it's hurting him. We should at least let him step out."

Beatrice shot her a sharp look. "He'll be fine. He's the only one of us who can possibly wield such an amount." *Her* eyes were not glowing. Nor were Damian's.

Thia looked around the rest of the circle, found no others. Only Quentin's. "He's getting all the power?"

She knew what that was like: Hell. She opened her fingers, but Beatrice and Damian held fast. She tugged. "Let go. It's too much."

She tried to shut off the outward flow of energy but had no more luck than when she had made a conscious effort to start it. It continued to out through her hands—and Beatrice and Damian wouldn't let go.

"Abby," she called across to her friend, "let go of his hand!"

"Leave it be," Beatrice hissed, her grip painfully tight.

"It's too much," Thia insisted. The glow of Quentin's eyes had gone from blue to white.

"He won't let me," Abby yelled, clearly alarmed. "I'm not sure he can."

Quentin shuddered. His chin dropped to his chest.

"Oh, God. It's killing him. Please," Thia begged. She backed away, digging her heels in as her arms became like the rope in a tug-of-war.

"He'll be fine," Beatrice said loudly as others began to look unsure. "No one is permitted to break the circle!"

"Let go," Abby shouted, struggling with the woman holding her left hand. Quentin, trembling violently, continued to grip her right. This was wrong, Thia thought. Beatrice was wrong. Yes, Idris needed to be stopped, but there had to be another way.

"It's mine to use," Thia said, gathering herself. Even if she didn't know how, the power was *hers*. "Mine to give. Mine to keep." She wrenched herself backwards and her hand slipped free of Damian's grasp. She suspected that this time he hadn't resisted.

The circle broken, power slammed back into her, white-hot and furious. As she stumbled and Beatrice released her other hand, she saw Quentin crumple to the ground.

● ○ ●

"You've been keeping too many secrets, *father*," Cormac said, and then grunted as he deflected a swipe of Idris's power.

The sorcerer roared in anger, tried again.

Again, Cormac deflected. Grinned. "This isn't your strong-hold with its restrictions and protections. And *I'm* the one who received new power tonight."

"It is still nothing compared to mine," Idris shouted back, his eyes glowing gold while he summoned more energy. "Not tonight. Not ever."

An icy wind slammed into Cormac, forced him back a few steps. Teeth gritted, he adjusted his stance and extended his arms, palms out. "*Adsoro,*" he murmured, and the gale swept back upon itself, returning to Idris.

"You've already lost." Cormac pitched his voice above the rumble of thunder as the storms clashed overhead. Despite the freezing cold, sweat poured down his face, stung his eyes. "The Cailleach's powers are out of your reach. Your Matthew is dead, and the Brigantium—"

"—will not survive this fight," Idris shouted over him. He stabbed his staff into the earth. "*Kristaje!*"

The ground rippled like the surface of a pond after a thrown pebble. Around them in the swirling Druid Fog, combatants struggled to keep their balance.

"The Cailleach's powers are not out of my reach," Idris said, his lips pulled back from his teeth in a skeletal grin. "They are shared between you and the girl. It will be my pleasure to remove them from you both."

Cormac felt a sick wash of fear before the earth beneath his feet heaved, tossed him up as wave after wave rolled out from where Idris stood, his staff the epicenter of a massive quake.

● ○ ●

Thia landed hard on ground which continued to undulate like a magic-fingers bed gone haywire. Behind her, the makeshift altar rattled, swaying wildly and sending steaming liquid over the sides of the cauldron teetering toward its edge.

"Hurry—we're losing ground," Damian bellowed, getting to

his feet. He extended his hand, helped Thia up before he then rushed to assist Beatrice in stabilizing the altar...by levitating it.

"Don't touch me, I'm fine," snapped someone to her right, drawing her attention.

Quentin, standing with obvious difficulty, was waving away Abby's offered help.

He wasn't dead. Thia hurried over, braced his arm to steady him. "I'm so sorry. I had no idea what—"

He shook her off and straightened. Her breath caught. His eyes glowed silver. "It was expected," he said tonelessly. "Too much too soon, that's all."

"Bullshit," said Abby, and Quentin leveled his gaze on her. She didn't so much as flinch, and Thia fought the unexpected but welcome urge to smile. She had seen Abby face down an entire bus-load of adolescent girls bent on retail mayhem. If Quentin thought she'd cower at a look—even an eerily silver one—he was in for a disappointment.

"In any case," Thia said quickly, "I'm glad you're all right."

"Thank you." He gave Abby one last glare before he shifted his attention to the ground. "There you are, you bugger." At the snap of his fingers, a cane rose from the trampled heather to fly to his outstretched hand. Instead of using it for support, he lifted it above his head.

"Ready or not," he shouted above the noise.

"Get it done," came Beatrice's sharp reply.

He slanted Thia a glance. "You and your friend will want to look away."

Not fast enough. The light that shot from the cane's silver top blinded Thia worse than a xenon high beam. From some distance away, she heard shrieking—that fell abruptly silent. Much as she wanted to look, she wouldn't be able to see if she tried. Behind her closed lids, her vision burned red. She pressed the heels of her hands to her eyes.

"Thia, come on," Abby said, pulling Thia's hand down and holding tight as she dragged her several feet to the right.

"But—"

"Here we go," Damian shouted next to Thia's ear. He took hold of her other hand. "The fog is clearing!"

Thia blinked hard, tried to usher away the jagged red after-image. She had been joined into another energy-chain, she came to understand when power began to travel through her, in one hand and out the other. None of it was hers.

Damian leaned in to speak in her ear. "*Expedio.*"

Thia's vision cleared. "Oh." Blinking, she looked around in surprise. "Thank you."

"Of course."

She stood as part of a line of people along the plexiglass. As Damian had said, the fog was clearing, laying bare a field of torn earth littered with bodies. Some moved; most did not. She couldn't locate Kendra in any of the pockets of continued fighting, and hoped she wasn't among the fallen.

With extreme hesitation, Thia considered adding a measure of her own energy to the mix. Just a teeny, tiny bit maybe... yes.

That was all it took. No sooner had she decided than she felt it happen. No special technique needed. No learned skill. She had only to think it, to wish it, and it was done.

She was careful this time to include a wish for it to be done gradually and not in such an amount that someone might get hurt.

Blue spheres flew from somewhere near Idris's broken altar only to burst harmlessly against the plexiglass. It was warded, she realized, seeing the telltale shimmer of color as sphere after sphere struck. Was there a limit to the protection, Thia wondered. Would the barrier weaken after a certain number of hits? Whoever launched the glow-balls seemed to think so.

Quentin ducked beneath her arm to stand at the front of

the line. He held his cane high by the glossy black stick. From its silver knob, bright light flashed. A jagged bolt shot across the Ring's ravaged field toward where two men stood silhouetted against the central fire.

The bolt struck something unseen above their heads and exploded.

Thia's breath caught.

"Shielded," someone said from her right. "Try again."

"No!" Thia broke free to step in front of Quentin and make a grab for the cane.

He held it out of reach, blocked her with his free arm.

"Please," she begged. "That's Cormac. He's on your side."

Quentin's silvered gaze narrowed, flicked from her to the fight between sorcerer and son.

"What's this?" Beatrice called. "Why have you stopped?"

Quentin looked again at Thia, spoke in a low voice. "You trust him? Truthfully, now."

"No."

His head tilted, brows quirked.

"But I know he doesn't want Idris to win."

"Fair enough." Quentin looked skyward and with a cryptic, "I think that one is his," shot a massive bolt into the clouds.

Thia yelled, reaching for the cane too late. She could only watch, breath frozen in her lungs, as Cormac doubled over and clutched his chest.

● ○ ●

Power. Pure, unmitigated power flowed from Cormac's storm and into his body. Too much, he thought. Already too much, and more coming.

Barely aware of Idris's shouts, Cormac opened to the energy, felt it shoot to the very tips of his fingers. Burning, pounding, demanding to be let out.

But he couldn't.

Not yet.

"*Sile trei sme*," he whispered and, spreading his arms wide, he brought down the storm.

● ○ ●

By the time Thia became aware that a roar of wind had joined the cacophony, the wall of water was nearly upon them.

"Brace yourselves! Take cover if you can!" Damian shouted as rain, blown horizontal on a gale, slammed into the plexiglass barricades and then, driven up and over, into the people. Any and everything was drenched in an instant. The folding table and cauldron crashed down with great .

Thia felt herself slipping, pushed by the flood of rainwater and unable to find traction on ground that had largely turned to mud. She grabbed onto Abby only to have Damian slide into them from behind. The three of them went down in a rolling, tangled mess of legs and arms and clothing.

A lone voice cut through the chaos: "*Kom mene brigo, sedaje rasta, sedaje winto!*"

Idris's voice, bellowing a bunch of nonsense as far as Thia was concerned, but that didn't mean it didn't terrify. She flung off what felt like yards of sodden blue-and-gold cloth which had gotten draped over her head and shoulders.

The wind pounded, hammering rain like nails through her clothes as she pushed to her knees. The barricades were down, scattered far and wide. The fighting throughout the Ring had lessened, thanks to the fact that hardly anyone could stand. Idris stood near the ruin of his altar. She couldn't see Cormac.

A gust shrieked overhead, hurling a column of rain straight for Idris. Simultaneously, a jagged needle of lightning struck the top of his shielding wards, causing them to flash a dull green. Shouting more strange words, Idris took a jerky step back, nearly tripped on a toppled altar stone.

Thia got to her feet, braced herself against the wind.

"What the hell are you doing, Thia, get down," Abby barked from where she and Damian were still trying to disentangle themselves. A flash of lighting briefly cast everything in an emerald hue, and a near-instantaneous thunderclap shook the ground.

Idris staggered, his cloak twisting around him in the wind. A blur of motion caught Thia's eye.

Cormac, racing toward Idris.

All around Thia, people stopped, their attention riveted as Cormac launched himself at his father. The tackle took both out of sight behind the ruined altar. There was a moment of stunned stillness, and then Thia joined countless others in a race to the Ring's center.

● ○ ●

Cormac was beyond thought, beyond anything but a desperate, all-consuming need to destroy. His hands wrapped around Idris's neck. He felt cartilage collapse, joints crack. Idris, his *athair*, his father, stared up at him through amber eyes wide with terror.

The raw emotion, the humanity of it, rattled Cormac more than a physical assault could have. His grip loosened...but he didn't pull away.

And because of that—because his hands remained—it did not matter that Cormac hesitated, that he might have made a different choice. A surge of external power, sent through the storm, used him as a conduit to get to Idris and destroy from the inside out.

Though Cormac didn't know it, he was screaming. A caustic, nearly unintelligible torrent of apology and regret. He didn't feel the burn of it in his throat. Didn't feel hot tears mix with the rain as it continued to pound, soaking him and the man who mouthed silent pleas for mercy that Cormac was unable to give.

He might have, but this was out of his control.

Idris stopped pleading. His eyes dulled. Beneath Cormac's hands, his father's pulse fluttered to a stop. And with it, the overriding current of power.

He heard himself then, hardly recognizing his broken voice. "*Athair.* Forgive me. *Inchóire.* I'm sorry." Sickened, disgusted, he unclenched his fingers, pulled his cramped hands away.

Idris's head lolled to the side, his eyes fixed and vacant.

Cormac stared, disbelieving. What had he done?

There was no time to consider it. With Idris's death, every bit of power he had amassed in his unnaturally long life shot back out into the world. The explosion of energy struck with enough force to send Cormac flying.

Too stunned to protect himself, he landed awkwardly, rolled several feet to come to rest on his stomach. He didn't move, just lay there and tried to retake the breath that had been knocked from his lungs. Tried to comprehend what he had done. What had been done *through* him. His actions had not been his own. He would not have done that by choice...would he?

Yet, he had not tried to stop it.

Could he have, if he'd tried? He would never know.

At last, Cormac raised his head. He had not been the only one bowled over by the outward rush of power. The field was a mess of churned earth and the fallen. The rain had stopped; the winds, calmed. The surge had cleared both storms, and the moon once again shone brightly upon the Ring.

He had killed his father.

Voices began to call out: some in uncertainty; others in an attempt to regroup. Cormac rose onto his knees, pressed a shaking hand to his mouth. A sound that was both a laugh and sob escaped.

He was free.

At the rage-filled cry of his name, he turned to find his

half-sister standing at the edge of the Ring. Behind her, two men held Thia's arms pinned between them.

"You owe me, brother dear." The blade of Cassie's athame gleamed. And when she held the tip to Thia's chest, directly above the heart, Cormac felt the blood drain from his own.

● ○ ●

Thia understood it had been foolish to run toward him, but at the time it had been an overwhelming impulse. If just now the slightest movement was not liable to result in immediate death, she would gladly kick herself.

Her gaze locked with Cormac's. He stood about twenty feet away, his expression unconcerned. Either he was an excellent poker player or he really didn't care. She wasn't about to take bets on which.

"Let her go, *claimsech*." The unfamiliar voice belonged to a man Thia had never seen before. He walked over from the smoldering ashes of the central fire to stand alongside the still silent, still unconcerned Cormac. His right hand held a kind of battleaxe. Dirt and other dark substances Thia really did not want to contemplate speckled his skin and what had once been a very fine dove-gray suit.

Behind him, an odd group calmly assembled. Grim-faced, menacing. Fierce. Whoever they were, they did not belong to the Brigantium.

Even the Brigantium's security team, standing at a distance with their automatic weapons and military bearing, managed to maintain a certain reserve, a polish which said that, while they *could* use violence, they would rather not. These people, however, dressed in all manner of clothing—everything from jeans and flannel shirts to delivery uniforms to what looked a lot like the red-vested usher's outfit from Granite Springs's Shakespeare Festival—were in themselves weapon-sharp and lethal. Not only *could* they use violence, but they *would,* and maybe even enjoy it.

Thia was astonished to see Kendra standing among them... and looking as if she belonged. Her expression held a deadly calm while she wiped the blade of a short sword clean on her sleeve.

Thia was going to have a long talk with both of her friends when this was over.

Assuming she lived through it.

"You've lost," the man told Cassie, and took an assured step forward. "Idris is gone. Your ranks are broken. Those who are able have run already or look as if they're about to. Release the woman and things will go a sight easier. Harm her, and you'll know no end of hell."

Cassie's laugh was manic. Brittle. "You dare to threaten me, *áploga?* I don't think so."

The man shifted his grip on the axe. Faint, blue flames flickered along the blade.

"Mr. Murphy speaks out of turn." A worse-for-wear Beatrice pushed past the group, with an even worser-for-wear Eben at her side. "But he speaks the truth."

Cassie scoffed but it lacked conviction, and Thia felt a flare of hope.

It was clear that Idris's death had thrown his people into confusion. Some had attempted to take up the battle where it had left off, but even Thia could tell they were floundering. Others simply keened, prostrate with grief, or stood watching from the outer edge of the Ring. Waiting, she guessed, to see how this standoff would go.

If not for her, would it all be over?

She clenched her hands at her sides, nails digging into flesh as guilt churned. She would never forgive herself if anyone got hurt because of her. But what could she do? Every option she came up with involved moving—which, with a knife poking her chest, really didn't seem like a good idea.

"This isn't over," Cassie yelled. "Not until I get the power from this one"—she set the knife point to Thia's neck—"and my brother"—bizarrely, that referred to Cormac—"pays the price for patricide. Conveniently, the one will bring about the other."

Cormac's expression had become easy to read: pure malice. Above his upturned palms, blue spheres hovered.

Cassie set her mouth at Thia's ear. "You and I have a debt to settle over Matthew first, though, don't we? And *that* will take some time, I think, to do right."

She vanished.

Cormac hurled the spheres—not at the shockingly absent Cassie but at the men holding Thia. They released her, tried to dodge. The glow-balls struck them both high on the chest and they collapsed.

Thia stumbled forward, off balance but free.

● ○ ●

Of Idris's surviving followers, those who were not broken in body or spirit scattered, running out of the Ring and into the moonlit countryside. Many of the Brigantium and Murphy's people gave chase. Cormac was surprised the latter didn't simply shoot them as they ran, but perhaps even mercenaries had a code of honor.

He watched Thia approach. She was a mess. Soaking wet, muddied and bruised with scratches on her face, her hair wild as a *bean sidhe's* and littered with bits of heather and soil. She was looking at him with an expression of relief on her lovely face and...something more in her eyes.

He didn't know what to say, what to do until she stepped up and did it for him. Her arms slid beneath his to wrap around his chest and she leaned in, rested the side of her head against his collarbone. Her breath feathered against his neck, and he struggled against a flood of emotion.

Almost of their own accord, his arms moved to hold her

close.

"Are you alright?" she asked softly. The understanding in her voice was an arrow straight to his heart. He might have trembled, or made some small sound because her arms tightened around him.

Holding him together even as she worked to tear him apart with all this damned *feeling*. With her. For her. Too much.

Panic clawed at him, sank teeth into his lungs. His soul. He pulled back, pushed at her shoulders. "I can't," he said, almost choking on the words. He pushed again, and this time she released him, allowed him to step back.

She looked as if he had kicked her. Or torn out her heart. He turned, striding away, and shifted into raven form.

She'd be fine, he told himself as he flew high above Brodgar. Her friends were there. They would look after her. Protect her. He banked left, headed out over the water.

He didn't know where he thought to go. He only knew he couldn't stay.

● ○ ●

Thia watched the sky long after she had any hope of seeing him, a black bird in a black sky. But she had caught a glimpse when he'd passed in front of the moon. He might do so again, and then she would know he hadn't gone as far as she feared he had.

He might change his mind.

All around her, power continued to hum, as inescapable as were the remnants of terrible emotions: violence, hate, fear, revulsion...death.

Glowing white spheres, much larger than the ones thrown as weapons, floated high overhead to light the Ring. Red glistened on the heather, on the grass, on the stones. Bodies lay all around. Some were shrouded in the black robes which marked them as having been aligned with Idris. Others were dressed with more variety, their heads covered by items that had belonged to them or perhaps donated in an act of respect. Black military jackets. Wool coats. A sweater. A tweed blazer with a bit or argyle sweater peeking out beneath.

"Thia."

At Abby's quiet voice, Thia turned, found her standing with Kendra a good distance away. A polite distance, she thought, and could guess why they looked so uncomfortable. They had seen her with Cormac. And they'd seen him push her away.

Tears spilled over on her way to her friends, ran freely as she was nearly smothered in a double-hug. So many dead, but here was life. Here was love.

"I'm sorry you came," she told them both, thinking of the horrors they had gone through because of her. "But I'm so grateful you did."

EPILOGUE

Thia stopped, looked out across the landscape. As best as her friends and a dowsing crystal could figure it, this was the spot she had been driven past last night. The spot where Lettie had died.

She took in the sloping, heather-covered hillside, the sea at its distant base, calm and gray beneath a washed-out sky. The small, unassuming harbor not more than a mile away.

How close her great-aunt had come. How differently things might have gone.

"Oh, Lettie."

She knelt. Earlier, she had collected a trio of white seashells from the beach near her hotel. She took them now from her pocket, laid them on a bare patch of earth. Then, because it felt right, she used her finger to draw a triskele around them. It was a traditional design Lettie had loved. Thia had seen it often enough in her great-aunt's home to know.

"I miss you," she whispered, inexorably sad. "I miss you so much."

Now, especially.

She shivered as she straightened, tucked her hands into her coat pockets. A pair of gloves would be—

With that thought came one of Matt, and her last memory of him. His pale, shocked face. The fear in his eyes. The blood. Everywhere, blood. Had that only been last night? Less than nine hours ago, if she were counting. It was only morning.

She could still be in bed, she knew, sleeping safe and sound in the Kirkwall Hotel...if she were able to sleep.

Oh, she was tired enough. Tired enough, probably, to sleep a solid week. But her mind wouldn't settle. Either it replayed the past or tried to envision the future.

Lettie had made Thia her primary heir. Eclectica, her house in Granite Springs as well as the one in London, along with the bulk of their contents and a substantial investment portfolio, were now hers, left to her in the will that had turned up in a search of the Swintons's apartment. That same search had also turned up a number of Lettie's journals and choice pieces from her personal antiquities collection. Beatrice had explained it all over coffee less than an hour ago—right before she had offered membership and training.

Thia hadn't given an answer. Yes, she needed to understand the power which continued to skitter in her bones. Kendra believed it was only a matter of time before Thia's body and the power would adapt to one another, but couldn't say how *much* time. Weeks, maybe months. Maybe more. Thia didn't think she could take "more," though it wasn't as if she had a choice. At least the pain had passed. The worst now was the fear.

Fear of the unknown.

The potential.

Could the Brigantium help with that? Maybe. Or maybe she shouldn't trust them. Lettie hadn't.

As to that, Beatrice's theory was that somehow Lettie had come to suspect Idris's infiltration. A reasonable assumption, since that had indeed happened. Yet Thia wondered if there hadn't been more to Lettie's concern.

Another worry was Beatrice's treatment of Quentin during the battle. Would that be Thia's future with them? To be no more than a tool—a weapon—to be used in times of crisis?

On its surface, such an idea seemed almost noble: personal sacrifice for the greater good. What better use of power could there be? But there were two problems. One, Thia had to be sure the greater good was what the Brigantium had in mind. Two, she needed to know that any sacrifices she might make would be done by choice. No matter what Quentin said, she didn't believe he had been given one. Could she risk putting herself in the same position?

Thanks to her friends, she might not have to. According to Kendra, much of what the Brigantium could offer in terms of training could be found in Granite Springs.

That needed more explanation, Thia thought, once again staring out at the sea. There was so much she didn't know about Kendra, about Abby—and Granite Springs in general. The idea that she had been surrounded by mystics, witches, and the like would take some getting used to.

But Granite Springs had become home. She may not have understood all the town was, but that didn't change how she felt about it. And Eclectica was hers now. She was responsible for it—not just the online branch, but all of it.

That should have alarmed her, considering how unprepared she knew herself to be. Instead she found herself smiling, her battered heart beating a little lighter in her chest.

There was her answer.

After taking a last look at the misty landscape and the small memorial she'd made to Lettie, Thia shrugged the tightness from her shoulders and walked back along the road to where her friends waited in the car.

She tried not to think too much about Cormac except to tell herself that the means of his freedom had been profoundly traumatic. He was entitled to do what he needed in order to cope.

That he had needed to push her away and leave hurt more than she would admit. But (as she kept telling herself) she'd get over it.

It wasn't as if they were friends, let alone anything...more. Until last night, she had believed him to be a lying, scheming murderer. He wasn't...well, he wasn't a murderer, anyway.

Really, it was better for her that he had gone.

Avoiding Abby's sharp gaze, she climbed into the car. The motor rumbled to life.

"Ready?" Kendra asked. Murphy had chartered a jet to take them all back to Granite Springs.

"For the airport, yes." Beyond that, Thia could only hope.

As Kendra executed a three-point turn on the narrow road, Thia took a last look at the flat gray clouds, where the black speck of a bird circled high overhead.

A black speck that might have been a raven.

ACKNOWLEDGMENTS

Many, many heartfelt thanks to my parents. Without your deep understanding and support, I would not be where I am, writing these words in particular.

Mom, I meant what I said in the Dedication. This counts as the long-ago promised travel book, right? (No? What about something with more pictures?)

Dad. You were watching late-night TV with headphones and crinkling graham-cracker wrappers in the next room while I wrote and edited all but the final draft. I miss you.

To family and friends, your interest and encouragement has meant more than I can say.

To the extraordinary people of Unicorn Gifts & Toys in Ashland, Oregon—I consider the day I walked in with my resume to be one of the most fortunate of my life. For so many reasons, thank you.

ABOUT THE AUTHOR

R. A. Finley is the author of the three published novels so far; a former animator of technical gizmos and systems which she cannot share due to nondisclosure agreements; an aspiring photographer and artist; a hobbyist knitter; and a graduate of the London Film School, Gnomon School of Visual Effects, and Southern Oregon University (not in that order).

A self-described middling adventurer, terminal eccentric, and gardening enthusiast, she is surprised to now reside in the Midwest. She may be found searching for a coffee shop to favorite, familiarizing herself with the local parks, and (some-times) posting on www.rafinleybooks.com and various social media (as @rafinley).

EXPECTED IN 2026

THE ACHILL BELL

The Wheel of the Year: Book 4

For news and updates: www.rafinleybooks.com

Read on for an excerpt of:

THE DARKEST MIDNIGHT

The Wheel of the Year: Book 2

It felt ridiculous to fear a dead man, but as Cormac walked the cold, deserted passageways of his father's underground stronghold, he did exactly that. Habit, he supposed. But dead was dead. The only ghosts Cormac might encounter lurked not in any actual darkened corner but within his own mind. The ghosts of memory. Of fear, pain, sorrow. Loneliness.

He ducked a low, rough hewn beam as he rounded a sharp turn. Either the long-ago people who had carved these tunnels deep into the mountain had been considerably shorter than Cormac's five-foot-nine or they hadn't the time—or perhaps permission—for comfort.

His boot slipped when the passageway, slick with ice, took a steep downward slant. Rather than slow, he increased pace. With every second the air felt a little thinner, smelled a little ranker; and the walls, already close enough, seemed to push in closer still. If not for the bargain with Murphy, Cormac would never have returned to Fiend's Fell.

The temperature was icy enough to chill even an American's beer, but Cormac was sweating beneath his jacket, the cotton of his shirt sticking uncomfortably to his back. It was absurd, this anxiety. As far as his Sight could tell, the stronghold was deserted. However large its current population might be, all must have accompanied his father to Orkney, and thus they either lay dead at the Ring of Brodgar or were on the run from there. Should any seek to return, it would require more time than Cormac intended to spend.

No, there was nothing to fear here tonight from his father's *thegnas*—his followers—nor from the man himself. With the memory, the *feel* of Idris Cathmor's death but two hours fresh, Cormac ought to know better than anyone.

His hands itched, their nerves not yet recovered from being conduits for so much power; his throat burned from shouting. Screaming, if he cared to be accurate (and he did not). He had put genuine emotion on display several times already this night, which amounted to several times too many.

When he'd seen Thia about to run headlong into the deadly protection spells that kept them captive within Brodgar. And again when he had held her while her body struggled to adjust to the Cailleach's newly-introduced powers. And, worst of all, when the Brigantium had used him as a conduit to kill Idris.

That had been the most public instance, no question. Even as battle raged throughout the Ring, Cormac and his father and their dueling storms had attracted a good deal of attention. It had been then, when Idris was down with Cormac's hands wrapped around his throat that the—

He shuddered, tamped down the memory before it could fully rise.

The Brigantium had seized the opportunity to rid the world of a perceived evil. He couldn't fault their perception or their decision. It was their method that currently gave him trouble.

The knowledge that, if they hadn't taken control from him in those last moments, he might have done the deed himself did not sit too well, either.

Guilt. It didn't eat at him, as the saying went. No. It invaded, thickened the blood and turned marrow cold. Threatened to transform him utterly if left unchecked.

He had nothing against it. Hell, he deserved it, did he not? Guilt over Idris, and over Thia too.

He rubbed his chest, the unconscious gesture doing nothing to ease the ache summoned by her name.

After a sequence of counterintuitive turns, Cormac entered a hexagonal antechamber.

Disbelief hit hard.

The doors to the most secure storerooms were wide open. Every single one. The wards that should have shimmered in Cormac's Sight were gone.

He didn't need to shine the light of his electric torch inside to see that every room had been emptied, yet he did. Nor did he need to enter them one by one, yet he did.

Nothing of significance remained. And, given the lack of any energy remnants—remnants that should have overwhelmed, considering what had been held within—the rooms had been magically scoured. He braced his hands on either side of an empty niche at the back of the room and dropped his head forward, his brow pressing onto the stone. Eyes closed, he breathed in the dank, familiar smell of failure.

The Achill Bell, promised to Declan Murphy upon pain of death, was gone.

THE DARKEST MIDNIGHT

The Wheel of the Year: Book 2

ISBN: 0-9893157-2-X
ISBN-13: 978-0-9893157-2-2
eBook ISBN: 978-0-9893157-3-9

**Available online from all major book and ebook retailers,
or ask for it at your local book store.**

For more information: www.rafinleybooks.com